About the author

Delvin Nelson was born in 1969 and lives in Blackburn in Lancashire with his wife and son. He has been an avid writer since he was eleven-years-old, whose only previous published work was a letter in the NME about the Manic Street Preachers. His literary inspirations are Iain Banks, Neil Gaiman, J.K. Rowling, Roald Dahl and Enid Blyton.

THE DEVIL EGG

Delvin Nelson

THE DEVIL EGG

Vanguard Press

A CIP catalogue record for this title is
available from the British Library.

ISBN 978 1 784654 42 9

*Vanguard Press is an imprint of
Pegasus Elliot MacKenzie Publishers Ltd.*
www.pegasuspublishers.com

First Published in 2018

**Vanguard Press
Sheraton House Castle Park
Cambridge England**

Printed & Bound in Great Britain

Dedication

For Helen and Dom

Acknowledgments

Thank you to my parents, David and Elsie, and my brother Ches. Also, thanks to Paul, and everyone else who read my work and offered much appreciated self-restraint when it came to giving advice.

Additionally, I would like to express my gratitude to everybody at Pegasus for their invaluable assistance and patience.

And in a time of ages come
The world shall split from dark and light
Wherein incarnates loom and grow
Sky and earth shall war and fight
Brethren will fall from high and low
Blood will spill and stain
This age of innocence suffering
As wretched pestilence will remain
Chaos likely will fill the air
And bring forth the unknown soul
The egg will crack and all will cease
The land will turn to foul
All who seek truth will find
The heavenly joys within
Beyond shaded realms divine
The fallen down, the sin
Then will follow emptiness
The silent screams will still
And darken blindly will then rise up
The world will have its fill
All will know as day's end
A saviour of another's womb
Will tend the war with raging fire
And reside within the earthen tomb

A poem and source of prophesy
Paul Joseph Cullen

In the year 988, three days after a vision of angels forewarned him of imminent death, the retired Archbishop of Canterbury, Dunstan of Glastonbury, called an abbot to his bedside and laid a clammy palm upon the other man's hand.

'Magnus,' he said, producing a small purple tome from the folds of his bedclothes, a volume he had confiscated from a malicious nun during a pilgrimage to Jerusalem after the vestal virgin attempted to use its esoteric powers to turn the region's wine into water and infect lepers with impetigo and sheep flu, 'I would like to be buried with this,' he stated. 'It is the first bible I ever possessed, a crude and battered text, but a humble treasure and more honest a ledger of commandments than the gold-trimmed volumes we witnessed in Rome, eh?'

Magnus nodded his head and spoke no words, for any response he might have made yield little significance in the telling of this tale.

'Place it in my coffin and tell not a soul,' remarked Dunstan, 'for my brothers may feel obliged to replace it with one of better quality.'

Magnus smiled and nodded his head once more.

'Do you promise?'

Yet again, unable to muster expositional justification for verbal function within the telling of Dunstan's legend, the abbot called Magnus simply bobbed his head up and down.

'The light is dim and my sight grows ever weary,' Dunstan said, 'so tell me with succinct words that you comprehend my wishes.'

Confounded by the paradox of having no communicative role within the context of how Dunstan's life arrived at its end and yet forced into an ethical corner by his dying brother, Magnus managed an affirmative cough.

'You are a good man,' said Dunstan. 'I have always known it to be true. Never once did I heed those spiteful rumours concerning you and that hunchbacked farm boy. Your verbal denial was never necessary for I have always trusted your will to be noble and spirit clean and have faith in Om's influence over your desires.'

And just as Magnus' consequence within the telling of this fable might indeed begin to exude a whiff of intrigue, the former Archbishop passed out of this world and rendered its telling nevertheless superfluous.

In 1508, when Archbishop William Warham demanded the tomb of St Dunstan excavated in order to win a wager with the Abbey of Glastonbury, the latter having proclaimed the saint was buried there, he discovered not only decomposed bones in the coffin but also a little battered book he took to be a bible. Warham was initially curious about the purple volume buried alongside the putrefied corpse, for no worm or insect had exploited it as habitation, which could not be said for the carcass of Dunstan. Fortunately, what Warham and, centuries earlier, brother Magnus had neglected to do was peek at the little purple tome's pages, for if either had they may not have proved holy enough to shun its unscrupulous virtues, for said book was no holy text. It was in fact the glumly infamous book of storms, *Humdinger's Thumb*.

Hadrian Otway Humdinger was appointed chief architect in the construction of Om's master creation, *the Known*

Universe. He was solely responsible for engineering many of its most remarkable rudiments. In addition to numerous elemental fabrics he developed several of the primitive life-forms that eventually roamed its seventeen-planet solar system, engraved the cosmos with star constellations and came up with a wide selection of pseudo-realms that holy (and often paramilitary) groups commonly refer to as the hereafter. Geomancer, Griffin Adler, in his biography about the renowned Seraph entitled, *The Origin of the Spatial* commended Humdinger for his vibrant use of colour, his imaginative and resourceful distribution of particles, and, most of all, his tenacious drive to promote the significance of mushrooms.

There is a sublime quality to all work of geomancy of that first age, Adler wrote, *whether of practical or aesthetic value, give or take a few early problems with the earth's gravitational pull, lopsided dinosaurs and the premature nucleosynthesis of supernovae, the Known Universe looks and smells today much as it did when it first came into being. Whether we are discussing Jean d'Orbais' use of undulating landscapes or the astrophysical* Door Handles *designed by George Gropius, ninety-nine-point nine percent of that original draft continues to function exceptionally well in the present day. Hadrian Otway Humdinger, quite literally, wrote the book on universal orchestration and* providentially *destroyed it immediately afterwards, for if such a text wound up in the wrong hands (or indeed, the right ones), less pious ethics than ours might undo every geomantic design Om made manifest.*

CHAPTER ONE
Attack of the clowns

The King and Egg were dining when the biplane's grumbling descent first became audible. They rushed outdoors in time to witness the troubled aircraft strike the baroque fountain beneath Hill House, watching as it churned the ground into a tsunami of mineral, dirt and atomised cherub creating a wave of debris to sweep over a twenty metre stretch of turf that included a recently laid gravel path contoured with cherry blossom saplings.

The little girl peered up at her pretend grandfather and searched his gallantly wrinkled features for signs of anxiety, finding none. She imitated his calmness, indifference that suggested such events were a regular affair around these parts, occurring every third Tuesday at precisely lunchtime. But then the King's demeanour shifted and, as his eyes narrowed and mouth tilted on one side, it became obvious all was *not* well.

Meanwhile the plane had vanished in a tumbling cloud of grit and sward only to reappear moments later moving at a much gentler pace having become imbedded in the land, a ploughing motion that gradually forced deceleration until the biplane came to a complete stop. And then, for the briefest of instants, nothing happened.

The two onlookers exhaled pent up breaths neither realised had been gulped. As a breeze tousled the girl's straight black hair and made her pink T-shirt billow at the waist, her pretend grandfather cupped a hand at his brow and squinted towards the unscathed yet inept aviator and emitted a tiny, incredulous hoot of recognition. Egg glared in the direction of their clumsy visitor presently hurling books from the fractured cockpit, liberating dozens of hard-backed tomes, sending them flapping and tumbling over the ground like deranged birds.

'I'll be a monkey's uncle,' the King declared and Egg regarded him with a bewildered frown. 'I do believe that is my old war buddy, Morecambe Pierpot.'

This made the girl laugh and she said, 'That's a silly name.'

Several white tendrils became unruffled from the King's thick hair in a gust of blustery wind, the tiny flurry transforming him into a reverential monument to himself. He stroked his solid, smooth chin ponderously and snorted another dubious laugh before setting off down the hillside with Egg trailing after him. The pilot cast a glance in their direction, two myopic eyes squinting over a pair of bent wire-rimmed spectacles. He continued to discharge volumes of hard-backed literature over the parapet of his plane before eventually scrambling out and dropping lithely to earth just as the King and Egg approached. The man scooped up several titles at random and, swiftly reading their spines discarded or stuffed them under his arm while kicking others over the ground in front of him.

Extending a hand for greeting the King hailed their caller in a friendly tone. 'That's no way to treat a library, Pierpot.'

The newcomer's laugh was a sound that implied he had perhaps forgotten how to. He pushed his twisted spectacles up the bridge of his nose and choked nervously on his reply while shaking the King's hand. 'I apologise for the unruly nature of my arrival, Reg,' he said, 'and also for the desecration to your grounds. If there had been time to wire ahead I would have done so.'

The King patted him powerfully on the shoulder. 'I'm sure you have a reasonable excuse.'

'Oh, I have an excuse,' Pierpot announced, 'but there's nothing *reasonable* about it I'm afraid.' He looked at the child. 'Hello there.'

Having not been introduced Egg decided to take matters into her own hands, beamed up at him and said, 'Hello. I'm Egg. Is that *your* aeroplane?'

'Actually, no,' Pierpot replied, fiddling with his spectacles again. 'I stole it from some chaps in hell.'

She laughed.

'There's nothing funny about hell, young lady!' He cast his eyes back to the King. 'It's quite a glum place, in point of fact. Not nearly as hot as we were led to believe, Reg, but definitely as sordid.'

The peculiar man's grim manner amused Egg. Scrutinising him, she committed to memory, in one visionary gulp, all of his quirky behaviour; how he continuously fidgeted with those misshapen specs, stooped when he walked despite exhibiting no physical encumbrance or protuberance, and his terrible haircut; little more than a reversed diadem of grey

19

curls stretched pointlessly around a head as shiny and hairless as a freshly minted penny. He appeared entrenched in his clothes rather than wearing them, attire so old-fashioned and mismatched they might have come straight off a charity shop mannequin. His arms piled high with scratched, scorched and still smouldering books he put Egg in mind of a pyromaniac librarian or perhaps a mad scientist researching the burning point of ancient works of prose.

'I have stumbled, quite inadvertently I might add, upon some rather diabolical information,' Pierpot informed the King. 'It would seem the forces of glumness are not overwhelmed after all, Reg, and are, in fact, attempting to raise another offensive against us. We must inform John Fate immediately.'

The King allowed himself a furtive glance at Egg before indicating with a nod of his head for them to retire indoors. 'The forces of glumness you say?' he asked as he led the ascent towards Hill House.

'Yes, yes, that's right,' Pierpot confirmed as he performed an elaborate hop and skip to fall in step with the King. 'Hell's *armies* are on overtime. I've been looking for signs in all the usual text and everything points to one indisputably deplorable conclusion: *imminent incarnate invasion*!'

While the King displayed no apparent alarm, Mr Pierpot's news inspired Egg to react with a short gasp of excited terror.

'If I have my facts straight, the resurrection of General Galbi's armies is impending. There can be no mistake when you...' Pierpot came to a sudden halt and twisted his body round to study Egg. The King stumbled on a few yards before realising he was alone.

'I'm sorry,' said Pierpot, 'did you say your name was *Egg*?'

The King cleared his throat, interrupting the girl's answer lest she gave the game away. 'Yes, that's right,' he said. 'It's a contraction of Megan, you know?'

Pierpot viewed the child with suspicion, one eye widening to the size and shape of a monocle lens, the other clasping shut. Finally, his bonce began to bob up and down, trusting in the word of his old friend, yet whispering over his shoulder, 'And who is she exactly?'

The little girl opened her mouth to speak. 'My granddaughter,' the King interjected.

Pierpot observed them both in turn, the convoluted calculation of their connection no doubt a challenging matter in his cluttered brain, but he was, ostensibly, satisfied by the explanation, and continued towards the house.

The King gave Egg a warning glance as they set out after their visitor already halfway up the incline. 'If my calculations are correct,' Pierpot went on, 'we are about to be engulfed in another epoch of incarnate gloom. It's what everybody's talking about down there in the bowels of hell: *war*. General Galbi's incarnate hordes sound confident this time, as though they have a surprise up their sleeve, some new weapon to utilise against…' He stopped again and swiftly turned back. 'So, you married then, did you, Reg?' he asked, studying both of them over his spectacles and casting another suspicious gaze at the girl. He swapped some books to another arm, almost dropping them in the process.

The King looked angry. 'I'm quite sure you didn't crash your stolen *Brunner-Winkle Bird* on my estate simply to categorize my marriage status, Pierpot. You mentioned something about *an epoch of incarnate gloom*?'

'Yes, yes,' the man remembered, allowing more pressing matters back into focus and set off once again with the King and Egg marching in his wake. 'We need to contact John Fate immediately. Or should I say, *you* need to contact him. I'm still a fugitive.'

When Pierpot abruptly stopped a third time, the King released a deep, irritated sigh, but their visitor's glance was aimed at the sky rather than at them. They turned and saw, what only moments ago had been a bright blue firmament suddenly filled with gloomy veins of malevolent weather; the entire expanse awash with extraordinary shades of miserable purples and greys.

'I think I may have been pursued!'

That was when the biplane exploded and a bright red haze of fire spat pieces of fuselage through the air to impale the ground yards from where they stood. Smoke billowed and drifted skyward.

'Perhaps it would be wise to continue this conversation indoors,' the King recommended.

Reginald Fielding was a simple man. His father had managed a successful stationery business during the last decade of the Futilities, a time when bureaucracy was rife and auditing a boom industry. *Fielding Office Supplies* excelled in a wide range of staplers, hole-punches and protractor designs and Thomas Fielding was one of the first manufacturers in England to introduce mass produced plastics to office trappings, the patenting rights alone earning him a small fortune. But alas, the notion of devoting his spirit to notebooks and extendable pencils caused Reginald to wake up gagging with fear in the night. He wanted more excitement out of life than absurd boasting like *a Fielding fabricated ductile leaf clasp is three times sturdier than the average fabricated ductile leaf clasp and half the price*! And while his mother was a proud activist who wiled away her time shoulder to shoulder with honest yet wrongly-done-to wage earners outside municipal buildings wielding placards (usually supplied *non-gratis* by her long-suffering husband) chanting proletariat songs at mill owners, Reginald had no stomach for militancy either.

A week after his seventeenth birthday, Reginald enrolled with the Contingency Plan's Paranormal Trooper Division. Sociable and morally charming, he rose swiftly through the ranks and after a year was appointed corporal and assigned to *HRH Edward VIII's* security detail, with duties consisting of travel roster and timetable inspections to ensure His Majesty's protection. He was also responsible for safeguarding His Majesty's out of hours schedule i.e. dinner parties, social soirees, and of course, the occasional game of gin rummy. And so it was, on 11th November 1936, after a game that lasted more than nine hours, during which, between them, the King and Reginald smoked fifty *El Rey del Mundo* cigars and swallowed three bottles of *Four Roses* whiskey, the title of Monarch was wagered in lieu of hard cash and, to Edward Saxe-Coburg's eternal shame, the crown was abdicated.

Of course, the private passing of the royal title was widely scorned and remains unsanctioned by reputable establishment figures, Reginald Fielding having no legitimate blood-right to the throne of England, yet less traditionalist members of the

Contingency Plan, at least those who consider a wager between two gentlemen a binding contract, adhered to its transition from the off if only to display their impertinence.

The King was not in the least haughty about this trophy appellation and as such, was not above making tea for old friends. And as he orchestrated the timpani of china and silver from elsewhere in the house, Egg concealed herself behind a sofa, spying on their guest as he roamed the sitting room, consumed with the absent wonder of someone who had never seen one before.

Morecambe Pierpot picked up a glazed ceramic bird, sniffing at the ornament before replacing it. Next he scrutinized a pair of plum coloured drapes at the window, staring at the material over the top of his glasses and running the cotton-work between finger and thumb tips. He moved on to a photograph frame, a sepia snap of the King in full military regalia, and held it an inch from his nose, turning it this way and that, twisting his eyes and features into curious shapes and positions to examine the image.

'So, tell me,' the King announced as he returned with a tray of sparkling cutlery, a steaming pot of tea and stacked cups and saucers, 'who was it shot your plane down?'

Startled, Pierpot almost dropped the banana he had been listening to. 'One can never be certain,' he replied, nervously disposing of the fruit behind a walnut cabinet. 'Definitely a low-grade homunculus, some substandard life-form tasked with keeping me under surveillance.'

The King placed the tray on a table and began to arrange crockery.

'Men of our reputation,' Pierpot went on, 'retain enemies beyond war. There are still a few rogue *Tin Men* out there who wish me harm.' When a ginger cat bounded up onto the surface of the table, Pierpot almost leaped out of his skin with a cry of, '*saints preserve us!*' He exhaled sharply with puffed out cheeks, a hand placed over his quickening heart then continued with his boasting. 'It may have been *VALDA Agents*. You know what utter, soulless automatons they can be. I did catch a whiff of *Devil's Breath* as I flew between Blackburn and Bolton, but that's to be expected over the A666.' He nodded towards the feline and queried, 'The moggy, is it witch-linked?'

The King chortled, reassuringly. 'You don't have to worry about old Gladstone there. I had him spayed by the Pope.'

'My propensity towards indifference all depends on *which* Pope,' Pierpot responded, distracting himself by running a finger across the ivories of a nearby piano and examining the digits for dust. 'Never did like cats, even before I knew there was a witch for each one.' He physically trembled at the thought and Egg squeaked a laugh before sinking behind the sofa. 'You know hell is full of cats? I was down there for more than twenty years, Reg. There's cats everywhere you look. Do you have any idea how long twenty years is in hell?'

'I see you're still a keen reader,' the King remarked, nodding at the mahogany bureau where Pierpot had clumsily heaped his rescued volumes.

'Oh yes... *What*? No, no, no,' Pierpot replied, bewilderingly as he received a cup and saucer from his host. 'All but one is camouflage.'

The King gasped and dropped a pair of silver pincers he had been using to transfer a lump of sugar to his own cup. They clattered noisily on the silver tray and Egg ducked down at the sudden sound. Gladstone thudded to the floor and found a place to hide.

The King glared at Pierpot. 'The only things one camouflages with books,' he said with dry lips and tongue, 'are other books.'

'That's right,' replied Pierpot, cheerfully, and slurped his tea. 'There are actually only three books in the Known Universe glum forces would deem important enough to shoot me out of the sky to retrieve. I've become rather a scholar on nefarious text recently and I'm sorry to bring this to your doorstep, Reg, but the truth is, I didn't have anywhere else to go. When I realised they were on to me I had to make a...'

The King distracted him by crossing to the bureau and rummaging through the literary pile. After a moment of searching he held up a small purple bound volume. 'This is a book of storms! You brought *Humdinger's Thumb* into my home knowing glum forces were on your tail? How could you be so thoughtless?'

Appearing unsympathetic, Pierpot sipped his tea before responding with, 'I saw it as my civil duty. I'm certain that, had the tables been reversed, had *you* needed to hide and *I* had a big house on a hill and a granddaughter...' he looked in the direction of the sofa, '... about that, Reg; doesn't one require children in order to acquire grandchildren?'

'Where did you get it?' the King demanded, waving the book at him.

'I might ask you the same question.' Pierpot grinned, nodding at the child, pleased with his rejoinder. 'Incidentally, I wouldn't draw attention to it by flapping it about like that.'

'*Where... did... you... get... it*?'

Appearing sheepish under the King's admonishing gaze, Pierpot said, 'I heard along the grapevine that glum forces were looking to expand their literary arsenal and thought if *I* got to all the books of power first I could...'

'You could curse one of your dearest friends by bringing it to his home?'

'I intended being rather less conspicuous, but as you are more than aware, I was shot out of the sky by ambiguous forces! I believed my escape from hell to be faultless, but someone must have followed me here.' Pierpot glanced at the book. 'Please, Reg, stop waving it about like that,' he advised, 'arcane devices are best left unobserved.'

The King lowered the tome. 'But I don't understand, Pierpot. Some of the most valiant and intelligent men in history have tried to obtain this book; how did an absolute dolt like you acquire it?'

'It's rather a curious story,' Pierpot replied, apparently unimpeded by the King's insult. 'You see, it's more like the book found me. I was a prisoner upon a zombie schooner crossing the vast Crystal Lake when suddenly the vessel was struck by an unforeseen obstacle and sank, taking me with it. I was immediately set upon by a school of *iron-tusked elephant sharks* and forced to kill the largest of them by wrestling one of its tusks out of its head and using it to open up the beast's gullet where I discovered...'

'The Thumb was in the stomach of an elephant shark?' the King asked in surprise.

Pierpot shook his head. 'You're not paying attention, Reg,' he said, repositioning his spectacles and sipping his tea before continuing. 'The map of where the book was *buried* was in the stomach of the elephant shark. I snatched it up and swam for the surface where, six days later, I was picked up by a fishing trawler and brought back to land. I set out on an expedition, following the map through many of hell's most dangerous…'

'What really happened, Pierpot?'

There was a moment of silence and then his old war buddy cleared his throat and said, 'I stole it from the Black House library.'

The King looked astonished while a tiny whimper of excitement came from behind the sofa. 'General Galbi's library?' he asked. 'You should have left the damned artefact where it was. Why bring it here?'

'I thought here might be the safest place to take it,' Pierpot confessed. 'Believe me, Reg, I had no idea incarnates were on my tail!'

'They'll soon be on my doorstep if they know what you took from them.'

Pierpot snorted, dismissively. 'I don't think it'll come to that.'

And then a sudden loud scream made both men turn to see Egg, one arm extended, forefinger pointing at the sitting room window where the powder-white and red-nosed, rosy-cheeked face of a clown smiled back at them.

'Of course, I could be wrong,' Pierpot remarked.

CHAPTER TWO
The Scent of Gloom

The erstwhile prince woke to see a sky marbled by the kinked and sinewy, interwoven fingers of trees. Simultaneous sounds of chirping, scampering and whispering animal voices vexed him immediately. Finding himself in woodland was almost worse than the bad dream he had been having and he sat upright with terror and glanced about him at the vast gallery of grooved and vertical boughs.

Prior to waking he had been back in the Futilities. Having avoided conscription by two diverse methods, the first being a royal bloodline and the second a spiritual inclination towards a sacred order known as the *Heyoka,* Rhodeburt Raven had been protected from active duty, but had visited every earthly city the war destroyed, observing the chaos from the safety of bunkers, command posts and neutral zones. In his dream, however, he had been entrenched at the very heart of violence, staggering between bullet-riddled bodies and mentally frazzled soldiers rushing each other with bayonets amidst a constant report of artillery. A quivering wreck, the dream him, the avatar in his bleak imaginings, stumbled from one bloody site to the next, a jittery coward served well by his witless whimpering and spineless ineptitude, an inglorious assortment of tools that, over the years, have helped him to survive.

The dream ended with a discordant sound, the noise heaven makes when it is torn asunder. He had time to look up beyond the smoke and the soaring airships, to glimpse a swirling, rasping rip in the sky, a laceration revealing a floating man, arms and legs extended in the shape of a star, silhouetted by blossoming sparks of torn cosmic flesh and anti-aircraft fire.

And then he awoke in the forest.

His last clear memory, before the oblivion of that nightmarish vision of Konigsberg in 1945, was sitting on a boulder beneath the ruined ramparts of his family home, scratching fingernails flush on grey stone to etch illegible words and pictures into rock. His head, filled to burst with madness, was suddenly host to a familiar, yet intrusive voice, and then, just as mystifying he was awarded the surprise acknowledgement of his brother's whereabouts.

His tangled black mane clotted with rotten leaves and scurrying insects, having long since dispelled with vanity as his ragged garments would attest, Raven dragged a pale and emaciated claw through the untidy coiffure, simply to remove it from his vision and climbed to his feet, sniffing heartily at the balmy air.

He smelled clown.

As he passed through the trees, listening to the twittering of birds in the interlaced kindling above, he recalled that all avian chirruping was fundamentally a battle cry; a territorial warning against potential invaders, and he correlated that confused whimsy with a far more ominous misinterpretation, *the jolliness and clowns.* A circus tent was not an indoor gala for fun and frolic but a morbid marquee crammed with madness, malevolence and misery. His blood boiled to imagine candy floss-chomping children led by the hand into such environments, terrible settings teeming with tediousness, terror and torture; too big for their cars, too small for their trousers, weeping/smiling faces intended to define sadness and joy in equal measure, clowns were a perplexing parallax of infuriating frivolousness.

The pungent scent of gloom and merriment brought him to the forest's edge where vibrant lawns replaced a shaded canopy, stretching away for kilometres, a landscape interposed with winding fences and prickly hedgerows, tumbledown outhouses and barns. He spied a tall, thin house erected atop a mound of earth, the epicentre of vast grassland. It was a lofty, spikey, century's old structure with spires that fractured a sky currently grumbling with foreboding cloud. Smoke climbed into the firmament from a fire in a distressed section of pasture.

And Spare Clowns roamed everywhere.

CHAPTER THREE
Amethyst Vampire Penguin

It was the very first time Egg recalled ever screaming and she was left feeling more embarrassed than fretful. She blamed her temporary misplacement of poise on the indecipherable exchange between her pretend grandfather and their accidental visitor, Mr Pierpot. Seeing the clown at the window seemed like a valid excuse to make their stupid conversation stop.

As their creepy observer tapped a long fingernail on the pane, a gaping grin opening its jaws wide and fogging up the glass, the King said, 'Quickly,' and motioned to the door. Pierpot snatched the Thumb from his grasp as well as several volumes from the bureau and rushed past. They crossed an expansive hallway encompassing oil on canvas portraits of Fielding ancestry, each image adorned in grubby shirts, dirty overalls or oily dungarees, and entered a much larger area which had, over the centuries, insulated three of its four walls with a comprehensive library, a fourth being mostly window. The King used it to look outside, pressing his face against the glass to gain a better peripheral view.

'I do hope the place is demonically sealed, Reg,' Pierpot remarked.

'Are we in danger?' asked Egg with a look of excitement.

The King turned to look at her and laughed with bravado. 'Not at all,' he said cheerily, which Egg immediately registered as a downright fib because in the entire three weeks she had known him, he had never done anything *cheerily*. 'We'll be fine. *Spare Clowns* are not the brightest bulbs on the Christmas tree.'

'Do you think that rogue Grimaldi was responsible for crashing my plane?' asked Pierpot. 'I wouldn't have thought a creature of low intelligence possessed such magic. They're foot soldiers at best and…'

When a curly green wig and snow-white features rose from beneath the sill behind the King, Pierpot's face turned almost as pale. When several more popped up, eerily slow and smiling with demented joy, Egg took a step backwards, toppling a large pot plant. Several more vibrantly bewigged and pastel-faced freaks ascended into view until there were at least twenty crammed against the outside of the window, staring menacingly in at them.

The King, who had yet to physically acknowledge them, simply said, 'Follow me!' and led them from the library, snatching a small figurine from a tallboy as they went. Packed into a small corridor at the foot of a staircase where no windows allowed for spectators, the King held the ornament up between finger and thumb. 'I have a plan,' he announced. 'This is the *Amethyst Vampire Penguin*. Spare Clowns are notoriously dim-witted fellows who only ever rise to the rank of minion and I would wager my life they do not know what they are here to retrieve. Several years ago, I battled a giant brainwashed mongoose in deepest Peru for this artefact. Whilst falling into a volcano and with the last spell of a dying witch I swam through molten lava to retrieve this trinket from *Tranche*, one of Orgo the Posthumous' blood nephews. As you can well imagine, in addition to being an incredibly sacred and exceptionally powerful artefact, it has much sentimental value. If this bauble was to fall into the wrong hands, or should I say, flippers, Om only knows what chaos might be unleashed in its name.'

'That's all well and good, Reg, but this is hardly the time to be bragging about your keepsakes,' Pierpot declared, glancing at Egg and rolling his eyes. 'There are more pressing matters at hand. You appear to have an incursion of Spare Clowns on your property.'

The King sighed and started up the staircase, urging them to follow. 'Parting with the Amethyst would be the equivalent of having my heart ripped from my chest and stamped upon with a spiked running shoe,' he confirmed, 'but if we can somehow convince these surplus circus dwellers it's the Amethyst they seek and not the Thumb, it may be a small price to pay for…'

Pierpot's face finally exhibited understanding. 'Very cunning, Reg, very cunning indeed,' he said. 'I never doubted you for a second.'

At the top of the staircase the King kicked open a set of French doors for them to venture out onto a small balcony. To the west the sky remained an unnatural swirl of gloomy colour and a cold wind burst forth as they stumbled against the parapet overlooking hundreds of painted circus entertainers amassed on the estate.

'What *is* the collective noun for clowns anyway?' Pierpot inquired.

'Right at this moment I'd call them an *Aggravation*,' the King replied as he observed the various circus folk below. Many were performing magic tricks, retrieving bunches of flowers from baggy shirt sleeves or sneezing confetti. A few executed energetic handstands while others hurled custard pies. There were even a couple of seals balancing beach balls, a dog wearing a frilly collar and tutu and an elephant dressed like Queen Victoria.

'Why are they called *Spare* Clowns?' asked Egg standing on tiptoe to see over the wall.

Glancing down at her with mawkish pity the King told her, 'When Om retained John Wood the Younger to create them, it's said he overestimated the amount the Known Universe would require and, as you can see from this diverse collection gathered below, produced a superfluous quantity. They were distracted by an explosion and watched as a Coco in a crash helmet was shot out of a canon followed by a ball of smoke. The poor performer painfully smacked into the side of Hill House before tumbling into privets. 'After all the circuses, theme parks, nightmares and fast food outlets were adequately supplied,' the King continued, 'something like two and a half billion residual jokers still resided in the Known Universe as well as all those ambiguous areas that exist between. And as you know, glum forces utilise idle hands for their purpose.'

'Spare Clowns are not to be confused with the *Heyoka*,' Pierpot pointed out, 'who are a holy order of Clown who derive from Native American history and whose impulse is simply to behave in an opposite…'

'Why didn't Om just *unmake* them?'

The King and Pierpot's faces seared with unease. The King cleared his throat and said, 'Because, my dear, that would be genocide!'

'Spare Clowns are typically nomadic,' Pierpot put in. 'They wander the Known Universe as mercenaries for hire. I've never seen so many in one place before. I fought one in Algiers in thirty-eight, you know? Blighter almost bit my arm off!'

'So, they're cannibals?' asked Egg with delight.

'That one was. Hadn't had a custard pie in months!'

When the King suggested, 'We need to attract their attention,' Pierpot waved both arms in the air and called out, '*YOO-HOO, HELLO DOWN THERE!*'

'That seems to have done the trick,' the King reasoned with an incredulous sigh.

Despite what they had been preoccupied with, be it tuning horns or tripping over imaginary objects and performing well-practised pratfalls, every clown on the hillside looked up at them. A Grimaldi retrieved an unfeasibly long ladder from a small leather suitcase, brought it to the foot of the wall beneath their balcony and began to ascend, yet with every step it placed on the ladder the ladder sank further into the ground and the clown made no progress at all.

'Allow me to handle this, Reg,' said Pierpot and, leaning over the bulwark, enquired, 'What appears to be the problem?'

A plastic bucket was passed through their ranks until it came to a Whiteface wearing a brightly coloured tie and a bowler hat with a large yellow flower protruding. The Whiteface disposed of the bucket's confetti over a nearby Auguste causing a nearby Contra-Auguste to laugh silently/hysterically. The Auguste kicked its acquaintance up the backside and both became engaged in a rib-tickling slap-fight. Ignoring the spat, the Whiteface punched out the bottom of the pail and raised it to its face to use as a loudhailer.

'We have reason to believe,' it called out in a high-pitched, helium-tinged voice, 'you are concealing a precious item. We have been charged with its recovery.'

The King provided their audience with a look of theatrical puzzlement before announcing, 'I'm terribly sorry but you must have us mistaken with another group of highly evolved monkeys. I have only a few trinkets about the place and am quite certain none of them are of value to *clowns*!'

'What about *books* then?' the clown enquired, gesturing towards the several tomes Pierpot was lugging under his arms.

'*Books*?' asked the King, nervously. 'Of course, you can have books. You can have every book in the house if it will remove you from my land.' He took a couple of innocent volumes from his friend and pitched them over the terrace. The first landed on a Grimaldi's foot causing him to hop about in pain, his pogoing action only stopping when the second hit him on the head and knocked him out cold. 'They are merely cookbooks and encyclopaedias, but feel free to widen your intellectual horizons if you must.'

'*ENOUGH*!' shouted the Whiteface. 'What need have clowns with silly books? We desire another object, something far more precious than cookery books and ency… encycl… other cookery books.'

The Whiteface was relieved of the loudhailer by an Auguste who pushed him aside. 'Give us the item we desire and we will leave your property forthwith,' it declared in a dull and deeply depressing monotone.

'This house was demonically sealed by Pope Innocent X so what makes you think you pose a threat?' the King enquired. '*You* cannot possibly get in and *I* have enough provisions to last the three of us months, so why should I surrender to your demands?'

'There are other glum and monstrous entities that will spit on your seal and dissolve it!' the Auguste threatened and many of its compatriots laughed, airing support for its defiance.

'But that would break a dozen diplomatic treaties and result in far more trouble for Spare Clowns than me and my friends,' the King reasoned. 'You must have subsidy from a very powerful source indeed if you're willing to risk unsettling a thirty-year peace process.'

'Oh, nice one, Reg,' Pierpot whispered, nudging the King's arm.

The Auguste guffawed miserably and said, 'You're just trying to trick me into giving you the identity of our employer.'

The King shook his head and laughed. 'Believe me I am more than aware that, due to your low status, you would not be allowed to know the identity of your employer.'

'Now you are… attempting reverse psychology in a subtle bid to antagonise me and force me to reveal who sent us.'

'Damn,' said the King, quietly to Pierpot. Then, to the clowns, suggested, 'What say you vacate these premises calmly and we will say no more about it? The Contingency

Plan doesn't need to know what has happened here and neither does General Galbi.'

Silence ensued.

'Or Callous Sacheverell,' put in Pierpot.

The Whiteface took possession of the loudhailer again, comically elbowing his rival aside. '*Enough of this*!' it screeched, angrily. 'Our instructions are simple. We are to obtain the object. So give it us now or suffer the consequences!'

Pierpot gently placed a palm on the King's chest and moved him away from the parapet, taking his place. 'Allow me, Reg. He looked down at the silly army. 'Look here, you lot, you've had your bit of fun and scared a little girl out of her wits, now bugger off!'

The clowns began to whisper angrily amongst themselves until the Whiteface appeared so annoyed his bowler hat shot off his head, catapulted by the swelling pressure of leadership. 'We demand you give us the little girl,' it said.

Egg gulped in surprise and then giggled. She hadn't had this much fun in all the weeks she could remember.

'Darn,' said Pierpot, stepping back. 'You seem to have antagonised the brutes, Reg.'

The King sighed. 'All right,' he called out. 'You win!' He held his arms up in a gesture of surrender. 'You have beaten my resolve. The article you seek is here.' He retrieved the Amethyst Vampire Penguin from his blazer pocket and held it aloft between forefinger and thumb.

'No, Reg! You mustn't!' Pierpot professed, playing along with the ruse and doing a hearty job of hamming it up for the sake of their audience. 'Whatever you do, don't give them the

Amethyst Vampire Penguin.' He stretched his neck out over the parapet and declared, 'It is far too magical an item for *clowns* to possess.'

The King sucked in a deep breath and avowed, 'You can have the precious artefact you were sent here to retrieve but only if you promise to vacate these premises once it is in your possession.'

Below, the clowns began to glance at one another in confusion until eventually the Whiteface started to laugh, followed by an enthusiastic swell of hilarity throughout the rest of the horde, as well as other forms of merriment expressed in mime. Very soon every colourful member of the sieging troupe exhibited a state of animated mirth. 'Do we *look* stupid?' the Whiteface asked.

'Well, frankly, yes,' the King acknowledged but only for the ears of his companions.

With its free hand the Whiteface retrieved a trinket from beneath its bright red kipper tie. It was an Amethyst Vampire Penguin on a gold chain. Several other clowns did the same.

'Your prized icon is ten a penny in paranormal circles,' it informed him and downcast, the King looked at the tiny statue in his hand, turned it over and saw, engraved on its base, the words, *Made in Taiwan.*

'Well that's just brilliant,' Pierpot complained. 'Now you've really gone and messed things up.'

Undeterred, the King retrieved what appeared to be a child's plastic ray gun from beneath his jacket. 'I was rather hoping we wouldn't need to resort to violence,' he said, gripping the balcony wall ready to leap over.

Egg smiled, jumping up and down on the spot and rubbing her hands together with delight while Pierpot appeared a little reticent about the idea.

And then the sound of smashing glass was clearly heard from another section of house and, in a very scary voice, the Whiteface called up to them, 'There's somebody beh*iiiii*nd you!'

CHAPTER FOUR
Ashok Kumar

In the early hours of an autumn morning in 1944, approximately a year before Rapture Bombs eviscerated Konigsberg and ended three hundred years of conflict, two ARP wardens dragged a man from the remains of a bombed-out Manchester church. On the night in question Dr Naveed Rajput was in residence at the *Salford Union Infirmary* when he heard gossiping nurses and members of higher echelon staff talking about an unusual patient. With a gentle, Middle Eastern air, coffee skin and a pair of enchanting hazel eyes Dr Rajput exhibited a handsomeness rarely met in twentieth century men. Yet these charms were overwhelmed by a shy reticence, and for this reason alone he never fell under the scrutiny of women; the only time his female colleagues ever acknowledged his presence was when he traversed hastily through the hospital with precious medical matters occupying his thoughts, as he did now having been summoned to examine this unusual man, forcing orderlies and nurses out of his way lest they be trampled underfoot.

For this reason, he was out of breath when he arrived at the guarded room on the third floor of the infirmary. One of the armed Planner's tapped delicately on the door and Dr Rajput was surprised to see John Fate himself appear and gesture him inside.

The doctor retained his usual expression of passiveness as he entered, nodding politely and saying, 'Good morning.'

'Doctor,' John Fate replied as way of salutation as he closed the door behind them, briefly wiping his nose on a handkerchief that he replaced in his breast pocket. In those days the Captain sported a moustache as well as his traditional black suit and tie which was generally in dire need of a good wash and iron. Throughout his long career, Fate always looked like he was going to or had recently returned from a funeral, and given the nature of the period this was usually the case. He was tall and trim; dark hair wiry and grey above the ears. His tresses hadn't whitened with age rather than happened overnight following a rather terrifying experience with a giant wasp.

The patient sat up in bed, looking bewildered and a little groggy after all the excitement of the last few hours. Seventeen people, including the church cleric had perished while sheltering from a Luftwaffe bombardment while he appeared to have sustained no injuries whatsoever.

As Dr Rajput began his examination he made mental notes of the patient's physical bearing; he was of average height and build with straggly auburn hair and a beard overdue a cut. The man's eyes were as brown as his own, yet the lids were framed with inflammation.

Looking up at him the patient smiled and said, '*Namaste*!'

Dr Rajput, who was taking his pulse, looked surprised and studied him more closely. 'Hello to you,' he replied persuading his patient to sit forward while he listened to his chest and asked, 'Do you speak any more words of my mother tongue?'

The man beamed pitifully and shook his head.

The doctor leaned him back on the pillows, placing the stethoscope to his ribcage. 'And how did you come by that Hindi phrase?'

'I... don't remember,' said the patient, laughing remorsefully.

'Is there anything you *do* remember?'

The unusual man glanced at Fate and then back at the doctor. 'I've been through this a hundred times already with him,' he said with a hint of irritability. 'The word *egg* seems important but I have absolutely no idea why.'

At this Dr Rajput stood up straight, observing him with a look of sincere bafflement.

'Is our patient well enough to be interviewed by my agents, Doctor?' Fate asked irascibly.

'By all accounts you have already asked him more questions than I am happy with. As far as his health goes, I can only say yes and no,' he confessed, leaning over the patient again and using one hand to gently pry open an eyelid to shine a small pencil torch into the man's pupil. 'What is your name?'

'I can't remember.'

'We're calling him John Doe,' said Fate. 'Is that appropriate?'

The doctor sighed. 'In India we called our unnamed, *Ashok Kumar*,' he replied.

'I like that,' the patient said. 'It sounds more exotic than John Doe.'

'Yes,' the doctor agreed, 'but exotic in terms of mysterious rather than glamorous.'

'Am I not glamorous?' the patient asked, smirking brashly.

The doctor shook his head. 'In medical terms you prove to be extremely interesting, but glamorous is not a phrase I would favourably use to describe you.' The doctor turned to look at Fate again. 'Perhaps we might talk outside?' Without a word, Fate turned and left the room with Dr Rajput following and closing the door behind them.

'So, what's your verdict?'

Dr Rajput glanced at the guards before replying. 'Your patient,' he said, drawing the Captain along the corridor, out of earshot, 'he is visibly alive, alert, communicative, exudes no foul rotting odour or physical indication his flesh is disintegrating and yet all of his vital signs, pulse, heartbeat and the function of his lungs, or should I say *malfunction*, indicate the man to be dead.'

'You're quite sure about that?' Fate asked, his reaction so animated that in later life Dr Rajput would, unjustly, visualise the Captain rubbing his hands together with glee. An orderly passed and they fell silent until he was gone.

'I am quite positive.'

He retrieved his hanky again and pinched his nose with it. 'When the first three doctors diagnosed him dead I couldn't be sure they weren't fuzzy in the head,' the Captain explained, 'so I had you brought up to verify it for definite because you have something of a reputation. I understand you're one of, if not, the most exceptional medical practitioners in this entire hospital, indeed the city.'

'I would like to think that even our sloppiest interns recognise a dead man when they examine one. There can be no mistake. This man is a definite walking corpse. Even Lords Crowberry and Sacheverell have beating hearts, organs that are perhaps full of spiky shards of ice, but beating hearts nonetheless. Your patient may as well be a shop window mannequin for all the good his bodily organs are doing to retain existence.'

'That's all I need to hear,' Fate replied with a cheery grin.

'Are you privy to anything that might explain the phenomenon?' the doctor enquired. If the Plan had clandestine interest in this unusual man, its Captain, famed for forecasting the future, was not about to discuss such matters with a general practitioner in a hospital corridor, but, out of curiosity, Dr Rajput thought it worth a try.

'Ordinarily, I'd have anticipated this evening's events, but it seems that the common cold interferes with my predictions,' he replied, gesturing with the hanky. 'Scripturally, there are hundreds of Cullen poems, half-forgotten god mythologies and mad old witch tales I can bend out of shape to apply logic to whatever phenomenon I wish,' he said, giving away nothing specific.

'An egg is a symbol of the origin of life,' Dr Rajput reasoned, thoughtfully, 'but it can also represent the bringer of the serpent.'

The Captain nodded and said, 'I can't help but wonder if our friend in there is a divine gift. What do you think; is your patient our enemy or our saviour?'

'He is not *my* patient.'

'He's your patient now, Doctor. You've just been enlisted to the Plan. I don't want anybody else examining him, do you understand? Whatever your current assignments are, offload them. Mr Kumar is your responsibility for the foreseeable future.'

The good doctor did not react for a moment and then humbly smiled and, gently bowing his head, replied, 'I am at your service.'

CHAPTER FIVE
The Turn-harp

'Quickly,' the King barked and ran back into the house, grabbing Egg by the hand and leading the way downstairs with Pierpot in hot pursuit. They dashed along wood-panelled hallways, up and down flights of creaky staircases, across tiled vestibules and antechambers, carpeted sitting rooms and games rooms until eventually they arrived at a subterranean kitchen to the rear of the property. The King barged through double doors, skidding to a halt on piebald tiles as Egg banged into his side and the hapless Pierpot, overburdened with his books, slid on by, colliding with a tower of saucepans at the opposite end of the room.

Egg gasped when she saw the man seated at the long preparation counter, hunched over a wooden bowl of *Potpourri*. He was dressed in scruffy, faded black clothes; a ragged shirt, suit jacket and unmatched trousers. His long, dirty black hair stood up like a drunken beehive while in other places it hung low across his features like a murky waterfall. His unkempt mane obscured most of the bowl he was eating from. Emaciated and pale, looking like he had just crawled out of a grave, the intruder glanced up through long and knotted tendrils and displayed two rows of manky white fangs gorged with red and purple scented dried petals.

'This is the worst cereal I've ever tasted!' he said, voice coldly mocking and sluggish.

The King still had the ray gun drawn and took the opportunity to point it at the intruder the moment they entered the room. 'Who are you and how exactly did you gain entry to my home?' he demanded to know.

The trespasser sat up straight on his stool, back audibly creaking and smiled wickedly at them as blood-red dye dripped from his chin. The sound of Pierpot upsetting more saucepans as he got up distracted the strange man and he watched the bespectacled fool re-join the others in the doorway, his musty books in tow.

'He's some vagabond burglar by the looks of him,' offered Pierpot, 'and definitely incarnate. This might be yet another infringement of diplomatic treaties, Reg. Don't worry I'm making a mental note of every contravention. An incarnate trespassing upon the property of a respected war veteran is a highly contentious…'

The stranger interrupted Pierpot by loudly blowing a raspberry with his lips.

'If you don't want me to blast your molecules into a billion pieces,' the King cautioned, working a mechanism on the weapon so it made a buzzing sound, 'tell me who you are!'

Egg was almost bouncing on the spot with excitement.

'If you don't already know, it's hardly worth my saying,' the intruder responded at such a leisurely vocal pace that time seemed to turn to stone as he spoke.

'Give us a clue,' said Egg with a giggle.

He glanced at her and the boredom that formerly decorated his pastel features became threaded with a grimacing leer. 'My father taught me children should be seen and not heard,' he said, voice grainy and menacing, yet his eyes devoid of expression as he continued to glare at the child long after his remark.

'Do not presume to reprimand my granddaughter, you villainous swine,' the King advised him.

At this the brooding burglar laughed, dribbling more red dye. 'If you must address me, old man, then I would be grateful if you refrained from comparing me to a *pig*! I am here to deal with your clown infestation and if you are not happy with this state of affairs I suggest you go and stick your head in a toaster!'

'Are you part of the Plan's community service initiative?' asked Pierpot. 'They have similar enterprises in hell, you know. It keeps the reprobates off the streets.'

Raven glared at him and asked, 'What know you of hell, silly-looking person?'

Nervously playing with a non-existent tie, Pierpot replied tensely, 'Nothing at all. I read a magazine article about it.'

'Did John Fate send you?' asked the King.

While Raven's eyes continued to inspect Pierpot he slowly turned his head in the King's direction, those two glum orbs eventually snapping towards the proprietor of the house and his face filling up with apparent revulsion. 'Because my name does not echo through the ages do not imagine I did not clap and dance with joy when chums of yours went early to their graves.'

The King sniffed and grunted. 'Yes, well, we all did things during the Futilities we now regret,' he said.

'Who says I regret them? For your information John Fate has no authority over me.'

'What lineage are you?' Pierpot enquired with genuine interest. '*Dumah, Eremiel, Haniel*?'

The intruder's eyes snapped back to Pierpot. 'Not that it is of any of your beeswax, odd, short-sighted cretin, but I am of *Hadraniel* descent.'

Pierpot was astonished by this genetic revelation and said, 'Your ancestor met Moses!'

'Are you a god then?' asked Egg.

When Raven didn't answer, just threw his arms in the air and laughed out loud, the child looked up at her pretend grandfather and asked, 'Is he a god then?'

'No,' said the King with a shake of his head, 'he's no god. His family may once have possessed dreams of becoming god-like and enslaving humankind, as many of his ilk did, but brave men and women put a stop to that nonsense thirty years ago.'

'He's a *turn-harp*,' said Pierpot, 'a deserter and a traitor to his people.'

'I prefer the term *existentially challenged* myself.' Raven giggled.

'How did you gain entry to my home?' the King asked. 'This building is demonically sealed.'

Raven stuck out one grey clad arm and pointed at a broken window high in the basement wall. 'Charms and rudimentary paranormal security systems do not affect defrocked Seraph as they might Spare Clowns,' he said. 'I simply jumped through your window.'

'Then my advice to you is to jump straight back out again,' the King said, gesturing with the ray gun.

'Worry not, your pseudo-majesty. I am here simply to exterminate an infestation and merely acquired access in order to haggle over a price.'

'I smell a fish,' said Pierpot.

'Is that some sort of slur, creepy man?'

'Not at all,' Pierpot replied. 'I'm suggesting you're demanding money with menaces and this siege is a ruse.'

'I agree,' said the King. 'It's one of the oldest tricks in the book. You infest my property with superfluous pranksters and then claim payment for their dispersal. Is that your despicable business, sir?'

Raven's response came with a large side order of pomposity. 'If that was my business then it would hardly be despicable. Such an endeavour barely registers as mischievous in my estimation, for the expulsion of clowns is a respectable pursuit. Do not insult me with suggestions of collusion for I would never be in cahoots with painted, imbecilic, aberrations such as those which currently surround your dwelling. I find clowns a foul anomaly. They are vermin and I am an exterminator and there is no…!'

'*Did* John Fate send you then?' the King asked, suddenly suspicious.

This line of enquiry seemed to anger the intruder. He dropped clumsily from his stool and groped the air with thin arms as though swimming through it, face writhing in a series of maniacal grimaces before declaring, '*I AM NOT JOHN FATE'S ERRAND BOY!*'

A long period of silence elapsed as Raven stood to attention, arms flat to his sides and said, 'I apologise for my outburst. Please could you point me in the direction of the nearest miserably daubed *Punchinello* for me to kill it.'

'And how exactly do you intend to *kill* it?' asked the King.

From beneath his grey rags the intruder produced the largest revolver any of them had ever seen and said, 'A bullet in the head usually does the trick!'

CHAPTER SIX
Army of Toys

The clowns were becoming restless at the arrival of their appointed leader, *Blanco the Magnifico*. This creature was less circus-friendly than his comrades and more resembled a disturbed child's nightmarish crayon drawing than a big-top artiste. His clothes were entirely white from a diminutive top hat strapped to his head with elastic down to an enormous pair of lolloping boots. Even his rotund nose was white, hair a shock of flaxen spikes and makeup pale and deadly like that of an imp. But the most significant difference between Blanco and his associates was his teeth: hundreds of asymmetrical pointed triangles, set in his gums like those of a shark.

'What prevents you storming this domicile?' Blanco demanded to know in a voice deep and gravelly like the sound wind makes in a coalmine. The clown he addressed froze and fell over backwards onto the elevated section of a seesaw causing the propulsion of a colleague, a Grimaldi who pointlessly flapped its arms and legs while tumbling through the air before striking an exterior wall and exploding in a shower of paint.

'Human magic, boss,' said a nearby Auguste, its bowler hat levitating when it pulled nervously on its necktie.

'Then we shall have to *do* something about that!' said Blanco with a maniacal grin.

At the advent of a plan several clowns began to laugh mischievously and then, as confusion settled over them, stopped and asked, 'What?'

'We will use our own magic,' said their leader.

'Do we get to eat them?' enquired another Auguste whose midriff was a helicopter.

Blanco smiled. 'Gouging on the inhabitants is our just reward, boys. How else will we fit these voluminous trousers?' When he started to laugh all the clowns joined in, even the ones who didn't get the joke. He raised a hand in the air and clicked a forefinger and thumb together. 'If there's one thing you can be sure of, boys, little girls have lots of toys.'

Raven twirled the heavy revolver round one finger in an impossible fashion as he headed towards the window.

'Wait,' said Egg. 'You can't just... *kill* them. That would be... *Jenny Slide*!'

The man in faded black stopped and slowly turned his head to look at her. He sniffed the air. 'Clowns are scum,' he said in a voice like creeping treacle, face writhing with hatred. When he turned himself completely around and stepped towards the child the King placed a protective hand on her shoulder. Raven scrutinised her, continuing to sniff the air. He stretched out a hand with the intention of poking Egg in the chest but the King stepped between them.

'That's enough!'

Drawing his hand back the turn-harp continued to stare at the girl, having to lean to one side to see past the King. 'Clowns are an abhorrence of nature,' he informed her. 'They are perverse and unnatural entities, betraying as they do every emotional convention in the Known Universe. They are a paradox of equal measures joy and sadness, not complex enough to possess free will and too ridiculous to exist properly. They are purely absurd and destined to die *in* absurdity.'

'I'll not let you kill them!' said Egg and struck the pose of a pugilist, two tiny fists rotating in front of her face.

Raven laughed at her pathetic gusto.

'Yes, I agree,' said the King. 'Killing them is highly unethical. Isn't there a more humane…?'

He was interrupted when the turn-harp stood up straight, coming almost nose to nose with the old man and, combing skinny fingers through his matted hair, said, 'I've listened to this type of sentimental duplicity for hundreds and hundreds of years. It's nothing but a schmaltzy deviation tactic. To kill something humanely is a contradiction in terms. Humans are a bunch of tragically confused orphans who think empathy will help them evade hell but take my word for it, nothing says thank you when you kill it. Nothing dies nicely. In death, some clowns perform inadvertent cartwheels while others engage in elaborate ballet moves, but eventually they all explode and splash on the ground. They all die morbidly, catastrophically and wretchedly as does everything else under this sun. There is no merciful method with which to employ murder. So I say, if the mood takes you, why not steal a smidgen of joy in the enterprise? I mean, what would *you* have me do Your Highness, drop *Rapture Bombs* on them?'

The King coughed awkwardly.

'Or perhaps you could disintegrate them with your ray gun.' Raven laughed. 'I'm sure it's environmentally friendly!'

'This?' the King said, holding up the weapon. 'This does not issue death. It's a teleportation device. It simply transfers a subject's molecular structure to another place in time like a Ladder!'

'Clown-friendly, is it?'

'You really are a morose little man,' Pierpot put in.

'You are mistaken, *bonehead*!' he said, glancing at the book-laden fellow. 'When it comes to killing clowns, *numbskull*, I am most serious, for it was a clown who murdered my father.'

This statement appeared to evoke a memory in the King, but he became distracted when Raven started to sniff the air around Egg again. 'How old are you?' the intruder asked the child.

'I'll be ten in two years,' she said.

'Ever kill anyone?'

Egg chuckled giddily while her guardian pulled her aside. 'What sort of question is that to ask an eight-year-old?' the King demanded.

'Asking her what her favourite ice cream is will not save her from these painted cockatoos laying siege to your estate. I am trying to educate the lass. And as I am offering my services to retire a few Cocos from your backyard I expected a little more gratitude. It's generally referred to as supply and demand.'

'Oh, so you do expect payment?' Pierpot asked.

Raven looked at him again and shook his head with frustration. 'I require no financial imbursement for assisting a few dozen *Poliaccis* to kick the proverbial confetti bucket. It's a hobby. But if you're in a generous mood you might give me that book you're trying so badly to conceal.'

There was a moment of icy silence. Pierpot glanced briefly at the King with a nervous flicker of the eyebrows while the King refused to meet his eye for fear of generating suspicion.

'Book, what book?' asked Pierpot, the attempt to feign ignorance lent little gravitas as he was carrying at least five under each arm.

'I would rather the clowns got their gloves on it than a vagabond of your ilk,' the King said.

'Very well,' Raven responded and put his revolver away, impossibly stuffing the huge object into the recesses of his ragged garments. He purposely bumped shoulders with Pierpot as he manoeuvred round the table, walking to the wall where he leapt to the sill of the broken window and hung there like a confused bat. After a moment he looked over his shoulder at them and, smiling peculiarly, said, '*Egg*? Wasn't that the first word Ashok Kumar spoke when they dragged him from that burnt out church?'

When Raven's eyes began to dance with excitement the King pointed the ray gun at him and said, 'She's my granddaughter.'

The turn-harp's head fell unsettlingly to one shoulder as though suspended on a dislocated neck. 'Many await her ascension,' whispered his syrupy voice. 'I would happily act as mediator in a trade. Keep the book. Magic books are for scholars and witches. Magic little girls however…'

The King shot him.

Egg and Pierpot gasped as, in a single flash of light, Raven's molecular structure imploded and disappeared. The King gasped too and, breathing heavily, turned the weapon to examine its settings. 'Damn and blast I had it fixed on short range.'

That was when the kitchen doors crashed open and, to their joint horror, hundreds of hexed toys: teddy bears, clockwork robots and dolls, marched noisily or rolled eerily in, each hitherto harmless artefact etched with a façade of evil and sporting some form of weaponry. A spring-operated tin Robin Hood fired a tiny arrow into Pierpot's shin and caused the man to cry out in pain while the King tried to fire the ray gun but to no avail. He checked the power gauge, twisted it and tapped it repeatedly with a finger, tried to fire again and still nothing happened, so he threw the device at the army of toys where a wind-up robot caught it, appeared to overhaul its settings and pointed it back at them.

'Quickly,' the King called out. 'Run for your lives!'

CHAPTER SEVEN
Sibling Rivalry

A sequence of loud popping sounds rang out followed by the rising scream of a disgruntled soul as a person materialised on the lawn in a swiftly degenerating puff of smoke. Rhodeburt Raven's anatomical structure was undamaged as he snapped instantly back together metres from where the King had disintegrated him. He patted himself down, feeling for missing limbs or reassigned aspects of his physical composition before emitting a sigh of relief, standing up straight and glancing around him at the cavalcade of freaks. The turn-harp smiled, brushed down his filthy grey and tattered shirt front, arranged his jacket at the shoulders and then addressed the troupe with, 'Who wants to die first?'

'Violence will not be necessary, brother,' announced a deep voice as a nudge from behind caused him to stumble. Raven spun on the spot, coming eye to eye with his brother, Blanco. Raven's hand went instinctively to his inner pocket when he realised the fat white clown was clutching the massive revolver.

'That's a neat trick,' he said.

'And what were you planning to do with this?' asked Blanco.

'Oh, that?' Raven replied with a snigger. 'It's a new type of dental floss, try it why don't you?'

'Did you truly think you might kill me with… *this*?'

'Actually, I thought we might make amends for old time's sake and plug a few *Merry Andrews* together, what say you?'

Blanco looked solemn. 'I say you're a disgrace to your holy vows, brother, and require penance,' he chastised while Raven watched his sibling raise the firearm above his head, open his mouth unnaturally wide and swallow the gun whole. Then the larger brother burped and sneered at the smaller.

High above, a great stratus of cloud snaked through with grey churned eerily, twisted into knots to form a clot of high pressured gloom and many of Blanco's infantry appeared spooked by the meteorological event.

'Have you lost weight?' Raven asked pleasantly, reaching out to twang Blanco's wide berth of trouser elastic with a finger.

Some clowns laughed at this.

'Have *you* lost your mind?'

Raven beamed and gently nudged the clown's shoulder with a clenched fist. 'When I heard you'd sustained our vow of clumsy and decked yourself out in this ridiculous apparel I said, no brother of mine would stoop to such moronic levels of reverence for it was a revolting clown murdered our beloved father.'

Blanco looked about him at his militia of circus entertainers before proudly pronouncing, 'Rhodeburt, it was *you* killed our father!'

The turn-harp grinned from ear to ear. 'Denial resides in one of our hearts that much is true.'

Exhaling sharply with impatience, Blanco the Magnifico waddled to and fro before his glum sibling. 'When the Rapture Bomb split us asunder, I retained the logic and sanity a black heart had yet to infect while you inherited every contaminated and insidious aspect of our father's son. You betrayed the honour of the *Heyoka*, the church you vowed to serve and the cornerstone of our holy mandate, the very principles you summoned as motive for murder. You cast these aside like…' Blanco gestured to his brother's outfit, '…old rags and now you resent the sight of the jester because it reminds you of your most iniquitous act.'

'Enough therapy, brother, let's rip each other limb from limb!' Raven declared, spitting on his hands.

Blanco shook his head, sombrely. 'If we re-joined forces out of respect for of our killed patriarch, we could shake up this entire universe, Rhodeburt.'

'Join forces with you? I would rather have a haircut from a crocodile.'

'Then, with a shameful heart, it seems we must engage in battle to the death after all.'

And with that Blanco reached a grasping hand towards his brother's throat. Inches from his sibling's pale flesh though, the clutching limb's progress became bizarrely prohibited. Repelled by some invisible force he was made to step back, making and unmaking a fist to test his authority over his fingers.

'We are stalemate,' Blanco said. 'It would seem not even a Rapture Bomb can deter a basic instinct. But if *I* cannot kill *you*, then *you* cannot kill *me*!'

Raven ran and leapt at his brother, punching Blanco squarely on the nose. The blow issued a honking sound the entire command of clowns heard with a shiver and caused the large incarnate to stumble backwards.

'You were saying?'

Blanco caressed his sore hooter and then scratched his big white head in confusion. 'Perhaps I retain some integrity which prevents me from killing myself,' he deduced, 'but look around you, brother. John Fate is not the only person with a *contingency plan*.'

'Let them do their worst,' Raven laughed, casting a vigilant glance at his nearest adversary. At Blanco's nodded command the farceur attacked, but Raven leapt aside, looped an arm around its insipid neck and whispered something in its ear. The Grimaldi's smile grew wider as its mind fought with furtive information before exploding in a cascade of colour that splattered Raven's clothing with paint.

'How it pains my heart to witness the repugnant depths you are prepared to sink,' Blanco growled through gritted fangs. 'You have become nothing short of a blunt instrument, brother.'

Raven attempted to wipe dye from his shirt but only managed to smear his hands with the vibrant colours of dead clown. 'You are a thing to be hated,' he said. 'I feel nothing but revulsion towards you. I detest, loath and abhor every one of your *comrades at laughs* too for they are a monstrosity and must be eradicated, but *you*, dear brother, *you* are the worst of them.'

The heavens boomed with thunder.

'Hate is a strong emotion,' Blanco remarked. 'I draw some solace that I at least inspire such *passion* in you.'

'Even if it results in *fratricide*?' enquired Raven gleefully.

Blanco smirked. 'Do your worst. I will endure. You forget; I have an army at my disposal.'

'No, brother, you have an army of *clowns* at your disposal!' He turned to regard a nearby Coco and asked it, 'Do you want to hear something *really* sad?'

The Coco looked at the pool of paint that decorated the earth close by. 'Not really,' it said, vigorously shaking its curly bewigged head, yet continuing to smile manically and trying not to appear frightened.

Raven continued nevertheless. 'The stone that will eventually mark the grave of each and every human being has already existed for billions of years just waiting for its titleholder to be born and then die,' Raven dramatically exclaimed for all to hear. 'Is that not the most depressing fact you have ever heard?'

Several nearby Whitefaces began to sob. The Coco started to panic and looked to Blanco for reassurance.

'Your parlour games won't work on battle-hardened commandos,' Blanco told his brother. 'These are die-hard soldiers and immune to dismay.'

Spinning on his heels Raven sidled up to a Whiteface. 'Did Blanco ever tell you about poor *Mr Fluffles*? He was my little doggy, old when our father found him abandoned by the roadside in the rain and after a few years he became lame in his back legs. One day I took him for a totter through the countryside and we sat under an apple tree where poor Mr Fluffles plonked himself beside me, put his tiny head in my lap and just died. I buried him under that tree and marked his grave with a stone created in the big bang.'

The Whiteface burst into tears before exploding in a close proximity of fine rain, splashing over its compatriots and leaving a puddle on the ground. In panic another Whiteface nearby did the same.

'My brother has never owned a dog,' Blanco told them in a sudden panic, 'for our father would never allow it. Don't fall for his miserable gibberish.'

Raven was already slithering up to his next victim, a nearby Grimaldi who froze in fear the moment the incarnate placed an arm round his shoulders. 'The love of my life, Miss Elizabeth Dixon,' he said, 'the lady I planned to wed and protect, the maiden who decorated my dreams with hope and longing, the very day I proposed marriage, laughed in my face.'

The Grimaldi, as well as three companions who had been standing in earshot, exploded in a loud rainbow of paint and tattered clothing.

'Do not listen to these lies,' Blanco implored his soldiers. 'My brother tricks you. He never owned a dog and what pitiful example of femininity would look upon his beastliness twice?'

'You,' said Raven, turning sharply and pointing at another Whiteface. The clown performed a somersault and then comically ran away. A Contra-Auguste who was standing directly behind it detonated in a puff of multicolour, so Raven glided up beside yet another flamboyantly nervous dupe and said, 'Or perhaps you, my good man, have you ever considered the fact that light and heat are not natural states of being; that without the sun, the earth would freeze and be entirely shrouded in darkness.'

The clown did not explode. It was a Harlequin and more stable than its counterparts. Holding its ground, it smugly smiled and turned to address the incarnate. 'We would still have the stars to light our way,' it announced proudly.

Raven's smile beamed brighter still for he liked a challenge. 'The stars, yes,' he said, nodding his head agreeably, 'and every single one that twinkles in the night's sky has been dead a thousand years.'

'*What*?' asked the Harlequin, looking anxiously at Blanco. 'Is that true?' Its manifestation fell foul to all the warped logic that held it together and it exploded just like the others had. Several of the survivors decided it was too dangerous to hang around and fled. Paint washed over Raven's face and clothes as he passed between the multitude of *Barnum and Bailey* buffoons conveying titbits of information like *when a TV set is switched off, all the little people inside cry* or *all dogs think they're immortal* or *all cats are*. And every time a clown detonated, colourful paint decorated his grim and faded garments until he looked far jollier than his quarry as he continued to turn and point at Whitefaces, Cocos and Grimaldis, causing them to scream and cowardly abscond or spontaneously combust into varied bright hues.

Blanco was horrified. 'You fools!' he shouted after them. 'Put your fingers in your ears. Do not listen to his deceit for these are invented sob stories.'

The clowns that remained tried to conceal themselves in inappropriate hiding places; one put his head in a flower pot while a rather fat Coco concealed itself, unconvincingly, behind the slender trunk of a cherry blossom tree. Others dived into hedgerows as though they were swimming pools. Still others sat on the ground and rocked back and forth, reciting carny lamentations and humming renditions of circus melodies.

And then Raven walked up to the giant white clown and asked, 'Shall we dance then, dear brother?'

'You won't get away with this,' Blanco warned him. 'My employers…'

'And who would that be?' And despite their obvious disparity in size, Raven grabbed his brother by his braces and lifted him off the ground with ease. 'Who engaged you and your troupe of dipsticks in this reckless affair? *Who sent in the clowns, Blanco?*'

Raven threw him bodily to the ground and Blanco landed with such a bump that it caused a localised tremor.

'You will suffer for this affront!' his brother warned him, scrambling backwards over the earth. 'Glum forces will hunt you down and make you pay for the atrocities you have instigated this day.'

Raven bent at the waist with hysterical laughter, his paint-spattered hair dragging on the colourful ground, coating what was left of its natural hue in garish rainbow shades. Suddenly the sound of his cruel merriment changed into a mad cackle, an insane screech that emanated from deep inside him. Nearby was a huge ceramic planter. The turn-harp saw it and grabbed it, lifting the large earthenware container high above his head he approached his hysterical sibling. And then...

And then forked lightning descended from a veil of clouds, a cosmic fissure that split open the fabric of space between them and swallowed Raven up whole.

CHAPTER EIGHT
Trapped

The King tore through the house with the gusto and haste of a man half his age, dragging Egg behind him and with Pierpot limping to their rear, mere inches from being savaged by an army of malicious toys. On more than a couple of occasions Pierpot had felt the hot beam of an energy bolt pass his ear as the King's ray gun, now in the hands of a possessed robot, discharged its laser. He even felt the breath of the teddy bears and dolls as they attempted to bite him on the ankles and buttocks, but thankfully managed to remain that valuable slender distance ahead of vicious teeth as the malevolent playthings chased after them. Laser bolts zapped past all their heads at such an alarming rate it was a miracle none were teleported to other points in the Known Universe. Instead, the stray beams of energy collided with tallboys, book cabinets and even a grandfather clock, transporting said artefacts Om only knew where.

The three humans sprinted at full pelt along tulip-wood panelled hallways, past shiny suits of armour and through luxuriously furnished rooms, each area becoming immediately destroyed and gobbled up in the absurd gears of war that pursued them. Eventually, having traversed the entire house, their frenzied dash brought them to an impasse, a lounge area furnished tastefully with lemon-coloured sofas, a rich damask rug and various cabinets of eastern European origin burdened with ornaments, but for all its exotic exclusivity, the room was a cul-de-sac and they were trapped.

As Egg and Pierpot crossed the threshold, the King slammed the double doors shut, held his palms against the wood and with eyes closed, spoke several words in a dead language. Egg was excited to observe her pretend grandfather utilise magic but equally alarmed when he was knocked off his feet as the toys slammed into the doors corridor-side, bending them inwards. Luckily, the magic held and the King was unharmed. They were protected for the time being, but able only to stand and watch as the entranceway buckled and swelled.

'At the risk of applying a glum spin on events,' Pierpot remarked, 'I think we're doomed.' He gestured at the wide expanse of window inhabited by several dozen zombie-like circus entertainers. 'There's no way out. Clowns roam the grounds and a host of psychotic cuddly toys want to break down the doors and murder us!'

The King glanced at him and then at where his faux granddaughter had been standing only to discover her missing. 'Where has that blasted girl got to now?' he asked, anxiously.

Pierpot gasped and exclaimed, 'Om preserve us! Have we left her in the corridor?' Apoplectic with worry, he rolled up his jacket sleeves, dropping his books in the process and snatched up a large figurine from a table. 'We have to go out there and rescue her.'

'I admire your nerve, Pierpot, but really, there's no need,' the King responded, puzzling his friend. 'She does this from time to time.'

Pierpot froze, the figurine held above his head and said, 'I don't quite follow.'

The King closed his eyes for a moment and drew breath up his nostrils. As tranquillity washed over him, he opened them again, looked Pierpot directly in the eye and explained, 'She has a talent for... disappearing.'

'You mean *hiding*?'

'No,' the King replied. 'I mean that she... disappears.'

Pierpot ruminated on this information, gradually lowering the piece of ceramic to his chest and holding it like a baby. 'I'm no expert on the matter, Reg,' he said, 'and Om knows I would never tell you how to care for your own grandchild, but in my experience, eight-year-old girls just don't do that sort of thing!'

'This one does,' said Egg, suddenly appearing at Pierpot's side and causing him to scream and drop the figurine.

'Egg's not your typical eight-year-old girl,' the King proclaimed.

'How on earth...?'

'There are men on the lawn,' Egg said, pointing at the row of clowns to indicate outside. 'They're wearing thick coats and scarves.'

The King hurried to the window and stood on tiptoe in order to see above the curly bright wigs and hairless white domes of the loitering carnival. Sure enough, in the distance, standing on the apex of hill, he saw a group of men dressed in bubble coats, woolly hats and mufflers. They were approximately a hundred yards from Hill House and appeared to have brought several large indefinable rectangular objects with them.

Pierpot, unable to cope with any more strange phenomena for the time being, was still pondering the abnormality of a disappearing little girl. 'Does John Fate know about your granddaughter's… *peculiar talent*?'

Continuing to scrutinise the men outdoors, the King said, 'John Fate is the last person I want to introduce Egg to, though now our home is under siege by, not only a bunch of bozos, but the paramilitary faction of Woolworth's toy department, it seems I'll be left with little option.'

'Should we survive,' reasoned Pierpot as a loud crash came from the corridor and the doors threatened to burst inwards again, yet mercifully continued to hold.

Egg joined her grandfather at the window where he placed a hand on her shoulder. 'You should have stayed outside,' he told her, crossly.

She looked up at the grinning freaks beyond the glass. 'I didn't mean to go out or come back in,' she said. 'It was an accident.'

Pierpot joined them at the window. 'You mean to say you have no control over this power?'

They both turned to look at him.

'It's much worse when she's asleep,' the King told him. 'Her subconscious has her popping up all over the show.'

'I once ended up in a wall cavity, didn't I grandfather?' The King smiled and hugged her to his side.

There was another loud crash out in the corridor and the doors bent inward some more so the King strolled into the centre of the room, taking Egg with him. They both chose large, lumpy ornaments from table tops and readied themselves for battle.

Pierpot remained at the window, observing the absurd line-up outside. He scratched his chin. 'The clowns asked us to give up the child,' he remembered. 'Perhaps they're not here for my book after all.'

'They can have her over my dead body,' the King declared and at the sound of more tumult in the corridor glared at those buckling doors, as did Pierpot now. They listened to desperate scuffling sounds and muffled voices and the unmistakable blasts of lasers resulting in the distinctive, effervescent *plop* of something being teleported or terminated. A moment later the crack in the oak panelling expanded as the hex the King had bestowed on the wood began to wane.

'For the record,' Pierpot said, 'I sincerely apologise if any of this *is* of my doing.'

'Think nothing of it,' replied the King.

And then the doors burst and splintered, discharging sharp fragments across the room. Forced to their knees, the King shielded his pretend granddaughter in enfolded arms as shards of wood rained down all around them. More laser bolts signalled the encounter was far from over and, unable to see anything because of a column of smoke that crept towards them over the parquet flooring, the three of them awaited their fate with dignity, Egg and her pretend grandfather still clutching their improvised weapons. And then gradually, as the commotion subsided, they were able to peer through the thinning smoulder and saw, to their terror, a fiery shadow emerge from the gloom. Pierpot gasped as a flaming teddy bear staggered forwards, furry paws groping at its own throat as it gagged for breath until a laser bolt slammed into its back and the animated object dropped down dead.

The obliteration of possessed toys can be just as trauma-inducing as firing upon actual life-forms. It is advisable the perpetrator seek psychological evaluation immediately.

Now they saw dozens of men dressed in thick coats, silver jumpsuits and gasmasks, each one armed with an emp-rifle. Mechanical voices issued counsel from their guns enquiring over the user's emotional responses following the skirmish. The sound of laboured breathing was perceptible too as the soldiers inhaled and exhaled oxygen supplied by their masks. The first person to enter the room was carrying Gladstone under his arm, the ginger feline angrily mewing at him. It dropped to the ground and scampered away to hide beneath a futon as the soldier removed his headgear.

'Your Majesty,' said the Planner nodding respectfully at the King. 'My name is Lieutenant Howard Bromberg of the Contingency Plan's Antarctic Research Facility in the Desolation Islands. A few minutes ago, we received several items of furniture registered to this address via an *Electra Galactic Distance Ladder*.' He paused a moment, glancing outside and at the Spare Clowns currently being rounded up by other Planners and then resumed his discourse by enquiring, 'Perhaps you might explain what exactly has been going on here?'

CHAPTER NINE
The Maw

Fear had long since exceeded its burden upon his heart and mind by way of acclimatization. Yes, he'd screamed when the King shot him with the ray gun, but that was only to be expected, nothing more than a spontaneous reaction to impending doom, for what sentient creature did not raise a startled eyebrow in the moment of imminent expiration? But the painful truth was that Rhodeburt Raven's soul was far too damaged to ever feel pure fear again. And this was the reason why:

As a child Raven's cot was a prison cell. He awoke every day to partitioning bars in a world that scorned him, made him feel weak, ridiculous and vulnerable. He would cry and his mother would rescue him from incarceration, take him with her wherever she went for the remainder of the day. But whenever his father was in residence, Raven remained in his cot. He had to be unobtrusive, silent as a ghost. His father had no time for noisy infants. As Raven developed, matured and grew into the strange, sinewy adult he became, that sense of captivity never left him and when his mother died, from natural causes (pushed from the highest tower of their family stronghold), Raven found himself alone in the world.

After Rapture Bombs fell on Konigsberg, humanity took to the streets in jubilation, embracing each other in tickertape downpours as air-forces performed self-congratulatory flybys. Good-hearted incarnates were welcomed into the human fold while the bad ones were allowed to secrete back into the shadows. Raven had already turned his harp by this point and so he was permitted to take part in the perplexing euphoria, mingling in the streets with beings who revelled in the defeat of his people. But in Raven's eyes, theirs was no true victory for it was not human forte that turned the war in their favour, but the arrival of a mysterious incarnate, a prophesised entity named *Heavenly Joys*. Raven despised their immodest rejoicing and loathed every person who tried to embrace him and started to entertain dreams of murdering them, all of them, one by one, with his bare hands, just as John Fate had taught him to do.

Following his mother's death, his self-contempt shaped his madness. Lunacy had always lingered on the fringes of Raven's psyche but now her body lay broken on the rocks at the foot of their family fortress it gripped his mind firmly. For years after the flesh stopped holding the corpse together, rotted clothes tried their best but eventually his mother's baby fell apart, separated and travelled and Raven arrived at a point of mental illness where he became convinced she had always been led askew on those rocks, becoming less vigorous of late. Morbidly, he worshipped her skull rather than the other bits and pieces wedged in crevices or carried off by birds. Parasites had their way with her tissue, but the skull remained close to where it originally fell and every day, during the course of his chores or play, the glum boy came to visit and converse with his dead mother's head.

And then one day it was gone.

His father issued instructions for it to be removed. There was not even a discoloration on the stone to utilise as a shrine and Raven realised he hated the man more for removing her skeletal remains than he had for pushing her off the tower in the first place. He had been so bewildered by her absence when she died, he needed that tarnished skull more than he had ever needed her living and breathing manifestation and now her complete absence was an effrontery even worse than her murder.

Grieving and angry, Raven surrendered to the Plan, pledging his allegiance and at the bequest of its Captain travelled to Konigsberg and strangled his father. The comic senselessness of it all tickled him at the time as he watched the colour drain from the fat man's face and told him, 'I am killing you to prove that killing is wrong, Daddy.'

And so, this was the sequence of events; his father killed his mother. Raven turned his harp. At the bequest of John Fate, Raven killed his father and then, whilst he still resided in that Konigsberg bunker, Fate ordered the city to be bombed.

He lost himself in the ruins of Konigsberg in the last days of the war, hiding in crumbled alleyways, laughing and crying in the shadows and praying for the death of his corrupted soul, but instead it burgeoned, grew into two separate organisms and when Death appeared, wreathed in grey rags and less burly flesh, He was confused by Raven's chaotic genealogy and

77

pointed a bony finger at him saying, 'What can I do with you? You are dead and yet more alive than ever.'

It had been his father's voice that disabled him in the rock garden before he woke in those woods. But there was something not quite right about it, something that appealed only to a mad soul like his. His father's features preoccupied his mind now, the crowfeet that turned his eyes into spiders and those brutishly distinguished lines that crisscrossed his pale, plump face. His mouth had been a constant black hole, shouting, snarling or laughing with unkind relish. He remembered other things too from the dream he'd had in the woods: the war-dead, droning aeroplanes and explosions in the sky, marching troops and jubilant humans, rolling tanks and doomed legions trudging towards death, death and more death. Human victory came at a mortal price, a triumph raised upon a colossal mound of corpses. Every dead Seraph wing was awash with the blood of a thousand human souls, so it was said. And if that was true, then his father's wings were saturated with the populations of planets.

He sat up in the snow and thought about the King's granddaughter. She was far too young to be of true value to his kinfolk, but there was definitely an aroma about her, an otherworldly stench that demarcated her as divine, as glumly significant. Raven recognised that stink of favour only too well after a youth spent paraded in front of comparable eminent types. But he must be wrong because, to the eternal anger of all living Seraph, John Fate had found her and her sisters and placed them in shackles.

When something came swiftly towards him out of the emptiness he was instantly roused from his reverie. A white spectre, a dilapidated creature packed inside layers of thick fur stood before him, eerily pointing a bony finger and demanding to know, 'Who the *hell* are you?'

'R-R-Rhodeburt Raven,' he stammered as he picked himself up out of the snow, feet and shins still immersed in the deep white crust. Wearing only the grey, paint-splattered garments of vagrancy, frayed apparel that symbolised both his state of affairs and mind, he felt the merciless cold infiltrate his bones and, glancing round the vast silver cavern, he asked, 'Where am I?'

'What were you doing at Hill House?' the eerie figure enquired and Raven could just make out a young and willowy face inside a bulky fur-lined hood, manly features that appeared almost skeletal, but definitely human and not the Glum Reaper after all. 'Did John Fate send you?'

This question made the incarnate exhale with anger, breath spurting from his nostrils like smoke from a dragon's snout. '*Why do people keep saying that*? John Fate is a fatuous toad and beneath my contempt.'

'So, what *were* you doing there, buddy?' the ghostly Eskimo asked. 'You almost ruined everything.'

It seemed to get colder. Icy burning singed the marrow in his bones and almost brought him to his knees.

'My only desire was to murder clowns,' he said.

The human skeleton, wearing what Raven now realised were several thick layers of animal pelts, began to cackle with laughter. 'Look, it's nothing personal, buddy, but your big nose almost ruined all our plans,' he remarked before striking a martial arts pose, moving flat hands around as though rolling an invisible ball. 'So now I'm going to have to kick your head in.'

'What are you talking about?'

The fur-buried carcass laughed again, chopping the air inches from Raven's chilly features. 'It's took us months to plan this afternoon's festivities and you turning up like you did almost spoilt it. You're not human, are you? Well I am, human and proud. Don't look my best, that's true, but I'm recuperating see?'

One of his Kung-fu thrusts inadvertently connected and Raven, feet still buried in the thick-set snow, fell over. Something slipped from his ragged shirt and came to rest on the ice. Both entities stared at the rectangle of purple.

'What's that?' the fluffy menace asked.

Raven quickly snatched up the Thumb and replaced it beneath his tattered jacket. 'Nothing,' he said.

'If it's nothing let me see it.'

Climbing back to his feet, Raven asked, 'Where am I?'

'Don't change the subject! What are you hiding, buddy? You took something from the King, didn't you?'

'It's just a book... an anthology of poetry.'

The slender Eskimo seemed disappointed, confessing, 'I hate poetry!' before twirling round suddenly with a lifted leg and kicking Raven in the belly, knocking him off his feet again. This time the heavily clad skeleton dropped on top him, holding one arm down with a knee and clutching his other to the snow with a claw-like hand. With his free hand, the malnourished Inuit retrieved the purple book and flipped through its pages with dexterous fingers. 'Humdinger's Thumb,' he declared, reading the inner leafs. 'You stole this from that fruitcake Pierpot, didn't you, buddy? What did you intend to do with it?'

Raven breathed heavily, fury getting the better of him. 'I was going to use it to kill my enemies,' he spat.

The multi-layered skeleton laughed some more. 'Am *I* on that list?'

'Perhaps,' he said, 'if I knew your name.'

The fuzzy figure got off him and wandered away, the sound of his footsteps crunching through thick snow echoing in the cavern. He continued to scrutinise the book. 'So it's not an actual *thumb* then? I never paid much attention in history lessons. I thought Humdinger's Thumb was a real thumb, you know, like *Gaap's Tooth* and *Moloch's Toe*.'

Raven got back to his feet, shaking snow from his clothes. 'Is there any chance we can make a deal?' he asked.

The human spectre turned to look at him and laughed. 'You want to make a deal?' he asked, incredulously. 'But I can just keep the Thumb. I could snap off your hand and take *your* thumb if I wanted. Then I'd have *the* Thumb and *your* thumb and then when it pleases me come back later and take your other thumb. Then I'll have three thumbs or five thumbs if I count my own.' It looked at its frozen hands. '*Five thumbs*! *Imagine that*! What else do you have to offer?'

'Only my nefarious soul,' Raven said, mournfully.

'I'll have to pass this by the boss first,' the fuzzy fellow said and Raven watched as he turned his eyeballs in their sockets and listened as his voice became deep and slow. '*Hello, Mummy, are you there*?'

A little unnerved, but definitely not afraid, Raven glanced round at the cavern realising an opportunity for escape when he saw one, but when he tried to move his feet he realised they were stuck solid to the ground, the snow acting like cement around his boots. He dragged and pulled at his legs to try to release them, but they were stuck fast.

'*It's Fletcher…*' the peculiar man reported in his sluggish monotone.

'*Yes, I know! I'll do it when I get back. Yes, yes… I* **SAID I'LL DO IT WHEN I GET BACK!'**

Startled by the human's roar, Raven's plans for absconding drew to a disappointed close as he became distracted by his jailer's peculiar behaviour.

'*Look, I'm in something of a pickle here…*'

'*No, it's…*'

'*That's not my fault…*'

'*No, I didn't eat any cats…*'

'*I gnawed on its leg a bit…*'

'*No, listen…*'

'**LISTEN!** *I would…*'

'*I would have done that but there was another person, an incarnate with a magic book.*'

What? Humdinger's Thumb. Did **you** *know it's not a real…?*'

'*Oh, you did? Well, that's why I'm calling. He killed your clowns.*'

'*Yes, you heard me right. His name is, Roddy…*'

'*Rod…*'

The thing that called itself Fletcher cast its eyeballs forward again, and asked in its normal voice, 'What did you say your name was?'

Raven sighed. 'Rhodeburt Raven,' he announced, impatiently.

Fletcher returned to his trance-like state.

'His first name's Roddy. His middle name's Burt and his last name's…'

'What? Are you sure?'

'Okay.'

Once again, Fletcher's eyes faced forward. 'She wants to know your bloodline!'

Raven groaned with exasperation. 'My bloodline is Hadraniel.'

Fletcher appeared as surprised as any withered corpse-like entity might at such information. 'Is it really?' he asked. 'One of your ancestors met Moses. Hadraniel eh, that's pretty remarkable. You know, Cruel Lord Crowberry's bloodline was Hadraniel.'

'You don't say,' replied Raven with a crooked smile.

Fletcher's pupils retreated again.

'He says his bloodline is…'

'How did you know?'

'Well, if you already knew, why ask me to…'

'Yes, but I don't understand why…'

'Yes, no, three bags bloody full!'

Fletcher's cognizance returned to the frozen cavern. He made angry fists of his hands and exhaled a tumbling blast of visible oxygen. 'Bloody parents,' he complained.

'So what did she say?' Raven asked.

The figure drew back its hood to better reveal bizarrely gaunt features, smiled and cocked an almost bald head on one side. Fletcher was possibly the ugliest human Raven had ever seen, but that might be due to illness, hadn't he said he was recuperating?

'She said to cast you into hell where you and your kind belong.'

'*What*?' Raven exclaimed, feeling the earth beneath his feet start to rumble. He looked down as a warm and rosy shadow began to melt the ice around his ankles. He still couldn't move.

'You were just in the wrong place at the wrong time, buddy.'

'What's happening?' Raven demanded to know as agonising heat began to invade his lower body.

'You're standing on a maw,' Fletcher told him, throwing him the book, his scrawny features screwed into a joyful grimace. 'You know what a maw is, don't you...?' The escalating temperature around Raven's legs became excruciating and got worse as he began to slide downwards into thawing ice. Fletcher sniffed a laugh and gestured towards the melting snow. 'It's where our enemies nip in and out of hell. Say hello to Satan and all his little helpers while you're down there, won't you?'

His mind went blank as the agony became unrelenting and he was sucked down through burning snow, earth and rock where, even in a state of stupor, confusion and pain, one emotional state did not feature, one reasonable response to such torture did not come to pass, for Rhodeburt Raven was immune to fear.

CHAPTER TEN
Grace Plateau

Lieutenant Bromberg's team of heavily armed research analysts had been studying feral cat populations on *The Desolation Islands*, a group of landmasses in the Southern Indian Ocean, when, rather surprisingly, a grandfather clock materialised atop a twenty-metre sedimentary rock formation swiftly followed by an eighteenth-century cedar wood tallboy and a bookcase. The islands were of particular interest to John Fate due to their mythology. Millions of years ago, when Orgo, Om's malevolent brother, plummeted into the frosty wasteland, a series of large scale volcanic eruptions shook the region. In subsequent centuries its submerged terrain became popular with nymphs, mermaids and numerous other types of leviathan and whenever cats, volcanoes and aquatic creatures appear in the same ecological vicinity together it is the obligation of the Contingency Plan to investigate said phenomena. So when antique interior furnishings pop up out of thin air the Plan is even more indebted to determine the cause of such illogicality.

'Using an *Electro Galactic Distance Ladder* we accessed the signals source and were able to teleport to Hill House just in the nick of time,' the Lieutenant explained to the King as he escorted them outside where many of the madcap invaders were still being rounded up. Having tried and failed to run away, oversized shoes impeding on their haste, the clowns were easily apprehended.

'We've managed to detain the remaining trespassers,' the Lieutenant remarked, 'including the notorious glum fugitive, Blanco the Magnifico. He'll be shipped back to Grace Plateau for interrogation.'

'What about the others?' the King enquired, as they passed a group of handcuffed clowns and he noted the worried expression on his pretend granddaughter's face.

'They'll be repatriated,' the Lieutenant replied.

'*Repatriated*?' the King asked, 'but Spare Clowns have no homeland.'

The Lieutenant briefly glanced at the child before prudently suggesting, 'I'm sure there's an absurdist district or two in Avignon culture where they'll be made to feel at home.'

This notion pricked the King's conscience but, in the hope he would never have cause to explain to Egg what it meant, purposely ignored her silent curiosity.

'Are abstract prisons still being built in this day and age?' asked Pierpot, oblivious to the caution adopted by his peers. 'I would have expected that in the two decades I've been away the manufacture of ridiculous pseudo-worlds would have been abolished.'

After such an eventful afternoon the King didn't possess the resolve to clarify what *Avignon culture* and *abstract prisons* actually involved and chose to point at the state-of-the-art EGD Ladder that had brought the Lieutenant and his men to Hill House, declaring, 'Will you look at that magnificent contraption,' and therein distracting everyone from complicated adult matters.

Familiar with teleportation devices, such technology having been used for decades, neither the King nor Pierpot had ever seen anything like the instrument Bromberg's team employed. It was so advanced that the two older men originally mistook it for an oversized standard lamp. This Ladder had none of the traditional pipes, pumps or bulkiness or indeed dispensed wheezing and burping noxious gases like its forerunners. This appliance was up-to-date and kitted out with all the latest technology: citizens band radio and a cassette player, LED readouts and a remote control. Typically, neither the King or Pierpot trusted the new-fangled machine, but it was a means to an end, even if that end was to avoid the controversial subject matter of discussing the pros and cons of virtual reality prisons with an eight-year-old.

'It's been an honour meeting you, Your Majesty,' Lieutenant Bromberg stated and the King had little time to look embarrassed before the four of them, Gladstone included, were steered beneath the Ladder's saucer-shaped apex. A blinding flash of light immediately followed by a short, sharp tug of stomach organs achieved a cosmic leap through the stratosphere, delivering them to a cramped cubicle on Grace Plateau.

Throwing back the drape the King stepped out onto a busy and brightly lit corridor. Similarly, curtained stalls stretched away in both directions along the passageway where military personnel, white-smocked scientists and clipboard-wielding clerks darted back and forth. Sandwiched as it was between stratums of reality, Grace Plateau currently found itself moored to Affleck's Palace in Manchester City Centre, yet, for various reasons, the fact it didn't sell shoes being one, Contingency Plan headquarters was off-limits to shoppers. In fact, it was inaccessible. Constructed from two thirds Accrington brick and one celestial strand (a languidly shifting material resembling billowing silk, but was in fact celestial deoxyribonucleic acid (CDNA), the DNA of God), the province was the last known residual presence of Om in the Known Universe.

Whereas cats took strange wonders in their stride, the three humans were dumbstruck by the populace of that corridor, standing in the Ladder Bay and marvelling at the multi-cultural community of alien visitors and heavily armed civil servants. Its employees dismissed the spectacle of living tissue walls and bumping shoulders with interdimensional species as normal, everyday Plateau life, but to the uninitiated, the location represented a chaotic utopia inhabited by giant rodents, beings with inside-out bodies and multi-limbed creatures jabbering in incomprehensible tongues.

'The kitty will require quarantine,' a diminutive woman with fat, stubby horns loping her skull remarked, causing the King to recoil having not seen her approach. He looked at Gladstone, patted him affectionately on the head and handed him over. Gladstone mewed with self-pity and betrayal as he was carried off but only Egg seemed to feel true sorrow for the moping moggy. Pierpot looked relieved to be feline free and the King became suddenly side-tracked by the approach of another female Planner, a tall incarnate woman leafing through forms attached to a clipboard.

'Follow me, please,' she said in a gravelly voice, a pair of exotic wings expanding from her shoulder blades, rapidly beating at the air and lifting her off the ground.

'*Phyllis*?' the King gasped as the three of them strolled in her wake.

Although of a similar age to the King, Phyllis Hartmann had retained a youthful physique whereas partisanship of Reginald's belly and hairline had become somewhat capricious over the years. Her pencil grey hair was tied up in a bun on her head and she wore bifocals, but apart from these vestiges of age, her Seraph beauty was an enthralling vision.

'Oh,' she said, flippantly, glancing over her shoulder and repositioning her spectacles. 'Hello, Reginald. I haven't seen you since... oh yes, that's right, the day before we were due to wed.'

An audible hush settled over their section of corridor as Egg and Pierpot, in addition to several passing extra-terrestrial eavesdroppers, gulped air and exchanged amused and prying glances.

'You're in luck,' Phyllis said. 'John is in residence and has a slot in his schedule.'

Pierpot leaned towards the King and whispered, 'Aren't you supposed to be keeping the girl a secret?'

'We have few options open to us right now,' the King replied in a hushed tone before quickening his pace to draw alongside their guide who had fluttered off ahead. 'Phyllis, it truly is a pleasure to... I mean to say...'

Mistaking his befuddled attempt to break the ice as an apology, Phyllis interjected by saying, 'An explanation isn't necessary, Reginald. There was no need thirty years ago and there's no need now. You ditched me at the altar. I'm completely over it.'

A sudden tumult came from behind them bringing everyone in the corridor to a halt and the Hill House inhabitants watched as a scuffle ensued between the newly arrived Spare Clown, Blanco the Magnifico and his uniformed handlers. The robust prankster threw Planners left, right and centre intending to fulfil his contract and attack the King and his companions. Dragging Egg behind him while Pierpot backed against a surging wall, the King prepared for an encounter but after seconds of disorder, a taser was utilised and the unruly prisoner was shackled and bustled off in the opposite direction, screaming blue murder as he went.

With giddy hearts calmed by the ensuing equanimity the King and his entourage set off along the corridor again.

Pierpot fiddled with his specs. 'I wonder; do *you* know the correct collective noun for a group of clowns?' he asked.

'A *Pandemonium*,' said Phyllis and the three survivors of the Hill House siege exchanged satisfied smiles and head nods.

CHAPTER ELEVEN
Battle-born

The beautiful glum witch, Leontine Pryderi, spun her scimitar around dexterous fingers, measuring each interval between strikes as she chopped, carved and jabbed at the encroaching horde of *Bos Torus*. Only hours earlier there had been a hundred thousand, a great swarm of solid, russet warriors, larger than the most purebred steer, pouring over the landscape. Their number had swiftly diminished as Pryderi and her Seraphim peers tore them to pieces. The Bos Torus once roamed the wildest hemispheres of earth, in prehistoric times, long before man was the planet's most formidable predator. A fearsome beast, immense and muscular, with four curved black horns sprouting from a solid head, in its prime it feared only one other mammal, the giant sabre-toothed tiger, and with good cause, for it was this vicious mammalian marauder eventually made the Bos Torus extinct. Now their existence was restricted to the malevolent chaos of glum worlds; a battle-born ogre for arrogant Seraph to exercise their blood-lust in lieu of slaughtering humans; a gory pursuit to entertain noble incarnates under the vulgar guise of hunting.

The witch wore black armour, to protect her from the more obstinate steers as she dove, sidestepped and physically climbed torsos of advancing oxen, tearing through packs with callous ease. She ducked a crude broadsword carved out of the bones of its wielder's ancestor and took off both its legs with her own weapon. Lance, axe and other makeshift armaments hacked and pierced the air inches from her flesh, but Pryderi effortlessly avoided every assault with gusto, spun on her heel, yellow, red and orange tresses whipping the air, lashing her foe with sweat as she deftly divided steer after steer from its bovine soul. A jagged carpet of corpses lay behind, beyond the bitter cold and grey bad-lands of *Marbas Gulf*; one of the most inhospitable provinces in hell where to survive its biting elements was, in itself, a trial. Dust exploded beneath her shifting feet as she passed through the horde, body after body turned into a pleat of carnage. She twisted and parried, sliced, diced and rolled, used the curved, lifeless rump of one steer to springboard at her next kill. She hacked off horns and heads, jammed her blade between solid shoulder blades, travelled with the corpse as it fell, estimating which imminent combatant was most vulnerable. Unsuspecting beast after unsuspecting beast was plummeted into eternal glumness under the razor-sharp edge of her scimitar and the massacre was repeated in a kilometre radius on both sides as noble-born incarnates, clad in their families' armour and colours wielded ancient Om-kissed weapons to take down the steer at such a rate the species might be rendered extinct all over again by teatime.

And then a thunderous crack erupted in the sky and a sickly grey heaven split in two. Black rain poured into the realm from another dimension. As the deluge lashed down hard upon them, incarnate and Bos Torus alike, the witch realised the firmament was pouring with blood. It soaked everything it touched, ran down the inside of her armour, stuck her multi-coloured locks to her head and stung her eyes. Grey wastes were quickly coloured-in red in a matter of seconds and she saw a further tsunami, an immense, dark wall of crimson ripping the mountains apart to the west and trampling the more distant oxen herds beneath it. The witch managed to slay three more steeds before hurling herself heavenward, hanging a dozen metres off the ground where she watched the destructive ocean of blood crash, catastrophically, over the plane. The full terrifying force of the tidal wave took the life of every organism that had not seen it coming. The fool-God known as *Marbas*, perceiving their blood sport a threat had inadvertently completed the annihilation of his acolytes and she laughed sharply and loudly so the half-remembered deity would hear.

Then the witch cast her eyes about at the curve of incarnate beings dotting the sky above the deep and crashing watercourse, their immense, sinewy wings unfolding

By the time the tidal wave had abated, flowing only inches deep over the surface of the land, the adrenaline rush that had sustained her killing spree had also receded and Pryderi waded past the bodies of battered and drowned steeds in a sulk until she came upon a particularly fat specimen and sat atop its belly to survey the day's hunt.

'You really have to admire the audacity of a seventh parallel tyrant who pitilessly sacrifices an entire species to save its skin,' spoke an articulate voice and Pryderi turned to see the tall, elfishly-striking figure of Lord Callous

Sacheverell, splashing through the shallows, gory waters up to the ankles of his black leather boots. He swept a gloved hand through short, dense white hair as he leered at her, two black pupils lending him an eerie grace.

'The fool-God forgot angels can fly,' the witch muttered.

'It gets you right here, doesn't it?' Sacheverell mocked, banging the chest of his armour with a clenched fist. 'The sacrifice, I mean.' Then he laughed, rolling a shoulder in its socket and came and placed a boot heel upon the corpse of the steer now rendered nothing more than a large brown atoll in a newly formed lake. 'You fought like a *goddess*, like *Anahit* herself. Your uncle would be proud.'

'Why do you speak of him in a past tense?' Pryderi scoffed.

The glum Lord looked mildly shocked and drolly suggested, 'Leo, please, let us not spoil what has been an eventful afternoon.'

'Slaughtering cattle is cushy work,' Pryderi grumbled, picking a hairy clump of mangy flesh from the dead steer and hurling it into the shallows.

'Why must the glass remain half empty with you?' he scoffed and took her by the arm, pulled her from the bull's corpse and placed his mouth on hers. She dragged herself from his grasp and calmly wiped her lips with the back of a hand, spat into the red estuary lapping their boots and turned and walked away.

'You've lost your appetite for sport, Leo,' Sacheverell goaded, watching her splash in the direction of the mountains where the tidal wave of blood had originated.

She stopped, turned back and looked at him. 'How can you wallow in this humiliation?' she asked, horrified. 'Every day we remain in exile is an insult to our dynasties. There are worlds out there we were born to preside over as gods. Gods don't hide in shadows. Gods don't practise their arts by slaughtering heifers. I get no gratification sanitising hell from grazing herds. Is that what we have become, Sacheverell, pest control for the underworld?'

'There is an eternity before us, Leo. There is no haste. One day the earth will be ours again.'

'It was never ours,' she snapped. 'For millions of years there was nothing to govern but germs and enormous lizards. Humans were much better sport than spores and dinosaurs, but we never truly governed them, did we? Om protected them. That witch allowed mercy and sanctuary. We had three hundred years to do with it as we pleased after she faded, a glorious time I thought would never end, but is long past now.'

The glum Lord sighed, folded his arms across his chest. 'When you have lived as long as I have, Leo…' he avowed, his voice as polished as his mind was prudent, 'you come to realise we are engaged in an ever-progressing state of play and that events do not simply conclude, they just alter perspective. There is always opportunity. This world around us…' he unfolded his arms to gesture at the landscape 'is merely a respite.'

She turned and walked away. 'Where are you going?' he queried, with a hint of hilarity.

'To find the lion,' she said over her shoulder, 'and when I do I'm going to smash its face in!'

CHAPTER TWELVE
John Fate

The Captain of the Home Guard was in his office, seated at his desk and sorting through that day's memos. As well as a notification that Spare Clowns and possessed toys had attacked Hill House, there were numerous other reports requiring his immediate attention: Satan-sightings in international coffee franchises, Behemoth attacks on potholers in Grange over Sands, the geomancer, Hereward Nery waking from a twenty year coma, the abduction of a Nefarious Logistics board-member by the Real Salvation Army, Incubus-rights campaigners criticising newspaper articles referring to them as *Succubus*, First Flesh Puritans demonstrating against the NME's passion for punk-rock music, on-going scandals involving unscrupulous scientists selling their gimmicks to unsavoury types and Friends of the Known Universe holding demos against *ASAP* (Availability and Sustainability of Alternative Powers) mining at the South Pole. But the only memo to pique his interest concerned Plateau staff complaints against time-tapered lunch breaks because he was hungry and the thought of food made his belly grumble.

Beside the pile of dispatches there was a Tupperware box containing a tinned-ham and brown sauce sandwich for should Fate ever be marooned on a desert island, swallowed alive and digested by a space whale or lost in any variation of additional ways out there in the furthest reaches of the cosmos, the only thing he would truly miss about civilisation was a homemade tinned-ham and brown sauce sandwich.

He leaned back in his ergonomic chair and sighed, glancing at his butty in its plastic prison as a sense of futility washed over him. It was a cliché for a man his age, but he really had had enough; enough of interrogating narrow-minded incarnates who wanted every human enslaved, enough of defending his own reactionary views when it came to ways of dealing with their enemies, enough of secrets and lies and enough of deciphering his dreams in relation to events in reality. The latter attribute was Fate's modus operandi, his great significance in the council that was Om's unofficial replacement; the Contingency Plan. He used a unique form of prognostic dreaming to make connections with day to day events. For instance, the King was documented in his vagaries, having visualised him, in a decade old dream, falling to his death alongside, of all things, a green dragon. The Captain's dreams were seldom literal but their metaphorical implications frequently justified investigations by the Plan. The dream of the King for example would probably have nothing to do with a real fall or a real dragon for that matter. Perhaps Reginald Fielding was fated to *fall out of favour*, or *fall for a deception* and become duped by an enemy represented in this instance by a dragon.

He leaned forward and sifted through the dispatches as two events clicked together in his brain. The Captain remembered a dream he once had about an absconded scientist called Dr Selwyn Tindal. He had visualised him riding a giant turtle. Finding the memo about the Behemoth attacks he reread the report. If memory served, Tindal was obsessed with Godzilla movies and often holidayed in Grange over Sands.

Check.

He leaned back again, his mind congested by thoughts of tinned-ham and brown sauce. He considered little else in his pigeonhole of reports worth casting illumination over for the time being, especially while his stomach was growling like a sore lion, so he drew the Tupperware towards him, deftly uncoupled its lid and lifted out the cellophane bundle. Satan-sightings, Incubus-rights, First Flesh Puritans and Friends of the Known Universe would all have to wait until his belly was mollified. But, as he started to unfasten the bound sarnie, a prophetic supposition struck him. The residents of Hill House were rescued by Planner's from Antarctica. Something about the EGD Ladder being sourced to the location stuck in his crow but he couldn't quite seem to attach two cerebral cables together, as if there was some sort of internal interference; hunger perhaps? His sandwich was unpacked and an inch from consumption but his mind was waving a flag and made him pause as he attempted to drag a memory up from that deep well of recall he relied upon for ongoing employment. A few more seconds and he would have it.

When the door burst open and Phyllis Hartmann fluttered in announcing the arrival of the King, the Captain heard the allegorical sound of a bucket tumbling back into the depths of a well as his mind lost grip on its symbolic shape. He dropped the sandwich into a nearby litter bin, knocked the Tupperware in after it and, silently reproaching himself, stood and said, 'Show him in.'

'He's not alone,' said Phyllis. 'There's a man called Morecambe Pierpot with him and a little girl called… Egg.'

Fate's eyebrows scuttled up his forehead with interest. He gestured for her to fetch them and as Phyllis took her leave, rubbed his aching temples, attempting to massage memory back; a slapdash ancillary for mental CPR. He strolled over to one of several glass cabinets decorating the compact office and stared at what the glass dome enclosed; the dismembered hand of Sir Charles Waterhouse. The image evoked a fleeting memory comprising a bear and an egg, but as before, he could not fully appreciate the vision before it was impeded upon by internal interference. Why hadn't he foreseen a child called Egg? That omission was highly suspicious. Perhaps it was a facet of growing old, along with a receding hairline, aching joints and a nostalgic longing for unhealthy sandwiches? Whatever it was it worried him. If he continued to disremember important facts and phantasms he would soon be out of a job.

Staring at Sir Charles' dissected appendage one last time, he chuckled to himself and then recovered his poise as Phyllis escorted two men and a child into the room. Fate sensed immediate evasiveness from the King and in his mind revisited the image of him falling alongside a green dragon. Standing next to the veteran was the epitome of idiocy, Morecambe Pierpot, a man Fate considered only able to enlist in the Plan during wartime, when the organisation was less choosy about membership. A lump of idiot like that would fail every aptitude test in today's administration, scoring so low he would not be trusted to mop floors. Finally, the Captain looked at the little girl who appeared distinctly interested in a large portrait of the paranormal war heroes, *The Harbingers*, the five champions posing in their orange jumpsuits. Her attention was then quickly seized by the spectacle of a stuffed gorilla wearing a cowboy hat and gun holster in the corner and then, with a mixture of alarm and delight, she caught sight of the skeleton of a parrot in its glass case that looked straight in her eye and cawed, *hello ducky*, to which the child exploded with giggles.

The King noticed none of this as, blushing, he attempted to attract the attention of Fate's PA who firmly ignored him and left. It was not until the door closed behind her that he finally acknowledged the Captain with a half-hearted smile and a nod.

'Welcome to Grace Plateau, Your Highness,' hailed the Captain and the King rolled his eyes with exasperation.

'There's no need for sarcasm, John.'

'Far be it for me to mock the only man ever to face down the *Kraken of Sabden Locke* and live to tell the tale,' Fate declared noticing the child's look of admiration for the old-timer. 'At the height of your soldiering career you battled *Martian Berserkers*, *dwarf Trolls* and *giant poisonous geraniums* and, as if that was not enough, you abandoned my PA at the altar. Tell me, Reginald, which of those fiery foes do you most fear today?' Laughing, he patted the King playfully on the shoulder before turning to consider Pierpot. 'And I see the rumours of your demise were wildly exaggerated.'

Pierpot smiled and said, 'Actually, no!'

The Captain's eyes furrowed with confusion. 'Then death suits you, old chap,' he remarked, finally turning to address the child, noting that her flitting attention was now detained by the disarticulated bear paw. 'I took that off a mad monkey that tried to assassinate Winston Churchill,' he lied.

The King and Pierpot exchanged knowing glances while Egg laughed.

'Is it the cold cruelty of assassins, the attempted murder of a historic premier or simply the word *monkey* that amuses you?'

'The word monkey,' Egg admitted. 'And that it was mad.'

The edge of Fate's lip raised itself in a sly smile. 'I can categorically say it was absolutely livid when I lopped that hand off. So, my PA tells me your name is *Egg*. That's a *very* interesting name to have.'

Seeing the gears of Fate's mind start to work the King was tempted to grab the girl and make a dash for it.

'Is your name truly *Egg*, or is the King playing a mean trick on me?'

Egg looked puzzled and glanced sheepishly up at her pretend grandfather before returning her peepers to the Captain and confessing, 'I can't remember my real name.'

The Captain's eyebrows ascended above mild suspicion to a level adjacent with intrigue. 'My, my, that's very, *very* interesting,' he said with frank excitement. 'Many years ago I met somebody else who could only remember the word *egg*.'

The little girl smiled and said, 'Do you mean Ashok Kumar? There's a pop-up history book in the library at Hill House and he's in it.'

'What an adorable young lady you are,' Fate delighted in saying, crouching in front of the child. 'So who do you belong to?'

The King coughed and told him, 'She's my granddaughter.'

'So, you must be *Princess* Egg then?'

Egg grinned from ear to ear and Fate laughed out loud, stood and grabbed her grandfather by the arm, dragging him towards the taxidermy gorilla where he leaned in close to the old man's ear and, in a more sombre tone, asked, 'What in the name of all that's shiny and holy is going on here, Reginald?'

The King played nervously with the lapels of his jacket, shifting his weight between feet. Eventually he snorted through his nose with defeat and took a moment to describe the day's events so far. When he finished he appealed to Pierpot to show Fate the book.

His bespectacled friend appeared cagey, enquiring, 'What book would that be?'

'The book, man, show John the book!' urged the King.

With a defeated breath, Pierpot dug a hand inside his jacket and brought it out empty, exhibiting nothing in his fingers.

Fate walked up to him and examined the man's unencumbered hand. 'What am I looking at?' he asked.

Rocking proudly on the balls of his feet and smugly sniffing at the air, Pierpot boasted, 'Why, this, my dear fellow, is Humdinger's Thumb, one of the three most dangerous texts in the Known Universe.'

Fate disguised his confusion and absently queried, 'Is it now?' running with the ruse rather than spoil the silly man's obvious glee. 'And where on earth did you procure such an arcane item?'

'Nowhere on earth,' Pierpot swanked. 'I actually uncovered it in hell, wedged between *The Occultist's Book of Baby Names* and a copy of Stephen King's *It*, in General Galbi's very own library.' He pushed his spectacles up the bridge of his nose with a noble air. 'Anyway, as I have already explained to Reg, it seems the forces of glumness are not overwhelmed after all and are, in fact, attempting to raise another offensive against us.'

'I see,' said Fate. 'And you thought a glum tome like Humdinger's Thumb falling into the wrong hands might prove unfortunate for humankind. Good thinking, Pierpot. However, since the passing Cruel Lord Crowberry there is nobody alive could possibly control a text of that magnitude.'

'Why Crowberry?' the King asked with curiosity.

Fate turned to look at him. 'Because, in the field of occultist paraphernalia, he was unsurpassed,' the Captain explained. 'His obsession with god-kissed odds and ends was almost as important to him as discovering *her* whereabouts…' And at this point, he looked at Egg.

'Do you mean, Chaos Likely?' enquired Pierpot.

'I've heard of her too,' said Egg with excitement. 'She's one of the Sinister Vessels.'

'At least the Thumb's out of harm's way…' Pierpot began to suggest.

103

'Talismans on that glum scale are best lost to both sides,' Fate avowed. 'Why don't you hold on to it for a while?'

Pierpot smiled and slipped the little purple volume that wasn't there back inside his jacket.

'I agree,' the King remarked. 'I'll sleep better at night knowing it's in our hands during a time of war.'

'*A time of war*?' asked Fate, apparently confounded by the statement.

Returning to Egg's side, the King laid a gentle hand on her shoulder. 'Wars never end,' he said, 'they just become moral and public inconveniences. The simple fact that people stopped dying in their droves doesn't mean war is over. General Galbi never surrendered and as Pierpot says, the Seraphim are stockpiling arms for another offensive.'

'This is old news, Reginald,' said Fate. 'The Plan has been aware of hell's arsenal for quite some time now. It is a benign threat.'

The King huffed, impatiently. 'And are we doing the same? Are we amassing armaments, I mean?'

'Armaments like this... *Thumb*?' Fate asked, gesturing towards Pierpot. 'A book that, whether in the possession of humans or incarnates, can only render annihilation for both sides?' He looked at Pierpot. 'Did the clowns see the book?'

'No,' he said, casting a burdened glance at the King.

'There was somebody else at the house,' the King confessed, 'an incarnate who managed to bypass my demonic seals. He didn't give a name but said he was of the Hadraniel bloodline.'

Fate seemed genuinely interested. 'What did he look like?'

'Moribund chap, dressed like a vagrant priest and in need of a good haircut. Oh, and he suffered quite the psychopathic repugnance of clowns. Somehow he knew Pierpot was in possession of the Thumb and wanted it in exchange for dealing with our mottled invaders.'

'And you refused to give it him, obviously.'

'Well, obviously,' the King replied.

Fate rubbed his chin, stroking the indentation beneath his bottom lip. Then he glanced at Egg. 'And what about the girl, did he show any interest in her at all?'

'Why would he?' the King asked, feigning ignorance.

'Yes, yes, yes, but *did* he?' Fate enquired with irascibility.

'She's just an eight-year-old girl.'

'Perhaps,' Fate said, 'perhaps not.'

The last thing the King wanted to do was bring unwarranted attention to Egg, yet at the same time he realised he had a code of duty to tell John Fate everything he knew. But divulging the truth to a man like Fate might be detrimental to the child. He was also more than well aware of Fate's ability to predict the future and reasoned the man may have already foreseen the events they were presently engaged in.

'You're keeping something back, Reginald,' Fate deduced.

'You're being paranoid, John,' the King replied with petulance.

'I'm paid to be paranoid.'

'My civil liberties were violated,' the King reminded him with the intention of changing the subject. 'My home was attacked. The very least you can do is investigate the matter.'

'I can only investigate a contravention of law if I have all the facts.'

The King shrugged his shoulders and said, 'I don't know what you mean.'

'Now, Reg,' Pierpot put in. 'I think Mr Fate makes a valid point. You *are* holding something back!' the former prisoner of hell submitted, making less than covert eye gestures towards Egg.

'Is this true, Mr Pierpot,' asked Fate. 'Are you privy to information I am not? Because if you are…'

'He doesn't know anything,' the King interjected.

'The girl,' said Pierpot, 'she's…'

'She's what? Not the King's granddaughter? The King has no children, and neither has he any siblings with which to bestow him nieces and nephews,' Fate announced, looking at the older man. 'So what's it going to be, Reginald? Shall I grant you all the protection at my disposal to keep you and the girl safe, which is significantly more security than you can offer, or shall I send you back to Hill House to deal with any further attacks alone?'

Exhaling a heavy sigh, the King looked down to see the child smiling back at him and said, 'Egg appeared in my garden a few weeks ago, just materialised out of thin air, in the centre of a *Devon hedge*; one moment it was a pretty shrub, the next a prickly prison for an eight-year-old. It was a sunny day and I was in a deckchair on the lawn when she just popped up out of nowhere. I'd barely time to remove my sunglasses when she disappeared again. It was astonishing. The hedge was completely ruined, mind.' The King snorted a laugh and squeezed the little girl's shoulder affectionately. 'Exactly twenty-four hours later she happened again and in the very same spot. I'd removed the bush by this time and so her influx was less awkward. Then she disappeared again. But on the third day, she reappeared and stayed. She has absolutely no memory of how she came to enter our universe and I only kept her a secret because… well, because I…'

'Because you feared the Plan would turn her into a weapon,' Fate guessed.

The King swallowed hard and nodded his head. 'Yes,' he replied.

Egg laughed. 'How could you turn me into a weapon?'

The Captain of the Home Guard bent in front of her again. 'Well, we could put some spikes here,' he said, tapping her on the shoulders, 'and perhaps missile wings along your arms.' She giggled and playfully punched him in the chest, causing Fate to tumble backwards onto his behind.

'Egg, that's not a nice thing to do,' the King scolded.

'I'm being a weapon,' she reasoned.

'Don't worry, I'm all in one piece,' Fate remarked as he got back to his feet. He wiped dust from his derriere and regarded the child with curiosity again. 'With all good intentions, and, out of a misguided wish to protect you,' he said, 'your grandfather has not been totally honest in his assumptions about your identity.'

'Protect me from what?'

'From me, would you believe?'

'*Why*? Are you a baddy?'

Fate smiled, briefly assessing the reaction of the others in the room before responding to the question. 'There are those who say I am and I imagine your grandfather is one of them.'

He walked to his desk and sat on its edge, picking up a paperweight in the process. 'From a certain point of view, I have done things that most people would deem morally inappropriate.'

'What does *deem* mean?' Egg asked.

Fate ignored the question. 'What do you know about Ashok Kumar?'

Egg grinned. 'His other name was *Heavenly Joys* and in the pop-up book he appears from behind a cloud and says, *egg*, just like me. There was a page with Chaos Likely and the Sinister Vessels *and* one about the Knight Watchmen.'

'And did the book explain what happened to Mr Kumar?'

The little girl nodded. 'Yes,' she said. 'He helped human beings win the war against Angels.'

'That's right,' Fate said with a smile, heftily pitching the paperweight, a tiny reproduction of the Lancashire countryside in a snowstorm, from hand to hand. 'Only, he didn't so much as *fight* in the war as provide humans with weapons that could impede our enemy's magic and turn it against them.'

'He was some sort of bomb,' she said.

'That's right,' Fate replied, tickled by her knowledge. The Captain was certain the King would take issue with his position and would, no doubt, explain it differently to her later, but he spelt out his own perspective anyway. 'Sadly, Mr Kumar died as a result of his participation in the Futilities. But we still have his weapons and all the science he provided us with to help fight the naughty Angels in the future.' He looked at the King. 'The moment Egg appeared on your lawn you must have assumed... well, what exactly did you assume?'

'I assumed nothing,' the King responded, squeezing the girl's shoulder again to reassure her.

'You assumed…' Fate continued, confidently, rising from his desk and walking to and fro, passing the paperweight between palms, 'not that Egg was here as another redeemer, because we are currently in a time of peace, but that she was something else entirely. Am I correct?'

Egg looked up at her grandfather. He shook his head and said, 'Don't be ridiculous!'

'Is it so ridiculous? It goes without saying, does it not, that when we were at war and in dire need of support, Om sent us Kumar. Now the war is ended and we have incarnates at bay, perhaps Om has made a different contribution to a different congregation.'

The King stepped in front of the child. 'When I leave Grace Plateau, Egg will be coming with me, John. Do you understand?'

Fate laughed and held up his arms in surrender. 'Reginald, I am *not* your enemy. I have no intention of getting on the wrong side of a revered war veteran. Whatever you think of me, I am in the business of good, not evil.' He glanced at the girl. 'But not all can be as certain as I when it comes to their principles.'

Pierpot glanced between the Captain and the King with a puzzled expression on his face.

The Captain looked at Egg and told her, 'Theoretically, I have no power to keep you here and have learnt first-hand the impracticalities of attempting to control glum magic.'

Outraged the King said, 'Egg has no glum magic! She's just a child!'

'As Callous Sacheverell was once just a child,' Fate replied and then suddenly, he hurled the paperweight in the girl's direction and, to the surprise of everyone in the room, including Egg, she swiftly raised a hand in front of her face and, with a protruding forefinger, shot a spark of blue electricity at the snowstorm that disintegrated it and filled the room with a replica snowfall.

As they left Fate's office, shaking snow off their clothes, the King brusquely instructed Pierpot to take Egg and wait for him while he went to talk to his erstwhile fiancée, finding her perched, bird-like on the back of a chair. When she saw him, Phyllis fluttered across the room to the top of a filing cabinet, pulled open a drawer and reached down to search through several folders. The King coughed to get her attention, but she ignored him. 'You were the last person I expected to see today,' he said.

Phyllis dropped to the ground and walked back to her desk, clutching a brown folder labelled *Distraction Tactics*. Her huge, elegant wings folded between her shoulder blades. 'I have arranged for a room at the Elysium Hotel here in Manchester…'

'There were unavoidable circumstances, Phyllis,' the King pleaded. 'You do know that, don't you? Leaving you at the altar was the most difficult decision I've ever had to make. I'm sorry.'

She sat and began to type.

'I was commissioned to look after the King of England.'

'You were meant to guard him, not pilfer his identity,' she grumbled.

'He always was rubbish at cards. Is there any chance at all we can…?'

'Stay out of each other's way for the foreseeable future? I don't see why not. *Goodbye.*'

He looked down, sadly. 'If that's what you want.'

Phyllis suddenly rose to her feet, wings unfolding to fill the space with feathers, her chair sliding noisily across the room in the kerfuffle. 'Soldiering has always been more important to you than actually living, hasn't it, Reginald? Now you're a retired and lonely old man you think you can suddenly replace all those *unavoidable circumstances* and *difficult decisions* with excuses, but you can't. The past is a fixed point. You don't get to change a single second of it. The war was more important than your personal life, I understand. Most people wouldn't, but *I* do! *I* do!' She laughed. 'And incidentally,' she suggested, justly, 'those are the two words you found so difficult to say to me all those years ago.'

CHAPTER THIRTEEN
The Grotto

Pryderi and Sacheverell spent the remainder of the day navigating the desert and its craggy highland, discovering and exploring several uninhabited passageways until they came across a tunnel with symbols carved into the stony entranceway. Because living in clouds was a well-worn divine mythology, simple-minded fool-gods like Marbas, chose to reside inside high mountain ranges. They descended the glum artery in the light of a firebrand, finally reaching a colossal cavern at its heart where thousands of flickering tapers burned and a vast collection of dazzling treasure added to the illumination. At the far end of the opulent grotto, upon a gilded platform, was the fattest, most repugnant lion either had ever seen, laid upon silk cushions, breathless and pouring sweat due to undue flabbiness, the simple task of lounging on pillows appeared to sap its energy. When Marbas saw them he emitted a miserable and fatigued groan that echoed through the damp chamber and, panicking, fell over sideways, noisily scattering pricey titbits about him.

'I've come to tear out your heart,' Pryderi told the half-forgotten god as she trudged across the natural room, kicking candles out of her path, the sound of her voice repeating several times as it ricocheted off the unseen granite above.

Marbas mumbled under his breath, mutterings the witch could only translate into cowardly, beseeching whimpers.

'In every dimension I have visited,' the witch said, 'I have come across pointless entities like you; vile and artless parasites, that prey on the life around them. As you greedily populated this world with an insatiable appetite for beef, I shall endure such voracity when I disembowel you.' She drew her scimitar and the trill of steel amalgamated with the reverberating sound of her footsteps.

Meanwhile, Lord Sacheverell remained at the cavern's entrance, a shoulder to the wall, utilising a small dagger to pick dirt from beneath his fingernails. He chuckled to himself at Pryderi's harrying words.

'*I... am... like you*,' the lion struggled to say between hefty inhalations of breath. '*I also... fell... from heaven.*'

The creature's spinelessness made her blood curdle. The fear in his voice blemished every word off his tongue with craven conceit. As Pryderi grew nearer, the lion rolled onto its rotund stomach and tried to crawl into the sanctuary of nearby shadow.

'You fell from heaven because you were too fat to fit on any clouds!' she mocked. 'But please, feel free to beg for your life, pleading souls invigorate my pallet.' Pryderi licked her lips demonstratively, while slashing the air with her blade. 'Sometimes it is no joy at all to kill a brave creature, but the way fat overlords whine and recoil fills me with joy. You tried to drown us and sent an entire species to its doom so there are no principles can save you or prevent me from twisting that portly head off its shoulders. No matter what language you use to express your terror and regret, all I hear is an entreaty for death.'

'Just kill the pussycat so we can leave this malodorous environment,' Lord Sacheverell urged from the cavern's ingress, his regal voice joining hers in the higher provinces of the cavity.

'What is precious to you?' Pryderi asked as the snivelling creature slid away. She was close now, close enough to smell its sweat-matted coat. 'What do you value? Is there something you can use as a bargaining chip perhaps; all this gold, a flavoursome soul or an offering of kin, some eternal secret or story? I like a good yarn.'

'Ask him if he knows any jokes,' a voice uttered from supplementary shadows behind her. Both Pryderi and Sacheverell turned with their weapons at the ready, pointing at the shady recess of cave. 'Here's one,' the voice went on. 'A priest goes to the post office with a bible wrapped in brown paper. *Is there anything breakable in there?* asks the postal clerk. *Only the Ten Commandments*, says the priest.'

A cold breeze rushed past them, snuffing out more than half the candles in the room. Pryderi listened to the remote echo of that jocular voice where it merged with the sound of their martial movements and tried to locate its source. And then, when a fat man with a long white beard, dressed entirely in red stepped into dim light, she wondered if it was some sort of trap the lion had organised. The fat man's outfit was smeared with dirt and his beard was in urgent need of a trim and a good soak. He dragged a bulky black sack behind him while his other hand clutched the stub of a fat cigar.

Lord Sacheverell snorted a laugh and put away his dagger while Pryderi was in no haste to follow suit. 'Away your blade, lady,' the fat man instructed, 'before you do yourself a mischief.'

'Who the hell are you?'

'*Who the hell am I?*' the fat man asked in an amused comical tone, putting the cigar in his mouth as he approached Sacheverell. 'Did you hear that, Callous, who the hell am I?'

'Leo, surely you recognise our progenitor?' Lord Sacheverell remarked, pointing a thumb in the fat man's direction.

'He looks like an unkempt garden gnome,' she responded, defiant in spite of a rapid sense of unease. *If Sacheverell hasn't taken his head off, he must be somebody of standing*, she quietly considered.

'I once visited a church in Thirsk, North Yorkshire, in the middle of a Sunday service,' the fat man said. 'When the congregation saw me, they screamed and scattered like mice before a cat. All but one climbed over themselves to get out of the place. This one chap though, he just stayed put, sat there on his pew, unimpressed. I walked up to him and asked *do you know who I am?* He said, *yes, I do. You're Satan!* And so I asked *aren't you afraid of me?* And the man shook his head and said *no*. I was curious and so, right before I tore his slimy soul from his puny flesh, I asked, *why* aren't *you afraid of me?* And do you know what his reply was? He said, *I've been married to your sister for the past twenty-five years!*'

Satan laughed out loud while Lord Sacheverell offered a respectful titter, filling the natural auditorium with eerily cheery echoes. Then a scraping sound emanated from behind the witch and she spun around just in time to see the lion's chubby tail slither into shadow and disappear. She barely had time to acknowledge her displeasure when a hand came to rest on her shoulder. The witch instinctively grabbed the arm and twisted it up the user's back.

'*Dear Lord*,' Satan exclaimed in pain, '*this one's got some spunk*!'

'*Leo*,' Sacheverell exclaimed, '*release him*!'

She gazed at the glum Lord a moment and then, exhaling angrily, pushed the fat man away. Satan stumbled, almost falling over his lumpy sack. 'I don't like being touched,' she warned.

'*Evidently*,' Satan replied, rearranging his grimy suit where she had creased it and chucking away his spent cigar. 'But more eminent folk than you have been disintegrated for less than breaking my arm, for I am *El Diablo*, I am *Beelzebub*, I am *Mammon*, I am dying for a slash, are there any toilets around here?'

'Have some respect, Leo,' Sacheverel chastised. 'This man is our oldest kin.' He stepped forward and placed a hand on the fat man's shoulder. 'Satan predates even Orgo as a Lord of glumness.'

'It's quite all right, Sacheverell,' Satan informed him. 'Obviously the young lady has not been keeping up her bible studies.' He snorted a high-pitched cackle.

'I've *heard* of you,' said Pryderi. 'But I was under the impression you were somewhat… *less jolly*.'

'Do not be fooled by this merry garb,' he told her, gesturing at his attire with two plump hands, 'for I am, physically speaking, only what is referred to in psychological terms as, *made manifest*. Originally, I was forged in the minds of humankind as a *necessary evil*, a monster created to fill in the scriptural fissures and scare babies half to death. More recently however I have become mixed up with this festive idiot, this cartoon symbol of humanity's greed, stress and disappointment and so a metamorphosis has resulted. I am no longer the horned, fiery demon with its spiked tail and trident, I am this tubby, rosy-cheeked mascot for a fizzy drinks company you see before you today. I think, in many ways it makes me scarier. The kiddies don't expect the fangs. But they love me, which is always a plus. As the holiest of holy mottos suggests, *get them while they're young*.'

'So what are you doing in this dreadful place?' asked Sacheverell.

'Potholing,' Satan declared, taking a moment to look solemn before bursting with giggles again. '*Your face!*' he laughed, pointing at the glum Lord. 'No, I'm just yanking your chain, Callous. I heard you guys were undertaking a bit of culling in the area and thought I'd come and offer you some *real* work.' He reached for the sack, dragged it over and dumped it at Pryderi's feet. Whatever was inside began to wriggle and writhe until it found freedom. The witch backed off when a pair of deathly white hands began to protrude and two sets of pallid and frail fingers gripped the rugged terrain, dragging the rest of the creature forward, a grey-wreathed organism with a paint-splattered black crow's nest for a hairdo and ragged clothing dashed with similarly vibrant colours.

The glum Lord looked mystified as he bent to observe the entity more closely. 'What sort of thing is this?'

'His name is *Craven*,' Satan informed them, kicking the man.

'*Raven*... my name is Raven,' Rhodeburt Raven said as he crawled fully from the bag and sat cross-legged on the ground before them, rubbing a spot on his flank where he had recently received several physical assaults. He glared up at Satan with hatred then looked at Sacheverell with less odium, a smile brightening his pale features. 'My liege, I am your loyal subject.'

The three incarnates exchanged amused glances.

'I discovered this dull being scurrying about in the bogs of Doloroth,' Satan explained. 'It has quite an interesting tale to tell about its consumption. Despite its obviously low status, it was recently involved in a coup to destabilise amity in the world above.'

'Is that so?' asked Lord Sacheverell, poking the prisoner with a spiky finger. 'Are you Seraph, creature?'

Raven smiled, nodded and choked on a laugh he tried not to emit and said, 'I am your loyal...'

'Yes, yes, I heard you the first time. What's your bloodline?'

'Hadraniel,' the prisoner said and they all laughed.

Through his jeering Sacheverell said, 'But of course you are; it is quite evident from your noble deportment and lavish wardrobe.'

'He came to my attention as an interloper,' Satan informed them. 'One of Galbi's Soul Squads captured him. You know the old saying, if you're not on the list you're not getting in, well hell has the same rules of admission. By all accounts, a human dropped this insect through a maw in the world above.'

'It's true, ugly thing it was too!' said Raven. 'Its name was Fletcher and it knew kung-fu. Please, my lord, I wish only to serve glum majesty and return it to its rightful seat of power. I yearn for servitude within the Seraphim legions that will one day...'

Satan smacked the paint-splattered man across the back of the head to shut him up. 'He does this a lot,' he pointed out. 'Stop grovelling, you miserable halfwit.'

Lord Sacheverell leaned in closer to the man. 'Have we met before? You seem rather familiar.'

'We have, my liege,' Raven said, excitedly. 'At Konigsberg towards the end of the war, you were there the day before... the day before...'

'The day before they dropped the bomb?' the glum Lord enquired with a grin before adding, 'Any history book will tell you that. But I have yet to read an account that mentions a wretched picador like you.'

Raven was tempted to reveal his identity, but the voice in his head told him it was a secret and he had to keep it that way for power existed in secrets and danger in revelations.

'I think I would remember a soldier in *painted* tunics,' Sacheverell teased as he scrutinised the fellow's features more closely. 'No, on second glances you are most certainly a stranger. Tell me, why are you covered in paint? Are you one of those pitiable circus followers who worship absurdity?'

'*I AM NO CLOWN!*' Raven interjected angrily.

Pryderi punched him swiftly on the chin and knocked the feeble man to the ground. Satan and Sacheverell appeared entertained by the prisoner's gall as well as the witch's cruelty.

Disinclined to raise his voice again, Raven muttered, 'Yes, it's true. I once amused myself with a desire to garb myself in big shoes and baggy trousers, but those times are behind me since I was rent in two.'

'My, what a morose little ghoul you are,' Lord Sacheverell commented as he stood up straight, treading on the prisoner's hand. And while Raven bit his gum to circumnavigate the pain, the glum Lord looked at Satan and asked, 'Surely hell has need of morose little ghouls?'

'Hell has need of air conditioners and toilets that flush,' Satan replied, laughing. 'Om once came to visit me down in hell,' he said, 'to inspect my unholy handiwork. She was surprised to discover the elevators and escalators all in working order. I informed Her we had recently obtained the soul of a remarkable engineer. She said it must have been an administration error and had the temerity to demand his return. I told Her *no* and She said if I did not do Her bidding She would sue me, so I replied…'

'*Where will you find a lawyer?*' Sacheverell interjected.

When Raven squeaked with laugher, Satan kicked him and angrily instructed, 'Tell the remainder of your tale, *cretin*.'

The turn-harp rubbed his bruised hip and gulped for air before saying, 'To my everlasting shame, I was forced to endure human company this day; at least I thought they were human. One at least was more interesting, *very* interesting. A little girl called Egg. She was in the care of the King of England and a man called…'

'Morecambe Pierpot!' said Satan, pointing a fat finger at both of them. 'Pierpot is mine, do you understand? He must not be harmed. I have no further interest in this matter beyond the return of that pompous fool to my clutches. This girl however...'

'She is our queen!' Raven announced.

Lord Sacheverell laughed. 'Preposterous,' he barked.

It was Pryderi's turn to bend before the prisoner now. She gripped his face in her hand and said, 'The Sinister Vessels are incarcerated, not even John Fate knows where. Their locations vanished with the geomancer, Griffin Adler.'

Raven sneered at her and said, 'I was in the company of soldiers many years ago when a vessel was smuggled through the deserts of Africa. At one point only the wall of a Bedouin tent stood between me and that divine spirit. The little girl smelled exactly the same as that itinerant sovereign.'

The witch snorted a laugh, asking, 'What are you, part Alsatian?'

'She smelled like moonbeams, starlight and fir trees,' he said, desperate for them to believe him.

'This creature's mind is broken,' she said, throwing back his head and standing up straight.

'There was something inscrutable about her, I swear,' the paint-spattered man avowed, gazing up at the glum Lord as though to implore his confidence. 'The last time I caught a glorious whiff like that was back in Africa.' He twisted his head round to observe the witch. 'I am no canine, my Lady, but my sense of smell has never betrayed me. Perhaps the Sinister Vessels are not all incarcerated? I have heard rumour at least one was unaccounted for.'

'How old was this girl?' Sacheverell enquired.

Raven looked back at the tall, blonde figure and blushing said, 'About eight, but that doesn't mean…'

'And do you recall how Sinister Vessels were officially identified?'

'Yes, of course,' said Raven. It was a bedtime story all incarnate families told their children. Some had tried and failed to defraud providence by faking its stipulations, baptising kin with relevant names, conceiving offspring on pertinent dates, forcing left-handedness upon their female heirs. 'The Sinister Vessels were born on a particular date according to prophesy,' the turn-harp spluttered.

'And what was that date?'

'It was the third of March.'

'And the year?' the glum Lord asked.

'Nineteen twenty-eight.'

Sacheverell held a finger in the air and made a revelatory *ah* sound at the back of his throat to indicate the puzzle solved. 'All five vessels were incarcerated in the last weeks of the Futilities, held hostage to ensure a peace treaty. Each was seventeen years of age, detained twelve months before their eighteenth birthday so their powers would never yield full effect. That was thirty years ago, you absurd little man; they'll be middle aged women by now, frumpy and ill-tempered hormonal time-bombs of no use to our or anybody else's cause. That is, of course, if John Fate did not have them secretly murdered which is a rumour that has visited my ears on more than one occasion. Immortal yes, trapped in the body of an eight-year-old, impossible. The very chronology does not add up.'

'There's something else,' said Satan, taking out a cigar and cramming it between his jaws. 'Tell them the rest, *moron.*'

'Pierpot,' said Raven, emphasising the Ps as popping sounds, 'he was in possession of a magic book!'

Sacheverell, looking bored of these constant adjournments and wanting only to dispose of the prisoner and leave the shabby cave once and for all, asked, 'What magic book?'

'Humdinger's Thumb,' said Satan as he wandered off to find a glowing candle with which to light his cigar. 'By all accounts Pierpot stole it from the Black House library.'

'Then he as good as stole it from me,' said Pryderi.

'Now your name rings a bell,' Satan said with sudden realisation, scooping up a stick of wax from the cavern floor. 'You and the General share chromosomes, don't you? Tell me, why are you scratching a living all the way out here culling vermin while your uncle governs all of hell's domains?'

She glared at him, and had Sacheverell not emitted an amused chuckle, might have taken the fat man's remark personally, such an affront leaving her with little option but to murder him. 'I am practising my skill for slaughter,' she said, a hint of menace in her voice, 'for the day he requires such amenities.'

Puffing on the stogie, Satan returned to their locale and, seemingly ignorant of the brief tension, continued with his discourse. 'I cannot account for the authenticity of this girl's divinity, but there is gossip amongst my allies, those who keep a tally on such comings and goings, that a powerful entity did recently arrive upon earth under much the same circumstances as the human redeemer, Heavenly Joys. If she is *not* our queen she may well be like him so it is in all our interests to discover her identity.'

'This fellow, Pierpot,' said Pryderi, 'he must be a very brave and resourceful man to steal from my uncle.'

'No,' said Satan. 'I have to be honest with you, he is very much the antithesis to both those adjectives.'

'Are you certain it is the Thumb?' asked Sacheverell. 'Lord Crowberry searched his entire life for the book and it proved elusive. Perhaps this bag of bones is spinning us a web of lies.'

'I have an advantage over Lord Crowberry,' Raven whimpered, 'I'm not off my rocker.'

Pryderi pointed a finger at him. 'Cease your tongue or I shall lop it off and feed it to the vilest monster this hemisphere has to offer.'

'My dear girl,' Satan exclaimed. '*I* am the vilest monster this hemisphere has to offer.'

'Here, allow me to do the honours,' Lord Sacheverell said, drawing his dagger and bending to the turn-harp.

Raven scuttled backwards until he collided with Satan's legs. He struggled to retrieve something from his rags, finally holding up a small purple book for them all to see and as the glum Lord froze and Pryderi gasped, Satan released a long pent up fart and said, 'Well bugger me!'

CHAPTER FOURTEEN
Evil Five

The King was downcast in the taxi ride to the Elysium Hotel. Pierpot tried to lift his spirits, reminiscing excitedly about their time together in the Contingency Plan. But it was of no use, the elderly man had a frown on him like a depressed tortoise. Not even when Pierpot regaled Egg with the story of how they collectively expelled a powerful demon from a possessed nun by tempting it into a jacuzzi filled with holy water could the aging Planner manage even a smirk. Egg thought Pierpot's affected re-enactment of the nun's high-pitched squeals and panic-laden genuflecting was one of the funniest things she had ever seen, but the King was far too depressed to find it entertaining.

Meeting Phyllis after all these years had opened unhealed emotional wounds and left him feeling fraught. It was selfishness more than rejection that bothered him, a familiar shame that had not troubled him in a long, long while. It troubled him now like an eel coursing through his innards, poking his delicate entrails with sharp spines. He was racked with guilt at a time when he least required emotive hitches.

The King had always justified his badly timed exodus from impending wedded bliss as his patriotic duty. Soldiering commanded it. Partisanship came before pleasure. What was one pair of derelict lives compared to hundreds of thousands saved by a pure act of altruism? In Phyllis' estimation, these words might make poor excuses and of course the reality was he had been more afraid of tying the knot than facing an advance guard of hellish miscreants because war seemed more logical than love. It consisted of practicalities men found easier to comprehend; following rules, rushes of adrenaline and moments of action, but *feelings*...? He could easily equate his emotional state during shoot outs or bringing down an enemy fighter or hunting reanimated troglodytes through perilous mines, but when it came to the slushy substance of romance such business was quite alien to him.

'Oh, I could tell you a tale or two,' Pierpot went on, repositioning his spectacles as the cab bounced over the road. 'Your grandfather saved my hide on more than one occasion. Remember Ecuador, Reg?' He crouched in his seat and spoke conspiratorially to Egg. 'I was taken hostage by sealions in the Galapagos Islands after saying something mildly tactless about their King, *Cohune*...'

'You compared him to an elephant seal,' the King muttered.

'That's right,' said Pierpot. 'I compared him to an elephant seal I knew back in the *Peninsula Valdes* called Wyse Roget and the sealion king wasn't too happy about that. Turns out Roget killed his favourite uncle when he was just a pup. The whole situation was a diplomatic fiasco from start to finish. Your grandfather dug a tunnel right under the main hall of Cohune's palace and smuggled me out the night before I was due to be executed. To this day I'm not allowed to visit any sea life centre in the world in case one of Cohune's relatives is incarcerated there. And then there was *New Rangoon*, do you remember New Rangoon, Reg? We were commissioned to bring back the *Rangoon Ruby*. Legend has it the jewel possesses magical powers, but what legend fails to mention is that the name *Rangoon Ruby* is above the front doors of about a hundred and fifty-six thousand Burmese restaurants. The first eatery we encountered was run by a bunch of python demons descended from a tangent bloodline of Egyptian incarnates called *Aapep* and the great, great, great, great, great, great, great, great, great, great granddaughter of the Indian Cobra demon, *Naga*. I mean to say if you don't like snakes, this lot are your worst nightmare. Anyway, to cut a long story short, I ended up swallowed whole by some fat, scaly gangster and your grandfather had to...'

'Save your skin for the umpteenth time,' the King remarked sharply, tearing his attention from the elapsing grey city.

'Well, yes, quite...' Pierpot mumbled.

'That was my job description,' the King stated, furiously. 'Every single assignment we were sent on, you botched it up and got yourself apprehended and I was forced to complete the mission single-handedly and then save your bloody life!'

'Exactly,' Pierpot responded, smiling and nodding at the child. 'We were a team.'

The King shook his head and looked back at the rain-soaked buildings, his mind fading out of the present and casting a nostalgic eye over the past. When he accepted

Edward VIII's security detail, a part of him reasoned it was the chance of a lifetime and nobody could begrudge him such honour, but in a microcosmic version of those events, he secretly recognised it as a way to avoid marriage. He did go to see Phyllis, intending to do the decent thing and explain his misgivings but in the end, said nothing about his posting as he discussed imminent wedding proceedings with his fiancée, helping to choose table decorations and colour schemes for the flowers. He cursed himself for his cowardice on many occasions and when the odds on the battlefield seemed against him, the King met such challenges head on with no self-regard, but not out of bravery, rather a sense of personal contempt. He put himself forward for every dangerous mission, even volunteered to work with a hapless idiot like Pierpot, a man others considered a jinx, throwing himself into every fight with the careless braggadocio of one already dead. And the irony of his valour was that he spent most of the Futilities, and subsequent years, attempting and failing rather miserably to get himself killed.

*****

When they reached the hotel, the King dealt with the formalities of their reservation while Pierpot observed a rubber plant between two elevators. He examined its large elliptical leaves, leaning towards Egg, who was pleasantly bored, and informing her, 'Did you know that a variety of fig-wasp pollinates the rubber plant, or the *Ficus elastica*, as we botanists refer to it. Now, fig-wasps can be separated into two distinct categories, one is a pollinating organism, the other a non-pollinating organism and while the pollinating fig-wasp forms a symbiotic relationship with the tree, the non-pollinators are parasitical, therefore, it is generally the case that even in the microscopic universe of fig-wasps and rubber plants there is a constant battle between good and evil! War is endemic, even in nature.'

'I like ladybirds,' said Egg.

'We're on the fifth floor,' the King announced as he passed them and pressed a button for the lift.

'The *fifth* floor?' asked Pierpot, looking somewhat alarmed by this information. 'Why are we on the *fifth* floor exactly?'

The King and Egg both looked at him mystified. 'What's wrong with the fifth floor?'

'I'm sure it's as cheery and luxurious as any other level but as you are doubtless aware, Reg, the number five and I have rather a belligerent history.'

The King rolled his eyes as a pinging sound notified them of the elevator's arrival and two steel doors slid apart. 'As it goes, this is the first time you've ever mentioned it in all the many, many years I've known you.'

'Well, suffice to say, the number five and I don't always see eye to eye, so being situated on the fifth floor is slightly unnerving to say the least.'

'I like the number five,' Egg commented. 'It's the curliest number.'

'Curls represent tails, my dear, and devils have tails,' Pierpot remarked as he watched his companions step over the threshold into the lift.

'In most cultures the number five is considered lucky,' the King said from the car, placing a hand over the sensor on the door to hold it ajar for his anxious friend. Pierpot appeared to have no intention of departing the foyer though and exploded with derisive laughter at the King's tender, as if he had made a celebrated mistake.

'The number five is an odd number. Odd numbers are *never* lucky numbers.'

Issuing an exasperated gasp, the King retorted, 'In China it's considered lucky. The Chinese believe in five elements; water, fire, earth, wood and metal.'

'They missed out *fungi*,' Pierpot said, tentatively putting one foot inside the car. 'Five is an incredibly *unlucky* number, Reg. There are five Sinister Vessels after all.'

'There were five Harbingers.'

'I tell you, five is an unlucky number. I was cast into hell on the fifth of May, nineteen fifty-five. That's four fives in a row, Reg. Spiritualists call sequences of numbers like that *Angel Numbers. Angel Numbers, Reg*! Do you need any further evidence of the glum significance of John Fate putting us on the fifth floor?'

Pierpot finally stepped fully onto the elevator, pulling his shirt collar away from his constricted throat and gulping.

'Fate didn't book our reservation,' the King informed him. 'Phyllis did.'

'So your argument is that because an incarnate you ditched at the altar thirty years ago arranged a room for us on the fifth floor I should stop worrying? Oh, I'm sure there are absolutely no sour grapes where she's involved.' Pierpot's words oozed with so much sarcasm they made Egg laugh.

'Five is a bad number for me. Three is a bad number for me, but compared to five, three's a raffle win.'

'You're being absurd,' the King said and reached towards the buttons and particularly the red glowing tile indicating the fifth floor.

Pierpot looked on with trepidation and then suddenly grabbed the King's arm. 'You think I'm being absurd, do you? The word itself is the closest anagram of *evil* in the English language, if you disregard *vile* that is. It's always been a bugbear of mine. I have suffered from myopia since I was five-years-old. When I was fifteen my father was murdered by Neo-Aztecs who worshipped the fifth sun by offering a human sacrifice every morning to ensure it would be reborn.'

The King uncoupled Pierpot's grip on his sleeve and pressed the button. As the doors slid together and the elevator began to ascend, he said, 'We have five fingers and toes on each limb.'

'Not only are you purposely disregarding thumbs in order to win the argument, Reginald, but you know for a fact I personally have a toe missing from my right foot. It was shot off by a man called Archimedes Quinn; Quinn as in *quintet* and *quintuplet* which are both nouns describing the number five.'

'It's just coincidence,' said the King.

'Coincidence was officially abolished in the 1612 *Happenchance Witch Trials*. Allow me to refer you to *panchadosh*. According to Sikh religion there are five evils: lust, rage, greed, worldly infatuation and ego.'

When the King rolled his eyes at her, Egg laughed again.

'Numerologists suggest the number five can be characterised as a risk-taker, deceptive, unstable and... don't quote me, quote the highly respectable fringe science of number buffoonery, *chaotic*! In England, the fifth of November is National Burn an Effigy of *Guido Fawkes* Day, an occasion when the entire nation is reduced to pyromaniacs performing satanic rituals by symbolically barbecuing a man who was born in the 1500s and captured on the *fifth* of November in the year sixteen hundred and... wait for it, *five*!' Pierpot pushed his spectacles up the bridge of his nose authoritatively. 'The fifth day of the fifth month is a glum calendar date throughout history: *Kublai Khan* became Mongol Emperor on May fifth 1260, *Napoleon Bonaparte* died in exile and some say by underhand methods May fifth 1821, on May fifth 1893 the New York stock market crashed and on May fifth 1920, US President Woodrow Wilson, leader of the free world, the very heart of all democracies, made it illegal to be a member of the Communist Labour Party. Need I go on?'

'Only if you wish to spend the night in hospital, you superstitious old fool,' the King replied. This less than subtle warning did not deter his unreasonable chum however.

'There are five points on a pentagram. Five is a *Fibonacci* number, a *Pell* number as well as a *Markov* number in mathematics, and we both know the comparisons between ungodliness and arithmetic, Reg! The most destructive hurricanes are rated as category fives on the *Saffir-Simpson Scale* and the worst tornadoes are rated as F-fives on the *Fujita Scale*. There were five horsemen of the apocalypse: War, Famine, Pestilence, Death and Obnoxious Skeleton and there were also five chillingly ruthless preadolescent protagonists in the *Iniquitous Blyton Transcripts*!'

The King laughed aloud, shaking his head scathingly. 'Blyton's reputation for iniquity is questionable,' he pointed out. 'She wrote children's stories, Pierpot. The very notion they were anything more than juvenile escapism is paranoid lunacy. If you read them under some form of satanic rapture, in a low voice and a glum cave surrounded by rats, spiders and bats, then yes, there's a palpable chance they'll seem creepy, but no more so than if you were reading the ingredients of a packet of boil in the bag noodles. As bedtime stories for kids, there's not a hint of foreboding on any single page.'

'Oh yes? What about *The Wishing Chair*?' Pierpot smugly responded, repositioning his spectacles again.

The King hesitated. 'Granted, The Wishing Chair is one of the most heinous paranormal books ever printed, but despite her name adorning the cover there's not a shred of evidence Blyton was actually responsible for inscribing that malevolent text.'

The elevator pinged and the doors slid apart. All three stepped out onto the crazy zigzag carpeting of the fifth floor. Hotel room doors and soft lighting led off in either direction along the passage.

'So, what's our room number?'

The King coughed to clear his throat and made a pantomime of reading the key fob. 'Room *555*,' he announced.

Pierpot came to a halt, almost collapsing beneath the sheer weight of this fresh revelation. 'That's three fives in a row, Reg! Three fives make fifteen.'

'And I suppose the number fifteen is unlucky because…?'

'Blyton wrote fifteen Secret Seven books. *Stesichorus*, the ancient Greek poet who was blinded when he wrote unflatteringly about Helen of Troy, died in 555 BC!'

'And what if nobody had died that year?' the King enquired. 'I suppose then you'd be holding *that* phenomenon up as a suspicious event?'

'Three fives make fifteen and in Pakistan, 15 is the number you call in an emergency.'

'We're not in Pakistan.'

'Reginald, we can't stay in room 555 on the fifth floor. In Roman numerals, five hundred and fifty-five is represented by the letters *DLV*. That's as good as *Devil*!'

'Only if you're illiterate,' the King snapped. 'The same letters also appear in the term *delusively uncivilized*, which is, essentially, an explanation for your current behaviour. Get a grip, man.'

'Yes, yes, of course,' said Pierpot with a reluctant sigh and, removing a handkerchief from his trouser pocket, he mopped at his sweating brow. 'You're quite right, Reg. I'm being ridiculously superstitious.'

Continuing along the corridor they quickly found their room. The King unlocked the door but, despite his assertion to the contrary, appeared in no haste to go inside, remaining on the threshold with a protective hand balanced on Egg's head.

'Is there a problem?' Pierpot queried at his shoulder.

The King cleared his throat, turned and headed back towards the elevator. 'Stay here,' he instructed them. 'I'll go check if the hotel has any other rooms available.'

CHAPTER FIFTEEN
Mr Anonymity Personified

On the face of it, the Plan was considered to be John Fate's private army and, particularly during the Futilities, his personal agenda and the wants of humanity had often converged. Officially however, the organisation was overseen by *the Tetrad*, a group of trustees the Captain of the Home Guard was expected to report to on a regular basis. Not that he always followed this strict code of practice, but from time to time he chose to involve them purely as a matter of course. Today, the trustees reacted quite irately to the Captain's summons; seemingly because he was unwilling to share much information on the phone, but most likely as a result of the get-together interfering with their Tuesday afternoon *Monopoly* session.

Preferring the oldest mode of transport in the Known Universe, *walking*, to traversing Grace Plateau's topography by golf cart, EGD Ladder or one of the many plastic slides used to access lower levels, Fate enjoyed the idea of being seen wandering the ancient hallways, a man of the people, mingling with grassroots Planners and *keeping it real*. And as well as recognising the social benefits, escaping his musky office, helped to dispel mental cobwebs and allow for clearer reflection. Today Fate reflected upon the thirty-year-old encumbrance that was Rhodeburt Raven's protracted existence. His foremost consideration as he remembered his recent conversation with the King and Pierpot, was that he had exhibited no untoward reaction when the turn-harp's identity came up, for only one other person knew of the Captain's deal with the incarnate, his onetime chum and compatriot, the renowned geomancer Griffin Adler. Adler, who had designed a weapons system harvested from the biology of a phenomenal man, had also earned a reputation for designing state-of-the-art virtual reality prisons known universally as *facsimiles*. A facsimile was a self-maintained forged environ where enemies of the Plan could be held indefinitely, often unaware they were in captivity. Fate regularly chastised himself for not incarcerating Raven in one such prison and, for that matter, Adler too. The geomancer had mysteriously disappeared a decade ago following a political change of heart and, many suspect, chose exile in one of his simulated pokeys.

When he arrived at the conference chamber, Fate was instructed to wait in a side office and so plonked himself down on a leather bench and leafed through a copy of *Lancashire Life*, idling over articles on drainage systems, a form of demonic mange in cows and a poem about a campervan sent in by a hippy. When the clerk returned, he replaced the dog-eared mag, stood and followed the administrator along the corridor and through a set of grand oak doors. Outside of Grace Plateau's industrial loading bays and facsimile generators, the chamber was probably the plateau's largest room. The design was minimalist; art deco sun beams and engraved pyramids decorated the walls, illuminated by sconce lighting. The ceiling was coved like an inverted bathtub and three chandeliers dangled like star clusters from its centre. A number of oceanic rugs, purchased from the avant-garde stalls in the alternative shopping arcade below, concealed the floor.

The Tetrad liked referring to themselves as *the* Tetrad, but they were in fact the *Other* Tetrad since the upheaval of their predecessors who damagingly mismanaged the Plan during the Futilities. That former foursome had been fusty old traditionalists, averse to change and miserly when it came to funding innovative ideas. But despite the incompetence of that erstwhile assembly, there were times when Fate preferred their parsimony and bland bigotry to the liberal-minded fluff proffered by these current commanders of democracy.

He sat upon an ornate wooden seat said to have belonged to a second cousin of King Arthur (a round table emergency chair), a single island of comfort in the bland expanse of room and waited until he was addressed. The council members arranged themselves along the far wall before a light source transformed them into silhouettes. After a moment of murmuring somebody spoke from across the way, the opening statement a desperate bid to convince him they had not been playing board games before his request for a consultation.

'We were rather busy auditing the recreational budget when you called,' the voice said. 'Have you any idea what the Plan spends on ping pong balls, Captain Fate?'

Protocol had long since demanded that the four members of the Tetrad remain anonymous. Theoretically, the Contingency Plan was a Socialist initiative and any Planner, from the person responsible for mending Grace Plateau's vending machines to highly decorated war veterans could be selected for undisclosed membership. Of course, there were three massive incongruities involved in this rule, the first being that somebody had to be responsible for selecting the first member and, therefore, would know the identity of at least one Tetrad member. The second was that no vending machine engineer had *ever* been promoted to the Tetrad (which was as it should be for there were far too many vending machines on Grace Plateau in dire need of repair). The third was that John Fate hadn't survived all these long years by not knowing the identities of his superiors and he immediately identified the voice commenting on ping pong balls now as that of Under Cromwell, First Lieutenant Second Bliss Company, a bunch of brave lads who gave their lives by abseiling into hell in 1944. The fact Under Cromwell was the only surviving member of that mission, having remained at base camp for the duration, was more an example of nepotism than heroism and always sat heavy in Fate's belly, but now the man was a Tetrad member the Captain was bound by principle to serve him steadfastly.

Putting a hand above his eyes, Fate squinted into the bright light, watching as three of the anthropoid forms moved inside the radiant, white glare. Ivy Mitford never moved. The 17th century witch, whose proposed curse on an irate rabble of villagers rebounded and petrified her, communicated telepathically and Fate despised the sense of violation involved, afraid the *Stone Witch* might do more than cut and paste her voice inside his cerebral cortex. In the early part of the nineteenth century when she had proved a frustrating agent, liberally prying into the heads of international secret-keepers, the Plan had her remains buried in the Sahara Desert to keep Mitford out of harm's way, seriously underestimating the range of her ability to haunt them. Justifiably apprehensive, they had her exhumed and no doubt placated with a seat on the Council.

Another Tetrad member was Sir Oswald Thistle, 13th Earl of Accrington. Fate had known Thistle for many years and the nervous wobble of his voice as well as a sodden lisp that prevented him pronouncing the letter *S* with any true dexterity or without spitting on those in close proximity was a clear giveaway. He also had no problem identifying Thistle because the man was so large his silhouette was the most prominent thing in the room.

However, when it came to identifying the fourth member of the council, the Captain was, exasperatingly, stumped. Beyond classifying the individual as male, Fate could never put a name or reputation to him. He was a mystery and wore his anonymity like a cowl, his physical designation constantly on the edge of the Captain's recall, yet always lingering just the wrong side of clarification.

'What ith it bringth you before uth today, John?' enquired Thistle.

'An infringement of Clowns at the home of the King of England,' Fate announced, leaning forward and attempting to put a face to one of the shapes conversing with him.

'Saw it in a dream, did we?' asked Under Cromwell with a snigger.

'No,' he replied, 'though I should mention a vagary concerning the King has previously been chronicled.'

Then illuminate us with your portentous reverie.

Mitford's voice in his head was awkwardly abstract and more troubling to his senses than that brilliant light, forcing him to look away briefly. There was no pain involved in the interaction; he simply found temporary possession discomforting.

'It was many years ago,' he explained. 'I saw the King fall to his death alongside a green dragon.'

'Not a Thpare Clown?'

'No,' he said.

'A dragon can be a thymbol of thin,' Thistle suggested.

But also of prosperity and power.

'To me the dream suggested a lost battle,' Fate said.

'A battle of war or a battle of spirit?' asked that unidentifiable member in his suave, ripened tone. It was definitely the voice of a man but beyond that irrelevant deduction Fate was flummoxed. He liked to think of himself as a collector of personalities, mannerisms and verbal characteristics, and having as adept a perception of physiognomies as any detective. He had happened upon the identities of the others by systems of subtle investigation, a process of elimination here and a good old understanding of the rules of *Cleudo* there, as well as trusting in old-fashioned gossip between Plateau clerks. But this fourth member remained elusive no matter how much he investigated or strained his mind, ears and eyes. The most vexing thing about the voice was that Fate was absolutely certain he had heard the silky-smooth cadence before.

Staring at *Mystery Man's* shimmering representation in the light he responded with, 'It's difficult to say. I would lean less towards catastrophic for the sake of optimism.'

'It does not sound optimistic for the King,' those exasperating vocal chords acknowledged.

'But it *wath* jutht a dream,' said Thistle.

The Captain of the Home Guard repositioned his buttocks on the solid wood. 'Dreams are my modus operandi,' he pointed out, 'as games of life, war and diplomacy are yours.'

A moment of uncomfortable silence filled the room and then Under Cromwell's syrupy voice enquired, 'When you say *The Game of Life*, *War* and *Diplomacy*, John, these are actual human customs you're referring to, not, let's say, strategy-based children's board games?'

Amused by the man's blinkered stupidity, Fate was about to respond with scorn when Thistle discreetly interjected by asking, 'Thurely thometimeth though, you dream for the thame reathon we all dream, John; for no reathon at all.'

'No,' said Fate, squinting in the direction of the fat man, 'some of my dreams are more mundane than others, I admit, but they always produce significance sooner or later. I should mention that the King came to see me earlier. He was with a man called Morecambe Pierpot and a little girl called Egg.'

'*Egg*?' asked *Mr Perplexing*. 'And is this little girl also an aspect of your dragon dream?'

'No,' said Fate.

Morecambe Pierpot, why is that name familiar?

Fate stuck a finger in his ear and shook his head to discard a sense of incursion. 'Several decades ago,' he said, 'the Plan investigated his liaison with a rival agent. Pierpot became infatuated with an incarnate woman. It was never clear if he surrendered important information or the whole affair was some sort of incarnate mouse trap...' a tiny gasp emanated from Under Cromwell's direction. 'And before the investigation was concluded he disappeared off our radar altogether, rumoured to have been incarcerated in hell.'

You mean to say the man is dead?

'He was in good health when I spoke to him earlier.'

'And this girl, this Egg person, what can you tell us about her?'

He sat further forward and carefully examined the blurred shape of *Mr Enigmatic* while considering his response. Due to Under Cromwell's recent misinterpretation of certain phrases, Fate couldn't help ruminate on other names for popular children's board games he might use to describe his frustrating inability to designate this man with a title, standard table top fayre such as *Guess Who* and *Connect Four*. Instead, he said, 'I think she may be on a par with Ashok Kumar. She too appeared out of nowhere and said the word *egg*.'

'In your opinion, Captain Fate, does she belong to our world?' *Mr Unidentifiable* enquired.

'No.'

When a phenomenon occurs a second time it is, consequentially, rendered much less a phenomenon. What are we to make of it? The first came in war-time when we most needed aid and now we receive a second in peace-time. What do you think it all means, John Fate?

He coughed to clear his throat and said, 'If our intelligence is correct, General Galbi has been stockpiling arms for decades now so perhaps Om sent us this other saviour in case of war.'

Cromwell laughed and said, 'Poppycock!'

'I'd like to return to the dream if I may,' suggested *Mr Inscrutable*. 'You say the dying King may have lost a battle of spirit, what does that mean?'

'I said no such thing,' Fate responded. 'I said I preferred to lean towards the less catastrophic, for the sake of optimism. Given a choice I would rather the King's falling was symbolic of a battle with his own conscience than one with an aggressor, but I cannot rule out foul play.'

'Do you suspect *the King* of foul play?'

'No. The man's as straight as a die. The idea of Reginald Fielding being dishonest is, quite frankly…' he purposely looked at Under Cromwell, '*balderdash*!'

In a whisper the Second Bliss Company First Lieutenant insisted, '*He did that on purpose. He knows about* Balderdash Thursdays!'

'But in your opinion, as a seasoned oracle,' asked *Mr Anonymity Personified*, 'could that green dragon symbolise an incarnate aggressor?'

'Yes, of course,' he said.

'Thank you.'

'Wath there anything elth thignificant about the dream?' asked Thistle.

After a moment of consideration, Fate said, 'No.'

'Do not dragonth lay eggth, John? Perhapth thith phenomenon, thith little girl called Egg, will cauthe the death of the King?'

There was a moment of eerie silence.

'I hadn't considered that,' Fate confessed.

'Becauthe you preferred the leth catathtrophic, for the thake of optimithm, perhapth?'

143

He did not respond. Fate got the feeling Thistle was accusing him of incompetency when all he had done was his job. He was now starting to wish he hadn't bothered reporting the incident at all.

'We apprethiate your ability to foretell future eventth,' Thistle remarked, 'and you've been an invaluable athet to the Plan and, although we do not blame you for jumping to concluthionth, ethpethially after your long immerthion in matterth of ethpionage, in reality, there ith no thuch ill-omen, ith there John?'

'I disagree,' the familiar/unidentifiable voice announced. 'John Fate has an almost spotless record. His vagaries have uncovered more murderers, marauders and malevolent machinations than any other agent on the Plan's books. If he suspects incarnates are about to murder the King of England, we should be on our guard and the King should be protected night and day.'

As infuriating as it was to not know the fourth affiliate's identity, having his patronage frustrated Fate even more.

'If we protected everyone who had a scary dream, we would run out of Planners fast,' Under Cromwell protested. 'And if we spread ourselves thin with security details then Grace Plateau and every region of the Known Universe we protect would be open to attack from insurgents and anarchists and Om-knows what else.'

Let us say, for the moment, that the King's life is in danger and that your dream really did have meaning, John Fate; how would you proceed?

'With caution, as always,' Fate responded.

'Yet more ambiguouthneth from the great John Fate,' taunted Thistle. '*What a thurprithe!*'

The Captain rose to his feet. 'Am I here to be made a fool of?' he demanded to know, glaring into the blinding light. 'I take great offence in the suggestion that my skills are engaged in trivial...'

Sit down, Captain Fate.

'*You all heard that, didn't you?*' Under Cromwell's lowered voice asked his associates. '*He was about to say* Trivial Pursuits!'

It is not your skill under scrutiny but your ability to function as part of a team. At times you must allow us to scrutinise your work as you would the efforts of those beneath you!

'Have I upset the Tetrad somehow?'

Omnipotence is allowed us, John, in all ways but one. Where are the vessels?

So finally, here it was: a thirty-year-old quarrel returning to bite him on the backside again. Remaining standing, the Captain shook his head with disbelief as he repeated a statement made many times in their presence. 'The whereabouts of the vessels disappeared with Griffin Adler.'

'Our predecessors allowed you *carte blanche* as far as the vessels were concerned,' said *Mr Unfathomable*. 'I cannot imagine a Planner of your standing allowing sole knowledge of their whereabouts to one man, Captain Fate.'

The Captain smirked into the light. 'Your predecessors agreed, quite wisely in my estimation, that the fewer people who knew of the vessel's whereabouts the better. What could you, or I, possibly wish to gain from such information anyway?'

'You could learn her glum secrets and use them against us,' Under Cromwell replied, his voice wobbling with blatant distrust.

The Captain looked angry as he asked, 'Have I not proven my loyalty to the Plan?' He ran both hands down his face in frustration and rage. 'I have stated, no less than a thousand times, standing in this very room, that I have *no knowledge of her whereabouts*! If you think I am a liar, don't beat around the bush, just come out and say!'

The silhouette of Under Cromwell shot to its feet and the man spluttered furiously, 'Your contempt for how this council spends its downtime is dutifully acknowledged, John Fate, but should you so much as hint at one more…'

'Sit down,' said *Mr Indecipherable*.

'But… you heard the insolent wretch; *beat around the bush*! He's brazenly namechecking popular board games as a way of undermining…'

'*Beat around the bush* isn't a board game, you paranoid ninny!'

'But… isn't it? Are you sure?'

With a deep sigh, the foursome's undisclosed adherent suggested, 'It may be wise to cut this discussion short. Put a facsimile in place to keep the King safe.'

'I've already made arrangements,' Fate replied, his anger receding slightly in light of Under Cromwell's embarrassment. 'The King and his companions are currently residing as guests at a hotel in the city.'

See no harm comes to them and allow for remote viewing. We would like to observe proceedings, especially given the divine significance of this Egg.

'As you wish,' said Fate and made to leave.

'Jutht one more thing,' spoke the Earl of Accrington. 'Thurely you wouldn't leave without mentioning the Thumb?'

He stopped and turned back to gaze into the dazzling light once again. How did Thistle know about the Thumb? And then he realised they would have remotely viewed his office and all his revelations about the King had been pointless because the Tetrad already knew the details. He heaved a sigh, hesitating as he chose the words with which to respond. 'As you are no doubt aware, Pierpot was not in possession of the book, though all three of them clearly believed he was which suggests to me somebody stole it and entranced them with glum magic.'

This Rhodeburt Raven, perhaps? What do you know of him?

The voice of the Stone Witch carried with it such intonation that Fate became immediately fearful for all the other secrets in his head for he had not yet mentioned the turn-harp's name. 'He sounds like a madman,' the Captain replied.

And what if this Raven is a madman proficient in understanding ancient arcane text, at least enough to tender its powers glumly?

'Then that is a *risk* we shall have to take,' said Fate, hearing Under Cromwell quietly snarl.

CHAPTER SIXTEEN
Room 410

They finally settled for room 410 on the fourth floor in spite of 410 being an Angel Number. Pierpot's last remark on the subject was that, *at least it didn't involve any fives, though I'm not completely comforted by the fact it can be easily divided by that terrible integer.*

The room was spacious, too vibrantly decorated in the King's estimation, a man who proffered earthen and pastel shades, but having spent a fifth of a century in hell, Pierpot gloried in its unashamed inclination towards garishness. A balcony lay beyond a concealed curtain and sliding door and on inspection of what other doors hid, Egg discovered two bedrooms and a bathroom. The King informed them he would be spending the night in an armchair while Egg slept on the sofa where he could keep a close eye on her and Pierpot could please himself as far as sleeping arrangements went.

Having nothing to unpack felt strange to the King who had never been able to unwind in hotel suites or billets until outfits were hung in wardrobes, a smorgasbord of toiletries displayed around sinks and storage for small clothes achieved.

Avoiding the usual half an hour of nomadic panic, absolute certainty he had forgotten something before locating it in a zipper section of a suitcase or entwined in a pair of Y-fronts, rendered him a nervous wreck.

Egg exhibited equal insatiable energy as she pressed her hands and face against the windows, misting up the glass before dashing to the sofa and hurling herself into its leathery plumpness and then darting back over the plush carpet to investigate every cupboard and drawer. Back at Hill House there were more rooms than either of them knew what to do with and she had explored every single one whereas now, the novelty of inhabiting somewhere unfamiliar filled her with delight.

'It's much more accommodating than my last abode,' Pierpot remarked as he examined the suite's geometrics in his own particular fashion, sniffing and listening to furnishings, intermittently repositioning his spectacles, 'but then I suppose sharing a narrow cave with a tactile thorn-ogre beneath the dilapidated privy of an Indian takeaway would be a preferred residence to the last place *I* resided.'

Egg came back to the sofa and turned on the TV. She began to channel surf and with each new image emitted a corresponding sound; a laugh, a comical cry of terror, a patronising sniff, a sympathetic whine or a single vowel of confusion.

'Thinking about it, I'd sooner exist for eternity in a damp cupboard with a flatulent jellyfish and a pot of contagious jam than return to *that* hellhole!' Pierpot announced, pulling faces at his own reflection in a glazed vase.

The King was still lamenting over his emotional wounds, considering how he had spent a lifetime recoiling from commitment and yet here he was, completely willing to put his life on the line for a mysterious eight-year-old girl who may or may not have been Chaos Likely. *Life was a funny old business.* He had spent decades trying to gain the wrath of a powerful nemesis for no better reason than to balance out the remorse he felt for dumping Phyllis at the altar just to spend retirement risking life and limb for a complete stranger whose destiny it might be to destroy the Known Universe.

'I expect it would be more relaxing in the fetid abdomen of a giant piranha than…'

'I need some fresh air,' the King announced, leaping from his armchair and crossing the room to the balcony. 'Don't let Egg out of your sight,' he instructed Pierpot before stepping out into a cool, evening breeze and sliding the door closed behind him to suppress the vexing sound of the ex-Planner's voice. The King went to the parapet where the air was brisker and the view more spectacular. The fourth floor of the Elysium Hotel awarded a splendid vista of the city at dusk where a multitude of twinkling lights delineated an immense sprawl of local civilisation. He lent against the bulwark, splaying both hands on the concrete and looked down to where a vehicle was leaving the hotel's street-level carpark, illuminating everything in its vicinity with coned headlights as it crawled through the dark to blend with the bulk of more fluid beams in the distance. He sighed, looked up at the full moon and the pinpricks of stars surrounding it and wondered if their initials were still imprinted upon that lunar surface; *RF 4 PH*. He had transcribed them in a hundred-foot letters with the heel of his boot to surprise her on a secret rendezvous, probably the only romantic gesture he ever really made.

A fluttering sound came to him and the King saw distant stars blink on and off when something passed in front of them. He became immediately guarded and took a step back into shadow. Was the enemy coming? Had whoever sent in the clowns that afternoon unleashed some fresh absurdity to try to take the child? If so, they would be obliged to leave him a lifeless husk because he was prepared to die to protect her. But then, as the shape grew more perceptible in the night sky the King relaxed. It was a comely figure steadily approaching, an avian-like carriage he had witnessed only a few of hours ago. She came swooping past the balcony, wings beating the air like flapping pennants. Ascending briefly, she turned full circle before eventually finding purchase upon the stone rampart.

He remembered Phyllis was gifted with nocturnal vision and sensed that, although he had backed into shadow, he stood out like a sore thumb and so felt a bit silly. He stayed in the corner however, swathed in self-denial, and watched her step gracefully down to the balcony floor, listening to the terse slap of her bare feet as they pad the tiles. She turned her back on him, her immense wings gradually collapsing and folding away between her shoulder blades.

'This city lures all manner of threats,' she said, her voice floating through the space between them, as sweet as it was succinct, nostalgically probing his memories. He had never forgotten that husky tone.

Admiring the swirling patterns of grey feathers on her back he sniffed and said, 'That's what the Plan's for, isn't it, to defend us from such threats?'

'And what if these days,' she said, finally turning to look at him, 'the Plan does its most remarkable work in the dark?'

'What are you saying?'

'This entire hotel is a construct, Reginald. John has requested you be contained at his pleasure.'

The King left the pseudo-protection of shadow and came to stand beside her at the parapet. Phyllis turned her attention back to the gloomy city while he stared, ponderingly, at her profile, anger and frustration fighting for the right to his emotions. 'Is he allowed to do that?'

'He has the backing of the Tetrad,' Phyllis said, glancing at him with sparkling green eyes that shone like emerald stars. 'He doesn't wish you harm, but equally, should the girl be a threat to the state of world affairs...'

'She's just a child,' the King exclaimed. 'John Fate is frightened of his own shadow.'

'A child who popped out of thin air and said *egg*,' Phyllis reminded him. 'Need I quote *Cullen's* poem?'

'Of course not, the damnable verse is etched upon my psyche as fresh as the day I first spoke it,' he told her, referring to the ever-enduring pledge versed on his first day of soldiering.

'If it turns out she *is* Chaos Likely then even you have to admit that a facsimile is the best place for her,' said Phyllis. 'At least it's a more secure environment than a quirky mansion in the countryside. Think of it as a temporary measure, until the proper checks can be made.' She turned back to observe the expansive map of twinkling lights against the black background of night. The King noted an audible sigh rattle from her.

'I appreciate the heads up,' he said, guiltily, and then considered Pierpot's recent articulations. 'I expect there are worse places to be incarcerated.' And then, acknowledging the grim look she flashed him, the King considered kicking himself. Morecambe Pierpot wasn't the only being in his vicinity who had been held captive by incarnates for decades on end. When Phyllis returned to the job of soldiering after their disastrous church date, she was captured by Cruel Lord Crowberry's forces in Europe and endured months of torture in a POW camp. As a turn-harp, she would have undergone the most atrocious degradation.

'My only concern is for the girl's safety,' he said. It was the King's way of telling her that his words had meant no harm, that all he cared about was the security of his fictitious granddaughter.

'Your work always did come first,' the incarnate responded and he realised she was chastising him.

'I suppose you're right.'

'You may as well never have existed, for all the life you consumed for yourself.'

As he looked out over the city he sighed too. 'I am a bumbling oaf of a man who needs a purpose in life. Slippers and a pipe, picnics and deckchairs, the Sunday supplements and roast beef dinners, these things are not sustenance for what I crave.'

'Tin medals and the insincere praise of parliamentarians?'

'My aspirations are far more humble than that,' he said.

'I understand,' she replied. 'Marrying me would have meant a lifetime of mundane practices.'

'Don't be silly,' he said, watching the breeze lift and play with her silver hair. 'In all my years I fell in love but once. I did wrong by you and have paid an emotional price ever since, despite what you might think.'

'You have no understanding of the glum thoughts that tormented me, Reginald. Anger and resentment, as human traits, these are rarely tendered with action. However ugly, they are simple emotions allowed to peter out with time, but for *Angels*... I have destroyed you over and over in my thoughts and dreams.'

'Do your worst,' he said. 'Burn me alive with those fiery eyes or plant a poisoned kiss upon my brow. Hurl my fat, aged body a kilometre into the night's sky. Punch a hole in my chest and tear my heart out with your perfect fingers, but do it now before my wits return and I remember my solemn oath to keep that little girl safe.'

'I have performed all of those atrocities and more, in private. I could have found you the very day you deserted me and bound you to my side with hexes, mesmerised you, forced you to walk beside me for eternity, but I would not have you come to me debilitated of choice. That is *your* penance, Reginald,' Phyllis said as she leaped effortlessly to the parapet. 'You must live with the shame of my forgiveness.'

As her wings unfolded, the King was knocked off his feet and fell against the balcony doors. Just before the love of his life left the hotel to soar over the dark city once more, she looked back, smiled and said, '*Whoops*!'

CHAPTER SEVENTEEN
Nocturnal Apartments

The water was so cold it froze his thoughts. His organs turned to stony glaciers inside his chest and he was unable to express this hypothermic hypothesis because every one of his senses had been neutralised by the iciness of seawater. Saltwater filled up his gaping jaws, throat and lungs until he considered drowning preferable to the bitter elements, but eventually they broke the surface and, gripping him by the collar of his grey and paint-splattered shirt, Lord Sacheverell dragged him over the shale in the pitch black night, both his captors striding ashore like great Krakens come to devour the world, while he flapped and kicked in their wake, the paltriest catch of the day, shivering and retching up bile. Dumped on the beach a yard from the groping tide, Raven watched the glum Lord's black boots crunch over the compact stone. Sacheverell's annoyance as well as humiliation at having to swim out of hell showed in his stiff gait and affected posture as the tall, blond incarnate stamped his feet and threw up his arms, hands dramatically twisted into claws, his very soul engulfed in fury.

Pryderi seemed more positive, sparkling with enthusiasm at the prospect of being back on earth. She had even enjoyed the transition from underworld to reality and had used the absurd duration to consider their options. 'We need to find earthly apparel,' she declared, bending to one knee and scooping up stones in a hand. 'Walking around dressed in armour will draw attention.'

Lord Sacheverell laughed, contemptuously. 'Oh, you think?'

She ignored him. 'We also need a place to hide.'

On hearing this, the glum Lord turned on her fiercely. '*Hide*? Leo, god's do not hide, we boast, we flaunt, we…'

'The moment we show our hand, John Fate will drop a Rapture Bomb on each of our heads.'

'He tried that once before,' Sacheverell declared with pride. 'I used an incantation and returned it to sender. Many hundreds of his traitorous turn-harps were blown to smithereens.' He looked back at the creature in grey as if only just remembering him. 'Did you happen to be one of them, *Craven*?'

'It's… *humph*… *Raven* and I am… *bleurgh*… no turn-harp,' their hostage spoke between heaves and coughs.

Lord Sacheverell returned his attention to Pryderi. 'This sack of dung is slowing us down,' he spat. 'Why don't we take the book and send his lowborn bones back to hell or wherever it is traitors go?'

'The smell of him turns my stomach but he may yet prove useful,' Pryderi replied, regarding the beach in both directions.

But the glum Lord was already standing over their prisoner, leering at him, menacingly. 'You are of little use to me, creature,' he said. 'How would you have me release the spirit from your flesh?'

'Kill him if you must, but do it quick,' Pryderi instructed with impatience as she continued to peruse the length of darkened shoreline. 'I think I hear somebody approaching.'

Lord Sacheverell bent before the man, lifting his head with one finger curled beneath his chin. '*Hmm, people,*' he said, licking his lips. 'My favourite appetizer!' He touched the ragged prisoner on his neck with a long, pointed fingernail and, just as he was about to open his throat, Raven raised a hand to his mouth and stuffed something into it, instantly chewing and swallowing. Sacheverell's smile died as he rose swiftly to his feet, taken aback by the man's strange behaviour. 'What did the creature do?'

Pryderi glanced over as Sacheverell grabbed Raven by the throat and lifted him physically off the ground. The glum Lord then hurled the turn-harp through the air where he landed several feet away with a crunch of gravel and bones.

'I do believe the simpleton swallowed a page of the book,' he informed Pryderi.

'He did *what*?' asked the witch as she made her way over to the inert pile of rags and turned him over with the toe of her boot. She dragged the purple book from his skinny fingers and flipped through its soggy pages. 'Why would he *do* that?'

In the centre of a grazed face, Raven's two brown eyes flickered open. 'To prolong my life,' he said, lifting up onto his elbows.

Pryderi placed her foot on his chest and pressed him back down into the shale. 'You *idiot*!' she snapped. 'Now the book may be useless. How is angering us going to prolong your life, *imbecile*?'

'Because I memorised the page before I ate it,' he said, laughing as he reached a weary finger to his head and tapped his skull.

They heard voices and turned to see a group of teenagers, faces hidden in the shadows of hoods, six anaemic, acne-pocked skeletons, in earthly dress, a couple smoking cigarettes, one carrying a football, all trudging along the shoreline towards them. Lord Sacheverell was already facing in their direction, striking a moored pose, legs apart and hands on his waist. His cropped blond hair gently stirred in the evening breeze. His current posture, which may have been considered regal in Seraph quarters was recognised as quite silly in human terms, amusing the advancing gang.

'Wha' y' doin' on our beach, lofty?' asked one of the humans, a particularly ugly chap with a large, caveman chin. He stepped up to the incarnate, initiating a face-off, bulbous features poking out of his hood like the head of a tortoise from its shell.

'I am afraid you are mistaken,' Lord Sacheverell informed the youth. 'This beach and that wall of stones and railings, the road and town beyond and every road and town beyond that, it all belongs to *me*!'

Laughter emanated from surrounding hoods. The smokers started coughing. Someone called out, 'Take his girly knife off him, Josh.'

The hooded youth reached for the dagger at Lord Sacheverell's waist, but in a flash, the incarnate ducked and turned in a complete circle and when he was facing the young man again, dagger drawn and pointed at the stars, Josh seemed to be less amused and animated, rooted to the spot. Black liquid dribbled from Sacheverell's raised blade, slithering over his knuckles. A moment later the human exploded in a cloud of dust leaving only the clothes he wore to flutter down onto the beach. His friends let out a cacophony of terrified screams and ran off back the way they had come.

The glum Lord chuckled and called after them, 'Your acquaintance is the first fatality in what will eventually be the gory massacre of all your loved ones and peers.' A rapid breeze flashed by his ear in the shape of a witch as Pryderi flew over the shoreline in pursuit of the fleeing humans. 'Do leave at least one alive to spread the message of my glorious return!' he bellowed, watching as she dropped directly into their midst and listening to the distinct sounds of hacking and yelling.

When she returned, her armour glistening with human blood, she carried several garments of clothing. 'Put these on!' she said, glaring at him.

Blackpool had become infused by the constant grey drabness of its terrible climate. By day its colourful buildings stood like gaudy gravestones, monuments to a bygone holiday era, while at night they served only to block out stars. A diverse range of events took place in these nocturnal apartments along the seafront, but in one particular chalet, a tenancy rendered almost obscure in comparison to the magnificent concrete and glass holiday homes surrounding it, a man dressed from head to toe in paint-stained rags sat cross-legged on a vibrant living room carpet, chanting in a dead language while an Angel and a witch looked on.

From the assortment of children's photographs and its chintzy décor, the place appeared to belong to an elderly couple who, given the layers of dust frosting every surface, must only have frequented the dwelling a few months of the year. Unopposed to violence, Pryderi was, however, relieved to discover the property abandoned. She had no desire to leave a trail of dead in her stead, not if it interfered with their plans. For all his nobility and his status as a legend of the Futilities, Callous Sacheverell was an uncivilised dolt when it came to the subtle matter of reconnaissance. If they were going to find and take the girl, they would need to proceed with delicacy and caution, even if that meant sparing human lives.

Raven was mumbling in a voice just above a whisper as he studied the Thumb, a ball of cerulean light hovering over the ground before him, constantly altering in size and shape. It materialised into a coffee cup and then a small dog. In the next moment it was a standard lamp and then suddenly a bird. From a bird it transformed into a pair of shoes and then a guitar, a ceramic phrenology head, a suitcase, a clock, a hairdryer, a cushion, a whiskey bottle, a pair of boxing gloves, a birthday cake and then a buckled bicycle wheel. This had been going on for quite some time and though it appeared to entertain the turn-harp, the ability to magic up tangible articles from thin air offered little astonishment for the more stalwart incarnates.

Eventually, the witch, now wearing a black sweater with a hood, purple drainpipe trousers and a pair of green deck-shoes, grew tired with Raven's uninspiring magic show and bent before the paint-splattered man saying, 'You seem to have mastered chapter one, can we move on please?'

Raven looked up at her, blinking rapidly as though emerging from a daydream or a deep trance, unable to remember who or where he was for a moment. As he cast his gaze around the building and realisation seeped back in, a little colour came to his pallid cheeks. 'Yes, yes of course,' he said. 'I'm sorry I... I became quite lost in thought.'

Sacheverell laughed. 'Supernatural trinkets have a reputation for subduing the weak-minded,' he announced, trimming his words with as much arrogance as he could muster. 'The Thumb is no anthology of party tricks, Craven. It is a highly complicated geometrical text that over the centuries has driven even incarnate intellects mad. How will a peasant like you channel its powers?'

Pryderi snatched the book from Raven's fingers and crossed the room. 'This is no spell book, clown,' she said. 'Tell me what was on the page you devoured and I'll promise to release you.'

Raven's voice came slow and grating. 'Please don't call me a clown!'

The witch turned to look at him, cruelly grinning. 'Hadrian Otway Humdinger helped construct the Known Universe,' she said. 'Even his margin notes embrace complex scientific conundrums; puzzles far too exclusive for a mind as base as yours to comprehend.'

The turn-harp lowered his head without taking his eyes from her. 'If the Thumb is a blueprint for creating the Known Universe,' he said, 'then perhaps, in the right hands, it may be used to *uncreate* it!'

Lord Sacheverell, struggling to appreciate the comfort of white training shoes, black denims and a red hooded cardigan with the words *Horny Devil* scrawled across the chest, snorted a sharp and sardonic laugh before marching up to a marble fireplace and angrily clearing it of ornaments. Family portraits, porcelain birds and a glass clock smashed on the carpet at Raven's feet.

'Do pardon my outburst,' the Seraph snarled, baring fangs, 'but I was rather under the impression that, when I take over this hodgepodge of a domain, I will require a place *to stand*. Floating through space for long periods of time can leave one rather nauseous I hear.'

'Surely you mean when *we* take over this domain?' Pryderi corrected him, glancing up from the book's pages.

'Yes, that's obviously what I meant to say,' Sacheverell replied unconvincingly. 'But we must respect tradition and consider that many Seraph have perished in their attempts to reintroduce me as their liege whereas you, my dear, as divine a specimen of femininity one could ever hope to meet, are perceived as riding your uncle's coattails!'

'The book's mine,' said Raven before Pryderi had a chance to react to the glum Lord's insult, and, to their astonishment, the Thumb sprang from her grasp, sailed through the air and landed squarely in the bedraggled incarnate's palm. 'See,' he said with a self-assured smile and immediately slipped it into the folds of his rags.

Lord Sacheverell pointed a wiry finger at him. 'You would do well not to forget who wields the true power here, creature! Do not presume to possess the proficiency to learn anything from that glum knick-knack other than its page numbers. The *right hands*, as you so amusingly put it, are these.' The glum Lord held up both palms for the man in paint-splattered grey to see.

Raven mimicked him by unfurling his own fingers for display, smiling wildly while Pryderi alleged, 'It would seem the Thumb disagrees.'

'Do you honestly believe the cosmic powers of the Known Universe would bestow this shabby, talentless twerp with its secrets?' asked Sacheverell angrily. 'That this scruffy moron could possibly sit upon a golden throne for an eternity while we stand either side as sentinels?'

'It's my birth-right,' Raven muttered through a black smile.

'What birth-right?'

'A lanky, elitist know-all like you wouldn't understand,' Raven muttered.

The glum Lord ran across the room and began to repeatedly kick him, striking turn-harp in his thigh and shins. Then he placed a single finger on the grey man's chest and lifted him up the wall, turning him upside down before dropping him on his head. Raven managed to reduce his injuries by reaching out with his frail arms, but still managed to sustain bruises and a winding.

'*THAT'S ENOUGH*!' Pryderi yelled, stepping between them. 'Enough,' she reiterated in the face of her comrade, who glared at her through snarling and slavering, wolf-like features as she gripped the chest of his hoody and pushed him away from his quarry.

Raven righted himself and brushed down his grubby clothes, all the while glaring at the Seraph. 'If you have another way of releasing your queen then feel free to implement it,' he suggested, arrogantly.

Lord Sacheverell scowled at the turn-harp as he forcefully attempted to sidestep the witch, but Pryderi held him fast. 'He means to bate you, Callous!' Pryderi warned him, pushing him back across the room.

'Why do you protect this vulgar swine?'

'Because we need him,' she said. 'The only reason we're here is because of the Thumb and given neither of us wishes to purée our brains with its glum magic this *vulgar swine* is, sadly, our only hope.'

'Don't call me a swine,' Raven's voice came from behind and the witch looked over her shoulder at him, displaying an exasperated sneer. Raven shrugged his shoulders and said, 'If there's one thing I hate more than clowns its pigs!'

Frothing with fury, Sacheverell pulled himself free of the witch's restraints, but rather than attack the turn-harp he lingered in the other half of the room. 'Only a few hours ago you were prepared to commit deicide by killing that fat lion; now you're protecting a lowborn creep.'

'I'm not protecting him,' she asserted, 'I'm *using* him until he proves impractical to our cause, at which point you have my blessing to flay, disembowel and decapitate the fool, but right now the Thumb is coupled to him so we have to sit tight, bite our tongues and observe.'

'I swear to Om,' Sacheverell spat through gritted fangs, 'if one more discourteous word glides off that moron's tongue, I will ram that book right up his hairy…'

'Surely even *you* can see past your fury, just for the time being, Callous,' Pryderi suggested.

'Yes,' he said, 'you're right, of course.' The incarnate Lord appeared to see sense in this strategy. He exhaled deeply and began breathing more evenly, laughing and reasoning that, 'I am, after all, the highest-ranking incarnate on Nefarious Logistics books, and the mental blethering of pinheads ought to be beneath me.'

When the turn-harp laughed Pryderi had to use all her strength again to prevent the glum Lord crossing the room, dangerously positioning herself between the opposed incarnates.

'Right, that's it, the bastard's dead!' the glum Lord declared. 'I tried, Leo, really I did, but this unwashed beast, this lowly parasite, this lunatic brother of a clown needs to be devoured. He's nothing more than a wretched foot soldier while we are demigods. How can you expect *me* to serve *him*?'

Inhaling the stale air of the chalet, Pryderi propelled the glum Lord further out of the turn-harp's earshot. 'The book and for want of a better word, the man, are a means to an end, Callous. We have spent the last thirty years licking our wounds, lamenting our losses, dreaming of a day when it would be in our power to reclaim glory. This is that day. That dream is in our grasp and when it is won...' the witch cast a cautious glance at Raven who was picking his nose, before whispering, 'When it is won we will destroy the book *and* the man in one fell swoop.'

Lord Sachaverell shook his head. 'This whole business is degrading for me,' he remarked as he released himself from her grasp and smoothed out the sweater where Pryderi's clasp had creased it. 'Magic swords, hammers, rings, shields *and* books are the thing of romantic lunacy. One always ends up serving the artefact and I will not serve a servant!' He glanced at Raven. 'Good day to you, sewer rat,' he said and then to Pryderi, 'Goodbye. I hope your pitiable venture pays off, Leo, but should it fail miserably I promise never to say *I told you so*!' And then the glum Lord vanished in a flash of red light.

Pryderi sucked in a lungful of fetid air and turned to look at the man in paint-splattered grey. 'Now I'm *really* mad,' she said.

'He would have betrayed you in a heartbeat,' Raven told her, his voice high-pitched and trembling. 'Yours is a name which carries no less glory than his.'

She was unpersuaded, nor flattered. 'It is not a name that will convince furtive allies out of shadows when the day arrives to conquer this ball of pus humans call a planet.'

Raven stood and stepped over the plush carpet, retrieving the Thumb from beneath his shirt and clutching it against his chest. He went to a set of patio doors, threw them apart and walked outside. A gust of wind tried to return him to the apartment but he prevailed and strolled out under the first-floor veranda with Pryderi stepping after him. Far above them the heavens were lit up like Christmas decorations.

Raven turned to look at the witch. 'I heard every word you said,' he admitted, looking sad and lost and when he smiled it did little to dissipate the pessimism imbedded in his features. His ashen flesh was made even paler in the moonlight. He resembled a ghost. 'I fear, with the power of the Thumb running through my veins, there will be no juncture in the future when I will be vulnerable to your assaults.'

'You don't frighten me,' the witch warned.

'I think, when I say things like that, I do, a little bit.'

She inhaled the chill night air. 'Callous was right about magic talismans,' she said. 'They end up mastering their masters. They do not belong in the hands of...'

'Of what?' he asked, daring her to complete her statement.

'In the hands of amateurs,' she said without fear or shame.

He snorted with defiance. 'I am no amateur,' he said. 'Sacheverell's memory has withered with age if he thinks me some lowly foot soldier. Mine *are* the right hands. Tonight, he cast himself as our enemy when he took his leave and that betrayal will be met with vengeance.'

Pryderi cackled at his melodrama. 'Those are arrogant words for a man who only just discovered how to produce a buckled bicycle wheel out of thin air. Remember, Lord Sacheverell's powers are colossal and *ingrained*, not learned from a book.'

Raven put away the Thumb and cast his eyes at the sky. He extended two wiry arms, aiming for the stars. From her position in the doorway, peering up at the firmament, the witch was amazed to see the turn-harp's fingers mine the pin-pricked blanket of night and twist the twinkling constellations out of shape as easily as dispersing still waters. She could hardly believe her eyes.

'That missing page you ate,' Pryderi speculated as she stepped out onto the flagstones, 'it must have been significant.'

'It was only the appendix, but as it now inhabits close proximity to *my* appendix nobody will ever truly know how to reference the Thumb but me.' Raven twisted the contours of the world above out of all cosmological fluency as easily as stretching a piece of elastic between his fingers and when he released the black ether, it bounced absurdly back into shape.

'Human beings fear magic and if my father taught me anything it's that fear is the greatest of weapons.'

Bewilderment danced in Pryderi's eyes as she asked, 'And who was your father?'

He giggled with excitement and placed a childish palm over his mouth to stem the laughter. 'Lord Sacheverell did not recognise me. I was no soldier when that narcissist had ambitions of glorification and instructed General Fleischer to defend Konigsberg no matter what the consequence.'

'General Fleischer? But he had no son, only a daughter.'

'Through the frosted glass of his vanity Lord Sacheverell cast me as a servile fool who followed him into battle, but I followed his misfortunes from other places, learning most from the glitter of generals who visited our fortress home of Moribund.'

'*Moribund*?' The witch's demeanour suddenly altered. She became slightly frightened, looking at him aghast. 'Moribund was the family home of Lord Crowberry,' she said.

'I knew him only as daddy,' Raven replied.

Pryderi backed away until her spine met with the cold brick of the building. 'Lord Crowberry was murdered by his mad son, Roderick!' she articulated and then gasped when everything fell into place.

'It wasn't madness turned my brother's hand,' Raven told her, looking suddenly repentant. He met her gaze with wrinkled brows, eyeballs expanding, almost spinning in their sockets and, laughing, said, 'Fate promised him riches beyond wealth and fame. Notoriety at a level with Om Herself would be thrust upon whosoever should bring an end to that futile war, that's what the Captain said.' He covered his smiling mouth with a hand again, exhibiting what appeared to be mock shame. 'Fiend Crowberry was a cruel man,' he reminded her, his mind apparently serving him with a series of awkward memories as his eyes continued to flit sightlessly. 'He bore my brother ill-will from the day he sought to take the polka-dot and parachute silk.'

She shook her head. 'You killed him!'

'My brother killed him,' Raven said. 'Or I did!' He looked confused. 'I am the vestiges of Roderick.' When he lowered his hands an unfurling smile was revealed upon his pasty lips, a joy that seemed absent from the grim picture of the rest of his face. His eyes became white flames set deep within his skull as something exuded from him, something glum and invisible and powerful enough to push Pryderi away, pressing her firmly against the wall, threatening to lift her physically as Sacheverell had lifted him earlier, the brickwork scratching her flesh through her thin garments. 'A third parent conceived the creature standing before you now,' Raven told her as he approached. 'His name was John Fate.'

The turn-harp threw his head sideways and the witch sailed through the air back into the apartment, slamming into a bookshelf and dropping to the ground in a heap of paperbacks and ornaments.

When Raven came in from the patio he had tears rolling down his pale cheeks. 'Please,' he said, 'let's never speak of this again.' He came to her assistance but flinched when Pryderi leaped to her feet. The witch punched him in the face, knocking him backwards where he toppled over a sofa and came to rest with his legs dangling in the air.

'We'll require ground rules if we're to work together,' Pryderi spat at the soles of his feet. 'Number one, if you ever try something like that again I'll gouge out your eyes and wear them as earrings. Do you understand?'

From behind the sofa came a stifled moan, swiftly followed by a maniacal giggle.

CHAPTER EIGHTEEN
1944

Monte Cassino was a tactical vantage point for Seraph armies as the mountain's zenith was considered inaccessible. Enemy command posts dotted the apex and hillsides and, hidden by foliage, they were at liberty to observe allied troop movements five hundred metres below where, amidst that tsunami of dust and frenzied organisation, the Captain of the Home Guard marched across a lively plaza with five infamous war heroes in his stead.

'Storming the Winter Line's pivotal stockade is an ambitious move, John,' said Azzarello Risso, the largest and unofficial leader of the Harbingers. The champions attracted inquisitive glances from the townspeople, but Risso more so, not because of his brawny physique crammed into a bright orange jumpsuit, but because, remarkably, he possessed the head of a pig.

'They say it'll make or break my career, Azz,' replied the Captain, laughing self-effacingly as he trudged towards that looming elevation at the end of town. Fate was well out of his jurisdiction in mainland Europe, out of place amongst all the khaki and camouflage, wearing his traditional black suit and looking more like a sightseeing politician than a man-at-arms. He had arrived by Ladder five minutes ago and would, with any luck, be back in his cosy Manchester office within the hour. 'Our intelligence suggests a number of snipers inhabit the hill. Your assignment is to neutralise these deadeyes. I don't want anyone up there who might impair *his* arrival.'

Risso snorted a laugh. 'What's so special about this geezer, John?'

'Words fail me, Azz,' the Captain said, sighing with pride. 'I think it's better if you just see him for yourself.'

Only the team's newest member, Wilhelmina Hippocampus, appeared daunted by the buzz of excitement surrounding their presence in Italy. She had been invited to join the Harbingers after her arcane skills were revealed by a local newspaper in her home village of *Little Wallop*. Following the capture of an intruder in her grandmother's house, Hippocampus revealed a rather individual method of interrogation resulting in the hapless thief confessing to an extensive series of crimes which included more burglaries, pilfering, pickpocketing, bike theft and the kidnap and ransom of a Border terrier called *Odysseus* belonging to Father Fickler, Little Wallop's incumbent vicar. The role of hero seemed to fit the witch less snugly than it did her counterparts and each passing truck and swooping helicopter or flash of a camera bulb seemed to make her jittery. She was unconventionally pretty, with a mawkish presence, straight black, unkempt hair hiding one side of pale features which were plagued by acne. Initially, she had resisted Fate's invite to enlist, but the Captain's famous powers of persuasion won through when he promised her the one thing she secretly craved more than money and fame: *affection*. Not his, that would have been highly inappropriate, but rather the regard of men the world over who would inevitably behold her as something of a pinup when her profile ascended and her embellished exploits reached the ears of available bachelors across Europe.

Having remained tensely silent since they'd arrived, she finally roused herself to speak and asked, 'What should we do with prisoners?' and noticed her shrill voice seemed to intrude on the conversation as they all looked at her.

'Don't do anything the Geneva Convention might bat an eyelid at,' Fate responded and then, for her neophyte ears, added, 'but never forget these glum forces mean to send you to hell.'

'I've a question,' announced the squat, plump and wrinkled witch, Rose Thicket. 'Can we keep souvenirs this time? Churchill wouldn't let me have that dreadnaught I confiscated at Sirte.'

Fate ignored her as the youngest and strongest of the team, the twelve-year-old Russian, Vadim Nabokov, burst with laughter and said, 'Only souvenir needed is look of fear on enemy face.'

'I understand the Abbey is older than most of the Seraph inhabiting it,' Risso remarked, rolling up his sleeves to reveal two hairy and muscular arms, 'so I assume there are damage limitations in play, John?'

'You won't be going anywhere near the Abbey,' Fate cautioned him. 'As I said, your job is to secure the hillside and take out the snipers. *He'll* take care of the rest.'

'I think St Benedict and I have a lot in common,' the lank-haired new recruit murmured, sniggering apprehensively and turning to look at her comrades at arms. She nodded at the mountain to her rear. 'It looks like we both understand the importance of solitude.'

Thicket sniffed and said, 'If you ask me, love, only a cruel sod makes pious folk walk all that way.'

Scurrying along in their wake was the usual hodgepodge of tabloid hangers-on: biographers, photographers, camera crews and war correspondents, as well as a few comic strip artists. This media circus was integral to the war effort, Fate insisted, for news of their escapades inspired hope back in *Blighty*. But more often than not this train of hack chroniclers, struggling to interpret what was actually happening, never mind what was being said, and in spite of their voices being drowned out by the sound of nearby manoeuvres, scribbled away in their notebooks nevertheless, inventing exploits and dialogue for Europe's civilian populations to lap up. Many of the brash comments and one-liners the Harbingers serialised adventures were famous for had been fabricated by dim-witted and hard of hearing journalists.

A common misconception the media had spread about Darby Dodd was that he could turn invisible. In fact, he was only able to alter his atomic structure and disintegrate into a fine mist. This was on account of being experimented upon by the enemy while he was a POW. Dodd's favourite prank was to fragment in this manner and allow his molecules to drift while the journalists inadvertently entered the grainy fog, upon which time he would burst back into existence and scare the living daylights out of them, much to the amusement of the young Nabokov.

Hippocampus watched him perform this gag now, a tiny smirk playing on her lips, a smile that had less to do with humour than disquiet and an encroaching odium for the stocky man's puerile behaviour. In reality, she would give anything to possess a corporeal temperament like Dodd's as well as his aptitude for entertaining his companions, but confidence evaded her wits and, along with it, a multitude of parallel social skills.

'Dodd, are you listening or playing silly buggers?' Fate chastised.

'Sorry, Cap, just like to put the wind up the scribblers,' he laughed.

'*Wind up the scribblers*,' Hippocampus reiterated, with a manic chuckle, desperately trying to fit in. Looking back at Dodd she said, 'It sounds a bit rude, doesn't it?' Her phoney laughter was a sorry attempt at ingratiation, the result of which was being either ignored or regarded with pitiful frowns by her colleagues. And as this comprehension hit home she came to a stop on the road, gaping dreamily at ether recently vacated by both the paranormal team of heroes and the gaggle of pressmen. As the dust disturbed by their tramping feet began to settle, the new recruit noticed a solitary figure standing in the plaza, a dislocated member of the media, looking back at her. He was a rather odd, gangly sort of fellow whose obvious lack of physical attributes visually broadcast his failure to be drafted. The young man busily scribbled something in a writing pad, tongue protruding attentively from one corner of his mouth, looked at her again and froze.

'Hullo,' she said, in a voice close to a whisper that only just managed to traverse the vacant expanse between them.

The gawky journalist smiled nervously and said, 'H-h-hello, Miss Hip-Hip-Hippo…!'

'Please, call me *Charmaine*.'

His smile faded, revealing a puzzled expression as he checked his notes before looking up again and asking, 'Why?'

'Because I loathe my birth name and Charmaine's a much prettier appellation, don't you think?'

'It's a-it's a-it's a lovely name!' the man replied, timidly. He coughed and then parted his hair with the fingers of his pencil hand, flattening oily tendrils to his scalp.

As Hippocampus approached, focusing on the writing pad in his grasp, she asked, 'Do you mind me asking what you're writing?' and the peculiar man cleared his throat and then refrained to use it, instead stepping forwards and awkwardly passing her his notebook. She read his scribbles aloud: '*All but insignificant beside mighty warriors like Risso and the prepubescent Nabokov and possessing magic rendered plain compared to Dodd's transformation skills and Thicket's ancient witchery, Wilhelmina Lucinda Hippocampus, the Harbingers' skittish newcomer, making up the numbers since John Fate decided five (despite it being an Angel Number and of all numerical digits, possessing the curliest extremity) a better sum of members than four, paces cumbersomely next to these historical giants, apparently pierced by palpable apprehension and with a nonplussed appearance of perpetual dread...*' Hippocampus looked up at him and smiled, saying, 'It's a shame you couldn't find a word beginning with *P* that means *dread*. You could have had *trepidation*. There's a particularly *pointy P* in that. And also, I haven't found a single full stop, but that's not a criticism you understand.'

'Punctuation is the very last thing I…'

'*Shh!*' she instructed, looking back at the text and reading on. '… *apparently pierced by palpable apprehension and a nonplussed appearance of perpetual* trepidation, *like a limping cocker spaniel next to four Tyrannosaurus Rex, she is meek and miserable in their midst, misplaced as a meaty mouse at a mass-meeting of meanly motivated moggies, mislaid amongst a…*' Hippocampus quickly ran her finger down the page until she reached the final few lines and what, thankfully, appeared to be a counter-argument 'but, *although at first glance one might assume the unctuous-haired maiden's presence superfluous, gratuitous even, on further observation of her companions, the immortal Risso, the naive Nabokov, the cocky Dodd and the unruly Thicket, perhaps a more vigilant fifth is required if the Harbingers are to endure beyond, not only this battle and this war, but their own infamy and inflated egos when chaos has ultimately been quenched.*'

When she finished reading Hippocampus continued to stare at the page. The journalist's face performed a series of emotions ranging between happy and sad via blustery concern and tortuous embarrassment. And then, finally, the Harbinger looked up and candidly smiled. 'You think I bring equilibrium?'

He nodded.

When a bulky military aircraft passed overhead, booming above them like a thunderstorm and blowing up another tempest of sand, neither of them seemed to notice. As the blizzard diminished, Hippocampus cocked her head on one shoulder and, blushing, handed back the notepad saying, 'Why, thank you, young man.'

The journalist smiled with a fragile confidence and stammered, 'Y-you're-you're very welcome!'

'None of your associates appear even slightly interested in me,' she observed. '*I* might as well be the invisible one.'

At this the journalist raised a finger in the air and pointed out that, 'It's actually a common misconception that Darby Dodd can...'

'Why did you decide to write about me?'

He coughed and considered a reply. 'Because,' he finally said, 'you have a... a rare quality. The others... well, they're strong or brave or magic whereas you... you're... well, you have an arcane demeanour.'

A frown lowered like a curtain over her timid face and uncertainty filled her mind.

'I... I mean it in a good way,' he said. 'I like you! What you do I mean... I... I like what you do.'

Suddenly, Rose Thicket's Lancashire accent cut through the raucous environment, '*Hippopotamus*, are you coming or not?'

'We're going on a mission up the hill to beat up some baddies,' the Harbinger informed him. 'Would you like to come along?'

'Oh yes please,' he said, visibly thrilled with the invitation. 'That would be... well, it would be...'

'Come on then,' she said, grabbing his hand and dragging him after her, calling out over her shoulder, 'You didn't tell me your name.'

'It's Sidney,' he replied. 'Sidney Seabrook.'

'Sidney Seabrook, the obsessive, essayist and stuttering Fleet Street star!' she announced with a hiccup and a laugh, as they hurtled through the settlement, past lines of marching soldiers and rolling vehicles, war-weary locals and centuries old, bullet-hole strewn buildings.

Machine gun and sniper bursts rattled out from the moment the trek up the mountainside got underway, Risso's immortal hide sheltering them from the worst of it while Thicket used magic to turn hurtling projectiles into harmless gusts of horizontal raindrops that stung on impact but were unable to penetrate flesh. Dodd avoided injury by dispersing himself atomically and drifting up and down the elevation at will. With less compulsion to dive into dense vegetation or behind large boulders, it amused him to watch his more prone cohorts narrowly avoiding mortal danger. And while Nabokov, the strongest member of the team, was relied upon to heave great sarsens out of the soil to use as shields, Hippocampus, being the Johnny-come-lately, was billeted with looking after the attending media, the majority of whom had retreated back to the Plan's encampment after the first flurry of bullets spat dirt around their ankles.

Whenever they came to the road that looped the mountain's rugged fascia, they were faced with having to leave the protective canopy of trees. Provided no shelter from a marksman's bullet, this was where Risso's future-seeing eye came into use. The origins of the Pig's ability to see forty-seven seconds into the future was a mystery even to him, a superpower attained in an unchronicled and equally unremembered epoch of his life and just one of many incomprehensible skills he brought to the unit in conjunction with invincibility, an innate gift for forcing enemies tell him the truth and an extensive knowledge of the musical compositions of singer/songwriter Barry Manilow (who, only being a year old in 1944, allowed the Pig to speculate that his own inscrutable geneses must have relied on some form of time travel). Harrowingly, the group were forced to wait up to fifteen or twenty minutes at a time by the roadside for him to assess immanent eternity for the safest instant to make a dash for it.

'By repetitively altering our tactics in this method,' Hippocampus commented to Sidney, her only companion in the leafy hiding place they had dove after sprinting maniacally across one section of tarmac, 'relying on Risso's notion of pending hazards, are we actually *altering* the future?' Her personal scribbler scribbled these words into his notebook. 'It makes my brain ache just thinking about how many dimensions our avoidance of death has generated in the last hour.'

On finding their first pillbox, a fabricated hut set into the oblique hillside and inhabited by a single soldier, Risso and Nabokov played *rock, paper, scissors* to decide who would take the sniper's nest out. Paying no attention to these selection tactics, the arrogant Dodd floated directly up to the concrete edifice in vapour form and began to tease the soldier inside, making him believe he was hearing voices and was going insane. He loosed off a few rounds of ammo which passed right through the imperceptible Dodd and kicked up earth and foliage for several metres around them. In the end, Thicket restrained the fighter's zealous charge by hurling a stone at him and knocking him out cold.

'Good work, Rose,' Risso said.

'*Good work, Rose*?' Dodd's detached voice protested. 'It was *me* did all the hard work, she just whizzed a brick.'

A sudden, sombre shriek melted the atmosphere and they turned to see Hippocampus kneeling over the body of Sidney Seabrook, the smitten reporter lying stationary on the ground. Her cries of woe, not only having the potential of giving away their location, but as unnerving to the soul as the esoteric whimpering of a ghoul at a bedroom door in the night, made each of them quiver with nervous fear.

'Nabokov,' the old witch ordered, 'shut her up before half the Wehrmacht come down on us.'

The youth, who was standing closest to the rookie, seemed confused about what to do and glanced back and forth between both witches for a moment before drawing back an arm ready to punch the blaring woman. He froze when her caterwauling abruptly ended and an unexpected silence, that seemed almost as deadly, settled on the area.

Only the tweet of a distant swift returned the world to order.

*****

They camped at the pillbox till dusk. Hippocampus was virtually catatonic, slumped against the trunk of a tree, refusing to respond to repeated enquiries about her mental state and, when not leafing through Seabrook's notebook, lips moving silently as her heavy eyes passed over the scribbled words, she simply stared into space like a stuffed cat.

The unconscious soldier was tied to an adjacent tree and as much ineffectual effort had been expelled to revive him.

When Risso eventually climbed to his feet and announced that Dodd was to stay behind and watch the witch, pressmen and prisoner, *The Disintegrating Man* was furious, exclaiming, 'The hell I will, *Porky.*'

'That's an order!'

'You're not the boss of me,' Dodd reminded him.

Thicket reasoned that, 'One of us has to stay behind and look after that poor mare and I never signed up to be no babysitter.'

'What and I did?' asked Dodd, heatedly as he got to his feet and approached the pig. 'If you're going up the mountain I'm coming with you.'

'I could carry,' Nabokov offered in his pigeon English. 'She cannot weigh more than bag of lettuce.'

Risso shook his head. 'Not unless you intend to carry the reporters and our captive too,' he said and pointing a fat, pink finger at Dodd told him without remorse, 'You're a reckless idiot. Taking out that pillbox on your own was haphazard at best. That reporter might still be alive if you hadn't…'

'Are you saying *I* killed him? None of us would be here at all if Fate weren't about to show off his brand-new toy, and from what I remember it was *Jerry* over there, the Seraph's Teutonic amigo, firing his metal Christmas present all over the shop what did for the scribbler.'

'Enough with the racial stereotyping, Dodd,' Risso warned. 'This isn't a debate. You're staying behind. The rest of us will continue with the mission. If you have a problem with that, speak to the boss when we get back.'

Dodd was furious. He glared after them as they clambered up the slope in the dark and then kicked and punched the tree Hippocampus was sat under unsettling the nerves of the journalists huddled close by. At one point he turned and stared at them, breathing heavily with anger. Then he looked at the inert woman and, his hatred turning to despair, dropped to his knees. 'It's not my fault,' he said. 'Terrible things happen in wartime.'

As a menagerie of nocturnal sounds replaced the Harbingers trudging and wheezing, the atmosphere in camp fell suddenly eerie.

'I was just doing my job,' Dodd insisted. 'I didn't mean for your friend to get hurt.' He looked at Hippocampus, placed a hand on her arm and shook it to encourage a reaction but when the woman continued to ignore him, he sighed with ignominy and asked, 'Can you even hear what I'm saying?'

'It's like you say,' one of the journalists spoke up, favourably, 'terrible things happen in wartime.'

Dodd turned to look at the man, his mood softening. 'I can't just sit here,' he said as his image began to fade, his physical form collapsing, becoming a cloud of dust. 'I can't just do nothing,' his displaced voice announced as the quavering mist shifted up the hillside after the others.

Hippocampus moved her eyes to look at the spot where the Harbinger had been but instead of a conceited hero, she saw only the German soldier tied to the tree opposite.

'Are you all right, missy?' asked one of the journalists.

The witch did not respond. Instead she crawled over the ground to the bound prisoner and, coming face to face with the insensible man, said, '*Wake up!*' When he remained unconscious she grabbed and shook him by his chin. 'I said, *wake up!*'

He blinked. His throat produced a groan and his face a grimace.

'I don't think you should be doing that,' one of the frightened journalists suggested while all three backed away into foliage.

'Doing what?' Hippocampus asked, still glaring at the prisoner, 'My job?' To the pressmen's alarm her mannerism changed from remorseful puzzlement to absolute wrath, her mushy eyes growing dark with rage and forehead slanted with arrowed creases. 'My job is to interrogate the enemy and if the enemy won't come out then I'll have to go in.'

By the time dawn arrived, Risso, Nabokov and Thicket had liberated more than a dozen pillboxes, bound at least thirty German soldiers to cypress trees and successfully reached the walls of the Abbey on the mountain's summit, without receiving so much as a scratch between them. Thicket sent telepathic word back to HQ to inform the Plan the mountain was secured and then the trio sat on the sloping hill under a baking sun to discuss recent combat.

'That was a close shave with the bayonet, Vadim,' the witch commented and loudly laughed.

'Close call?' the young Harbinger complained. 'Crazy Hun tried to take off ear.'

Uncharacteristically, Risso laughed too.

'Is no laughing matter,' said Nabokov. 'Ear's my best feature!'

Their hilarity was cut short when a thunderous detonation sounded in the air above them and clouds seemed to draw apart, moving consciously out the way to prepare for a happening. The Harbingers watched with puzzled expressions as the sky opened up, splitting apart with piercing golden shafts of light; peeling like a fruit to reveal a divine pulp beneath. For the briefest of moments there appeared to be two suns in the blue firmament and then, with an ear-splitting popping sound, one imploded and became a small object hurtling forwards, spinning randomly through the ether, light propelling from it in exploding columns.

'Fate resorted to catapulting them in now, has he?' asked Thicket.

'It looks like a person,' said Risso, a hand above his eyes to protect them from the blaring light as he got to his feet.

They began to watch more out of curiosity than wonder as the figure tumbled closer, rotating dizzily in the air, head over heels in a constant airborne forward roll and, as he grew nearer, they heard the unmistakable sound of screaming. If this was Fate's new weapon it was certainly the most bizarre armament any of them had ever seen. The figure ascended to fifty metres above their present location on what looked like a trajectory to send him right over the mountain, when suddenly a change of direction dropped him swiftly onto the ancient Abbey. There was a blood-curdling crash followed by a swell of dust and a tremendous ground quake.

'What the hell was that?' asked a voice beside them and the pig turned to see Dodd emerge on their periphery as Thicket and Nabokov got to their feet.

'If that's some new-fangled Ladder, I'll stick to me bus pass,' Thicket remarked, passing Dodd on her way down the hill.

'What are you *doing* up here?' Risso asked Dodd, furiously. 'Didn't I tell you to watch the girl?'

The affronted man sniffed and shrugged his shoulders. 'I just thought I'd be more useful…'

'We had no use of invisible man,' said Nabokov.

'Oh yeah, so who do you think blindsided that looney kraut with the bayonet then, eh? He'd have taken your head clean off if I hadn't…'

Risso purposely bumped the man's shoulder as he passed, following Thicket on her way back to camp but then both Harbingers stopped and looked back when a series of explosions erupted from the Abbey's grounds.

*****

What took six hours to scramble up in darkness took only one to descend in daylight and when Risso and his comrades finally reached camp they were surprised to find everyone but Hippocampus and the dead Seabrook missing. The three journalists were soon located, however, hiding close by in long grass and as they were rounded up remonstrated about returning to the vicinity of the lank-haired witch.

'What happened to prisoner?' Nabokov asked as he watched Hippocampus cradle the deceased journo in her arms, stroking the man's thin hair.

Rose Thicket, who had already heard the tale of horror from one of the trembling pressmen she'd found in the woods, said, 'She ate him from inside out.'

And Hippocampus looked up, eyes red from crying and voice scuffed with sorrow, and said, 'I was just doing my job.'

CHAPTER NINETEEN
The Unfastened Room

Holding a cushion to her chest, large green eyes peeping over its silky perimeter and flitting between the TV, her pretend grandfather, currently studying a trouser press instruction manual, and Mr Pierpot, transfixed by the contents of the mini-bar, Egg felt unusually downcast.

She wasn't used to feeling sad, as far as she knew. Her life pre-amnesia may have involved tremendous bouts of sorrow, but she had no memory of it. Trying to remember had become a dangerous pursuit, for it was attempting that type of nostalgia that caused inadvertent teleportation. It was like being a part-time ghost incapable of maintaining a normal existence in the here and now. And should the condition continue into old age, dementia would see her zapping all over her retirement home.

It didn't matter if her memories never returned, not really. She would be more than happy living with the King. The only thing she knew for certain, though uncertain how she knew it, was that he was a good man and would take care of her. His compassion had been evident from the off. When she appeared in his garden, dressed in rags and smeared in dirt, face festooned with grey rivulets of smudges where tears had driven a watercourse through the caked muck, the King had taken her under his arm and escorted her to one of the many bathrooms in Hill House where he left her to shower and freshen up, trusting and caring about her welfare instantly.

But she couldn't risk thinking about that now, about how grubby and upset she had been, for if she did then the temptation to remember why might override her resolve not to think about the past.

By some means, a duplicate hotel suite seemed to have replaced the original. Egg could see through its blurry and transparent field, a fake casing that rendered her companions fuzzy ghosts. She saw the King glance up from his manual and perform a double take before leaping to his feet with alarm and running to the sofa. Although she realised he couldn't see or hear her any more, she waved and called out, '*Look, I'm still here.*' He tore away the cushions under the illogical impression she had been swallowed up by the piece of furniture, his movements seeming irregular, reduced to a sequence of jump-starts like a flicker book image. And when Mr Pierpot joined him in his panic, their voices sounded sluggish, muffled and far away.

She got off the other sofa in that other room and passed right through her grandfather's and Mr Pierpot's spectral forms, the very notion of it making her shiver. And as she walked away the image of the hotel suite faded and eventually vanished completely until she was left standing in a cold, abandoned room dressed only in her pyjamas. Her breath trundled out in front of her like a lacklustre party horn as she hurried to the door and peered out along a bare, concrete

189

corridor strewn with shards of plastic sheeting, loops of wiring, fast food cartons, empty cement bags and other forms of what appeared to be worksite refuse. Some of it blew around her ankles as she made her way along the passage, carefully avoiding treading on anything sharp or nasty in her bare feet. She glanced into each small and empty cell of a room she came across, noting the clutter, the sort of waste that typically littered abandoned building sites. Given her circumstances, Egg ought to be afraid, but something about the place registered as safe. It matched the sense of wellbeing she felt on Grace Plateau, so excitement, rather than dread, rose from her belly to her chest as she continued along the corridor beneath flickering strip lights and metal ceiling frames empty of tiles, peeping curiously into empty rooms until, to her delight, she found one occupied.

A fat man was sat in an office chair, absently rotating back and forth, a small pot of ice-cream in one chubby hand and a tiny plastic spatula in the other. He wore a dark blue T-shirt with white lettering across the chest that read, *CPG*. A pair of light blue jeans appeared stretched to extremity. The man's eyes concentrated on the grey screen of a computer monitor. After a moment he seemed to sense being watched and turned to see her standing in the doorway. He stopped breathing and looked back at the monitor with unease, tapping the screen and then the keyboard with the only fingers free to him before slowly turning back, exhaling breath and nervously saying, '*Hullo!*'

'Hello,' said Egg, stepping inside where it was warm. There was an electric heater plugged into the wall.

'You're Egg,' the man said.

She nodded and asked, 'Do you work here?'

He turned completely around in his chair with his ice cream and spoon held at arm's length. 'This is where I work my magic, yes,' he replied.

'Can you *do* magic?' she enquired with interest.

'Oh, I'm not as good as you.'

'*I* can't do magic.'

'Is that what the King told you?'

'What's your name?'

'It's Zack,' Zack said.

'What does your T-shirt mean?'

Zack looked down and ran a little finger under the logo. '*Contingency Plan Geomancy*,' he revealed. 'I'm in charge of stars, the ones outside your hotel window. This,' he stated, indicating everything around them with a wave of a hand, 'is just the foundations of the facsimile you... up until a moment ago, inhabited.'

She looked round at the interior of the office, surprised at how real it all seemed. 'So none of this is real?'

Zack laughed. '*This* room is real, but the other one, the one in the hotel, that was a facsimile.'

'It's really quite simple, Egg,' a voice from behind her said before she could ask Zack what a *fat slimy* was, and she turned to see John Fate leaning in the doorway, wiping cement dust from his lapel and smiling like a lizard. 'I bet you like colouring in, don't you?' When she nodded her head he said, 'Well think about how eager you are to shade in all those empty horses, boats and farmhouses with your colourful crayons. Those black and white pictures are lifeless and dull outlines until you add your imagination. That's really all that happens here. Zack augments the lifeless and dull outlines with *his* imagination. Geomancers create fake worlds, little environmental deceptions we call facsimiles. They come in very useful in espionage and warfare and make rather splendid penitentiaries.'

'Like prisons?'

'Exactly like prisons,' said the Captain.

'Am *I* a prisoner?'

He snorted a laugh. 'Up until a moment ago, I suppose you were. But only for your own protection.' He came forward, crouching before her as he had done earlier when they met in his office. 'The room your grandfather and Mr Pierpot currently reside in is counterfeit, designed purely to protect you from... less urbane types, shall we say?' His smile became more slanted and more reptilian, unreliable as smiles go, as though even the Captain of the Home Guard wasn't falling for his own blather. 'You're already proving to be something of a phenomenon, Egg. Facsimiles were considered inescapable and then you just up and decide to pop out of there, as easy as opening a door and stepping through it. That's a bit unnerving for people in my line of work. Your accommodation was a temporary arrangement, a respite while the Plan investigated the incursion at Hill House. It was also a rather resourceful way of keeping you under tabs, just while we tried to figure you out.'

'So I *am* a prisoner?'

His smile evened out but remained ominous. 'I prefer to think of you as our guest. Your grandfather asked you not to teleport, which in my book was sound advice, and quite honestly I had not anticipated your ability to leave the suite entirely.'

'If I'm a guest that means I can leave if I want.'

Zack laughed and Egg looked at him. 'Leaving the hotel suite is one thing,' he said, 'but leaving Grace Plateau? You're still trapped in its parameters, even here. It's multi-layered see, a bit like an onion. It spans rather a large section of the city and its surrounding townships and parishes. You could pass through dimensional wall after dimensional wall for weeks and weeks and always be within the limits of the plateau. Unrestricted exit and access are virtually impossible.'

'This is Grace Plateau?'

Zack nodded his head.

The little girl appeared confused. 'But we left there yonks ago.'

'It's very complicated science,' explained Zack.

Fate placed a hand on her shoulder. 'You shouldn't have left the hotel until we were satisfied you weren't in any serious danger,' he informed her.

'Or, equally, that you are not seriously dangerous,' added Zack.

'Why would I be dangerous?'

'Because you're a miracle, Egg,' Fate answered honestly. 'And you're a mystery to us, an entity we don't fully understand.'

'A UFO,' said Zack, 'only without the flying bit.'

'We can't allow you to simply wander around freely. For one thing, it would be a dereliction of my duty as Captain of the Home Guard.'

Egg looked at both of them in turn before frowning and saying, 'That doesn't seem fair. I haven't done anything wrong.'

Zack spooned ice-cream between his gums. 'But we don't know if you will in the future, do we? We've yet to determine if you're friend or foe.'

'You might be here to save humanity from an imminent incarnate uprising,' Fate said, flapping his arms about dramatically, 'or you might be here to destroy our world entirely.'

'I don't want to do either of those things,' she told them.

Fate and Zack looked at each other. The Captain of the Home Guard stood up, patted her on the head and said, 'Zack and I are grownups and grownups don't believe in coincidence.'

'Because coincidence was outlawed during the Happenchance Witch Trials of 1612,' stated Zack.

'Why would I want to destroy the world?'

'For no other reason than because you can,' Fate said. 'Take a walk with me. There's something I'd like to show you.' He went to the door and out into the corridor.

Egg smiled at Zack and said, 'Goodbye.'

He waved. 'Bye,' he replied, 'oh yeah, and please don't destroy the world just because you can.'

She ran after the Captain and as she caught up with him an inexplicably strong breeze blew along the hallway, throwing her hair around her face.

'I'm sure you're aware by now that your grandfather and I don't exactly see eye to eye on most matters,' Fate said as she ambled along beside him, the both of them moving at a luxurious pace. 'I'm not a bad man, Egg. I've just had to make very tough decisions in my time as Captain and I admit that many of them were ethically ambiguous to say the least, but they were decisions that needed making and I didn't see anybody else volunteering for the task. Whatever I have done, it was always for the good of humanity. Those words sound like a tainted axiom these days, but they're the truth. Do you know what a cliché is, Egg?'

'Is it one of those purple and green fruits with spikes?'

'No, that would be a *cumquat*. A cliché is a tired old phrase deprived of value due to overuse, but is a steadfast and dependable fact nonetheless. Your grandfather, for example, he's a cliché.'

As they progressed along the passageway, Egg noticed it change shape around them. Colours faded and contours altered; a similar metamorphosis to the one she had witnessed leaving the hotel suite was taking place. The rectangular hallway remained, but its walls were revealed to be skeletal frameworks of steel piping and the floor became wood planking. They were elevated, striding along a scaffold a hundred metres off the ground, a steel gibbet that extended fifty metres square around the offices where Zack *worked his magic*. When Egg looked down, she was delighted to see hundreds of people scurrying about like worker ants, wearing blue overalls and yellow hardhats, all adorned with the CPG logo.

'Wow!' she said, the wind whipping her hair vertically a moment and making her giggle.

'Marvellous, isn't it?' said Fate, but he did not marvel for long. After a brief glance over the edge of the platform he continued with his constitutional and his dialogue. 'I'm so glad we have a chance to speak confidentially. The King is a decent sort, but rather a stubborn old man; especially, it seems, in matters concerning *you*, his unauthenticated kin. What he fails to realise is that he's just one person and this world is jam-packed full of nutters who will cast themselves as your enemy. My organisation is better equipped to shield you from said nutters. Incidentally, do try to keep the King away from any dragons.'

Ignoring the random comment about dragons, Egg asked the Captain, 'Why would somebody want to be my enemy?'

They arrived at a steel-mesh elevator and Fate held the gate open for her to climb aboard, entering after her. 'Sadly, the most placid and cheerful entities on this earth often provoke animosity for just those characteristics. The very fact you did not exist upon this plane of reality a month ago will incite many undesirable factions into hysteria.' He pressed a button and the elevator began to descend. 'Somewhere in the Known Universe there will be a half-forgotten god, cult or glum fiend who considers you a more than adequate keepsake for their mantelpiece or dungeon or suitable subject for sacrifice. I deal with this nonsense on a daily basis, Egg, and so I believe that shielding you from such an uncomfortable truth is simply denying you important information you may need to protect yourself. What frightens me most about your mysterious manifestation is that my dreams allowed me no prior warning, for that is where *my* talents lie, in prophesising the future. The last otherworldly entity that arrived here without warning was…?'

'Ashok Kumar!'

'Precisely,' said the Captain. 'Though admittedly, I was suffering from a terrible cold at the time.'

As the elevator descended, Egg was surprised by the amount of labour and construction happening simply to keep a single facsimile running smoothly. It looked like thousands of Planners were employed in the process, hurrying to and fro, hoisting equipment, noisily shouting orders at one another, welding girders and climbing ladders and pushing wheelbarrows.

Fate said, 'Many people already assume you are *Chaos Likely*.'

Egg tore her eyes from Grace Plateau's sprawling topography and looked up at him in surprise.

'Allow me to quote from a poem written many centuries ago by the prophesier, Paul Joseph Cullen; *chaos likely will fill the air, and bring forth the unknown soul, the egg will crack and all will cease, the land will turn to foul!*'

'You think I'm the egg in that poem?' she asked, excitedly.

He shrugged his shoulders and replied, 'I hope not. On this matter my understanding is a little clearer than most. You see, I have it on good authority that you can't possibly *be* Chaos Likely, and not just because she would be almost fifty-years-old by now but because her identity has already been divulged to me. You're not nearly as old as that, are you?'

Egg giggled. 'Of course not, silly!'

'I thought not, but there are many peculiar people in the world that will utilise bespoke logic and consider you to be her. They'll want to steal you away, desiring the glum power they imagine resides in your bones.'

Egg cringed and looked up at the steel framework ascending behind the Captain. There appeared to be at least twenty levels beneath the facsimile of the hotel suite, despite it only residing on the fourth floor of the Elysium Hotel. 'Where are we going?' she asked.

'I'm taking you to the *Unfastened Room*,' he said, 'so-called because it has never been tied to reality. We utilise it as a record system. Anything that ever happened in the Unfastened Room happens forever in its own splintered dimension and is eternally open to observation. We tend to do all of our most important work in there, to document it thusly.'

'It must be a *big* room,' Egg said.

'On the contrary,' Fate laughed. 'It's no bigger than a broom cupboard. It was the sight of an ancient geographical phenomenon and is one of the reasons why Grace Plateau is allowed to exist here.'

'What was the *jog raft free normal one*?'

'The geographical phenomenon,' Fate corrected her, 'is a patch of land where a blessed man's blood was spilled.'

Egg's eyes expanded with insightful interest. 'Is it where the *Knight Watchman* was almost killed?'

'Very good,' said Fate, impressed. 'The King has done a sound job in educating you.'

'It's one of my favourite stories,' she replied. 'Centuries ago, Om needed people to watch over the Known Universe when she went on holiday and so a tournament was held where all the strongest men… I don't know why they had to be men, but it was the olden days so I suppose it must have been okay then… and all the strongest men in the world came and competed for the position of Knight Watchman and when the winners were chosen a man lost his temper and...'

'A man called Reverend Christophe Clovis,' Fate informed her.

She nodded her head with excitement. 'He lost his temper and tried to kill them.'

'He tried to kill only one of them,' Fate informed her, 'and because the Watchmen had already been blessed, the man's blood was holy and so when it seeped into the ground it made that patch of land holy too.'

'Where are the Watchmen now?'

Sporting that shifty smile of his again, Fate said, 'Living in Northern Spain last I heard,' and Egg had the definite impression he was telling lies.

The elevator touched ground with a bump and Fate opened the gate and led the way out, across what now appeared to be a vast aircraft hangar towards a set of huge sliding doors. Egg was still fascinated by the towering construct behind them, its highest levels submerged in cloud. The building had altered again just as the hotel suite and the corridor had done earlier and though she could still see the scaffold enclosed summit it appeared to be blended with an indoor sky.

At the hangar doors, they were met by a short, gargoyle-looking clerk who handed Fate a clipboard. He signed a document and they left, crossing an airfield where dozens of biplanes lined the paved terminal and unusually shaped zeppelins were anchored by guidelines, their bulbous forms bobbing half a kilometre above ground. Fate led her to a rotund metal hut beyond a runway and once inside, Grace Plateau's flimsy white corridors became discernible again, an interior space that by far outreached the physical parameters of the metal hut's exterior.

'Everything is something else here,' she said.

'Impressive, isn't it?' Fate responded, noting the joyful bewilderment on her face. Planners marched everywhere dressed in uniforms or suits, carrying guns or clipboards respectively. A few alien-looking life-forms were escorted past, some with ankles and wrists in manacles. A Seraph flew overhead trailing word-processor printouts behind him.

'Is it magic?' she asked.

'It has a slither of magic at its core,' Fate said. 'Griffin Adler rewrote every physics book we threw at him to design this place. He was a brilliant scientist, a fugitive now of course. Should you ever run into him, be sure to say hello from me.'

They turned a corner at the end of the silken corridor, strode past offices where various species and extraordinarily dressed people sat waiting to be admitted or dismissed. Egg soaked up every detail of the exotic location, marvelling at its majestic diversity, until Fate finally stopped and turned to look at her. 'You told me you were familiar with the legend of Ashok Kumar,' he stated and she nodded her head. 'Well, you're about to witness a moment in his life from more than thirty years ago. Not many people are privy to this information so I'd appreciate you keeping it under your hat.'

Egg absently put a hand to her head to check if she was wearing a hat as Fate opened a door and led her into a fairly ordinary room with two chairs and a desk. It resembled a police interrogation suite and was relatively unimpressive compared to all the wonders she had witnessed on the way here. On the desk was a yellow box that resembled a child's toy complete with two bulky and colourful buttons, one red the other green. Fate closed the door behind them, went to the desk and produced a square of plastic from his pocket, which he inserted into the box before pressing the green button.

For a moment nothing happened. And then the door opened, only it wasn't the real door because Egg could still see the real door closed behind the image. She watched two men drag a third into the room. To her astonishment, one of the men was John Fate, only younger and sporting a moustache. Another had dark skin and Egg assumed he was Dr Naveed Rajput (there was a lever on page two of the pop-up book at Hill House that when you pulled it, Dr Rajput rose up behind Kumar's hospital bed with a stethoscope in one hand and a crescent sword in the other and a speech bubble attached said, *say aahh*!). She watched the men lay their insentient companion on the table. The unconscious man was thin and pale, had long brown hair and a scruffy beard. Egg put a hand over her mouth when she saw gaping wounds in his shoulders and chest as well as bloodstains on his tattered clothing. The man was unmistakably Ashok Kumar. The image flickered as time sped up and Kumar was suddenly conscious, screaming and shouting, grappling hysterically with his friends. He tried to sit up but his companions restrained him. Eventually he returned to a lethargic state and lay back, completely subdued.

'*Did you see what happened?*' the young, moustachioed Fate in the transmission asked the doctor.

'*They say seeing is believing,*' Dr Rajput replied, '*and yet I am incapable of trusting what my eyes so recently observed.*'

Everything sped up like fast forwarding a video tape and when the images resumed a regular pace again, the man on the table was awake, raising a hand towards the doctor, clutching the medic's arm for support.

'*You are out of danger, Mr Kumar,*' Dr Rajput told him, helping him sit up, placing an arm behind his patient to prevent him tumbling from the table.

'*What happened*?' asked Kumar.

'*A miracle,*' said Fate.

Kumar looked at him. '*I dreamt I was… falling.*'

Dr Rajput sighed and said, '*it was no dream, my friend.*'

The bearded man's eyes narrowed and he beheld the Captain and then the doctor with a bewildered stare before looking sullenly at the floor. '*Then I was flying,*' he said.

'*I wouldn't exactly call it flying,*' Fate commented with a chuckle. '*Your coordination left a lot to be desired, but you hit your target and caused enough destruction to put the wind up General Galbi and his forces.*'

Kumar put a hand to his bloody T-shirt, pulling it away from his chest wound and, despite the clothing's sticky red mess, the flesh beneath was smooth and unbroken.

'*I don't understand.*'

'*That is the nature of miracles,*' said Dr Rajput and the image became unnaturally elongated, juddered and disappeared and Egg and the current version of John Fate were left alone in the room.

'I don't understand,' she said.

The Captain smiled without humour and sat on the corner of the desk. 'We were fighting a war,' he told her, 'a war, I might add, we were losing. When Om disappeared, she left us to the mercy of Seraph. They're not *all* bad, I suppose. Most just want peace like the rest of us, but others wanted earth for themselves. Nefarious Logistics have been behind every human conflict in the last three hundred years, influencing mistrust, affecting misinterpretation, whispering in the ears of madmen. The Futilities was a war we were bound to lose until Ashok Kumar fell out of heaven. Ancient prophesy referred to him as *Heavenly Joys*. The event you just witnessed occurred in the aftermath of an assault on an enemy stronghold in Italy. Kumar was to teleport to the location and assist allied forces in the big push, only he fell out of the sky and his impact completely destroyed an entire fortress. Moments later, as you just witnessed, his body was completely healed. It was a macabre and difficult resolution, but one that turned the tide of the war. We learnt a very interesting fact from that assault; that Kumar's blood was toxic, not to humans but to incarnates. We finally had a weapon to match their glum magic. After Italy, we improved and modified the science, trained Kumar, battle-hardened him and then released him over the city of Konigsberg.' Fate glanced down at the floor, resembling the look of sullenness Kumar had exhibited a moment ago. 'I have never witnessed devastation like it. We rained hell upon incarnate armies and those who did not retreat or surrender died or split asunder. A more honourable and principled man, a man like your grandfather perhaps, might have declined such a project. But today, that man would be a slave to malevolent glum Lords like Callous Sacheverell and Fiend Crowberry.'

'What happened to Ashok Kumar?'

Fate sniffed, reached behind him to retrieve the cartridge. 'He died... eventually,' he said, voice full of sadness. 'But not before he started to remember things.'

Egg's eyes bulged with intrigue now. 'What things?'

'Dreams mostly,' he replied, 'well nightmares, actually. He said he remembered meeting one of the Sinister Vessels, the one called *Sally Cakes*.'

Egg smiled. 'That's a *unigram*,' she said, excitedly.

'You mean *anagram*,' Fate corrected her. 'Yes, it's one of the Sinister Vessel anagrammatic names, an approximation of *Chaos Likely*. But that's not all. Kumar told me another facet of his dream, a matter that has never been made public. He told me they'd been romantically involved and there was the possibility of a daughter.'

Egg gasped with amazement and tried to remember.

CHAPTER TWENTY
Satan in the Mini-Bar

Technically, Pierpot had endured more than twenty years dehydration whilst immersed in hell, so the prospect of raiding the mini-bar burst with irresistible excitement for him. But instead of frost-encrusted refreshments, on inspection of its contents, he discovered a vast and sweltering volcanic landscape and when a swelling eruption of deafening sound emanated from the metal appliance, resulting in a spectacular crescendo of blistering lava and boiling steam exploding inches from his nose, he slammed the door shut and thought it best to remain thirsty.

Egg and the King appeared to have no knowledge of the incongruous happening, so he considered it a hallucination brought on by the day's disquiet and softly laughed at the notion of a hotel fridge containing aspects of hell. Armed with this sound logic he, cautiously, reopened the mini-bar only to stare upon the same steaming rivers of scoria that cracked and scorched the ground, dividing the landscape into towering precipices of burnt stone. These were flanked by fiery pastures and singed black mountain ranges, dotted here and there with the seared remains of mortals.

Another rumbling ascended from the back of the appliance until a massive burst of flame and smoke bloomed like an esoteric firework in Pierpot's face and Satan's voice clearly called out: *DESIRE SANCTUARY AND IT WILL BE PERMITTED*!

And then the King suddenly yelled, 'Dear Om, where has she got to now?' and Pierpot slammed the refrigerator door shut again. He was surprised to see his friend closely examining the sofa where, only seconds ago, Egg had resided but was now unoccupied and so joined in with the search for the missing child, for no other reason than to take his mind off Satan being in the mini-bar. When they heard a bump followed by a giddy yelp emanate from the bathroom, the King crashed through the door to discover his pretend granddaughter upside down in the tub amongst a bent plastic bath tidy and several hotel issue shampoo bottles. Relieved, he lifted her out, swaddled her in his arms and carried her back to the sitting room. 'You frightened me to death,' he said. 'What happened to you?'

'I was with John Fate,' the child told him.

She was immediately placed on the ground and studied at arm's length. 'What did *he* want?'

'Did you know this room isn't real?'

The King heaved a sigh, went to the door and opened it briefly to reveal the corridor gone and in its place a swirling black corpus of scary nothing. He closed it and came back to his pretend granddaughter, kneeling before her. 'Did he hurt you?'

She shook her head.

'What I mean to say is he didn't... take a biopsy or anything like...'

Pierpot interjected with a cough and nudged the King's shoulder. 'I just thought I ought to mention it, Reg, but the mini-bar seems...'

'Help yourself,' the King replied, misinterpreting the man's concerns, 'John Fate is footing the bill.'

'We're being held prisoner,' Egg announced.

'I know,' said the King, 'apparently it's for our own good.'

'The mini-bar,' Pierpot continued with frustration, pointing at the possessed contraption at the other end of the room, 'it appears to be...'

'Yes, yes, take what you will!' his friend snapped irately before returning his attention to Egg. 'Is that what Fate wanted to talk to you about, this counterfeit apartment?'

Shaking her head again, Egg said, 'He showed me a weird film of the day Ashok Kumar was made into a bomb!' With squealing laughter, she added, '*BOOOOM!*' and Pierpot leaped into the air, his spectacles flying off his head.

'That's not even funny,' the King chastised her. 'I wouldn't trust John Fate to shake my hand for fear it might end up in one of his glass cabinets. Do you remember the one in his office? The one he said belonged to a mad monkey? He lied to you. He took that limb off Sir Charles Waterhouse in a duel. Sir Charles is a good friend of mine whose only sin was to defend the honour of a woman Fate accused of murder because he saw it in one of his silly dreams.'

'Ashok Kumar's my dad,' she announced.

Both the King and Pierpot, the latter bending to retrieve his twisted eyewear, froze and stared at her, engulfed in a thick soup of confusion, exhibiting puzzled facial mannerisms as they assessed the likelihood of what they were being told.

'That's impossible,' said the King. 'Kumar died thirty years ago.'

'But he dreamt he and one of the Sinister Vessels had a daughter,' Egg said. 'And it feels true somchow.'

The King got to his feet, staring at the child with unease. Without taking his eyes off her he started pacing the room, one hand cradling his chin until finally he stopped and clicked a finger and thumb together. 'John's messing with our heads,' he proposed. 'He can be a shrewd individual when the mood takes him. He's told you this to distract us, to keep our minds busy with a ludicrous jigsaw puzzle while he achieves some more deceitful goal.'

'I think he's nice,' said Egg.

'*Nice*?' the King laughed, incredulously. 'John Fate might be many things, Egg, but nice is not one of them. People like him rarely are. A righteous man, perhaps, but *nice*?' He shook his head. 'Did he tell you how the Plan discovered Ashok Kumar's amazing powers?'

She nodded. 'Yes,' she said. 'My dad fell on an enemy base and...'

He crossed the room and grabbed her by the shoulders again. 'Perhaps that's how it's remembered in history, as some sort of jolly mishap, but those of us who were around at the time recall it very differently. The public prefer to think of Heavenly Joys bungling his Ladder trajectory and reducing an enemy stronghold to ruins by accident, like he's some sort of slapstick, silent movie star. Salvation arriving in the shape of a divine man falling from the sky has a certain irony about it; a falling incarnate overwhelming fallen incarnates. The entire episode chimes with poetic justice. Anybody with an ounce of practical judgment knows Kumar's flightpath was interfered with that day. Fate needed to boast about this almighty weapon he had created and, in doing so, put the fear of Om up a tenacious foe. Believe me, Egg, Monte Cassino was a well-orchestrated piece of propaganda and no happy accident.'

This new take on events made Egg quite cross and she sulkily folded her arms across her chest.

'Do try to understand,' the King said, 'though John Fate is not strictly our enemy, he wouldn't think twice about dropping *you* on...'

'*THE MINI-BAR'S A MAW*!' Pierpot blurted out uncontrollably and the King and Egg gasped in fright and turned to look at him.

'Excuse me?'

'I just thought I'd mention it,' the ex-Planner said, nodding at the appliance across the room. 'The mini-bar's a maw and that's all there is to it, nothing to do with me, it was like that when I got here.'

The King turned on his haunches and squinted at the contraption several yards away. 'The mini-bar is a gateway to hell?' he asked.

The ex-Planner nodded.

'Have you gone completely mad?'

'Not completely, no, but I fear I'm dangling perilously on the precipice. If I open a wardrobe and find *Orgo the*

Posthumous swinging from a coat hanger, I think that'll be enough to push me over the edge.'

'A porthole to hell you say?'

Pierpot nodded again and then looked terrified as the King got to his feet and marched across the room. 'It's not a good idea to look in there, Reg,' he pleaded, shuffling over to hide in a nook in the wall, peeping round the edge of the alcove just in time to see the King place a hand on the refrigerator's handle. The ex-Planner squeezed his eyes closed and listened to the sucking sound of a vacuum seal becoming separated from its casing.

'*Holy Om!*' the King called out. '*I don't believe my eyes.*'

'*Close it, Reg!*' a visibly quivering Pierpot begged. '*I beseech you to close it before we all get sucked into that damned domain.*'

'There're seven different types of *nuts* in here.'

Pierpot's eyelids flicked open as he stepped warily out of hiding. '*Nuts*? It's a profane trick, Reg! Satan knows I'm allergic.'

'It's no profane trick, Pierpot,' the King informed him looking back. 'It's a fridge full of snacks and...' and then the King gasped. 'Where the *hell* has she got to now?'

CHAPTER TWENTY-ONE
A Glum History

'In 1719,' said Pryderi, rising off the ground and drifting, effortlessly upwards through the rainstorm, welcoming the splatter with arms opened wide and stepping effortlessly onto the chalet's roof, 'when invading Spanish forces attempting to overthrow King George were defeated at Glenshiel, a volume of text was discovered amongst the treasury of occult items Jacobite supporters brought with them.'

Raven sat sulking, slouched over the Thumb to protect it from the torrent. He had made the arrogant mistake of elbowing the witch aside when she attempted to translate its arcane text over his shoulder, criticising her knowledge of primary malevolence, forgetting, momentarily, the witch's long association with men like his father and ventures to seek out ancient glum weapons with which to enslave mankind, god-kissed articles such as swords, amulets and, more specifically, books.

'Other items unearthed, such as demons' brews, the matrix unguis of a zombie cat and several one-eyed hell-frogs, were the archetypal trappings of everyday go-getting occultists,' Pryderi forged on, squatting, precariously, at the roof's edge. 'The Thumb, which was considered less threatening than a hag's cookbook by unschooled Georgians, was stashed away with the rest of the esoteric contraband and transported to London. While nestled amongst this cache of paranormal articles it was said to have absorbed the warped energies of the surrounding objet d'art, and, invigorated with this assimilated magic, managed to escape. Only when the hoard of confiscated armaments arrived in the capital was the manuscript, which Robert Walpole believed stolen, considered truly valuable, for what self-respecting thief neglects gold, silver and enchanted ruby jujus to pilfer a worthless book?'

A low, rumble of vexation arose from the turn-harp, contradicting his attempt to appear impassive. The sound grew into a repetitive chant of, '*Yes, yes, yes,*' and a resultant statement of, '*I get the bloody picture!*'

'But in 1766,' Pryderi continued, grinning proudly in her arrogance, 'when Henry Cavendish discovered *Hydrogen* there were many in the Plan who grew suspicious of the asocial physicist, questioning how such a secular notion could be conceived without glum assistance. It wasn't until 1798 however, thirty-two years later, after Cavendish famously exposed the mean density of hell, determining it, "*very mean indeed*", that his research practices were actually investigated and he was arrested whilst dining at the *Royal Society Club*, where the Thumb was discovered upon his person. The book was sent north again, locked in a vault on Grace Plateau, located at that time in a Manchester public house called *The Sow's Stern*. There was scientific outcry over the physicist's incarceration and more controversy was sparked when Prime

Minister William Pitt described the Plan's heavy-handed techniques as a witch hunt. What the Plan deemed too wide a leap of scientific achievement and a series of discoveries unborn of natural intellect, Cavendish's supporters argued was the Plan's antediluvian attitude and blatant disrespect for science. Cavendish may have gotten away with it too if it hadn't been for one small detail; it was the late eighteenth century and he was the only boffin in the Known Universe working on a thermodynamic weapon's system.'

'Consider me effectively disciplined,' uttered Raven's sugary and sarcastic tone, travelling sluggishly up from the sodden garden, 'but your acquaintance with a book's history is by no means evidence you can actually…'

'While the Thumb was safely back under lock and key,' Pryderi interjected, arms placed behind her head as she leaned back on the damp tiles and stared up through the downpour at the stars, 'it was studied by some of the sharpest minds of the day. For twelve years it underwent rigorous scrutiny and analysis by respected intellects of the time, men like Sir William Herschel, John Dalton and Sir Gwynn Adler, grandfather of Griffin Adler, when finally, on the 24th February, 1810, it was mutually decided by all genii involved, men whose very lives and reputations were dedicated to unearthing the volume's secrets, that Cavendish had slipped them a forgery. When this news arrived back in London, the prisoner was sent for but his cell was discovered empty.'

A stone clattered over the roof slates, narrowly missing the witch's head. She sat up sharply and peered down at Raven who gave no indication he had moved and was still leaning over his precious tome.

'In 1840, William Robert Grove invented the electric light and was immediately arrested under the Walpole Act and held for questioning on a count of harbouring illegal incarnate material, but while his property and laboratories were thoroughly ransacked, the Thumb proved evasive. And then in 1911, Ernest Rutherford developed the model of the atom and the Plan, which had spent a hundred and thirteen years harassing and arresting every science boffin that proposed a hitherto unthinkable theorem thinkable, finally deciding to initiate brilliant minds rather than terrorise them. They installed him in a facsimile alongside a man called Hans Geiger. Whether Rutherford had prior insight into the Thumb or not, these men successfully split the atom and devised a technological theorem that a decade later would allow Griffin Adler to build Rapture Bombs out of Ashok Kumar and, in the process of defeating incarnate forces, turn you into a morose and twisted freak!'

'Have you quite finished?' Raven asked, slowly turning his head around to look at her.

'Not quite,' replied Pryderi. 'The Thumb was thought to have perished in a fire at a storage facility and disappeared from public scrutiny for more than sixty years, until this Morecambe Pierpot stole it from my uncle's library in hell and brought it back to earth.'

'So what's your point?' Raven asked, irritably.

The witch shifted closer to the edge of the roof, glaring at him. 'My point is if all those so-called gifted people could not fully divine its secrets or wield its power what possible chance does a div like you have?'

Raven got to his feet, a confident smile woven into his pale features as rain splashed off two pointy cheekbones. He looked at a section of garden and mumbled a line of prose from the Thumb in a language merging Ancient Greek, Old Persian and Timeless Gobbledygook and, in a brief explosion of light a little girl appeared before him.

CHAPTER TWENTY-TWO
Chaos Likely

Something grabbed her stomach innards and snatched her from the room. It had nothing to do with teleportation brought on by her reminiscing. This was abduction, clear and simple. Initially it felt like hunger, a physical state Egg had no memory of; the closest she had come to it was hankering after a pink wafer in the middle of the night, a haphazard yearning that culminated in her zapping straight to the larder. But she imagined this was what starvation felt like, ghostly and bony hands grasping the meaty bits inside her and twisting them about. She knew it was abduction rather than hunger because, for one thing, she'd eaten more than her fair share of cake at lunchtime and for two, she was currently spinning through the folds of the cosmos.

The sensible thing to do was to fight it, do what her grandfather had taught her and try *not* to teleport. So Egg distracted herself with the most predominant thought in her mind and…

She was standing on a sloping cobbled street, surrounded by stocky houses of black stone. It was night-time and the dark masonry rendered the buildings almost invisible. Close by, a group of teenagers were inclined against a car, feverishly chatting and smoking cigarettes. Egg hid behind a large oak tree that was so huge its roots dislodged nearby paving stones. When she scrutinised the rowdy group Egg recognised her mother instantly, an acknowledgement that almost sent her whizzing off through the cosmos again as she mentally strived to evoke memories of her. She looked a bit like her. They had the same diminutive stature, round face, sparkling green eyes. She didn't seem particularly majestic or especially malevolent for that matter; just a moping adolescent girl dressed from head to toe in black and with her hair dyed vivid purple.

'It's Siouxsie and *the* Banshees, divpot, not Siouxsie and *her* Banshees!' Sally Cakes scolded a gangly boy with a rainbow Mohawk standing next to her. When she sharply punched him the boy flinched and rubbed his arm.

'*I know, I know*!' he exclaimed with embarrassment as the others laughed at him.

'So why did you say Siouxsie and *her* Banshees, then?'

'I don't know,' he answered with a sad shrug. 'I thought it was like Adam and *his* Ants.'

When the girl started laughing again, her fierce cackle filled the night with scary echoes and Egg looked up at the black sky as if watching the sound ascend towards the moon. Mountains loomed over the craggy rooftops delineating an undulating skyline that blocked out stars and Egg briefly wondered if the stars were made by Zack. By the time Egg looked back all the kids were busy taunting the gangly boy, punching him or hurling empty plastic pop bottles and cigarette butts at him. Egg couldn't help but laugh too, but the moment she did the entire gang fell silent and hers was the only voice in the night. As they glanced around for the source of this external mirth, Egg stepped out of hiding, waving at them and saying, '*Hullo.*'

The girl with purple hair stood up straight and asked, 'Who the hell are you?'

Smiling, Egg replied, 'My name's Egg.'

After a short, intense silence, another girl, head shaved but for one curly lock of blonde hair that spiralled down her face, snorted a chuckle and said, 'Yeah and my name's *Chips.*' The punky group burst with laughter.

'Yeah, and my name's *Bacon,*' somebody else said.

'My name's *Sausage.*'

'And you can call me *Pencil,*' said Mohawk and when Sally punched him on the arm again, Egg thought it was really funny and chortled with delight, bending double at the waist.

The gang regarded her with suspicion, studying her with puzzled expressions as if she was an alien. When she finally managed to restrain her humour and approached them Egg became distracted by the boy with the Mohawk, staring at him, preoccupied with the gawky youth to the point of obsession and, gaping into his deep blue eyes she gasped when she realised he didn't have a soul. And then, to their annoyance, she began assessing the rest of the unruly bunch, arriving at the same awful conclusion, that, apart from Sally Cakes, none of them were real.

'What do you think you're gawping at, squirt?' asked Mohawk when Egg's gaze returned to scrutinise him again.

Egg turned to look at her mother and said, 'You're the only one that's real,' causing more hilarity to spill forth from

Sally's group of friends. Sally appeared troubled rather than amused by this information. In fact she stared at the child with what looked like well-acknowledged fear.

'Why do you say that?'

Egg pointed at Mohawk. 'He's not really real! He's a ghost or something.'

'Why don't you go and f...!'

'*Who the hell are you*?' Sally repeated. She looked so scared it started to alarm her associates, especially when she began examining them with the same wide-eyed curiosity as the child.

'I'll deal with the brat,' said Mohawk, stepping forward and, towering over her as he did, in any normal circumstances, she would not have stood a chance, but the moment he attempted to grab hold of her, Egg sent him wheeling backwards over the car with just a thought. It had not been intentional. She had rejected him as easily as if they were the opposing poles of a magnet, which was enough to scare the living daylights out of the others and send them fleeing in all directions, all except Sally.

'*It's the kid out the Exorcist!*' she heard one of the boys yell out as he darted away.

Sally grabbed Egg's pyjama top and shook her, asking for the third time, '*Who the hell are you?*'

'Is your name Sally Cakes?'

Seething with irritation, the girl asked, 'Didn't anybody ever tell you not to answer a question with a question?'

'But is it though?'

'What if it is?'

Egg smiled, took a moment to consider her response and then said, 'John Fate is holding you prisoner.'

She let Egg go and looked up and down the street as if scanning the area for evidence it was a windup, that at any moment a film crew might emerge and her friends would resurface and make fun of her for being such a sucker. But none of that happened.

Mohawk's multi-coloured do slowly poked up over the car bonnet.

Looking back at Egg, Sally told her, 'I've often suspected that... well, it's weird, it's like I remember stuff in dreams mostly, but it's like... it's like I've been seventeen far too long.' The young woman looked frightened, manically raking through her purple mane with both sets of fingers. 'What makes you think my friends aren't real?'

Egg shrugged her shoulders and said, 'I didn't mean to upset you. I'm sorry.'

'How did you do that to Toby?' Sally asked and when Egg glanced at him peeping over the car, the colourful spike of hair quickly descended. 'Could you teach *me* to do that?'

A little taken aback, Egg replied, 'I think *you* gave me the power.'

Sally cocked her head on one side, squinting at the child as she calculated what this meant. And then her eyes widened and she put both hands on her belly and gasped. 'That's impossible.' she said. 'This is some kind of windup or a nightmare.'

'John Fate says you're Chaos Likely, that you and Heavenly Joys had a baby,' Egg blurted out.

Sally glared at her. '*Chaos...*?'

'Chaos Likely,' repeated Egg. 'You know, one of the Sinister Vessels?'

The older girl's fingers gripped the hem of her black, mohair sweater and lifted it to reveal a black T-shirt beneath decorated with a circular tribal design in white swirls and spikes. Scrolled through the pattern in silver thread were the words *Chaos Likely*.

'That's the name of our band,' she said. 'I thought it up in a dream. The others hated it. Toby said we should call ourselves *Erotic Autopsy*. But I knew this meant something. I knew I'd dreamed it for a reason.'

'It's because it's your name,' Egg told her.

'But my name is Sally Cakes.'

Egg glanced at the boy behind the car and he gulped and dropped out of sight again. She looked back at Sally. 'People think you're going to destroy the world,' she explained. 'That's why they've put you in prison.'

The young woman laughed. 'I've dreamt about that too,' she said. 'I dreamt I started a war and annihilated everyone. I stood on the edge of a ravine looking down at a black, smoking ruin where the entire world once existed and there was a vast multitude of men and women there with... they had the heads of dogs and there was an old man called *Adder*? No, Adler. His name was Griffin Adler.'

Suddenly, a loud thrashing sound descended upon them along with a strong gust of wind that blew their hair and clothes against their bodies. They looked up into a spotlight shining from the undercarriage of a helicopter. Egg turned to see, further along the road, two massive armoured vehicles and dozens of armed Planners advancing towards them. 'We have to get out of here,' she said.

'How?' asked Sally, frightened and confused as Egg ran across the road back to the tree.

'Bloody hell!' said Mohawk, leaping to his feet and running away through nearby bushes.

The last thing Egg saw before her feet left the facsimile and she was sent spinning back through the cosmos was Sally Cakes, wide-eyed and terrified, engulfed in torchlight, kneeling on the ground and surrounded by armed soldiers.

And then Egg was in a rain-soaked garden. A few metres away stood the peculiar man who had offered to kill the clowns at Hill House. A woman suddenly thudded to the ground beside him, as if she had leaped from the roof of the small house behind. The man ran a spindly hand through his paint-knotted black hair, leering down his nose at her and smiling with wicked glee.

'Hello, Egg,' he said.

But Egg only heard the first chilling syllable, *hell*, before a memory struck her about her name; *egg* had been the last syllable she heard before...

*****

She tried desperately to return to the hotel suite as she spun through the maelstrom; the place between places, a topographical limbo. But try as she might Egg could not bring that earthly domicile beneath her feet. She started to panic at the thought of never returning and for a brief moment, as she drifted through nowhere, she remembered everything.

She was seated in the front carriage of a rollercoaster just tipping over the crest of a high section of rusted track, screaming with elation as a gust of cold air blew through her and when another voice screamed at her side, turned and saw a strange man with cold black eyes sitting in the next seat.

Egg disappeared.

Suddenly, she reappeared in a rowing boat in the middle of a gigantic lake, surrounded by ice-capped mountains. It seemed the most idyllic place on earth, a picture postcard landscape. She sighed with relief.

'*What a whopper*!' somebody called out and, turning, she saw the same strange man reeling in a large marlin on a fishing line.

Egg disappeared.

She reappeared in an opera box. The world was in darkness and a theatre audience held its breath as the curtain rose. Egg lifted a pair of opera glasses to her face as that huge, velvet drape ascended into the roof-space with a spine-tingling squeak accompanied by incoherent music played by an orchestra of skeletons. A ballet was taking place and lots of emaciated men trooped across the stage spinning on their toes. When she leaned forward, squinting through the glasses, she saw the same strange man with cold black eyes performing a daring pirouette.

Egg disappeared.

She appeared on the back of a horse, her small arms gripping the gingham shirt of its rider. The horse was galloping at speed over desert and, looking over her shoulder, Egg gasped at the sight of a dozen or more Native American Indians in hot pursuit, their wild stallions kicking up dust.

Some fired arrows, some rifles. The same strange man with the taciturn eyes was amongst them, whirling a tomahawk around his head and patting a palm against his mouth to produce a loud warbling sound.

Egg disappeared.

She found herself standing on an uprising escalator in a shopping mall. As the escalator neared the next floor, he appeared at the top so she turned and began to run down, having to knock bag-laden shoppers out of her way.

Egg disappeared.

She was on the moon, staring out of a large glass helmet at a grey and lifeless environment. Her breathing was shallow and loud in her ears. Where the lunar surface curved away there was eternal blackness with only the blue sphere of the earth hovering three hundred and eighty thousand kilometres away.

'*Cut!*' somebody yelled and she turned to see an entourage of personnel holding various bits of moviemaking equipment: sound booms, lights, clapperboards and cameras.

'Scene twenty-one, take twelve,' called the strange man with the cold black eyes.

Egg disappeared.

CHAPTER TWENTY-THREE
Pierre de Zoet

While Egg swam through that cosmic maelstrom, Grace Plateau was abuzz with news of an eight-year-old girl infiltrating the facsimile of a Sinister Vessel. John Fate was livid, not just because of the incursion (such an event hardly brightened up his day) but mainly because in less time than the news had taken to reach his ears, terms like *Sinister Vessels*, *facsimiles* and *incursions* were being bandied about by domestics and maintenance staff alike. And it was entirely his fault. The Tetrad would have his badge for this.

Presently, a red light blinked on one of the telephones on his desk. He realised it would be them calling to verbally deliver his P45, no doubt a pleasant game of *Kerplunk* having been disturbed by the current hubbub.

He had passed on highly confidential information to an infant thinking he had the measure of her and that he was simply testing her knowledge on all matters incarnate. Ashok Kumar had required similar analysis during the months he resided on Grace Plateau, but the ability to wander in and out of heavily hexed, high security areas without so much as a scratch was a feat of transit not even *he* had accomplished.

Conversely, it was an ability that might prove valuable to the Plan, as well as overturn his imminent sacking, if he could harness it.

The telephone stopped ringing. Fate sighed and reached for the other phone on his desk. Putting the receiver to his ear he dialled the number five, five times, a number he had hoped never to use again. The line buzzed a moment and then whistled shrilly before a jovial French accent sang, '*Bonjour*!'

'Mr de Zoet? It's John Fate.'

The man on the other end of the line emitted an extensive exclamation of fondness, sounds of joy similar to little girls in the presence of kittens frolicking in pink wool. 'Monsieur Fate, how long it has been since last we spoke. And longer still since you desired the aid of Pierre de Zoet.'

'What makes you think I *desire* your aid, Mr de Zoet?'

'Because, of course, you are not a man who calls up to chitty chatty about the yesteryear and have a rather biased view of my *vocation*.'

'Yes, well there's no need to sound so smug!' Fate sighed again, realising he was probably making a big mistake, but it was the only way he knew of controlling the situation. It had worked before, kind of. 'I have a problem that is rather more in the realms of your parameters of expertise than…'

'*Monsieur Adler's*?' de Zoet concluded.

'Precisely,' said Fate. 'It's a containment issue and I require rather than desire your assistance. If there was any other way…'

'Monsieur Adler is generally the *go to* guy to solve such issues, is he not?' asked the Frenchman.

Fate briefly closed his eyes with exasperation as he explained, 'Mr Adler and I have had a parting of ways? He retired some years back.'

'Disappeared up his own facsimile is what *I* heard. And what was the cause of this *estrangement*?'

'That matter has got nothing to do with my present proposal,' Fate told him.

'You are mistaken if you think that,' said de Zoet, 'for men like Monsieur Adler and I are kindred spirits. There is a moral code between geomancers of all breeds, Avignon and Orthodox, an unspoken…'

'I'll give you *Enceladus*.'

'Ah, a Saturn moon for my collection,' enthused the Frenchman. 'Another fifty and I shall have the complete set. I shall prepare immediately. What is the tender?'

'I require a state of the art construct,' said Fate. 'It will need to be completely invulnerable. More than an upgrade or some hastily thrown together *oubliette*, do you understand?'

There was laughter on the other end of the line. 'I am surprised you have no one else to meet these demands, but then there is a saying in my country, *wise rarely outwits want*. Do not get me wrong, I am extremely flattered you desire… *require* my input, but what makes you think I can create a superior realm to those of Monsieur Adler's?'

'Because, Mr de Zoet, you are devoid of scruples.'

'Scruples are an obstacle in this matter?'

'You might say that.'

'Then I am *indeed* the right man for the job. Monsieur Fate, you seem to be exhibiting character traits of an almost *Machiavellian* nature. Am I to understand that you wish me to apprehend and contain certain individuals with unwarranted fervour?'

'Nobody must come to any harm, do you understand? I don't want another fiasco on my hands.'

'There is a risk in all things. If you wish to secure my skills, then you must consider the dangers secondary.'

'Put no lives in danger.'

'I will require an address,' said de Zoet.

'It's room 410 of the Elysium Hotel in Manchester. A little girl will be attempting to return there by means of teleportation. You need to grab her before she arrives. I reiterate, she must not come to any harm, do you understand?'

'Not even a little bit harmed around the edges?'

'Not a single hair out of place.'

Pierre de Zoet replaced the receiver on the back of a dwarf woman who scuttled off on all fours through the luminous cavern. He smiled, his cold black eyes watching as she pushed herself inside a service pipe set into the wall and disappeared, calling out, '*wheeeeeee*!' as she descended. Another pipe close by became ingress for a very tall man in a pinstripe suit and bowler hat, carrying a briefcase and an in-operational umbrella. He entered the cavern feet first, unfolded to a standing position and strode with a wide gait across the grotto, graciously tipping his hat as he passed by. De Zoet, in green overalls and balaclava, nodded amiably and walked from the mouth of the cave, out into a much larger environment beneath a dramatic orange sky. Nearby, a series of bizarre market stalls were erected, selling everything from eyes and lips and variations of other bodily parts to dreams, secrets and the *sins of the righteous*. An epic canvas of purple mountains was their backdrop, a delicately swinging painting that effectively gave the impression of distance. De Zoet listened as a stallholder demanded words as payment for a set of ears he was selling, but not any old words would do, they needed to be luxurious, silky smooth ones from rich vocabularies like *plinth* and *diatribe*, *consensus* and *vex*, *mongrel* and *serpentine* and *phalanx*.

A cloud rocked back and forth on steel wiring, high up in the ethereal rafters of that barmy biosphere, perforated with blinking light bulbs. Sweet music rained down in hundreds of thousands of liquid notes that burst and sang on touch. Lamps, park benches, bicycles and the odd pet became susceptible to the harmonious downpour and fractured as easily as whimsy in a dream.

After the market place, and escorted by a number of yapping Papillon puppies, their colourful wings flapping a breeze throughout his journey, de Zoet unwound a length of string from his pocket and cast it across a wide fissure in the earth where a bumble bee with constantly altering psychedelic colouring chased and caught it and kept it aloft to allow the man to transcend a bottomless crevice by walking on the cord. When he arrived safely on the opposite side, he let the twine go and it turned into a flare of sunlight, frightening off the mini beast.

A blue and black tiger passed and De Zoet ran his fingers through its wiry fur. A set of clothes: pumps, trousers and a T-shirt with nobody inside, wandered by.

He arrived at a colourful doorframe set into no wall, turned the handle and stepped through. When de Zoet closed the door behind him, it banged against a casing set into a brick wall and there was no colourful cavern to be seen around its perimeter, just the room's solid interior. On this side of the door the world was quite logical and boring. There was a grey filing cabinet, a desk and an old-fashioned typewriter. The table was inundated with objects, piles of rolled up scrolls and tiny bell-jars inhabited by plastic flowers. The rest of the room was inhabited by podiums supporting bigger bell-jars housing mechanical scenes, many of which had begun actively clicking away when he entered. He went out onto a balcony through a set of French doors and stood a moment, marvelling at the panoramic view. His fortress was situated in a district solely devoted to the absurdist arts of Avignon geomancy as ascribed by Pope Bernadette XII. The sun-bleached world stretched away in brilliant bright blues and greens in an epic vision of a summer dream, spread over a landscape as magnificently as it had spread through his imagination before creation, its colours both sickly sweet and madly melancholy. From that small stone balcony, high above such an arena of unnatural splendour, de Zoet could build entire continents of absurdity in which to incarcerate John Fate's enemies.

On the balcony's parapet was a small metal box with two green buttons decorated with arrows, one pointing up the other down. De Zoet pressed the down button and the entire terrace descended, accompanied by a shifting, crunching sound as the brickwork behind rearranged itself. Balconies both above and below moved in accordance and ten seconds later each one stopped with a jolt, having become matched to a different set of French doors.

De Zoet re-entered the building which was now a replica of a busy Parisian train station platform in 1936. Steam billowed from huge locomotives as ladies in furs and pearls walked by with baggage-laden servants in their wake. Men in fine tailored suits and fedoras smoked cigarettes with the swagger of athletes. De Zoet removed his balaclava and shook out his unkempt black hair. His green overalls attracted little attention from the landed gentry who simply cast him as an engineer. He walked to the end of the platform where a gold and filigree clock hung above the station and checked the time, intermittently glancing at his own wristwatch, calculating the correct moment to trip the *gimmick*. All the finest geomancers implanted gimmicks in their work; back doors and absurdist portals with which to enter or escape unnoticed. This one required him waiting until the second hand of both timepieces ventured into ascendancy, at which point he could pass back into the present. Not only was it a brilliant device for bypassing lengthy journeys, but a very clever way of avoiding pursuit. He alone knew how to leave the Peculiar Palace and not even an astute mind like Griffin Adler, who doubtlessly used similar personalised devices to access and depart his own constructs, could possibly guess at these precise and intricate sequences of events.

It was a close-knit thing. Just as the second-hand of his wristwatch reached its twenty-eighth indicator, the second-hand of the platform clock touched its first. The Frenchman stood on one foot, put a little finger in his right ear and asked a passer-by, 'Where will I find the *Trevi Fountain*?'

The passer-by looked at him suspiciously and said, 'Why, it's in Rome, you fatuous plebeian.'

De Zoet was instantly transported to a busy Rome street. He turned to see a tiny, provincial building kitted out as a gift shop and, narrowly avoiding being run over by a scooter, hurried across the highway to where the shop's proprietor was busily stacking white, ceramic effigies of the Coliseum. The man looked up with less surprise than alarm when he recognised his visitor. 'Senior de Zoet,' he said, nervously. 'I hope the Armageddon is not upon us?'

'I'm here for my tools, Luigi,' de Zoet informed him.

'This is bad, no?' asked Luigi as he guided the Frenchman hesitantly through his air-conditioned shop and, by way of a beaded curtain, into the sweltering house beyond. 'I should make no plans for the future?'

'You presume too much,' de Zoet laughed.

They found one of his sons in a sitting room and the proprietor instructed the boy to take over the cash register. Luigi's diminutive grandmother was also in the room, surrounded by boxes containing statues of saints, fridge magnets, decorative cups and tea towels. 'Nonna, I must ask you to vacate the room also,' Luigi instructed her.

The elderly woman looked aghast, as though he had asked her to jump through a window. '*Leave*? I haven't left this room in fifteen years. Where would you have me go? I should sit on the pavement and burn?'

'Five minutes, Nonna,' Luigi pleaded.

'I would go into the shop, but it's full of foreigners,' she complained as she got up from her seat. 'Five minutes, he says, like this is not enough time for an old woman to die.'

'Go to your room, just for five minutes.'

'*Go to my room*? You are sending your Nonna to her room now? What has the world come to?'

'Si, si, I have important business to discuss,' Luigi informed her as he escorted the little old lady out. When he returned he rolled his eyes to the ceiling with implied exasperation before dragging the armchair she had been sat in away from the wall. 'The scissors there,' he said, pointing them out on a table. De Zoet passed them over and Luigi used the pointed steel to dislodge a skirting board. He reached inside, his arm disappearing up to the shoulder and when he removed it he was holding an ornate blue box. 'Nothing good can come of this,' the shop's proprietor said, but Pierre de Zoet's only reaction was to smile, roguishly.

CHAPTER TWENTY-FOUR
A Disciplined Machine

When the girl disappeared, the witch's pleasure was supplanted with intense anger and she snapped her head round to glare at the turn-harp, demanding to know, '*Where did she go?*'

'Don't worry, I have a lock on her,' Raven announced, holding forefingers to each temple. He clenched his eyes shut and shuffled back and forth adopting a crooked posture that, under normal circumstances, might have amused the witch but now only served to vex her. 'I'm pursuing her across a number of alternative dimensions even as we speak,' he declared, tapping his head and looking exceedingly un-*chosen-one*-like.

'*Bring her back then.*'

'I can't,' he told her. 'There's somebody else involved, a second magic source has latched onto her. She's on his hook already, but she's trying to get away. She's very strong, very stubborn.' His eyes remained closed until he faced the witch and then slowly opened. 'My endeavours have been obstructed.'

'What are you talking about? Who has obstructed you? Is it Callous? Is it Fate? Who is it?'

'The magic is…' Raven gasped, shaking his head 'of Avignon abstraction.'

Pryderi was more dumbfounded than puzzled. '*Avignon*? What the hell are you talking about, *Avignon*?'

'I can't compete with it,' he told her, 'it's the very cradle of absurdist mysticism; the foundation of all that is weird, strange and downright silly.'

'I thought you were half clown,' Pryderi said, harshly, 'downright silly should be easy for you.'

He looked at her with hurt in his eyes and said, spitefully, 'There's nothing I can do.'

'You have one of the three most powerful books of glum magic in your possession. Use it. Do the thing with the stars and get her back here, *now*!'

Raven looked exhausted, his spirit wilted by failure as he heaved a tragic sigh, turned and stalked off indoors.

The witch was furious. 'Where are you going? Get back here. We had her in our grasp. Are you just going to give up as easily as that?'

When he returned a moment later with a vase, two saucepans and several serving dishes stacked in his arms, the witch believed he was robbing the place in one final act of defiance before surrender. She raised a palm towards him and the paint-splattered man lifted off his feet, the vase and cooking utensils spinning out of his grasp and rhythmically thudding to earth an instant before he splashed face down in the sodden plot.

'We have a pact,' she informed him.

'*Ah uss wyin amubba ammoaff*!' came Raven's muffled response.

'What?'

He pulled his face from the mud with a slurp and spitting and blinking rapidly exclaimed, 'I was trying another approach.'

Ten minutes later Raven lay on his back beneath the stars again, continuing to study the Thumb's influence on that patchwork quilt of twinkling lights, rain beating down on his blanched face. All around him stood ornaments and flowerpots, jugs and pans, anything he had been able to lug from indoors with the capacity to collect rainwater. Pryderi had returned to her perched position on the chalet's roof, casting a watchful eye over the darkened neighbourhood.

'You have until dawn, insect, at which point I will degenerate every bone in your body and leave you a sagging bag of breathing flesh,' she instructed him. 'You see, I *can* be merciful when I choose.' She cackled loudly at her own glum humour and lay back on the roof's tiles as if the effort to sit up had been vanquished by her vicious remarks. 'Brute force I understand,' she said, 'but astrology is a feeble science.'

'This isn't astrology,' Raven spluttered, and in a lower tone added, '*you gaudy-haired imbecile*!' He lay the open Thumb pages down on his pigeon chest as he rubbed his weary eyes with knuckles. 'The Thumb's magic has more comparison with biology and physics,' he declared. 'The Known Universe is a complicated entity. Every pattern of stars, belt of planets and baleful black hole, these cosmic stations have purpose. They are galactic cogs, pulleys and wheels; an interstellar circuit-board. This entire universe is interactive. The moon controls the oceans, the sun heats and lights and juggles the planets, causes jungles to grow and deserts to crack. The cosmos is a disciplined machine.' He stopped kneading his eyeballs, picked up the book to revisit its pages and added, 'And as with all machines, there is opportunity for a spanner to be thrown into the works.'

During his oration, Pryderi silently descended from the roof. She kicked him hard in his ribs. 'Did you just call me a *gaudy-haired imbecile*?'

Rolling into a spineless ball, Raven yelped like a puppy and said, 'No, I'd be too scared to say something like that to a scary lady like you.' He sneered over his shoulder at her, signifying his true sentiments and then cast his eyes at the patch of grass beside him. 'Come and see what I can see.'

Her initial reaction was to protest, but instead she lowered herself to the soggy ground in surrender. Side by side they stared upwards through the drumming rain, blinking briskly and acknowledging the ancient black firmament and its spotting of silver. And then Raven stretched out an arm, let his fingertips delineate a certain cluster of stars and moved it about in the night sky as easy as shifting silver coins on a black counter. He inserted the fingertips of his other hand into a second constellation and twisted and dragged it across the galaxy allowing it to mingle with others for the first time since the Known Universe came into being. He did this several dozen times until a whole section of sky was as black as coal while directly above them existed a bursting profusion of light spelling out a familiar statement: *death to all clowns*.

'Get over it,' Pryderi groaned, rolling her eyes.

The turn-harp briefly removed one set of singed and smoking fingers, blowing on them before reinserting each digit and twisting slowly left and then sharply right, and releasing the new constellation where it span wildly in what resembled perpetual motion. When a sudden flash of lightning hit the garden, they both leaped to their feet with excitement, watching as the forked heat blasted an ornate vase propped up in the grass. The bright, blade of light decanted to a silver orb, bobbing upon the liquid content of the clay receptacle. Another lightning strike descended to become suspended over a saucepan and then a third over a fruit bowl and on and on until the entire garden was beset with glowing globes of starlight atop decorative household objects.

Raven swept back his soaked black hair and, hugging the Thumb to his chest, smiled as a mesmerising vision of bodies began to appear and disappear in rapid succession, each at the core of that concentric pattern of illuminated knick-knacks. Collectively, each bright orb reached out a limb of light to its neighbour as the wild sequence of incandescent figures came and went. The outlines were mostly human, yet every now and again the contour of a wing or some other unsightly appendage posited it neither human nor incarnate: a tail, horns, a surplus of heads. It was a process that continued longer than it was able to sustain wonder and just as they began to grow bored, imagining it going on forever, a shape materialised and stayed. And as the hypnotic lights expired and the garden returned to darkness and silence, to Raven's dismay, he saw that their prisoner was a Seraph female gasping in horror and pain and sinking to her knees beneath collapsed wings.

'That's not right,' he said, frantically flicking through the Thumb. 'I was trying to locate John Fate,' he declared as their jailbird tried to lift herself off the ground, a process prevented by intense pain as lightning passed between every object in the garden again, an electricity grid that exploded in a blast of energy where the Seraph lay, causing her to scream and collapse.

'You must work for him,' Raven surmised, clicking his fingers together. 'Did I select the wrong workstation?'

'Why would an incarnate work alongside a tyrant whose objective is to wipe us all out?' asked Pryderi, pacing back and forth.

'*Who are you*?' the prisoner mumbled.

'You have the opportunity to fulfil the obligation of your bloodline, Seraph traitor,' said Pryderi, ignoring the her question. 'Tell us where to find the girl and we'll kill you softly.'

'*What girl*?'

'Chaos Likely,' said Raven.

Amidst all that obvious pain and terror the prisoner seemed to find their demands amusing and said, '*She doesn't exist.*'

The light course swelled and shocked the woman into submission again. This time she was thrown onto her back, one wing bent uncomfortably beneath her.

'She was in the care of the King of England and Morecambe Pierpot this very afternoon,' Raven announced. 'I smelled her. You are one of John Fate's civil slaves, are you not; one of his novel office pets? I expect they came to him for help.'

The Seraph woman attempted to sit up. '*You were lied to,*' she struggled to say. '*Chaos Likely is nothing but a...*'

She was unable to finish the sentence as a circuit of energy passed through the arrangement of receptacles and boiled the marrow in her bones, forcing the woman into an agonised kneeling position, upper torso twisted painfully out of all natural shape. Her wings cast themselves slowly to their full span and for a brief moment she was a gothic memorial to an erstwhile majesty, but when the balls of light faded and the current of electricity ended, she dropped to the ground dead. A foul-smelling white smoke drifted gently from Phyllis Hartmann's scorched flesh as a deferential silence settled over the garden and the magnitude of what they had done settled, quite profoundly, over the turn-harp and the witch.

CHAPTER TWENTY-FIVE
Kerguelen

Rain soaked the outer side of the glass dome. He looked down at a damp and dreary Manchester and the grey blur of whimsy and steadfastness that in no small proportion he helped to maintain. John Fate often came up here when guilt niggled at his thoughts. Something was wrong. Life had become unfathomable and his dreams had not anticipated it. Why hadn't he seen the arrival of Egg, the attack on Hill House, the incursion of Sally Cakes facsimile? Why had all these significant events been closed off to him? In only a few hours his world had turned inside out. And then, when Phyllis failed to answer the intercom and she wasn't behind her desk, a need for isolation crept up on him and, as he'd traversed Grace Plateau to this, its highest and most remote region, anxious whisperings reached his ears, stories about missing workers, a clerk who had been seen vanishing from a corridor and the absence of other Planners, those who hadn't turned up for meetings, who hadn't arrived home or went to the toilet and never came back. Had they been abducted? Had Phyllis been abducted? Was it an act of aggression, the instigation of imminent war? Was he ready for another war?

Down below people mingled like ants as shops and businesses closed for the night and the population became nothing more than dots dashing back and forth from this distance… distance… *distance*?

*****

Blanco the Magnifico was manacled to a vertical gurney, accompanied by two heavily armed Planners and a third man, Benjamin Swift, the warden of Seven Gates Penitentiary. Swift, with his wavy blond hair, smooth complexion and athletic physique, was seen by many as a new breed of Planner, a next generation partisan. It mattered not that he had been in short pants when General Galbi first attempted to enslave humanity; Swift was a modernist, a man of his time and not a paranoid has-been like the Captain. Fate disliked him, not only because he had risen expeditiously through the organisation on an agenda of popular rhetoric and as an obvious contrast to men like himself, but because if Swift really was the future of the Plan then Om help them.

'This is all very spur of the moment, John,' Swift commented as Fate swept wordlessly past, taking a seat across from the clown in the Unfastened Room. Overlooking his rudeness, the warden typed a code into the gurney's control panel and its metal hinges squeaked as they pivoted Blanco into a seated position.

Fate quietly studied a file he'd requested along with the prisoner's transfer. He switched on the room's recording equipment while selecting several crime scene photographs from the folder, fanning them out across the table. 'Do you recognise any of these puddles of paint?' he enquired.

The clown emitted a disdainful laugh as he looked to the warden for moral support, finding none. 'Is the Captain trying to be funny?' he asked, 'or just insensitive?'

Fate smiled and confessed, 'Insensitive was entirely my stratagem.'

Blanco grunted. 'If somebody eviscerated dozens of *your* compatriots do you think *you'd* recognise their colourful after-stains?'

The Captain glared at him a moment before asking, 'Is that a threat, Mr Magnifico?'

The clown laughed again, looking pleased at having disgruntled the man. 'I'm speaking hypothetically, Mr Fate.'

Sharply sniffing the air, imbibing the foul stench the clown had netted after just half a day in Seven Gates, Fate continued with his line of questioning. 'I've always been fascinated by the nature of paranormal entities,' he said. 'Spare Clowns for instance, they're renowned for enjoying their own company, a preference for solitude, not roaming the English countryside in packs. Normally you might see one, maybe two together on a street corner, making toy animals out of balloons or performing mime outside fast food outlets.'

'*Racist!*'

'So, how come as many as three hundred of you were observed to trespass on the King of England's estate this afternoon?'

The clown sat forward, or would have had he the physical freedom to do so, which essentially meant all he managed was

243

to stick out his chin. 'His sovereignty isn't official,' he said, 'and if it was, as tax-payers, we have an Om-given right to encroach upon lands sustained under levy. These monarchists are parasites, Captain Fate.'

The Captain laughed at this as he retrieved a medical report from the dossier, looking up at the prison warden. 'It says our guest here is of the *Hadraniel* bloodline.'

Swift nodded. 'That's right,' he replied, 'but we found charring in his DNA suggesting he might be one half of a single organism split under rapture.'

The Captain frowned and looked back at Blanco. 'You have a very narrow and elitist bloodline for someone who reviles the monarchy,' he said, leaning back in his chair and gazing at the clown's sad-painted eyes. 'It is particularly elitist in fact. Where it did interbreed, those houses were eventually made extinct by civil war and out of puritanical spite. Cruel Lord Crowberry had his blood kin executed to protect the clarity of his lineage in the event that one day his son, Roderick Crowberry might inherit the throne of hell.'

At first Blanco appeared angry and then he found it difficult to conceal the arrogant pleasure that rose up in him like lava in an active volcano, the mere mention of his father's name inspiring pride. He emitted a stifled laugh the size of a mouse squeak and said, 'My brother and I are the last of our house.'

Fate's jaw twisted in consideration. 'If you're Blanco then I expect your brother goes by the connotation *black*. *Raven* perhaps?'

The clown nodded. 'When we were separated, every vile sentiment of our soul resided in his manifestation,' he revealed. '*I* am no killer. I am only what was leftover; the holy vestiges you might say.'

'Did your brother ever mention me?' Fate asked, briefly glancing at Swift.

'Not that I recall,' Blanco replied and then giggled as he added, 'My father once used your name to describe canine faecal matter he was scraping from the heel of his boot, but it would be amiss of me to repeat such vulgarities here.'

'So the invasion of the King's estate was some sort of anti-monarchist protest, was it?'

'Yes, that's right,' Blanco grinned. 'These supplemented blue bloods really get up my hooter.'

One of the Planners sniggered, but quickly composed himself following a severe look from the Captain.

'So you didn't go there for any other reason; to steal something or to kidnap somebody? This was a purely pro-republic convention? Who was your ringmaster?'

Blanco smiled devilishly and said, 'I'm not at liberty to say.'

Strands of relevance and revelation briefly interwove in the Captain's mind, a sensation he had become unaccustomed to recently. He decided to chance his arm. 'Does *she* have a personal vendetta against the King?'

'Not that I'm aware of, she…' Despite the frozen happy sentiment permanently painted upon it, Blanco's face suddenly appeared horror-stricken.

'*She*?' asked Fate, revelling in the prisoner's anxiety.

'She, he, you all look the same to me. I just exist to entertain,' the clown responded, doing a lousy job at covering up his mistake.

Fate was excited about the prospect of having solved one part of the mystery, but he needed confirmation, more evidence. 'Evasion won't earn you any brownie points, Blanco. Give me the name of this ring-*mistress* of yours and I'm sure we can make some sort of deal. If you truly are the heir to a respected Seraph legacy and not some shackled servant then you'd be candid and rejoice in your proprietor's downfall.'

'Not on your nelly!' Blanco said, exhibiting razor-sharp teeth in a frustrated frown. 'I don't like you,' he said. 'My father loathed you, but my brother...'

Fate got to his feet and addressed one of the armed Planners. 'Take this lowlife away. He's just another disposable pawn in some overzealous creep's fantasies.'

'That's not true,' Blanco protested. 'I was promised a reward.'

Fate slammed a hand on the table. 'Your mystery mistress doesn't reward clowns! She doesn't even respect them. She sends them to die in her name.' He indicated the crime scene photographs depicting puddles of paint. 'What could she possibly promise you; acres of undulating pasture for you and your people to erect marquees?'

When Blanco spat black phlegm, that splattered and dribbled down the Captain's white shirt, Swift poked the console panel with a finger and the gurney bent sharply forwards, banging the clown's head on the desk before resetting in a seated position.

'*Ow*!' Blanco said, after a pause.

Fate sat down and asked, 'Why would you die for the glory of a faceless entity?' as he wiped his shirt with a handkerchief proffered by one of the armed Planners.

'I wouldn't be the first luckless disciple to tie his wagon to the endeavours of a faceless entity,' the clown replied, a statement Fate was certain referred to the mysterious Tetrad member, a fact that when fused with what his own thoughts were already telling him made the Captain shiver. He decided to play his trump card and tossed another photograph on the table, the image of a scorched wind-up robot holding a ray gun. It made Blanco smile with pride. 'I had such dollies when I was young.'

'Do you recognise this ill-fated toy?'

'Yes,' the clown said, 'it belonged to the child.'

'That's a rather dangerous bit of technology in its pincers, wouldn't you say? Did that belong to her too?'

'Possibly,' Blanco laughed. 'You know what kids are like these days.'

'Fortunately, the robot didn't do any real damage with the weapon otherwise you'd be facing a triple murder charge,' Fate told him, 'but worse than that you'd be facing disgrace amongst your people. Clowns who commit murder are feared throughout the Known Universe, but clowns who murder children… that's just not tolerable in any circus.'

Blanco looked worried. 'I only brought the toy to life. I didn't accessorise it.'

'*You*?' laughed Fate. 'You're just a patsy. You don't have the glum clout to animate inert objects. Somebody used you as an arbitrator, somebody who didn't want to be seen or connected with the attack on Hill House and didn't care if one of those toys picked up an Electra Galactic Distance Ladder and zapped the King of England to the other side of the planet.'

'I mesmerised some toys,' Blanco remarked, getting angry again. 'I didn't have time to carry out a full-scale risk assessment. No harm was done and even if this…' he gestured towards the robot's picture, 'metal chap had managed to blast the child with the gun, she'd only have been transported to the Desolation Islands.'

Fate now glared at him, keenly, saying nothing and hoping Blanco would realise his mistake.

'Well, I mean, that's where the King's furniture ended up, isn't it? The worst you could possibly accuse me of is giving the brat a cold.'

John Fate continued to glare at him while his mind constructed the edges of a jigsaw yet to be fully realised. 'How did you know the furniture went to the Desolation Islands?'

Blanco sniffed. 'I… I guessed. No, I didn't guess, I overheard. No, I did guess.'

It was all suddenly making sense. Everything that had been nagging him, dancing on the tip of his tongue, waving an equivocal flag in front of his eyes, it all became composed in one enlightening moment. Blanco's inadvertent testimony had weaved all of the day's events together; the ray gun, the endeavours of a faceless superior and the Antarctic Research Facility located in the Desolation Islands. The evidence had been there all along, Fate had just been prevented from seeing it.

'John, what is it?' asked Swift, concerned by the Captain's apparent comatose state.

'Has he had a mental breakdown?' asked Blanco. 'You can't pin this on me. Everybody knows he's a complete stress-head.'

And then Fate got to his feet and turned to one of the soldiers. 'Is Lieutenant Bromberg still on Grace Plateau?'

The man nervously cleared his throat. 'He took the opportunity to visit a recreational wing while his team stocked up on...'

'Did he *leave* yet?'

'He leaves in about twenty minutes, sir,' the soldier said.

Bromberg and his men had retired to an east wing recreational quarter for the duration of the afternoon as they were obliged to fill in incident reports and equipment acquisition request forms before attending a debriefing as well as mandatory counselling sessions (they may only have battled possessed toys but the Plan followed strict policies and guidelines concerning any military engagement). When Fate and a company of Planners arrived at the facility, bursting in with emp-rifles drawn, they found it empty, except for one man slumped in an armchair, his eyes opened eerily wide and staring fixedly at a nearby wall.

Fate crouched to examine him. 'Everything's falling into place,' he said to the puzzlement of his entourage.

'Who is he?' one of the Planners asked.

'Hereward Nery,' Fate replied.

'Why do I know that name?'

The Captain looked up. 'Because he recently woke up from a twenty-year coma,' he said. 'And it looks like some villain just put him back in it. This isn't good. Nery was a geomancer and chief lab assistant for Griffin Adler back in the day.'

As he got back to his feet, Fate finally understood everything; why he hadn't been able to anticipate events, why his dreams had failed to warn him about the girl. His intuition had begun to tingle back to life the moment he considered the Distance Ladder and the significance of the ray gun coordinates, helped by the fact that coincidence was officially banned following the 1612 *Happenchance Witch Trials*.

He addressed the soldier beside him, simply to air his suspicions. 'Why did the robot set the ray guns coordinates for the Desolation Islands?' and when the soldier shrugged his shoulders, he clarified, 'Because they were familiar to whatever glum magic possessed it!'

'I don't...' the soldier responded, mistaking the Captain's rhetoric for conversation.

And as Fate tried to tease the complete truth out of his own head by massaging his temples, a voice suddenly beseeched him to *help us*. It arrived with a barrage of ice-cold pain that almost brought him to his knees but then a salvo of comprehension that made the pain worthwhile because he now knew why he had been prevented prior warning of all these substantial happenings and more importantly why he had been unable to identify the Tetrad's fourth member. The person behind this plot was using Mitford's telepathy, not only to disguise her identity, but to counteract Fate's oracular gift.

'Sir?' one of the Planners exclaimed with concern.

The Captain looked at him. 'What's your name?'

'Private Tippet, sir.'

He looked at the next man. 'And you?'

'Sergeant Grey, sir.'

'Tippet, you're coming with me. Grey, get a company of Planners together. Find Bromberg and his team.' He rushed to the door with Tippet on his heels and then turned to readdress Grey. 'The Lieutenant and his men are traitors,' he said. 'Be prepared to use ultimate force if necessary. If you need me, I'll be in the council chambers.'

And with that they left.

It took three minutes for Grey and a team of more than a dozen armed Planners to reach the loading bay where Bromberg and his men were currently assembled. Occupying a steel gantry high above the industrial-sized Ladder located on the west side of the hanger, the sergeant called out, '*LIEUTENANT BROMBERG, YOU ARE ADVISED TO REMAIN ON GRACE PLATEAU FOR FURTHER DEBRIEFING*!'

Thirty metres below, on the hangar's east side, Bromberg and his team appeared to be transferring wooden crates from the Ladder rather than to it for exportation. Indeed, as Grey watched, another box materialized in the glowing blue light of the Ladder.

'*YOU ARE ADVISED TO CEASE AND DESIST*!' Grey called out and Bromberg and his entourage immediately stopped what they were doing and, in an overtly casual manner, made their way to the teleporter, removing the newly arrived box from its circumference and sliding it clumsily across the hangar floor.

'*LIEUTENANT BROMBERG...*'

It all happened so fast.

Before Grey could complete his instruction, dozens of emp-rifles opened fire. Caught off guard, he and his team dropped to the scaffold's mezzanine floor as blue bolts of energy disintegrated into sparks against the steel parapet. Electronic voices uttered therapeutic advice from every expended weapon, echoing infuriatingly around the hangar walls and adding to the chaos. Below, Bromberg's team hurried to pack themselves into the radius of the Ladder, ready for conveyance. Grey's men managed to return fire, injuring one of the traitors just as the loading bay walls ignited in flickering blue light and the Ladder rescued all but the injured man. The sergeant sucked in breath when he realised the turncoat held a remote device and called for retreat, but his team separated and scrambled to different ends of the gantry as a massive explosion ripped through the bay.

Slamming and locking the hanger hatch behind him, shutting out the intense heat and fire that had breathed on his neck and shoulders as he guided most of his men to safety, Grey utilised a portal in the door to see flames and a plume of black smoke envelope those who had fled to the gantry's opposite end only to find their exit locked.

As a massive explosion shook the plateau, Fate crashed through the chamber doors and was immediately blinded by the spotlight rigged to the back wall and forced to use a forearm to protect his retinas from the light source. He saw movement, somebody heading towards an emergency exit. When Tipper arrived, Fate snatched the man's rifle and extinguished the illuminations.

It is a standard emotional reaction,' the emp-rifle opined, *to experience nihilistic sensations of gloom in the hours following the deployment of a weapon. Please seek immediate psychological assessment.*

'Get after her,' he instructed Tippet, returning the man's weapon and the soldier left in hot pursuit of the person responsible for all of Fate's recent woe. The Captain leaped the Tetrad's now unlit pulpit where each member of the council lay slumped in his or her version of death; Under Cromwell with a knife jammed in his ribcage, Rowland Thistle tied up in a repulsive knot of broken limbs, the Stone Witch, Ivy Mitford, with a wound of raw flesh about her neck where she had been throttled while next to the witch, draped over a chair, limp and lifeless as a discarded suit, lay the remains of the elderly oil magnate, Sir Clement Kerguelen, of *Kerguelen Mining PLC* and executive director of ASAP (Availability and Sustainability of Alternative Powers).

When Fate heard a croaky female voice in his head he went to the body of Mitford. *She fooled us all* that voice fluttered through his mind less butterfly-like than vulture, while her lips remained motionless and eyes stared ahead as they had for hundreds of years.

'Was it Kerguelen's wife?'

'Yes,' Mitford's dislocated voice affirmed and then the last words to ever project from her thoughts said, *'the Harbinger.'*

CHAPTER TWENTY-SIX
The Peculiar Palace

For some time Egg lay awake on a cold, hard floor, her eyes tightly shut, too afraid to acknowledge her whereabouts. When she finally opened them and viewed the spectacular golden lobby surrounding her, the massive vestibule of an ostentatious mansion, a dwelling far more remarkable than Hill House, her jaw dropped with apt wonder and she clambered to her feet, so captivated her panic dissolved completely. She was in some sort of palace belonging to an Emperor from a bygone era, a period when profligate splendour was not frowned upon and dazzling chandeliers and grandiose architecture were considered evocative rather than provocative. Bejewelled tendrils like glittering stalactites dangled from the ceiling, the forest of ornate liana a metre out of reach, while beneath her feet waxed tiles perfectly reflected her image and made her giggle as she turned on the spot and visually gulped every mesmeric element of her location.

Then she stopped to inspect a baroque terrace overlooking the oceanic atrium, the centrepiece of a vast wall of mirrors that extended around the entire room. Two white-stone staircases with hulking gold banisters, twisted serpentine-like up either side of the veranda resembling the stairways heroines in old black and white movies ran up to a soundtrack of swirling orchestral music.

Had she seen any old films?

Her first consideration was that the clown exterminator lived here and that after she had escaped from the garden he had discovered another way of extracting her from the Plan's dubious hospitality, for she had certainly not volunteered her attendance. The last thing she remembered was a surly, black-eyed stranger pursuing her through a succession of freakish nightmares. And, oddly, despite casting her mind back to these moments, she remained in the decorative building rather than zap away to somewhere else.

'*HELLO,*' she called out and the *O*s echo receded momentarily, venturing along unseen passageways deep inside the mansion, eventually re-emerging like a verbal boomerang, its adventures having been to no avail.

'*HELLO, IS ANYBODY HERE?*'

She saw a glimmer of light reflected in a mirrored wall a few yards away and searched for it in the wide-open space. In due course her eyes landed upon a moustachioed man dressed in a yellow military uniform, the sort of apparel that, two hundred years ago, was worn by army generals while these days it was more likely to be seen on a member of a brass band. The moment she spotted the soldier, he marched hastily towards her, leather boots clacking over the buffed ground and an accompaniment of chains and medals jingling elegantly where they dangled from his uniform. He seemed to be dripping with trinkets, the laurels of victory, all down the left side of his frockcoat, big bright medallions on rainbow ribbons. Finally standing before her, the soldier systematically stomped both feet, coming to attention with a salute and beholding Egg with deference.

'Mademoiselle,' he said, by way of greeting.

'You're not the strange man with black eyes,' she remarked.

The soldier seemed puzzled by this statement, his curly moustache wobbling curiously on his top lip as he considered it and then he coughed and said, 'I am at your behest.'

'I don't know what that means,' Egg responded shyly, her cheeks glowing red with embarrassment. 'Where am I?'

'You do not know where you are?'

She shook her head and listened as their conversation repeated around the vast hall, dispersing a syllable at a time.

'Ah, then we are having something in common, for I have not the... how you say, *nebbia, nebbioso*.'

Egg laughed. 'I don't understand.'

'Si, si, these are words I find *difficile*.'

'*Difficult*?'

'You speak *Itiliano*?'

'Never had *one* lesson,' she announced, proudly.

'But you are a *natural*,' he said with surprise. 'Italy is a beautiful country. Have you been?'

She shrugged her shoulders. 'I might have,' she replied. 'I don't remember. My dad's been though. He blew up part of it.'

The soldier gasped.

'You just called me *Mademoiselle*. Isn't that French?'

He froze and then physically deflated. Even his moustache seemed to droop listlessly. 'All right, all right,' he said, in a patently English accent, holding up both hands in surrender. 'I'm not Italian and I'm not French. I don't know *what* I am. It just gets so boring here sometimes. I try to maintain a sense of the exotic, some pretence just to keep from becoming so utterly jaded and bored.'

Egg felt sympathetic. 'I understand,' she said. 'I get bored too sometimes. Is this Grace Plateau?'

'*What*? Of course not,' he said and laughed and then became immediately miserable again, looking as if he might sob. 'This place is the antithesis of Grace Plateau.'

'What does *anti faces* mean?'

'You're not very smart, are you?'

'I'm only eight.'

'Antithesis means… well, it means… it's something to do with opposites, isn't it?'

'It must have a name. Everywhere has a name.'

'What, this place?' The soldier sniffed and wiped a finger under his nose. 'Oh, this place has all sorts of names. Some call it the *Fortress of Eyes*, some *the Dream Nightmare Theatre of Horrible Horror and Dismay*.'

'Who calls it that?'

'Other people,' he said, 'the ones who show up from time to time like you did just now, out of nowhere.'

Egg scanned the foyer again. 'It looks like a palace.'

'I think it's a sort of purgatory,' the soldier said, 'and I'm here to be punished for my sins.'

'What sins?'

When the soldier shrugged his shoulders, two golden epaulettes bounced up and down either side of his head. 'Om knows,' he replied. 'I once taped the top forty off the radio. They say that's illegal. All I know for sure, well, I'm pretty certain, I suspect anyway, is that I've been trapped here for centuries… decades… a long time in any case.' He sighed and then, quite dramatically, said, 'Trapped like a thing that's trapped in a trap.' He ended his affected monologue with a slap to the head. 'Do we have to talk? Banal chitchat makes my brain ache. What's wrong with silence? It's such a dull social obligation to natter away about…' A ferocious howling came from somewhere in the building and the ground began to vibrate. The burnished, jewelled vines tinkled like a timpani orchestra as the walls and ceiling shook. '…where we are and why we're here? I mean, if we're quiet then perhaps the terrible thing that always happens next won't happen because we won't attract…'

'What was that noise?'

The soldier wrapped his arms around his head with frustration. 'It's inevitable,' he said. 'I try to alter the sequence of events by changing the subject matter but it doesn't stop you asking the one question they always ask, *what was that noise?*'

Another mighty roar set the entire building a tremble.

'Is it an earthquake?'

The soldier shook his head and told her, 'That's another question they always ask. As if all the loneliness and boredom isn't enough, I'm asked the same tedious questions over and over; *what was that noise? Is it an earthquake?* If we talked about something else instead, ignored the loud roaring and the ground tremors that always precede the arrival of the dragon…'

A sudden ear-piercing screech and a loud pounding pulsed at close proximity. Egg looked around her to try to work out where the noise was coming from, finally seeing, where the two staircases embraced the golden veranda, the humungous head of a green monster as it burst through the stone balustrade, an intrusion that sent rubble and dust hurtling across the lobby floor. The dragon's body heaved against two corridor walls and a ceiling that hemmed it in on the first storey, cracking masonry, causing it to cascade in great powdery chunks until the creature became jammed in the alcove, frantically twisting its head and fore-shoulders, thrusting this way and that, trying to break free.

She considered what John Fate had said about keeping her grandfather away from dragons and gasped.

'Too late,' the soldier announced. 'Here comes *Old Scorcher* to burn you to a crisp and eat you up for supper.'

'Is that what usually happens when the dragon comes?' Egg asked.

The soldier looked at her with astonishment. 'Now that's a question I've not been asked before,' he said, looking delighted. 'Usually, when the dragon comes, the visitors run away screaming. The dragon chases and catches them, chars them with its fiery breath and then eats… *where are you going*?'

Egg had set off at a run towards the nearest staircase leading to the trapped leviathan. It seemed like the maddest thing she could possibly do, contravening every piece of health and safety advice given to her by her grandfather and yet, if it

259

was such a course of folly why did it feel just and exciting? Under the circumstances, she was convinced she'd never outrun a beast of that magnitude if, as the soldier described, the dragon's arrival regularly resulted in visitors being burnt and eaten alive, so shouldn't *she* try to alter the chain of events?

'Are you mad?' the soldier called out as he raced after her, sword and medals jangling like Christmas tree decorations in a draught.

'I don't think so,' she called back. 'Are you?'

'I have nothing to fear,' the soldier laughed. 'The dragon isn't here for me. It comes and eats the other people and I escape every time.'

'Have you ever tried to slay the dragon?'

'Who do I look like to you, *Billy Idiot* from *Numptytown*? Slay the dragon? I'm a soldier not a... a...'

'*A Dragon slayer*?'

'Exactly,' he agreed still on her heels.

'Perhaps slaying the dragon is the thing you're meant to do?'

Panting and furiously pumping his arms and legs, the soldier frowned. 'Perhaps this is *your* purgatory and it's *your* duty to slay the dragon?'

'I'm only eight,' Egg responded, her bare feet rhythmically slapping the smooth ground, arms thrusting at her sides, driving her forwards. 'I can do lots of things other eight-year-old girls can't but I'm sure slaying a dragon isn't one of them.'

'Well *I'm* not doing it! I'm a real person, you're not!' the soldier argued, boots beating a swift tempo over the shiny floor.

When she finally reached the stone staircase Egg launched herself up the first few steps before hiding behind the curved marble banister. To her disappointment there was no accompaniment of swirling orchestral music. A moment later the soldier joined her, wheezing unhealthily, sword drawn.

'If you think I'm not real, why did you chase after me?' Egg asked.

'Because... because... you're an eight-year-old girl and there's nothing gallant about running in the opposite direction when an eight-year-old girl plays chicken with a dragon.'

Above them the creature continued to groan angrily as it pulled and slammed against the walls and ceiling encasing it.

'Has anybody else ever run at the dragon?'

'*Are you kidding*? Who'd be stupid enough to do that?'

Egg laughed and crawled up a couple of steps, stopped momentarily to survey the area and then went up a couple more with the soldier reluctantly following. When they had ascended to a point level with the mansion's first storey, both lay flat on their bellies and peeped over the top step where one of the dragon's huge fore-claws sat.

'Usually you run away,' said Egg, 'and the dragon has a reason to break free and jump down and chase after you. But today it didn't see you because you ran towards it instead.'

'We've changed the order of events, so what? Is that necessarily a good thing? Old Scorcher will just eat you all the sooner.'

That great front paw twisted in their direction, forcing them to slide down a step or two to prevent being pushed off the staircase or risk razor sharp talons dissecting them.

'This is rather more danger than I'm used to,' the soldier told her.

Egg laughed. 'Danger is a foot,' she said.

'I'm glad you think it's funny. So what do we do now?'

She looked at him. 'Now you slay the dragon.'

The soldier appeared to consider her suggestion for a moment, and then descended the staircase on his bottom. 'No, no, no, no, no,' he said as he went.

Egg slid down after him. She quickly caught him up, grabbed the back of his frockcoat and digging her heels into the marble steps prevented him from going any further. Eventually, exhausted by the struggle, he lay back and looked up at her, pleadingly. 'I can't do it,' he said. 'You're talking about killing another living creature. It doesn't seem right somehow.'

'It's *not* really living though, is it?' Egg said. 'None of this is real. It's all just a test like you said.'

'Of course it's bloody real! It's as real as I'm lying here!'

She glanced at him with a forlorn expression and the soldier sat up straight with alarm. 'Why did you look at me like that?'

'Like what?'

'Like I'm a deluded fool,' he replied.

'I didn't,' she lied, guiltily.

'Yes you did, you looked at me as if to suggest...' he gasped and said, '*you don't think I'm real.*'

'You're not,' she said. 'That's why the dragon never eats you.'

The soldier got to his feet, coughed and dusted down his brightly coloured uniform. 'The existential purpose of my being here, trapped in this Om-forsaken place, has not failed to occur to me, you know? During the decades, years, months, whatever length of time I've been imprisoned in this fortress, I've had many thoughts of a, shall we say, philosophical nature. But I always arrive at the same conclusion. I *have* to be real. What's the point of me if I'm *not* real? And if there's a single, microscopic thought living inside me concerned with the notion of not being real there must be a me to be concerned about to have the thought inside. Do you see what I'm saying?'

'No, not really,' said Egg, shaking her head.

'Well, a supplementary point to all this relative ambiguousness is that if Old Scorcher's real too then the chances of me surviving a conflict with it are slim indeed and may result in me *not* being real for the rest of eternity. And, just for the record, if anybody around here isn't real, it's you. I mean, seriously, what real person runs *towards* a dragon?' The soldier nervously scratched at his chin, sniffed and, appearing defiant and sad at the same time, looked at the sword in his hand. He seemed to admire the way it shone and glinted with light as he turned it from side to side. Then he looked at Egg. 'If anybody asks, you'll tell them I was brave, won't you? You won't mention all this complaining?'

Egg mimed zipping up her mouth and throwing away the key.

He glanced up the stairway, drawing in and puffing out a deep breath. 'Right then,' he said, 'I suppose there's a first time for everything, so here goes.' He pushed out his chest with one last sigh and, with a courageous shout of, '*CHARGE*!' raced up the steps like a madman, waving his sword round his head as if it was a helicopter propeller.

'Excuse me,' a jittery voice spoke in Egg's ear and she turned to see an elderly knight in shining armour standing on the staircase behind her. 'My name is *Sir Baluster the Bravado*. Have you by any chance seen a dragon hereabouts?'

Egg gasped in horror. She turned and ran after the soldier. Knights in shining armour slew dragons, not soldiers in yellow uniforms. Ahead of her she saw the brave man vault heroically off the top step and onto the dragon's paw, thrusting his sword through its tough scales. As Old Scorcher writhed in pain the soldier was thrown into the air and ricocheted lithely off a nearby wall, clattering to the ground. Egg reached the top of the stairway just in time to see him bound to his feet, dart beneath the beast's belly and slice it effortlessly from one flank to the other and, as the green monster twisted in pain and anger, she ran alongside it, diving into the first doorway she came to, hankering down and peering round the wall as the dragon thrashed about emitting a bloodcurdling howl and, in its death throes, inadvertently destroying what was left of the adjacent area. When it died, the huge beast settled in the passageway, its fat abdomen expanding to fill up the corridor, puffing out against the walls like an inflated hovercraft skirt, crushing elegant pieces of furniture and toppling every portrait it had not managed to disturb in its living fury.

Egg breathed a sigh of relief, stood in the doorway and dusted herself down. When she heard a smarmy voice say, 'Bravo,' she turned to see four strange men clapping their hands and smiling at her.

CHAPTER TWENTY-SEVEN
Raven's Gambit

In 1962, the Captain uncovered a terrorist cell operating in Wigan calling themselves *ADAM* (The Anti-Deity Autocracy Movement). They had no particular political agenda other than a wanton desire to kill Seraphs and cause mayhem and despair when and wherever the opportunity presented itself. John Fate spent three months monitoring its members and, in particularly, a Planner by the name of *William Spark*. Spark lost, not only a leg after a mishap with a hand-grenade, but also his partisanship, thereafter flagged as a potential *Thomas* (of the doubting variety) having displayed signs of discontent and acrimony whilst recuperating from his injuries. Some suggested the mishap with the grenade hadn't been an act of misfortune at all, that, whilst engulfed in a glum stupor, Spark had pulled the pin wittingly. While under surveillance, he was observed meeting with numerous unsavoury types, most significantly anarchists linked to *The Real Salvation Army*, a terrorist organisation with a long and terrible past. When Fate eventually had Spark and the anarchists apprehended on charges of conspiracy, a highly controversial letter was discovered upon the ex-Planner addressed to a tea shop in Kent. It contained plans for the potential homicide of the five *Sinister Vessels*. A subsequent search of the Kent establishment heralded more arrests and a large cache of anti-incarnate paraphernalia. Several more contentious letters, addressed to somebody called *Uncle Elk Emergent* were revealed and, after close analysis, verified as politically significant. Uncle Elk Emergent was interpreted to be an anagram of *Clement Kerguelen*, the name of a highly respected industrialist and member of the British House of Lords. Lord Kerguelen made his fortune mining ore and was an extremely influential statesman as well as a high-ranking member of the Contingency Plan. Additionally, in 1946 he wed the disgraced Harbinger, Wilhelmina Hippocampus.

An inquiry determined that it was actually Kerguelen's wayward son, Fletcher who was mixed up with anarchists and he had used his father's name in a boastful and unruly attempt to cast aspersion upon the establishment who, he considered, to be too lenient towards incarnates. When the case against the Real Salvation Army, Spark and Fletcher Kerguelen went to trial a year later, every shred of evidence, all the incriminating letters as well as a number of proudly written confessions and indubitable witness statements, had miraculously disappeared. Lord Kerguelen personally stood up in court and demanded, not only that the Plan should make a full apology, but also a sizable pecuniary donation to scientific research of his choice. It was that day in court, without the Stone Witch's telekinetic abilities to impede upon his identity, that John Fate heard the man's voice, the same voice which had eluded him in successive attendances at meetings with the Other Tetrad. It was a burden on Fate's heart and soul that he had not made the connection earlier, but then, he was not supposed to; Wilhelmina Hippocampus had seen to that, having pervaded and controlled her husband for the last decade and finally murdered him along with three other council members, the bodies of which the Captain was currently watching being placed into body bags.

He felt nauseous.

'Captain Fate…' said a reptilian clerk appearing at his arm 'it appears that a segment of ethereal coupling has been irreversibly damaged in the bomb blast. I've had connecting sections of corridor sealed off to prevent further corrosion.'

Fate nodded, still reeling from the shock of multiple assassinations and exploding bombs happening on his watch. 'Is there anything else to report?'

'Yes, sir. The list of absentees currently stands at thirty-five.'

Fate glanced around him, sighing at the spectacle of disaster; emergency service workers attending the dead council while dozens lay injured in the corridor outside. Encircled by broken glass, dazed Planners and gloomily veiled bodies, the state of his world had completely altered in the last half hour. If it was chaos The Real Salvation Army intended then they had achieved their goal, but sadly, the Captain had a sneaky suspicion this wasn't the case.

'Are the missing Planner's insurgents running for the hills or hostages do we know?'

'I'm guessing hostages, sir,' said the clerk and then, after clearing his gravelly throat, said, 'Phyllis Hartmann is on the list.'

The Captain felt something grow tight in his belly and became lightheaded. His discomfort had nothing to do with his PA's disappearance. Neither was it a physical representation of his sense of culpability as he stumbled and reached for the wall. How could he have anticipated an attack of this magnitude? If it hadn't been for that toy robot resetting the ray gun's coordinates to a region of Antarctica where a recent memo revealed Kerguelen's business interests had built drilling rigs, he might never have overcome the mental block at all, not that it had saved many lives.

'Captain, are you feeling okay?'

He nodded and waved the clerk away, using his other hand to massage an aching temple he considered how both the attack on Hill House and Grace Plateau had been a complete diversion and that, presently, he was the only person who knew why. There had been no attempted coup or breach of truce or even a futile effort to cause horror with violence. When one factored the lab technician, Hereward Nery into the proceedings, there could be only one explanation for today's succession of well-organized atrocities; the anarchists were after Griffin Adler's gimmicks, the secret doorways the missing geomancer wrote into facsimiles designed to detain the five Sinister Vessels.

'Everything happened so *abruptly*,' Fate said to nobody in particular, and then, spotting Sergeant Grey giving orders for his men to take the Tetrad members down to the morgue, he stepped over the encased portly corpse of the Earl of Accrington and roughly grabbed the sergeant's arm, taking him by surprise.

'Captain Fate,' he said, coming to attention.

'Forget all this nonsense,' Fate told him. 'I need you to take ten good men to the Desolation Islands. Find Bromberg and his team. It's my belief they were involved in a plot with Wilhelmina Hippocampus to steal confidential information and...' he placed a hand to his belly as it writhed with pain, 'I think I think I'm about to be pilfered.'

The Captain dropped into a plastic seat at the other side of a grubby Formica table where Rhodeburt Raven, garbed in paint-splattered grey rags was hectically cramming junk food into his mouth, fistfuls of chips and greasy burgers. Fate glanced about the café's bright interior as rain beat against the window and then peered out at the ancient buildings and population of Manchester beyond. In large reversed yellow and red lettering, the word *Clarabelle's* arched across the pane. He briefly watched civilians ramble by with unleashed umbrellas overhead and then back at the table in front of him at what looked like a tinned-ham and brown sauce sandwich. Just that morning he had dreamt of such a sandwich. Had it been more than a hankering? Had he predicted his last supper?

'They say,' great chunks of masticated potato, beef and bread flopping from his mouth as he spoke, 'that you can never really know a person unless you've loved or hated them intensely.' Raven sat up and burped, acknowledged Fate for the first time and wiped his smirk on a grubby paper napkin before instructing him to, '*Eat up!*'

Fate scrutinised Raven's ashen features almost obscured by lank hair, a flow of dusky locks that even dangled in the man's food. A paradox played on the turn-harps face; Raven appeared as young or old as one wished to perceive him, generating a childlike, unabashed soul that had been so easy to manipulate towards familial betrayal years before, all tethered to an aged and jaundiced shadow of insanity.

'*Who* says?' asked the Captain.

'*They*,' replied the incarnate, allowing his eyes to flit around in their sockets as though watching a dizzying display of looping flies. 'Those mysterious and erudite busybodies we apply as a barometer for all social injustice.' Raven laughed. 'You look old, John; well beyond your prime.'

A waitress brought three cheeseburgers and a large plate full of fries to the table, plonking them down amongst the dozen or so empty food containers and wrappers already there. 'Keep 'em coming,' Raven instructed her, leaning back in his seat and smiling at the woman. Then he leant forward, saying to Fate, 'I have come to realise there are two categories of humanity.' He sniffed and wiped his nose on the back of a hand. 'There is the shallow egotist who builds temples in the worship of surplus foodstuffs and there is the insignificantly meek who number in their billions and starve to death on every fragment of land on this insipid dust ball.'

'Where's Phyllis Hartmann?'

Raven settled back in his seat, sniffed the air and wryly smiled. 'I don't recall the name.' He laughed, scooped up a handful of chips and crammed them into his jaws.

'She's missing, along with thirty-four other people.'

'Was she the turn-harp I fished out of your office? How's *Blanco* by the way? I expect you picked him up after that fiasco this afternoon.'

'Is she dead? Are they all dead?'

'We seem to have wandered off the beaten track here, John. Can I call you John?' Raven mopped his mouth again,

270

leaving a gap in his monologue should Fate wish to reply, but the Captain just continued to stare at him, so eventually he went on. 'My opening statement about never really knowing a person unless you have loved or hated them intensely, that was no babbling declaration of narcissism on my part. It was an attempt to introduce myself as a potential adversary in the troubles to come. All eminent figures in culture have their rivals, Mr Fate: Cain had his Abel, Odysseus his Poseidon, Mozart his Salieri. And so, I welcome the opportunity to confront you as an equal in both mortal and intellectual combat as the Known Universe slides back into apocalyptic war.'

'And did you confront poor Phyllis as an equal?'

'Sadly, no,' Raven replied. 'She proved to exhibit no equivalent aptitude for this type of banter and as a result *stopped living*. What she failed to realise, as she abided by her mislaid loyalty and under the delusion that bravery is somehow a virtue, was that I would just find another of your white-collar slaves to interrogate and eventually torture to death. And indeed, I amassed a pile of bodies akin to genocide.' He picked up a cheeseburger. 'If she had not been so stubborn and told me exactly what I wanted to know she might have saved all those lives. But imagine my surprise when finally the information I sought came to me and I ventured to the little girl's location to find her not there.'

'So somebody in the Plan gave her up?'

'Oh, don't be so paranoid, John,' said Raven. 'I spent an hour snapping many of your minions in two and not one secret was revealed. Not until a fat star-maker by the name of Zack bounced into my sights.'

Fate ignored an impulse to dive across the table and strangle the monster, breathing deeply in through his nose and saying, 'It's lucky I moved her when I did then.'

'My brother, how does he fare?'

The Captain leaned over the table and said, 'You can't win.'

With half a cheeseburger already devoured, Raven spat soggy bread and meat as he mumbled, 'Is that why you moved her, because you're so confident of my defeat? I don't think so. Have you any idea of the profound agony they all suffered? I am showing you a courtesy I did not this... *Phyllis* person. By inviting you to this top-notch restaurant I'm allowing you the dignity of parity, John. So, do be kind enough to show me the same respect and just tell me where she is.'

'She's under my protection. Somewhere you'll never find her.'

'*Protection*?' laughed Raven. 'Is somebody trying to harm the child? As I recall the last time a person of her abilities was exposed to this world, it was *you* he required protection from.'

'We obviously encompass different connotations of the term *protection*.'

'We obviously encompass different connotations of the English language, John. Talk proper or I'll make you pay for your sandwich.' Raven laughed out loud, snatched up more fries and sucked them down. 'You moved the girl because you *fear* me taking her,' he said through a mouthful of chips. 'You have no real power to hide her because the source of that power derives from *my* kind. Left up to you and your little band of office clerks, you'd have to continue lopping pieces off fallen angels to build your clumsy, inhumane weapons and storage units and the brutality simply doesn't suit you, whereas it comes naturally to me, John. Eat your sandwich.'

'I'm not hungry. Are you working for Hippocampus?'

Raven stared at him and frowned. 'What the blood and stomach pills are you going on about now?'

'When the Plan locates me, which shouldn't take them too long, you'll find it rather tricky to leave this building in one piece.'

Raven laughed again. 'Don't worry about that. I have an ace up my sleeve. And anyhow, your gauche bombs have already made me half the man I was, what are you going to do, dice me into quarters? How *is* my other half by the way?'

'It's over,' said Fate, ignoring his question again. 'I've sent a platoon to the Antarctic to apprehend Bromberg.'

'John, really, as much as I respect you, you're coming across like a blathering idiot. I really don't have a clue what you're talking about.'

'Of course not,' Fate said, derisively. And then his mood changed. It occurred to him Raven might be telling the truth. He sat back and wryly smiled. 'What were you doing at Hill House this afternoon?'

'A bit of existential pruning,' said Raven with a face-wide grin.

'But why were you there?'

'It's a free country.'

'What do you recall prior to your arrival?'

'What do I *recall*?' Raven smiled mordantly and rolled his eyes in his head. 'I recall cloudless blue skies and endless summer days sprinkled with the innocent laughter of a contented little boy who danced and skipped and squeezed rabbits into jam jars.'

'No really, indulge me,' suggested Fate, 'before you arrived at Hill House this afternoon, where were you exactly?'

Raven continued to chomp on his fries a moment, but as he considered his response his jaw's chewing motion slowed and finally stopped. He looked up. 'I was moping about my derelict homestead, begging Om's help to find me a clown or two or three or four to chomp on and then a holy miracle occurred.'

'So you just happened along to the King's estate inadvertently?'

'I go where the mindless slaughter takes me,' he said. 'But I've outgrown my petty loathing of circus folk now. Painted jugglers and tumblers no longer gratify my wanton appetite. I have a new obsession.'

'So I see,' Fate said, gesturing to the heap of food receptacles and specimens decorating the table.

Raven smiled. 'Not this muck. I'm talking about Chaos Likely.'

'I thought you were after the child.'

'What do you mean?' Raven wiped cheese from his lips and hair.

Something struck Fate then. He glanced at his sandwich and then back at the glum fool across from him. 'How did you stumble upon the Thumb? Your father, with all the amenities at his disposal, strived to find it for centuries and then you just turn up out of the blue at a location in the English countryside and *there it is*! No, I'm not having that. We've both been deceived today. We've been played like the brass section of an orchestra.'

Raven looked uncertain as he tried to decipher Fate's words. 'I am *nobody's* trombone,' he complained.

There was a flash of light and an armed Planner appeared in the café's vacant aisle. Raven took no notice of the soldier, but when Fate pointed at the incarnate the Planner aimed his emp-rifle at the rogue. A moment later another soldier arrived, followed by another.

'It seems your bringing me here was a mistake after all, Raven,' Fate informed him.

'There are more things in heaven and earth. I like to think I'm open-minded enough to believe the Known Universe still holds surprises from time to time, don't you?'

More armed Planners arrived. Raven laughed and stuffed more greasy fries into his cheeks. 'When I killed him, my father that is, I was doing you a favour. You are the only person who ever promised me glories untold. I asked you for asylum and, well, technically, you put me in one. You treated me no better than a mangy old dog. When do I get my reward for killing pops, John? Give me the girl called Egg and we'll call it quits.'

'Haven't you worked it out yet? Egg isn't Chaos Likely. She's just a random, ten-a-penny miraculous event. She's an eight-year-old girl who doesn't belong in our universe. She's not evil incarnate. You were a fool for bringing me here, Raven. I'm not indebted to you. I told you all those years ago, you'll never be part of the Plan because of the blood that runs through your veins.'

'But that blood doesn't only reside in my veins, John,' the incarnate said, reaching across the table, 'look, it's on my hands too.'

'That's ketchup,' Fate told him.

The turn-harp giggled and licked one palm. 'So it is.'

Another Planner arrived on the scene and another emp-rifle was pointed at Raven's head.

'Is this some type of ruse, John? If you're trying to convince me that charming child I met this afternoon is not the chosen one, I must beg to differ. I smelt power all over her: immense glum energy. And I sense that you fear her.'

'The desire you possess for notoriety, the longing to be more than your father's murderer, it's blinded you to the basic facts,' Fate told him. 'Chaos Likely was seventeen when she was apprehended, not eight-years-old, and that happened over thirty years ago which would make her almost fifty now. Egg is a mysterious astral occurrence, but a Sinister Vessel? I don't think so.'

Raven shook his head. 'Nice try,' he said, producing the Thumb from his rags and waving it in the air. 'But all the signs suggest otherwise.'

Fate snatched the book from his fingers. 'This thing is nothing but a haunted trinket and as good as useless,' the Captain told him, scrutinising the ancient tome as Raven grasped tentatively in its direction. 'It was decoded centuries ago and to the ruin of many good men. If it had any true, practical power the Plan would have used it as a weapon of mass destruction when it was in our possession. Instead we stuck it in a vault and forgot all about it and somewhere along the way it was stolen and dangled like a carrot in your face.'

As the turn-harp's fingertips came within touching distance, Fate stashed the volume beneath his jacket. 'Think about it, Raven. What your father endeavoured and failed to locate in a lifetime, in a single day was salvaged by an idiot like Morecambe Pierpot before being purloined by an incompetent head-the-ball like you. Does that make any sense at all?'

Raven appeared nervous, his glum confidence bruised. His dark eyes seemed to sparkle less arrogantly and where they did, doubt inhabited their contours. And then he gasped. 'I heard his voice!'

'You heard whose voice?'

The incarnate glared down at his own hands, mouth twisted in an absurd rictus grin. 'He's supposed to be dead. These very fingers strangled the life out of him, but his voice spoke to me and led me to the Thumb.'

'You heard your father's voice?'

Raven looked up and abruptly laughed, incongruous madness returning. 'Let's not talk about that, let's discuss the girl. Where will I find her?'

'Raven, Cruel Lord Crowberry is dead!'

'*I SAID I DON'T WANT TO TALK ABOUT THAT*!' Raven's face expanded in a mask of wild horror for the briefest of moments, before calm resumed. 'What you don't appear to understand, John, with all due respect, is that you *need* me. You need my moral deficiency to guide you. Humanity has plunged into glumness for thousands and thousands of years. Look at all you outlaw with doctrine. That you require a set of strict guidelines to stop you randomly killing each other was the original indicator for imperfection, and, as such, established a need for immediate and stringent discipline. The very fact that for several thousand years, despite religious principle to the contrary, you and your *ilk* have continued to plunder ethics with a deep, reprehensible, enthusiasm is clear evidence you are no less nefarious than I. We are the same when it boils down to our marrow and the cravings in our hearts. There is no difference between you, me and these gun-toting, salaried lackeys of yours. If there was a button on the table in front of you that would wipe out every Seraph in the Known Universe would you even hesitate to press it?'

'No,' said Fate.

Raven laughed, raucously. 'Oh, we must do this more often. I haven't had this much fun in years. But, alas, if you're not prepared to hand the girl over, we have nothing more to discuss.' He rose to his feet and a rush and report of activity ensued as Planners primed and aimed their emp-rifles at him, intent on tearing him asunder if he tried to vacate the premises.

'I'm sorry, I can't allow you to leave,' Fate informed him, standing and obstructing the way.

For a fleeting moment Raven's features exhibited a combination of confusion and anxiety. Then he laughed. 'You can't keep me here, John.'

'Oh, I think I can.'

'I'm sorry to disappoint you, but if I don't walk out that door in the next few seconds, *my* friend will have no option but to kill two of *yours*! That worthless veteran, Fielding and his ridiculous sidekick, are my prisoners and my associate is under strict instruction to massacre the pair should you and your substitute army try to keep me against my will.'

Fate thought about his vagary concerning the King's death and the overall absence of a green dragon in the vicinity swayed his hand. 'I'm taking you into custody,' he said.

Raven's smile widened with surprise, pushing his cheeks up his face. 'No, really, John,' he tried to explain, 'should one of your pet dogs try placing me in shackles the King and his fool *will* die.'

'That's a risk I'll just have to take, isn't it?' Fate said, confidently. 'Somebody arrest this piece of shit!'

Raven looked suddenly disappointed. He looked around the room and said, 'You all heard me warn the pompous idiot,' and the moment he stopped speaking a bulky object fell past the restaurant window at high velocity, hitting the pavement outside with a deathly splat and Fate turned to look just in time to see a jade figurine of a dragon shatter on the ground beside the body of the King of England.

CHAPTER TWENTY-EIGHT
Confessions of an Albatross

Room 410's balcony wall imploded and, despite sustaining a gruesome head injury in the blast, the King leaped in front of Pierpot and fought like a lion to protect him from the witch hovering in the smoking fissure. All the hexes and martial deceptions a lifetime of soldiering had awarded him, as well as whatever heavy objects were on hand to throw, proved low calibre ammunition compared to the arcane knowledge she drew upon, but they were enough of a diversion for both men to slip out of the room.

Mercifully, the facsimile had been removed and the world beyond was no longer a swirling black corpus of scary nothing. Now all they had to contend with were hotel fire doors closing automatically as the building's alarms began to peal, creating an assault course for the hysterical pair. As was customary in all desperate games of cat and mouse though, especially ones involving human beings and monstrous, otherworldly adversaries, while the King and Pierpot sprinted for their lives, the witch's demeanour, exhibiting a smug lethargy and spiteful confidence, combined with a vain decision to disintegrate each door she arrived at, effectively stalled her pursuit.

'We need to limit the potential carnage,' the King announced as they reached the roof. They came to rest behind a large aluminium air-conditioning unit, the beat of rain on the boxy contraption at their backs sounding like a stampede of ants. 'This building is already fated for disaster,' he went on, 'so if we can hide then Pryderi will focus all her destructive powers on the hotel rather than demolish half of Manchester and sooner or later the Plan will turn up and rescue us.'

'Leontine Pryderi? Are you sure that's who it was?'

With rain and blood streaming down his face the King nodded. 'I recognise her from Kampar when she helped capture RAF Kuala Lumpur for the Japs.'

'Good heavens, Reg, you know she's one of General Galbi's nieces, don't you? Do you think he sent her to retrieve the...' Pierpot slipped a hand under his jacket and fell anxiously quiet as he realised the Thumb was gone.

'The turn-harp stole it back at the house,' the King guessed. 'That morose scoundrel mesmerised us and made us look a right couple of numbskulls in front of John Fate.'

Pierpot hunched his shoulders and puffed out his cheeks with defeat while the King rubbed an arm across his brow where blood continued to ooze from the deep cut on his forehead. They both felt the entire building tremble from explosions happening deep within it and heard the shrieking voice of the witch in a frustrated bid to locate them.

'I apologise, Reg,' Pierpot said, unexpectedly.

'For what?' the King asked.

'For all the trouble I've caused. Not only today but through all the years we worked together. I've been nothing but an albatross.' He removed his spectacles and wiped raindrops from the lenses.

The King looked at him and sighed. 'You know you never actually told me why you were in hell,' he pointed out.

The ex-Planner shook his head and with a self-deprecating laugh, set about clarifying his troubled past. 'Do you remember my commission to Marrakesh? Well I met a witch there called *Strega* and fell madly in love with her, silly old fool that I am.' He replaced his spectacles and shook his head again. 'The whole episode was a confidence trick. She had friends in Nefarious Logistics and was just using me for espionage purposes. I told them nothing of course. All I gave them was the sort of conditioned guff they taught us in basic training, you know the kind of thing, cake recipes and horticultural flimflam committed to memory for just such encounters? I've always been a loyal soldier if I haven't been a very practical one at times. I realised Strega had esoteric qualities the moment I laid eyes on her and should have gotten on the first camel out of there, but I chose instead to court the devil in more ways than I realised, swooning like a schoolboy as she groomed my aging ego with her arcane powers of seduction. Eventually I managed to escape her clutches and kept my head down for almost five years, living like a fugitive, unable to come in from the cold because I was afraid John Fate might think me a traitor; you know how paranoid he can be. And then, while I was in Tibet, I received word Strega bore a child, *my* child in fact. A boy named *Darren*, which, as you know, is *Ancient Sabdonian* for…'

'Satan,' the King interjected.

Pierpot nodded and said, 'Precisely. Now, of course, I had no option but to get word to the Plan about this boy and when I did a detachment of Planners were sent in to apprehend them, but they evaded capture and before I knew anything about it her allies caught up with me and banished my soul to...'

'Why was it so imperative you got word to the Plan about this child?' the King asked with concern.

Pierpot looked wistful, sighing deeply before saying, 'She was a very beautiful and enticing lady. I'm telling you that so you don't think I threw my ethics, loyalties and career out the window for the first pretty minx to look at me twice. She was a temptress, one of the very best in the business actually. Well she would be, wouldn't she, due to who her father was... *is*?'

'Wait,' the King said in disbelief. 'Are you saying you were engaged in a romantic liaison with... *Satan's daughter*?'

His friend nodded. 'I certainly know how to pick them, don't I?'

The King's bottom jaw fell open for a moment and then slammed shut as he gulped on air and said, 'I seem to recall you giving me a rather xenophobic pep-talk when I first shared my feelings with you concerning Phyllis. I'd say your starry-eyed misdemeanour overshadows mine considerably, wouldn't you?'

'There's no need to gloat, Reg.'

'*Gloat*?' mocked the King, 'you fathered a child with the spawn of the Devil, Pierpot. A moment ago you were swearing your allegiance to the Plan while in the next breath you're confessing to being the begetter of Satan's grandson.'

'When you say it like that it *does* sound rather grim.' Pierpot admitted.

'*Grim*?' the King exclaimed. 'You've sired a devil. I always considered you a clumsy old fool but this, well this just takes the biscuit. In all my years of active service, danger never played such fancy with my emotions or intruded upon my sense of self-preservation as it does today. When you brought a circus to my front door I forewent my right to disregard your predicament, allowing you the benefit of doubt, supporting you in your hour of need, despite the jeopardy you placed us all in. You mentioned nothing about Satan having a bounty on your head or being taken advantage of by his daughter or, for that matter, attempting to have his only grandchild incarcerated by the Plan.'

'It didn't seem relevant.'

'*Didn't seem relevant*? Pierpot, you're the Devil's son-in-law.'

'There was never any legitimate, binding ceremony.'

'Oh well, that's all right then,' the King laughed, bursting with sarcasm. 'I'm sure under the circumstances even the Prince of Darkness will abide by civilised protocol and not hold you personally responsible for the exploitation and attempted imprisonment of his brood.'

'I realise I'm in a bit of a jam, Reg, don't think I haven't spent the last couple of decades reflecting upon my misadventures,' he explained, wretchedly, 'but the truth is, I was deceived. And the real injustice was spending twenty years in hell for no better reason than I was in the wrong place at the wrong time. At the first opportunity I escaped and came to you for help. How was I to know you'd be sheltering an eight-year-old girl who may be Chaos Likely. And for the record, you chose not to divulge that rather significant piece of information, not until we were in John Fate's office.'

The sound of the rain replaced their quarrelling voices, a relentless buzz like a badly received radio transmission. And then the King sighed and said, 'You're right of course. I haven't exactly been above board, have I? I suppose you did what you thought was right and I wouldn't be much of a friend if you couldn't come to me in an emergency.'

Pierpot's face twisted into a smile as he repositioned his specs. He might have cried if he hadn't had his tear ducts damaged thirty years earlier in a space vacuum. 'Thank you,' he said. 'I'm flattered that you consider…'

And then the roof detonated in an outburst of debris and Leontine Pryderi rose from the fiery fracture.

'Follow me,' the King declared and, crouching, ran parallel with a channel of electrical cables, pipes and ducts. The two men turned right at the roof's low parapet and followed its edge until they were alongside another building a floor higher than the hotel and separated by an alleyway at least seventy metres deep. A steel ladder ran up the wall through a mezzanine balcony only a few metres away. The King launched himself from the roof of the Elysium without hesitation, landing gracefully inside the steel cage. Pierpot wavered however, the toes of his shoes dangling over the perimeter of brick as his friend silently waved him on.

'I thought you said we should limit the city's destruction by staying in the vicinity of the hotel?' Pierpot asked the sky above, too petrified to look down.

'Oh, to hell with what I said, just jump, man.'

Pierpot shook his head and appeared to faint, tumbling backwards behind the parapet. A moment later he peeped over the wall. 'Save yourself, Reg.' he called out. 'Leave me to my fate. I'll keep her busy while...'

'Don't be a damn fool, Pierpot! Get yourself over here right now! This is no time to grow a spine.'

'I'm a liability!' the man reasoned. 'What value is my company? I just bring you trouble and...' He stopped talking when the King's gaze lifted with fright. Pierpot looked over his shoulder and saw a swelling black cyclone sucking clouds from the sky as well as brick and mortar from the Elysium. The witch was at its core, floating like a goldfish in a murky and tubular bowl, staring right at him with glaring red eyes and a mouth full of teeth that would make a shark covetous. Pierpot pushed his spectacles up the bridge of his nose, sprang to his feet and the roof's parapet and heaved his entire body through the air. He landed inside the mezzanine cage and the two men leaped up the ladder as a bolt of lightning destroyed the gantry beneath them, sending its singed remains crashing noisily to the alley below. They climbed frantically to a sloping roof and scampered over slippery tiles, skidding and sliding on the slate and flinging themselves desperately at skylights and chimney stacks as if they were buoys on a heaving grey ocean.

Both men managed to traverse a street or two before the witch swept down and effortlessly took the King, carrying him off into the night sky. Pierpot furiously cursed the woman as he balanced on the roof's inclined apex, waving a fist in her direction as well as spitting a variety of swear-words after her.

When a finger tapped him on the shoulder he went cold and slowly turned to see the sneering pale features of Rodeburt Raven, flinching when the incarnate laughed and said, '*Boo!*'

*****

Pryderi was tasked with guarding them while Raven had a prior engagement with his *greatest adversary*; just one of many euphemisms the mad turn-harp used to describe John Fate, *worthy opponent* and *esteemed nemesis* being two others. The King considered the turn-harp's ego noticeably improved since the last time they met if he now admired a man of the Captain's standing as his equal/enemy rather than a horde of humble clowns. He wondered why Pryderi didn't just kill them and have done with it and after several minutes sitting against the damp parapet enveloped in awkward silence, the King attempted to make conversation, if for no other reason than to irritate the witch.

'I can't imagine your uncle will be best pleased when he hears about this,' he commented, repositioning two aching buttocks on the wet, gravelled roof.

Pryderi laughed and leaned over the elderly man, taking his face in her spikey fingers. 'I've prompted more wars than you've had hot dinners, *Your Majesty*. I've also murdered more monarchs, *real monarchs* I might add, premiers and rogue gods throughout the Known Universe than you ever resigned incarnates to hell, so do you really think I give a damn what my stupid uncle thinks?'

'I met him once,' remarked Pierpot, vaguely. 'Well, I say met him, I was actually spoon-feeding gruel to a paralysed cephalopod beneath the Black House while the General was torturing a hobgoblin in a chamber nearby. But I did hear him laugh aloud with cruel gratification at one point.' His melancholy features turned thoughtful and he asked, 'Don't you have a sister?'

Continuing to grip the King's features in her claw, Pryderi cast her fiery gaze at the ex-Planner. 'Do not speak of that treacherous wench and do not think for one moment that my pitiful uncle's indolent existence on the throne of hell is emblematic of the attitude of all incarnates. He grows idle with power while it is the frustration and anger raging in the hearts of the rest of us you need to fear.'

'So you're working for a turn-harp these days?' the King asked, with a hint of pity in his voice. 'I recall a time when Leontine Pryderi stood at the right hand of Emperors and high-ranking Seraph leaders. Still, work is work I suppose.'

The witch looked at him, drawing his face closer to hers, digging her nails into his aged flesh. 'Those impudent men stood at my *left*, you pompous old sod,' she declared with a volley of phlegm. 'I have been sidekick and subordinate to *no-one*! Soon the day will come when *I* sit on the only throne that matters and all other seats of power will be used as kindling at the foot of bonfires where... where...' Her eyes flashed white as she became distracted by something neither human could immediately distinguish. Then the King realised she must have a telepathic link with her mad associate and that the turn-harp was sending her a portentous message, telling her something that would not be in his or Pierpot's best interest. When her anger dissipated, the look of fury on her face transforming into a contented and malevolent smile, he knew without doubt they were about to die.

Releasing his chubby cheeks, the witch stepped back and, employing a series of esoteric hand gestures like a form of celestial sign language, she lifted both of them from the surface of the roof. Pierpot wrapped his limbs tightly around the King, whimpering nervously as they were cast over the parapet and left dangling above the street.

'I will not say it has been a pleasure,' Pryderi remarked, smiling cruelly as the two men struggled in vain to return to the building's apex, 'but I have to admit, killing the King of England will embellish my reputation somewhat. Thank you for this unique opportunity, Your *Highness*!' She cackled hysterically, throwing her flame-haired head back and casting those wild screeches at the black sky.

Wind molested the King's white fringe and caused his clothes to billow up around him. His feet attempted to make purchase on the air as he struggled to retain some dignity while wrestling with his friend's grappling limbs. And as Pierpot's frightened sobbing echoed through the night, the King looked at the witch and bravely said, 'My death may embroider your reputation in the eyes of your glum peers, but on the most part it will incite disgust and when Egg discovers the truth, she won't rest until she finds you.'

For the briefest of moments Pryderi looked worried, but then her fear was surpassed by haughty confidence and she grinned at him and said, 'I'll crack that egg when I come to it.'

'So be it,' said the King.

And then, with yet another variation on smiling wickedly and to the sound of Pierpot's inevitable objection, the witch dropped her arms to her sides and gravity sucked the two men towards death. And amidst this transitory moment of mayhem, Pierpot tried to bring to mind any titbit of training that might alleviate the symptoms of a high velocity collision with a pavement. Ironically, although he could remember a herbal remedy against alien bowel parasites, how to confuse a two-headed python and what woodland leaf to rub on a zombie bite, he knew no prevention or cure for his current ailment.

Fortunately, the King did and, deploying some form of meditation technique, managed to reduce their plummet from a reckless plunge to a jaunty tumble. The trouble was they were still falling at a rate that would kill them on impact. When the King placed both hands on Pierpot's chest and began pushing him away, the ex-Planner, confused and fearful the veteran was forgoing their friendship in lieu of his own survival, tried to hold on tighter.

'Let go, you idiot!' the King instructed him, face purple with mental exertion. And then Pierpot was slammed in the torso by an invisible force which rerouted his descent in an L-shaped trajectory and blasted him through a nearby window. He shot across a living room and collided with a glass cabinet, smashing a collection of crystal decanters and brandy goblets, the deluge of which coated him like snow as he hit the carpet. He picked himself up and returned to the window as one of the flat's two elderly occupants, a Chinese lady, apoplectic with the injustice of having her sitting room invaded and destroyed, screamed at him in her native tongue and grabbed a nearby ornament to hurl at him. The statue glanced off Pierpot's right ear and out through the broken window and the ex-Planner watched it travel down to the morbid scene below; a falling jade dragon that, when it hit the tarmac, showered the sprawled body of the King with glossed fragments of dried clay.

A chill travelled the length of Pierpot's spine as he realised his friend was dead and, instinctively, he glanced up and saw the witch leaning over the roof. When she hissed at him, he ran to the apartment door which had more locks on it than a bank vault and while struggling to unfasten them had to defend himself against a fresh offensive by its two elderly inhabitants who rained a torrent of blows down on him with a wok, an umbrella and a cricket bat. Pierpot finally gained access to the corridor and ran as fast as his pounding heart could take, only travelling a few metres when instinct twisted his belly and he stopped and turned to run back towards the geriatric Asian couple. A loud crash came from behind him and, glancing over his shoulder, he saw the witch fall into the corridor along with the vestiges of a decimated ceiling.

The Chinese man now had a pair of *nunchucks* and was busily twirling them about his upper abdomen as Pierpot approached, narrowly missing the ex-Planner by a hair's breadth, but inadvertently knocking out the old woman. Pierpot ran on, risking one final glimpse behind him before disappearing into a stairwell, and seeing the witch disintegrate the luckless duo and pass straight through their vaporous forms to continue with her pursuit.

He dashed up three flights of stairs and out onto the roof, running directly to the edge to look down and see the same unnerving crime scene from a higher perspective, this time including several armed Planners peering back at him.

When Pierpot turned to leave he found himself face to face with Leontine Pryderi. 'Your turn,' she said, nudging him with a pointed finger and forcing him into a seated position on the low rampart.

'You killed the King,' he spat at her, trying to keep his balance on the wall. 'They'll bring back burning for this.'

She laughed and said, 'Start flapping, old man, there's a pavement down there with your name on it.'

'When the girl finds out what you've done...'

'*What*? What will she do? Cry into her pink, pony-patterned pillows?'

'She'll tear this world apart to find you.'

The witch sniggered. 'Tearing this world apart is her birth-right. She is fated to obliterate this feeble sod of earth.' Pryderi put a hand on his chest and calmly pushed him backwards to the building's edge.

He tried to grip the wall with flailing fingertips as he felt himself reach tipping point and his stomach performed a sickly summersault as he was about to topple over. In desperation and panic he spluttered, '*She goes by the name of Buhrmann now.*' and the witch, looking puzzled, clutched his shirt in her fist and dragged him back to the safety of the roof. Sprawled on the ground, having been swiftly hauled from the brink of death once again, the ex-Planner began mentally establishing how to maintain self-preservation.

'What are you babbling about?'

'Your sister, Biel,' he said, 'it's how she managed to disappear. She married a farmer from Leipzig and changed her surname to Buhrmann.'

'And you know this how?'

Panting with anxiety, Pierpot glanced at the roof door. 'Is that Planners I hear coming up the stairs?' he asked, confidently. 'You're running out of time, Pryderi!'

292

She grabbed him viciously by the neck. 'And you're about to run out of oxygen. What do you know about my sister?'

Pierpot stubbornly shrugged his shoulders, smiling through his pain and then, as Pryderi applied more pressure on his throat, started gurgling, his boggling eyes wide open. The witch appeared to revel in the sound of his choking until a commotion on the stairwell a few floors below distracted her. She released him. 'This is a trick.' she implied, looking at him dubiously. 'You're just trying to buy yourself time.'

As he massaged his sore throat Pierpot told her, 'If you kill me you'll never know what happened to Biel.'

She was suspicious, knowing the old fool would say anything to save his skin. How could she be certain it was the truth? And then she answered her own question with a revelatory smirk and, grasping him by the collar of his tweed, said, 'I know just the person to loosen your tongue,' and dragged him into the air as a dozen armed-Planners stomped onto the roof to find it vacant.

CHAPTER TWENTY-NINE
Automata

Davis, Red, Sweet and Grimes were their names and they wore tuxedos in a style that suggested all four were unaccustomed to such apparel. She knew their names because they were printed on large badges pinned to their chests. Davis' tux was at least two sizes too small, his uncovered wrists and ankles making him look like he had experienced a three-year growing spurt overnight. The man smiled at her with malicious charm, drooled black spit down his chin and offered her a blue cocktail. She gasped at the sight of his teeth, hundreds of terrible yellow daggers that glimmered in the light from the room's single chandelier.

'No thank you,' Egg told him. 'I'm only eight.'

He glanced anxiously about before saying, 'I'm sorry, we don't appear to have any *child's* cocktails.'

Red looked equally ill-fitted in his formal wear, but thankfully far less sinister. The expression on his face was one of constant distaste as though his top lip was coated with a foul odour. He thrust out his chest, ran a hand through mousy hair and comically waddled away from the others, saying, 'Well I for one don't see what all the fuss is about. It was just a silly dragon.'

Sweet was almost drowned in his apparel, shaved head barely visible over its collar. The tux was no larger than those Davis and Red wore, but Sweet was so short that, on him, the garment resembled a two-berth tent while Grimes fit his tux rather better than his associates, though his shirt was buttoned up wrong and one of the jacket sleeves was missing. He stood sulkily in the room's centre, resembling a statue devoted to melancholy. His long, thinning hair was parted down the middle above browbeaten features. He had a forlornly bent spine and mournfully hung shoulders that lent him a look of uber-boredom.

'It makes no difference to our predicament,' he groaned, 'if the dragon's dead or alive. We're still prisoners here. We're still incarcerated.'

'But this little girl's a blooming hero,' said Davis, in a sickly-sweet voice. 'She defeated the *Menace of the Vestibules*, pretty little thing that she is. How many people in the three hundred years we've been here do *you* remember thrashing that big lizard? None, that's how many. Anybody who batters Old Scorcher tastes of strawberries and cream in my book.' And then Davis struck a contrite expression and, perspiring, swept brown and oily tresses from his forehead with a paper serviette. 'Not that I intend devouring you whole, my little scrumptious ball of meringue. Not that I even imagine a nibble on one of your little pink fingers, you exquisite little...'

Thankfully, Grimes interrupted this mortifying and cannibalistic monologue by saying, 'So there's no dragon? It hardly changes our circumstances. We're still trapped in this Om-forsaken and pitiless pit of pointless peculiarity.'

'I could have battered the dragon,' Sweet's high, croaky voice announced from behind them as he zoomed about the room intermittently banging against walls or into the glass panes of cabinet windows like an erratic windup top. 'Nobody ever told me to batter the dragon. If you'd just asked I'd have gladly run out and head-butted that scaly beggar any day of the week.'

'You absolute liar,' Red reproached him, farcically. 'We've been here three centuries and never once in all that time did you ever, ever, *ever* attempt to fight the dragon, ever, *EVER!*'

'That's only because nobody said they wanted it fighting. If you'd have mentioned it sooner I'd have given the fire-breathing sod a right booting.'

Egg put a hand in the air to get their attention. 'I didn't kill the dragon,' she informed them, 'a soldier in a yellow uniform did.'

'A *soldier*?' asked Red, anxiously. 'What soldier?'

'I think he might be dead,' she replied, gesturing in the direction of the deceased leviathan, currently filling up most of the doorway. The dragon squished him.'

'If you ask me, I think we all might be dead and this is hell,' Grimes interjected. 'I think I died of sinusitis when I was a boy. I sneezed and my brain shot across the room.'

Red snorted a grotesque laugh and joked, 'What brain, *stupid?*'

'*Come and have a go if you think you're hard enough,*' shouted Sweet and threw himself harmfully at a wall to represent how he might have handled Old Scorcher if he had been given the chance, leaving a Sweet-shaped impression in the plasterwork.

'Would you like a liqueur, a cigar perhaps?' Davis asked, producing both from behind his back.

'Children don't smoke cigars,' Red scoffed. 'It makes them sick. Why do you all have to be such complete and utter dunderheads?'

'Ignore him, Egg,' said Davis. 'His mum dropped him on his head when he was a baby. And then again when he was three, three and a half, four, six, twelve, thirteen.'

'How do you know my name?' Egg asked with a puzzled expression.

'It's written on your badge,' Davis informed her, pointing, and when she looked down Egg was surprised to discover a name-badge pinned to her pyjama top.

'That's strange,' she said. 'I don't remember having this earlier. Am I dreaming?'

'I'll tell you what *is* dreamy,' said Davis, glaring at her with his eyes wide, as if she was grilled and garnished and offered up with a lemon slice, 'eggs with a dash of pepper and a slither of... oh, I'm so hungry I could eat a...'

'*Geronimo!*' shouted Sweet, distracting Davis as he crashed into a nearby table and tumbled over it.

'I think Sweet might have killed himself again,' grumbled Grimes.

'No, I'm fine,' said Sweet. 'I just broke my neck in seven places.'

'*Ooh, ooh,*' exclaimed Red, excitedly. 'I once broke my leg in *two* places, once in Scarborough and once in...'

'The *tibia*?' asked Sweet as he got up off the ground.

'What? No, no. Listen to what I'm saying; I once broke my leg in two places, once in Scarborough and once in…'

'The *femur*?'

'You're doing that on purpose!' Red protested. 'You're deliberately misunderstanding my joke just to annoy me, well I've got one thing to say to you, Sweet, it's not big and it's not very clever.'

'Are you still talking about your leg?' he asked, 'or have you moved onto your head? If you have, you're only half right.'

Red began to laugh like an excited schoolgirl. 'Yes, yes, I *am* only half right. Half right and half…'

'*Pterodactyl*?'

'What? Don't be ridiculous, Sweet,' Red admonished. 'How can I possibly be half Pterodactyl?'

'No, Red. There appears to be a Pterodactyl in the doorway.'

They all turned towards the entrance where a brightly coloured creature with skeletal wings hopped from one spindly leg to the other, the carcass of the dead dragon directly behind it.

'That's not a Pterodactyl, Sweet,' said Grimes. 'It's one of the storks.'

'My mistake,' said Sweet. 'Where was I? Oh yes…' He ran across the room, collided with a sofa and tumbled over it out of sight.

The stork said, 'The boss wants to see you,' and turned to climb back over the dragon.

'*The boss*?' asked Red, excitedly with exultant tears bubbling over his eyelids. '*The boss* wants to see *us*? Oh, Om be praised, the boss wants to see us. Finally, we're saved. We're going to be released and redeployed. Oh, at last. *At last.* Three hundred years of torment over. I know I've been rude about his eminence in the past, accused him of cruel abandonment, but I've always praised his sense of fundamental decency. It's been a challenge, having to live in this hell-hole with the rest of you, but now he's given us the opportunity to move on and put all this behind us I can't help but feel a teensy-weensy bit of respect for the old French sod. After all, haven't I always said, what doesn't kill you only makes you stronger.'

'I think I broke my spine,' said Sweet.

Red began to collect items from the room: statues, books and ashtrays. 'You can say what you like about ambiguous glum magic labyrinths, but quite honestly, where would we be without them?' He laughed aloud with what appeared to be nostalgic joy. 'Remember the *ringworm*? Remember the endless nights of coughing and the blocked-up toilets? That's all behind us now, of course, because we're about to be released. And, fortunately, I haven't aged a single day, which is a bonus. I'm still the handsome fellow I was when I first entered this esoteric fly-trap and I'm pretty certain there are thousands of beautiful girlies out there who have mourned my absence, whole generations of women tendering the fable of Red down through the ages, mother to daughter. Imagine it chaps; freedom at last? I can almost smell it. Can you smell it? *I* can smell it. To celebrate, we should...'

'It's the girl he wants to see not you, pinhead!' the stork added and left.

Red's eyes bulged with rage.

'That's just typical,' moaned Grimes.

'And she looked ever so tasty too,' said Davis, running his tongue over his fangs.

From the back of the room, Sweet asked, 'Can somebody ring an ambulance?'

Egg and the stork climbed over the dead dragon and then marched along an expansive and once elegant passageway now festooned with dints and cracks and smashed furniture. Hung at intervals along the walls were damaged portraits of genetically identical men, transformed only by their affluent attire, each based on a different historical period. Egg recognised him instantly; the black-eyed stranger who had chased her through the cosmos. He was a lean, proud and handsome fellow with a thick black mane, always parted down the centre with eyes as black as obsidian, but a blackness which lent no gloom to his features, only absurdity and if anything, rendered him quite stupid-looking.

She stopped briefly to appreciate the view from a tall window, marvelling at the strangely coloured hedgerows and trees that grew throughout a huge estate of gardens, parklands strewn with fern and fauna the shape and hue of which she had never seen before, all of it perforated with equally peculiar wildlife: blue bunny rabbits, anthropoid cows and polka dot sheep. People wearing historical fashions meandered through these fabulous meadows or rode fantastic animals to and fro. Several flying contraptions passed by, crafted from steel and wood, coughing and spluttering great clouds of acrid grey smoke as they defied gravity and logic. In the distance, a cluster of cumulous clouds floated only a few feet above the ground, immersing the upper torsos of a large group of ramblers, so that they resembled a huge downy caterpillar with hundreds of human legs.

'We shouldn't keep him waiting,' the stork said brusquely when she lingered too long and Egg hurried after him, disappointed to leave the vista.

'Where are we exactly?' she enquired catching him up.

The stork snorted and muttered under his breath, '*Another bloody logician*!' then looked at her and more loudly enquired, 'When you say *exactly*, are you asking for precise latitude and longitude coordinates or exploiting a hackneyed expression in order to acquire a less precise response, which if you ask me is pretty symptomatic of the entire modern educational system today.'

'I just want to know where I am,' she said.

'Well, in philosophical terms you're here, aren't you? In spooky, otherworldly terms, *you're nowhere*. But in paranormal geographical terms I suppose the truth is you currently inhabit one of many concrete arteries inside *The Peculiar Palace*.'

'Is it really called the Peculiar Palace?'

The stork nodded. 'It's all a bit pink bananas and flying jellyfish round these parts,' he said, 'anything goes, know what I mean? You know what they say about enough monkeys and typewriters? Well this is the place where that zany hypothesis happens twice a bloody day, only it's not monkeys it's evil space piranhas and it's not typewriters it's cerebral matter disintegrators.'

Egg giggled as they turned a corner into another corridor and passed more fake portraits and lavish furnishings.

'You laughed because I said *monkeys*, didn't you?'

She nodded.

At the end of the passageway there was a large oak door guarded by two more storks. Her guide nodded at his comrades as they approached and raised a feathered arm to tap on the door.

'That's not any sort of egg I ever clapped eyes on before,' she overheard one of the storks whisper.

'*Infantile*, yes, *egg*, no,' said the other and sniggered.

She was ushered inside. 'His Grace will be with you *shorty*,' her escort announced and she heard his associates outside in the corridor chuckle. 'Oh, I do apologise, I mean, *shortly*.' He saluted her, spun on one leg and ambled out.

Egg ignored a brief spell of muffled laughter from the other side of the door as she surveyed the dimly lit room. Sunlight leaked in through velvet drapes at the window and a lamp burned on the wall. It was a gloomy domicile with torrents of dust tumbling through slender columns of penetrative light. Dozens of what appeared to be automata made of brass, silver and gold sat atop podiums covered with domes of glass. These windup contraptions turned in slow sequences of jittery movement, decorative characters and scenes coming to life beneath shiny bell-jars. She examined one of the appliances up close; a couple in Victorian fashions lent towards each other to kiss and following each mechanised smooch the lady stood up straight, slapped the man across the face and made his ornamental head spin on his shoulders. Beneath another glass dome there was a representation of a giant, reaching an arm into a house through a window. Each time the giant retrieved a doll-like figure from the domicile a larger version of the doll, even larger than the giant, rose up through the base of the apparatus and booted him squarely in the rear. In another, a bird fed its hungry young with what appeared to be diminutive people. And in yet another, a soldier dressed in yellow charged at a dragon and the great green beast collapsed dead upon him. As the delicate cogs turned in each casement, the machines repeated their actions and Egg searched for the dome that might contain four strange men in ill-fitted tuxedos. When she finally found it she smiled and watched one of the figures continually bounce off every surface.

'Do you like my mechanical children, Mademoiselle?' enquired a French accent from the shadows. Egg spun round, searching the room for its owner and then, carefully, approached the dusty old velvet curtain, the only place a speaker might hide. She threw back the drape and was blinded by the sun. Egg covered her eyes with the back of a hand until she could see again, the light casting a cosmos of murky spores about her.

'Down here,' the voice said.

She blinked and looked down at her feet.

'Too far,' it rebuked, 'up a bit.'

She lifted her vision, but all she could see was a wiry black spider crouched in a grimy corner of the window frame. 'Oh,' she said, 'you're a spider.'

'At the moment, yes,' the spider replied.

'I don't like spiders.'

'*I* don't like saxophones.'

'What does that mean?'

'Oh, I'm sorry, I thought we were playing the, *I don't like game.*'

'No,' said Egg. 'I meant I find it a bit icky talking to a spider.'

'Do I frighten you?' the spider enquired, proudly.

'A bit,' she replied. 'What did you mean you're a spider at the moment? Are you not always a spider?'

The creepy-crawly laughed. 'I am a spider *a lot* of the time because I find it is the thing most people are afraid of. But I am a man *most* of the time. Some people are afraid of me even then. I chose to be a spider for you, Egg, because you are not afraid of men.'

'I don't like clowns much.'

'Ah, yes, *Clourophobia*. There was a time every child loved a clown, now they are a thing of nightmare. It is a cultural phenomenon I think, like being *lactose intolerant* or *allergic to nuts*, a nauseating trend.'

'I don't think being allergic to something can be called a trend,' Egg pointed out. 'I think you either are or you're not.'

'Maybe you are right, but rabbits too I have noticed have become tarred with the *scary* brush,' the French accented spider went on. 'More and more people are afraid of rabbits these days. I think it is a form of post-modern irony. I do not understand it myself, but profoundly admire its illogicality. People want to be afraid of things that are not particularly fear-inducing which makes my job simpler. What will they be afraid of next I wonder: spectacles, zip-up cardigans, portable walrus cleaning kits? Did you know Sigmund Freud was afraid of trains? The world is full of silly people me thinks.'

'Spiders *are* scary though,' Egg avowed.

'Yes, especially when they do *THIS*!'

Egg jumped back with fright, but when nothing happened, she started laughing. The spider hadn't even moved. 'When they do what?' she asked, a little embarrassed for the part-time arachnid.

'What?'

'Nothing happened,' she pointed out. 'Your voice got a bit *shouty* but nothing else.'

'I didn't grow ten times the size and change colour?'

Egg shook her head, giggled and said, 'No.'

'Well, *that's* humiliating I've been practising it for ages.'

Egg stepped towards the window again. 'So who are you when you're not being a spider?'

'My name is Pierre,' the spider told her. 'Pierre de Zoet, free enterprise geomancer, employed by those who require quality work under clandestine circumstances, and you, little one, are my prisoner.'

'Oh,' said Egg. 'So, is this *your* palace then?'

The spider laughed. 'Yes. You might say that for I constructed it. There is no actual physical production involved in the elegant generation of such a surreal form. Everything you see, smell, feel, hear and touch, it is all in my mind.'

'This big mansion and everything in it, the dragon, the yellow soldier, me, we're all inside your head?'

'That is correct.'

'That's clever,' she admitted, genuinely impressed.

'Why thank you, little girl. You have exceptional manners.'

'My granddad says it costs nothing to say please and thank you,' she informed the spider.

'Your granddad sounds like a very decent man.'

'Oh, he is. He fought in the Futilities,' she said.

'Did he really? The Futilities, how wonderful. I'm a veteran myself you know. Of course, for many, that war is best remembered as the *Fatalities*. Numerous souls perished when heaven and earth decided to knock ten shades of bodily seepage out of each other. The human won on a technicality no less, and one day the post-human will exact his *vengeance*.'

'But good will always conquer evil,' said Egg.

The spider laughed, scornfully. 'Good gracious me, no,' it said. 'Evil will always win, for it is *evil*. Only evil conceives the fates of men while *good*ness is what fights and dies. But there is nothing good about war besides its passing into history. Do you know, I think I'm going to enjoy chatting with you? You are probably one of the most delightfully loquacious guests I've had the pleasure of incarcerating.'

'Why did you try to kill me with your dragon then?'

'Old Scorcher is here to kill Sir Baluster the Bravado, not you. I was surprised to hear the yellow soldier slew her. Usually the fool runs away and she eats whoever's left behind, but I never for one moment planned for the dragon to eat you, little Egg.'

'Why is it meant to kill Sir Baluster?'

The spider said, 'Because Sir Baluster killed Om's brother, Orgo. That's his eternal punishment you see.'

'Wasn't Orgo a baddy?'

'As I say, I am a private enterprise geomancer, little one. It is not only enemies of the Plan I capture and bestow with a purgatory all of their own. Monsieur Fate instructed me no harm was to come to you. However, I have other benefactors who are not so *timid*, shall we say?'

'John Fate asked you to take me prisoner?'

'Indeed he did.'

'So my grandfather was right,' she surmised, 'he can't be trusted. So, does that make you a baddy too?'

De Zoet laughed again. 'Little Egg, there is no such thing as good and bad in my business, only commercial perspectives.'

'What does that mean?'

'It means where financial benefit is involved, there can be no such thing as a guilty conscience.'

'So, you would imprison anybody in your facsimile if they paid you enough money?'

The spider, if such a thing was at all possible, looked appalled. 'You have the gall to refer to my art as *facsimile*? My work is unique and far superior to the television sitcom sets those boffins and buffoons at Contingency Planning churn out like cardboard dolls houses. The Plan employs tin-pot scientists. *PIERRE DE ZOET IS AN ARTISTE*!'

'Actually,' said Egg, making herself laugh, 'You're a spider. What would happen if I squished you?'

'You'd go to a special hell for spider-killers.'

'If I'm in this room, in this house, which is all in your mind and you're just a spider, what would happen to me if I bashed you with a rolled-up newspaper?'

'You would be bashed too, obviously.'

'But I can't be in two places at once,' she reasoned, casting her eyes to a nearby table where there were piles of old newspapers. 'How can I be inside your mind if I'm out here looking at you?'

'But you're not looking at me; you're looking at those potential cudgels.'

Egg crossed the room, picked up a yellowing broadsheet and, rolling it into a tube, returned to the window.

'Little Egg, if you proceed with this ridiculous attempt to…'

She raised the rolled-up paper above her head.

'Don't do it, I'm warning…'

The newspaper came down swiftly.

'*MERDE*!'

When Egg lifted the rag there was a black smudge on the windowsill. She smiled, but then stopped when the building began to tremble, losing her footing and tumbling backwards into one of the mechanisms which fell to the floor and smashed. She looked down, surprised to see a representation of Hill House dash across the floor. When everything stopped rumbling and juddering and Egg lifted her gaze to the window again, instead of seeing a bizarrely coloured landscape stretched over the horizon there were just two huge jet-black eyes.

CHAPTER THIRTY
The Jubilant Hag

For obvious reasons, Wilhelmina Hippocampus disappeared from public life after Monte Cassino. She spent a year in Little Wallop, wallowing in her misery. During the course of those dismal twelve months, struggling with self-pity and shame and ownership of her sanity, she inhabited the half-life of a broken soul who simply bumbled from one grey mood to the next, gripped with grief and obsessed with her disgrace. The war trudged on without her and concluded in humanities favour and while the world celebrated that victory, Hippocampus found no solace.

Repatriation had done little to comfort her. The tiny hamlet she grew up in was populated by the same family and friends who cajoled her into joining Fate's paranormal cranks. If she had only trusted her instincts, declined the Captain's ill-fated offer of celebrity, whatever indignity they might thrust upon conscientious objectors would not have stung with the same ferocity as attaining abject failure. She had always known, in her heart of hearts, that she was incapable of the civil capacity to be a champion. She just didn't have the confidence. Her peers had argued to the contrary and insisted it would be a *wonderful opportunity* and she now realised their support had been self-serving, a profitmaking scheme for Little Wallop's uninspiring tourist industry which, in her estimation, laid the blame for all that went wrong at their doors.

The Harbingers survived the scandal, despite replacing her with an idiot like Hubert Dazzle who turned out to be one of Lord Crowberry's spies and whom, even in the maelstrom of her melancholy, Hippocampus observed to have less aptitude for paranormal pursuits than a conjurer at a child's birthday party. And later, when Darby Dodd was killed at the *Wolfs Lair*, the Harbingers reputation boosted in the wake of his sacrifice, the *Enchantress of Snakes*, Lady Valona Boon was recruited to replace him. Hippocampus saw it as a move to erase the stain of dishonour brought about by its former female participant. The aristo's engagement was a statement, a well-orchestrated publicity stunt by John Fate. In those days the public willingly trusted landed gentry and Boon was a blue-blooded filly, applauded by Plan superiors who normally poo-pooed the Captain's choices. Hippocampus had no blue blood. She was a blue-collar nag, a poster-girl for proletariats, a failed attempt to entice working-classes towards patriotism and the unachievable notion of *wonderful opportunities*.

Loathing grew on her like rot with every heroic exploit she heard on the wireless or read about in a newspaper until the media coverage of their adventures began to feel like personal taunts, barbed re-enactments directed at her as well as intended to whitewash the memory of Sidney Seabrook, the drippy journalist killed in action, the only member of the press entourage ever to take notice of her. Sidney had been forgotten about in the tumultuous public response to and aftereffects of what she did. In order to propagate a legacy he was denied his martyr status, elapsed by history while fantasists continued to make up stories about *The Pig* and *The Hag* and *The Russian*. And as the ethics of the world seemed to change, caring more about her ignominy and the ill-fated soldier who shot the poor journo than the poor journo himself, her ethics also changed. She and Sidney shared an injustice as headline-grabbing ink-hearts continued to hurtle after Risso and his associates and neglected to transcribe the truth about Monte Cassino. And so, in lieu of saving his life Hippocampus decided to keep his memory alive by verbally despising the nature of war and the voracity of men like John Fate as well as the egos of Harbingers and Seraph alike. Taking her story to Little Wallop's Member of Parliament, Clement Kerguelen, she would highlight the profound tragedy the Plan tried to flout.

And then she had a better idea.

It was a way of sending John Fate a message when she courted and later married Little Wallop's MP. Should the Captain be smart enough to translate it, it would have read *despite a year spent licking my wounds, I never surrendered entirely to misery or the sort of altered perceptions you did when it comes to who your enemies are.* She reinvented herself by adopting gentry, emulating the aristocratic star Fate effectively replaced her with, and for all intent and purpose hid in plain sight, biding her time, building an empire of sorts with which to afford a momentous riposte. And in his ignorance, or was it arrogance, Fate failed to notice her even when she was embedded in the lifeless husk of her joyless husband and manipulating the Tetrad and the Plan in turn.

The Captain never smelt a rat.

At certain times of the year, Todmorden was shrouded in an hour's more darkness than neighbouring municipalities. This was because of a high valley that loomed over the town, precluding moonlight. Its electricity supply was also feeble, having to traverse kilometres of countryside. The streetlamps were old and their frosted casings obscured by the joint accumulation of fly cadavers and fossilised bird faeces.

And so, glumness was common in the region.

William Spark possessed noble features: piercing blue eyes, sculpted cheekbones and a Romanesque slab of nose that impressed upon those who met him an image of refinement. But the moment he opened his mouth to speak he revealed himself a dullard.

'All right?' the balding man asked, adding a respectful nod as Hippocampus appeared before him on the cobbled street. Only moments ago, she had narrowly escaped Grace Plateau after John Fate's interference in her plans and so her communications with *The Real Salvation Army* had been brief, allowing very little detail or organisation. Bromberg had confirmed the necessary gimmick Hereward Nery had yielded to him and having paused just long enough to convey this information to Spark, and to momentarily marvel at her own ingenuity, she had travelled directly to the environment. Although there had been no time to assess the dangers or put in place a backup strategy, the witch was confident that all her years of clandestine preparation would win through in the end.

She looked down her nose at Spark. Yes he was a dunce, but he was a dunce that could be trusted, an ally to the cause, not only a loyal bodyguard but an accomplished and enthusiastic torturer as well as a first-rate sycophant; a more dependable tool than staunch companion. Hippocampus felt a quiet indulgence by having the man at her side, which was more than could be said for that much disputed fruit of her womb, her enduringly ailing and psychotic dunderhead of a child, Fletcher. If the midwives had switched babies on her in the maternity ward she would not have been at all surprised.

'This it then, is it?' Spark enquired, digging his hands in his trouser pockets and glancing around at the black stone buildings.

'This is the street, yes,' said Hippocampus remembering the locality from the remote security footage Fate had installed upon the child at her bequest. She trailed a withered hand through long tendrils of greying hair to remove it from her face as she stepped carefully over the cobbles, eyes flitting up and down the thoroughfare. The only sound in that vast glumness the *clip*, *clop* of her heels and Spark's limping gait on the stones. 'Fortunately, the gimmick worked,' she remarked with a smile.

Spark chuckled and replied, 'Dismembering the cat wasn't easy.'

Hippocampus came to a halt and gazed at the surly man; a breeze blew her lank mane across her face again. 'What are you talking about?'

He leaned in, conspiratorially. 'The bloody thing wouldn't sit still while I lopped its tail off.'

She rolled her eyes to the starless sky. 'The instruction was to *indulge a bystander with a genuine animal tale*, not to hand over a freshly severed limb. You were supposed to regale a stranger with a true story involving a worldly creature, Mr Spark.'

He chortled with delight in his own stupidity. 'So how come I still managed to gain entry?'

Hippocampus considered his query a moment and then enquired, 'Did you verbally express how you came about the flea-ridden appendage to a stranger?'

He nodded.

'Then destiny intervened,' she said, smiling again. 'It is a good omen. I have waited too long in the shadows to blunder at this late stage,' she announced, striding away with the lackey hobbling at her heels. 'After tonight there will be no more hiding. Gods and incarnates have had their wicked way with this world far too long. It is time a new administrator took office.' She spoke as much to fill the void with sound and verbalise her own excitement as to converse with the flunky.

'There's a new sherriff in town?' Spark offered.

Hippocampus laughed. 'Very good,' she said, impressed. 'Yes, a new sherriff in town. I rather like the sound of that.'

They walked further under the bleak canvas of sky. Eerie silence and opaque shadows swelled around them, amorphous objects made manifest by their imaginations. After they had traversed a good hundred metres or so and noticed no sign of life, no people, moving traffic or the sound of hooting owls or mewling cats, Hippocampus came to a stop again and Spark stumbled into her back. 'What is it boss?'

'I am certain this was the place,' she said, scrutinising the sight. 'I saw her there, by that tree.' She pointed across the road to the aged trunk Egg had hidden behind and then looked to where earlier she had witnessed Sally Cakes and her gang standing around a parked car. 'Fate's remote security footage on the child definitely showed this part of town. The Vessel was with several of her friends and when the little girl showed up…'

Tuneless whistling distracted them. They turned and watched a plump elderly lady, stooping with arthritis and the weight of heavy shopping bags, stagger across the street and enter one of the semi-detached bungalows nearby.

'Spark, I do hope you are up for a bit of excitement?' the glum witch enquired.

'Well, she's a bit old for my taste but…'

'I'm referring to your aptitude for violence.'

'Oh, you know me, always up for a bit of the old *wounding with intent.*'

They made their way across several lawns to the bungalow the old lady had entered. Hippocampus tried to see into the lobby through the frosted glass of the front door, but all was opaque. Wrenching on the handle she discovered it locked so gestured for Spark to intercede. Her assistant stepped up, brought his head back and then swiftly forward, smashing the windowpane with his forehead, then reached inside and unlocked the door. They went in, moving guardedly along the dark hallway until they found the OAP seated on a stand chair in the lounge, just a lumpy silhouette in the dusk, feet surrounded by bags of shopping. It was as if the senior citizen was waiting for them.

Spark found a light switch.

Hippocampus snorted a laugh when she recognised her old war buddy. 'My, you haven't changed a bit,' she said, approaching the hag. 'But then you always were a wrinkled old prune.'

'Takes one to know one,' replied Rose Thicket, sniffing and shifting her buttocks on the stand chair. 'You're too late. She's already gone. John had her shipped out about half an hour ago.'

'Well then,' Hippocampus said, stumbling angrily through her thoughts, 'you are rather unlucky because my friend, Mr Spark here, has a unique talent for bodily torment. It's said his mother had the most horrendous pregnancy and labour and that even the midwife lost two fingers during the birth.'

'Torture it is then,' agreed the elderly witch.

'You appear unruffled by my threat of violence, Rose,' the glum witch noted with suspicion, head hung low and grey locks dangling like vines before her face. 'Do you assume I will have him go easy on you for old time's sake?'

'Torture hasn't started yet,' the hag said. 'It might not be as bad as what you're making out.'

Spark appeared impressed. 'Rose Thicket, eh? You're quite a legend.' He turned to look at Hippocampus. 'Shall I tie her up, boss?'

When she nodded, Spark pulled a cord from a standard lamp and began wrapping it around the apparently helpless war veteran, tying her limbs to the stand chair. The Harbinger made no effort to oppose him and started whistling with a look of mild disappointment on her weathered face. She looked less like somebody concerned with imminent torture than she did somebody waiting for a bus even though Spark tied her arms so firmly the rope chafed her flesh.

Hippocampus leaned over the Harbinger and asked, 'Where did Fate send the vessel?'

'Somewhere you'll never find her,' Thicket replied.

'And where would that be?'

The Harbinger looked at Spark. 'Have you started yet?'

Jumping to attention, Spark snapped back one of her fingers and to the confusion of her aggressors, the old woman laughed.

'Tell me what I want to know and no further harm will come to you,' the anarchist leader warned. As she strolled back and forth Hippocampus carelessly swiped a hand over shelves and table tops until the living room carpet was festooned with broken porcelain birds and cracked family photographs.

'I told Fate first time I laid eyes on you, *loose cannon that one*, I said, *never be a team player.*' Thicket remarked. 'Plan should have dealt with you thirty years ago, love, would have preserved a lot of lives today if it had.'

Hippocampus harrumphed at the accusation. 'It wouldn't have preserved poor Sidney though, would it?'

The hag looked puzzled and asked, '*Sidney*?'

This only made the glum witch madder. 'Sidney Seabrook, the journalist Dodd killed at Monte Cassino.'

'Oh, you mean Frank.'

'*What*?'

'Terrible shame what happened to Frank. Frank Pickup his name was. Didn't you know, love? He was hired to make

317

googly eyes at you, so you'd feel special. I thought you knew. I thought that was what all this nonsense was about.'

The last thirty years of Hippocampus' life flashed before her eyes. It felt like confronting the incongruous and unspoken truth of a nightmare in reality. The very idea that John Fate continued to manipulate her, to change the rules of the game, even now in her ultimate moment of triumph, made her sick to the stomach and infected with such a level of malignant hatred that no extent of vengeful aggression could rectify her soul.

'*YOU'RE A LIAR!*' she screamed, frightening Spark. 'Sidney Seabrook had an elderly mum who lived on the coast. I corresponded with her till the day she died ten years ago. I wrote to her every week and she wrote back.'

'I'm sorry to break this to you, love, but it was probably some lass in John's typing pool wrote those letters. Sidney Seabrook never existed so his mother couldn't have existed. Frank Pickup was unmarried and an orphan, if that's any consolation.'

Hippocampus slapped the Harbinger across the face and then glared at Spark who took a moment to acknowledge what she wanted before snapping another finger. The old woman jumped up and down in her seat in delight and Spark sighed and scratched his head. All of his hard work seemed to be having none of its customary effect. 'Could you ask her to be a bit more professional, boss?'

Hippocampus grabbed Thicket by the face, moulding her flabby cheeks into doughy clefts. 'You're a liar and John Fate's a liar. This is a charade, a distraction technique, but it won't work. I'll just find something *you* love and kill it.' When Thicket glanced sideways, at the only remaining photograph

318

on the mantelpiece, a portrait of a young moustachioed soldier, Hippocampus released the witch's face and snatched it up. 'Do as I command and no harm will come to this devilishly handsome fellow.'

The old witch's hilarity abruptly ended. She calmed herself, looked at the sepia image and then at Spark and finally back at Hippocampus before a sniff burst the damn of her seriousness and she exploded with giggles again. 'That picture came with frame. *They all did.*'

'She's a bloody nutter,' said Spark. 'Maybe I should tell her a joke; use a bit of the old *reverse psychology*?'

'You're a seer,' Hippocampus suddenly remembered. 'You can see my future as it exists within your lifespan.'

Amidst an attack of maniacal giggles, a bout of physical hilarity that caused her chair to bang up and down on the floor, Thicket said, 'It's no skin off my nose. Give me your eyes.'

'*Give you my…?*'

'Come closer,' the Harbinger instructed, calming down, 'let me stare into those pickled eggs.'

Hippocampus did as she was told and, cautiously, leant forward feeling the witch's prying gaze stir the embers of her consciousness. 'You see me, don't you?' the glum witch enquired, excitedly, jealous of the fact she could not witness the same wonder and future glories the Harbinger saw. 'I am prominent am I not? I am as powerful as any queen. What am I doing? Am I sitting on a throne? Do I bedeck a stamp? I demand you tell me, *hag.*'

The Harbinger cackled and said, gloomily, 'With every reading of future events, curses serve as consequence.'

Spark bent back another finger, really cheering the old dear up. '*Stop tickling*,' Thicket pleaded, bobbing up and down with pleasure.

'It's no good,' said Spark. 'She just won't comply.'

'So what becomes of me?' Hippocampus nagged.

Thicket tried to regain her composure. 'I wish I could be of help, lass, I really do,' she said. 'I'd like nothing more than to give you good news. Visiting me in the wee small hours has been a real joy, but I'm afraid I looked into me future and all I could see was your boy. Fletcher Kerguelen will soon set sail. It's as certain as you are doomed to fail.'

'*Fletcher will set sail*? What the hell does that mean? And incidentally, is it really necessary to speak in rhyme?'

'Do you know what, you're quite right it isn't,' said Thicket. 'The rhymes were just a ruse while Plan erected this prison.'

'Stop doing that! It's disturbingly wholesome.'

'*Prison*?' asked Spark. 'What does she mean *prison*?'

'You were trapped the moment you walked in me door and now you'll stay here for evermore.'

Hippocampus looked about her, evaluating the validity of her environment. 'Check outside,' she commanded Spark who shuffled over to a set of flowery curtains and tugged them open.

'*Oh shit!*'

'What is it?' the glum witch asked, coming to join him at the window and observing quite a different setting than the rural, cobbled street she and Spark had traversed only minutes ago. Beyond Thicket's garden was a concrete courtyard decorated with various coloured geometric shapes demarcating demonically-sealed pathways as well as sports courts. These were cordoned off in places by rhombus-wire fencing and all in the shadow of a huge grey wall with barbed wire coiled along its summit. The wall was one of a quadrangle of brick and mortar structures no doubt running around the entire property. In each corner a watchtower extended ten feet above the wall, inhabited by a floodlight and armed Planners. As Hippocampus and Spark stood there, transfixed by the scene, one of the floodlights was turned in their direction and engulfed the room in blinding light, forcing them to protect their eyes from its probing luminosity.

Spark closed the curtains as Hippocampus rushed back to the bound witch and said, 'For years you showed John Fate what the future had in store, why not me?' She held Thicket's face in one claw-like hand again.

'Fate had a nice bum on him whereas you're a bit on the scrawny side, if you don't mind me saying so.'

When Spark arrived by the witch's side, he pulled a finger right off her hand and waved it in her face, but Thicket just roared with uncontainable merriment.

'Harbingers and incarnates aren't the only ones with magic tricks up their sleeves and I've refined my skills over the years,' Hippocampus announced, her eyes becoming black orbs. She bent over the hag and she seemed to fill the entire room with menacing shadow, an expanding gloom that sent Spark stumbling backwards in surprise and falling over a nest of tables to the ground. She inhaled sharply and the whole space began to buckle and crack with the force of being sucked towards her lungs, the disgraced Harbinger's jaw dislocating and growing to the size of a doorway. Spark could only look on as, kicking and screaming, yet all the while creased with cackling mirth, the Harbinger was completely consumed, chair and all, down the glum lady's gullet. A moment later everything returned to normal except for the Harbinger and the chair and the sound of Planners trying to knock down the front door.

Spark got to his feet. His boss looked exhausted, but smiled at him. 'I was not... in her future,' she said between gasps of breath, 'because... she did not have one. This is how we shall commence henceforth. This is how... we build... our *legacy.*'

'Yes, boss,' Spark replied and then silently gasped.

'What is it?'

He slowly raised a finger to point at her. The dignified lines of wisdom that once crossed the woman's aged flesh were suddenly wide and bright red gulleys delineated by fire. Her confident smile fell all the way to terror as burning pain ignited beneath her skin. Her jaw dropped open again, but this time spewing forth golden light that blinded more profoundly than any prison tower beam. Spark tumbled backwards for a second time, coming to rest against the wall as Hippocampus began to flounder, arms lashing about in panic until finally she froze, paralysed in the centre of the room.

And then boom!

The front door of the bungalow yielded to soldiers as Spark witnessed the transitory explosion of Wilhelmina Lucinda Hippocampus. And as the glum witch disintegrated entirely in front of his incredulous eyes, Rose Thicket returned to the land of the living, untarnished and wiping bits of murderer from her frock. The door of the lounge burst open and a dozen Planners rushed in pointing emp-rifles at the anarchist who sank to his knees, pleading for his life.

Still wiping bits of baddy off her, Thicket chuckled and gestured at the coward, saying, 'Book him, lads.'

CHAPTER THIRTY-ONE
Battle Bizarre

Nostrils flaring angrily, two flushed cheeks heaving with panic and eyes as wide as moons, Egg's gargantuan host appeared extraordinarily livid about what she had done to him. 'Little girls should not practise such malice!' de Zoet blurted out, frosting up the window while Egg hid the rolled-up newspaper behind her and gawked in fascination at the colossal visage outdoors; those black eyes bigger than beach balls and the Frenchman's slender pink nose resembling a playground slide hung over a cherry and waxen cemetery of a mouth. He appeared to be wearing a pair of gold pyjamas which lent him the illusion of a Las Vegas crooner.

'Are you big or am I small?'

'I would have thought that was patently obvious,' de Zoet snapped, continuing to seethe about his recent assault. 'Didn't your grandpa teach you that taking life is a sin? How would you feel if *I* was to swat *you* with a colossal issue of *Le Monde*?'

'I don't understand how you were in danger if it only happened in your mind,' Egg reasoned.

De Zoet guffawed at her effrontery. 'I can assure you, Pierre de Zoet was in no danger. My concern is only for the poor insect.'

'Spiders aren't insects,' Egg informed him, 'they're… *archaeologists*!'

'The *arachnid* was causing you no mischief, little Egg. It was so small and ineffective compared to you. Why would you squish it?'

'Because it was icky!' she exclaimed.

'I sense a cold heart beating in that infantile chest,' the Frenchman responded. 'You are not a *good* Egg, you are a devil.'

'If the spider was a figment of…?'

'*Not a figment!*' de Zoet barked, further insulted. 'My mind's eye generates the manifest. I am an *artiste* who paints in flesh and bone, not some O-level Morpheus only able to confuse and bewilder with psychological gibberish. You need to stop thinking this a dream, little one.'

'If you were still in that spider when I whacked it…?'

'The existential conventions of the Peculiar Palace are too complicated for a little girl to comprehend,' de Zoet expounded, breathlessly. 'But just for the record, you cannot possibly harm me. I am a divine spirit in this environment. There is nothing in this world, be it man or beast that has not come by way of my cerebral exertion. In these terms, *you* are no more substantial here than the spider, while I am a…'

De Zoet gasped when Egg disappeared, casting two massive, disbelieving black irises desperately about the room. 'Where did you go? You think you can hide from god?' And then he felt a tap on his shoulder. He gulped, resigning himself to what this implied and, sighing, peered behind him. His eyes expanded in their sockets with terror as he took in the sheer density and height of what was standing there. He had to look up and up and up to see her properly. Egg had become much more than a giant, she was almost cosmological.

She kicked him up the backside and briefly lifted him off the ground. '*How dare you molest me?*' he said.

Surrounded by the elegantly landscaped gardens and grounds Egg had observed from a corridor window earlier, the two of them now resembled mighty leviathans from a Japanese sci-fi movie. Tiny people and animals gathered around their ankles, astonished by the phenomenon.

Egg kicked him on the shin and he hopped on the spot, causing a localised earthquake and shaking the diminutive population off their feet. '*Stop it, you cruel viper!*'

'Only if you send me back to the hotel,' Egg demanded.

'You are my prisoner,' de Zoet reminded her. 'I shall do with you as I please. I have the permission of John Fate, as well as the *savoir-faire* of much gloomier individuals than he.'

Unimpressed by his declaration she kicked him on the shin again. 'What does that even mean?'

Ignoring his painful shinbone and playing pompously with the lapels of his gilded pyjama jacket, de Zoet smiled up at her and said, 'So-called do-gooders turn a blind eye to my arts just as eminent Lords of glum magic wish you equal bad fortune. The consensus is you are a burden to both sides of the eternal struggle. So you are here, under my jurisdiction. And though you may possess a little magic of your own, over the years I have collected many secrets and know a thing or two about a thing or two.' And with that de Zoet sucked in breath and his body began to transform. He grew outwards, muscles, veins and tendons expanding beyond natural dimensions like bubbling liquid oozing over a saucepan. His facial features altered also, mouth widening to reveal fangs, flesh turning scarlet, eyes and forehead bunching up in escalating creases and folds. His clothes tore from his body and fell like tickertape rags on the tiny population below. Dragon scales slithered from his skin while bony spikes poked out his spine and ivory studs protruded from his skull.

'*YOU GAMBLE WITH YOUR SOUL WHEN YOU PESTER PIERRE DE ZOET,*' the beast decreed in a voice not unlike the sound one makes talking into a steel bucket. '*I AM A CREATURE BORN FROM THE FIRES BENEATH THE KNOWN UNIVERSE AND ABETTED BY THE AVIGNON POPE, BERNADETTE XII, WHOSE ANCIENT DOMINION OF ALL LIVING AND DEAD THINGS IS A CRAFT SHE TAUGHT ME WELL!*'

Egg waited until he had finished both his transformation and boastful statement before pulling off a far superior metamorphosis by swelling up to three times the Frenchman's size and eight times more visually horrifying. When her transformation was complete she was not only the scariest monster the Peculiar Palace had ever seen but the most terrifying creature that had ever existed in any dimension or in any form of reality since the first sound in the Known Universe. Her skin tone did not alter hue but became armoured by glistening scales while her head bulged out of shape on the right side only and several eyes popped into existence, bloating with disproportion. Her gaping mouth revealed a cavern of stalactite and stalagmite fangs which protruded from putridly green gums. And as if her scary form was not bad enough, just as she reached the pinnacle of her transmutation, Egg exploded and became a cloud of gaunt black wasps that subsequently enveloped the Avignon geomancer with a thousand stings, causing a swift reversal of his mutation and the palace's inhabitants to run away screaming, seeking out hiding places from the swarm. The wasps eventually regrouped and reformed in the shape of an eight-year-old girl and she laughed at de Zoet's form, dressed in rags and presently scrabbling at dry earth with bare hands as if tunnelling his way to freedom.

Denizens of the palace emerged to surround them.

'I want to go back to the hotel.'

The geomancer sat swiftly up on bare knees. 'But of course,' he said with apparent compliance. 'I will see to it as soon as I defeat you with my unsurpassable knowledge of illogicality and farce.'

Egg rolled her eyes and asked, 'You and whose army?'

De Zoet climbed back to his feet and, wiping dirt from his hands said, 'Allow me to respond to that arrogant cliché with a less verbose deed.' And then he squinted into the distance and, when she followed his gaze, Egg was surprised to find the hulking palace and its citizens were now many kilometres away. She pouted with confusion as a sudden rush of activity occurred. Every door and window of the fantasy fortress seemed abruptly obscured by an exodus of brightly dressed individuals. Out they squeezed from each and every architectural orifice, to come sprinting over the landscape towards them, a constant flow of brightly uniformed soldiers rushing over the exotic lawns. The soldiers were dressed in much the same fashion as the one who slew Old Scorcher, only these uniforms were cherry red, lime green, sky blue and powder pink and they came swarming over the grounds, crashing through hedgerows and flowerbeds and splashing through ponds.

And then the west wing of the palace erupted in a billowing cloud of wood, stone and roof tiles as enormous black dragons emerged from the structure, finding purchase on the air and flying in the wake of the multi-coloured army.

Egg laughed with excitement, a sound de Zoet found both confusing and disappointing, so, attracting her attention with a tap on the shoulder, he nodded in the opposite direction and the child turned to see, far, far away, a black cloud winding through the sky. It resembled a huge swarm of insects or a lesser flock of migratory birds, but then Egg realised it was made up of biplanes and B52 bombers and even more dragons. The great beasts furiously flapped their enormous wings, pounding the ether as they soared between the large aircraft, a thousand things in the sky all at once.

'I have mined your deepest fears and brought them to life,' bragged de Zoet. 'You are afraid of war because Monsieur Fate will make a bomb out of you but you fear dragons by proxy. The dragon signifies death, but not your death. You are far too young to fear dying.'

Despite his recent failed confrontation, this new confidence in his efforts to defeat her had Egg slightly worried, but she continued to smile as she suggested, 'If these are horrors from my imagination then I can control them.'

'That would seem a logical conclusion,' de Zoet remarked with a knowing grin, 'if I had not brought something to infect said manifest fears with ferocious venom.' He brought a hand from behind his back and exhibited an ornate blue box. 'Do you know what this is?'

'Is it chocolates?'

Wicked relish made the black-eyed man grin as he removed the lid. A glum vapour wafted from the container and de Zoet sharply sniffed at it, sucking smoke up both nostrils.

'When Orgo the Posthumous fell,' he said, 'his fading contaminated the earth and created hell. This is what remains of his malignant energy. Incarnates call it *Gods Vein*.' He reached inside the box and retrieved a snaking cord of sickly red sinew. 'It is farmed in a locality known only by a few and with just one whiff of its toxins I am able to suffuse your worst nightmares with increased horror. With one draught of this malevolent haze you will not only be my prisoner, but become my slave. How do you imagine I was able to disarm your predecessor, Monsieur Kumar?'

Egg gasped. 'What did you do to him?'

De Zoet glanced towards both approaching armies before returning to his monologue. 'I merely introduced him to the *Heavenly Joys* of eternal slumber,' he told her with delight. 'I amalgamated his glum soul with my magic kingdom, as I am about to do to you.'

The ancient lump of tissue twisted and trembled in the geomancer's hand, its effervescent vapours bursting and dancing in his palm. And then it defined itself with shape, transforming into a gruesome looking imp with red and wiry flesh, fierce eyes and a mouthful of yellow needles for teeth.

Egg reached over and tickled it under the chin and the imp swooned and fell over. 'What have you done to my ghoul?' de

Zoet asked, looking cross. 'Why do you continue to be so chirpy and uncooperative in my plans? You are turning out to be the most exasperating lodger I ever allowed through my doors. At this particular juncture, most little girls would be screaming and begging me not to let the monster eat them, not befriending the frightful beast. When a god of fathomless glum magic knowledge presents you with a ligament from Orgo the Posthumous you should show a bit of respect.'

'I'm not frightened of a monkey,' Egg said.

De Zoet coughed on incredulous laughter. 'What have monkeys got to…?' He stopped talking and looked at the grisly creature in his palm which had transformed into a chimpanzee. It was still oily red in texture, but definitely a primate. A black tongue slithered across the critter's top lip. De Zoet sighed and shook the ape to the ground and the animal responded by leaping at his ankle and biting him. The Frenchman danced a jig with the ape firmly attached to his leg until Egg came to his rescue, bending and scooping him up, cradling the creature in her arms like a baby.

Limping back and forth and moaning in pain, de Zoet swore in French then he sat in the grass glaring at her. 'I hate you,' he said.

'That's not a nice thing to say, is it, Kevin?'

'*Kevin*?'

The monkey made a respondent monkey sound and de Zoet rolled his eyes and shook his head.

Egg stroked the ape until it fell asleep. A moment later it vanished entirely. She turned to look at the advancing army and dragons that had emerged from the dilapidated house and flapped a hand in their direction. Their colours and physical casings, everything that made the creatures logical, vanished until all that was left was a sea of grey, skeletal beasts. And then she turned to hell's flying fiends and with a similar gesture brought their glum colours and images to the surface.

'So you have changed their hue? It is still *I* who commands them!' de Zoet commented, sounding only half as confident as he had earlier.

Egg clicked her fingers and became an exact replica of the Frenchman causing her opponent's haughty features to sag with desperation. He stopped caressing his monkey bitten ankle, got to his feet and looked at the oncoming hordes in panic. Then he relaxed and, laughing, looked at the pretend him. 'I am no less myself for this conceit,' he told her. 'They will know instinctively which of us commands them. You will just have to stand and fight, little Egg.'

Amused by the inevitable situation, the geomancer moved to a position of safety and settled on a grassy mound where he was determined not to be trampled by the advancing throngs. He looked at the approaching military horde and squinted with curiosity, forehead furrowed. 'That's curious,' he commented, turning towards the other him, 'there appears to be somebody riding one of the...' His voice petered out when he found himself alone.

Egg clung to the dragon's grey scales with the very tips of her fingers and giggled with excitement as she bounced up and down on its rearing spine. '*CHARGE*!' she called out and the immense troop of foot and dragon sprinted, scuttled and soared faster over the plain. She spotted de Zoet equal distance between both fantastic armies and, foreseeing a terrible mess when the two collided, imagined the extraordinary heap of broken dragons and soldiers with a squashed Pierre de Zoet at the very bottom of the pile.

But then both of the large infantries as well as every aircraft and mythical lizard the French geomancer had conjured up suddenly popped out of existence with the sound of a thousand bursting balloons and Egg shrieked with joy as she was propelled forward, striking the ground and rolling over and over in the dirt, eventually stopping with an athletic spring to her feet. She whooped with delight, looking round for the Frenchman and feeling a bit silly to be standing alone in the middle of nowhere in her pyjamas.

Acknowledging that her cowardly rival had either run off or was hiding somewhere, Egg decided the best thing to do was to return to the palace. Briefly impressed by its breath-taking contours on the hazy horizon she contemplated restoring it, now that she had doubtlessly conquered the environment, and turning the dwelling into a holiday home for her and her grandfather, but then quickly erased that idea from her thoughts, reasoning that her grandfather would hate the place. The Peculiar Palace was far too absurd a location for the King's sensible tastes.

After walking through the pounding heat for quite some time, dazzled by the sun's sparkling rays, Egg realised the turreted bastion seemed to be moving away from her. Huffing with exhaustion, she peered up at the buttery orb in the sky and noticed indistinct shadows shimmer over its curved surface and she laughed when she realised where she was. After taking a moment to consider her options which were either to melt under that heat or use her magic to escape, she chose the latter, crouched with one knee on the ground, eyes remaining fixed on that brilliant curve of sunlit heaven and felt the muscles in her legs tighten and the dusty earth beneath her tremble and sag as it formed a deep crater, drawing her down into it. She instructed the earth to rapidly regain its shape and, like a stone from a catapult, was boosted into the air. A frosty wind sucked at her cheeks and clothes and she grew colder the higher she went until the whites of the bright sky transformed into milky creams and pinks and became penetrated by more defined shapes: massive skewed images that floated in the atmosphere resembling framed portraits and book shelves, curtains and desk-lamps and various sticks of furniture bent all out of perspective by an inflected force-field of glass.

*****

Egg burst from the automata, bounced off the ceiling and fell onto a table, demolishing it and yet another of de Zoet's magnificent machines (a mechanism exhibiting the gyrating image of a man being carried through the sky by a witch). She crashed to the carpet and rolled onto her back and looked up to see an Egg-shaped imprint in the plaster above.

She started to laugh.

The door flung open and the three storks rushed inside, one of them exclaiming, '*What the hell…?*' as he assessed the situation, which, even by the typical standards of everyday events in the Peculiar Palace must have struck him as odd. 'Where's the boss?' he asked when he spotted Egg lying in the dust.

'He's hiding behind the curtain,' she giggled, climbing to her feet and brushing down her clothes.

All the storks stood immediately to attention when they saw the drape shaking and noticed a pair of bare feet poking out the bottom. 'What would you have us do with the sprog, boss?'

There was no response.

'Boss, it's me, Squirrel. Should I lock her in the dungeon?'

Eventually, de Zoet's frazzled features peeped from behind the gaudy material and, smiling nervously, ignoring the presence of the child, he said, 'Yes, if it's not too much trouble, Squirrel.'

'No trouble at all, boss. Right, you're coming with...' When the Squirrel tried to step forward he found himself unable to move, as if he was frozen to the spot. 'That's weird,' he said, 'it's like I'm frozen to the spot.'

Egg went to the curtain, dragged it off the geomancer, snatched the ornate blue box from his sweating palms and instructed him to, 'Tell them to show me the way out.'

'Yes. Of course, that's another option,' de Zoet realised, pulling the curtain back around him. 'Guards, could you show her the way out?'

Squirrel looked confused and asked, '*The way out*?' He glanced at his brothers in arms and then, with a chuckle, back at his cowering employer. 'But boss, she's still breathing. She's still got all her arms and legs. Aren't you going to pull something off her before she goes?'

'No,' de Zoet said with a nervous smile. 'That won't be necessary.'

Egg smiled proudly as the storks exchanged confused glances and then Squirrel looked at de Zoet again. 'Is this a good time to ask for a raise, boss?'

Pierre de Zoet slowly shook his head.

CHAPTER THIRTY-TWO
The Desolation Islands

They all felt it, a piercing internal bite of cold as the EGD Ladder cast them unto a rocky outlet amidst sprawling white palatial scenery. And when that Antarctic sting bit, Sergeant Grey was grateful for every extra layer of clothing that had caused him and his men to sweat profusely back in the hangar on Grace Plateau. And just as abrupt and disturbing as that severe cold was the utter silence and the incessant stillness that pervaded the province, an extreme lack of stimulus that was known to send people crazy. The glacial continent was the least populated environment on earth and equally renowned for being the bleakest. Beauty existed here; the ice-shelves were spectacular, resembling colossal ocean liners set against pure blue waters, but the monochrome monotony, the landscape's sterility and solitude proved too intimidating for most.

A curtain of frost blew off a nearby crag, a vertical flurry of tumbling rime that provoked Grey and his men to raise their weapons and send their hearts and minds racing as they ensured their safety with cautionary glances at seemingly harmless sections of the elevated environment, the rugged cliffs and stony outcrops which reminded Grey of the cavity strewn veneer of old men's teeth. He was almost blinded by the bright sun and turned away to gauge the faces of each proficient squaddie that had accompanied him. Ten good men the Captain had said and Grey had rounded up ten comrades-at-arms he would be proud to have by his side in any combat situation. There was not a veteran amongst them. They were a young and tough taskforce, a small detail of battle-acclimatized warriors who had seen action in the underworld as well as numerous alternative realities, skilled and resilient soldiers he trusted implicitly. A couple were even well-suited to the wintry environment, glacial-honed commandos who had fought their fair share of polar beasts, from bears to tigers, chimera to yetis, kappas and kelpies. The others, respectable First and Second Bliss Company operatives, soldiers with whom Grey had spent the last seventeen years enduring skirmishes along the borders of hell.

Grey signalled for them to move off in three groups of three, extending the radius of their search. The coordinates Bromberg had utilised had been adjusted slightly so Grey's team did not arrive in the exact same location, for fear of ambush. They had arrived half a kilometre west of the spot, on a flatland of flint grey rock encroached by sheets of bone-chilling snow. After the three *Alpha Teams* moved out, Grey was left with Private Tippet and the two men advanced vigilantly through the desolate country, scouring the infertile region with the barrels of their emp-rifles.

'Sergeant Grey, sir,' Tippet whispered, his breath drifting out in front of him to disperse in the merciless air, 'is Fletcher Kerguelen behind the attack on Grace Plateau?'

Grey glanced at the man as he stepped cautiously through the Om-forsaken zone, rifle constantly held at eye level, and asked, 'Who told you that?'

'I overheard the Captain talking to the dead witch in the council chambers,' Tippet replied. 'It was the disgraced Harbinger killed the Tetrad and she and her son have links with the Real Salvation Army.'

'All I know is that Bromberg is a traitor and he's hiding out on this frozen rock. The Lieutenant is our objective.'

'Yes, sir,' said Tippet.

They hiked through sub-zero temperatures as a blizzard blew off the mountain peaks. The crisp snow was deeper in places and consequently more treacherous and as a frost fell softly around them, impairing their vision, they had to become more vigilant about hidden alcoves or sharp, ice-moulded rocks that might cause severe injuries should they wander off path.

Grey remembered the winters of his childhood, the cold that numbed his fingers when he made snowmen in his parent's garden and the lopsided, half-completed igloos he and his brother would erect. Snow was a luxury to children, an excuse for a day off school and the only seasonal upshot offering free entertainment, it also arrived at a time of year when kids bubbled with excitement about impending celebrations; an additional pleasantry to the season of magic and toys and delicious foodstuff. But the snow that fell here was of an entirely different species. On the Desolation Islands the cold didn't just numb a careless man's fingers and toes, it snapped them off. It didn't simply chill a chest, it froze all the sap inside.

After about twenty minutes spent trudging through the imbibing landscape the radio on Grey's shoulder hissed and vibrated against his collar bone. He released one hand from his rifle to operate the transmitter. 'Alpha leader responding, go ahead.'

'Alpha six calling alpha leader, we've located a structure about a klick west from our arrival point. It looks like some sort of drilling platform.'

'Alpha leader to alpha six, sit tight and observe. All alpha teams make their way to Alpha six's location.'

Grey and Tippet set off at a brisk pace in the direction their comrades had taken, frosty wind stinging their faces as they hiked through deepening snow, a ghoulish squall whistling through the stalwart cliffs above. A few minutes was all it took to reach Alpha six's position and Grey and Tippet joined them on their chests against a natural snowbank overlooking a deep gorge in the terrain where a hundred-metre-high steel platform was erected. A huge steel piston had been driven deep into the floor of the chasm. Grey lifted a pair of binoculars to his face and surveyed the worksite, moving from worker to worker, recognising half a dozen men before he found Bromberg on a steel gantry beside a man holding a clipboard. Bromberg was pointing at something and Grey followed the direction of the Lieutenant's arm. And what he saw astonished him. Ascending slowly and hauntingly from a large shaft gouged in the ice, dangling on the end of a winch, was the insentient body of a woman. She twisted eerily on her towline, her coffee-coloured skin glistening under the worksite lamps, as she was hoisted over the heads of the traitorous Planners, arms and legs hanging limply and long black hair obscuring much of her upper body.

Grey dropped the binoculars and turned to provide his companions with a look of confused terror.

'What is it, sir? What did you see?'

He shook his head in disbelief, glancing at each man before speaking. 'That's how they hid her,' he said, making no sense. He gripped the arm of the soldier to his right and, staring intently at him, said, 'She was buried where her brother fell so that her spirit left no trace.'

'Sir, who do you mean?'

Grey gulped and said, 'Om! I'm talking about Om!'

The Alphas exchanged surprised looks and then Private Tippet asked, 'What are our orders, sir?'

As another of Grey's Alpha teams arrived at the location, the three men tramping swiftly through the snow and joining them at the hummock, he sniffed the cold air and tried to deal with what he had just witnessed. He had a decision to make. There appeared to be between twenty-five and thirty heavily armed Planners manning the machinery below and if rumours were true and Fletcher Kerguelen was also down there with members of his anarchist group, Grey's team would require backup.

'Get a message to the Captain,' the Sergeant ordered, suddenly pulling himself together. 'Give him these coordinates and inform him we need at least another ten men.'

The soldier got onto his radio immediately as Grey turned to the newly arrived Alpha team. 'You three circle round as far east as you can and wait for my instructions.'

The men automatically set off through deep snow as Grey put his hand to his radio. 'Alpha two team do you copy? This is Alpha leader… Alpha two team, come in.'

There was a buzz of static and then a chillingly playful voice came over the radio. 'Well hello, Alpha leader, how nice of you to join us on this brisk summer's eve. You'll find the climate rather inconsiderate down here on the islands but even *you* have to admit, this place is one of nature's true marvels. My buddies and I just stumbled across three of your chums cowering out here in the cold. I think I'll take them hostage in the likelihood of…'

Grey gasped when he heard the sound of a gunshot over the radio and its replicated resonance from a couple of klicks away. Laughter came over the airwaves. 'Drat, I didn't *mean* to shoot him,' the voice announced. 'My mother will have my hide for that one; you know what parents are like! It's these chunky gloves, I just can't seem to control my index finger on the…'

There was another gunshot both over the radio and from afar. 'Oh dear, that was rather clumsy of me. I've gone and killed two of your Alphas, Alpha leader. I can be such a maladroit fool sometimes. Let's hope I'm dexterous enough not to inadvertently…'

Bang. Bang.

CHAPTER THIRTY-THREE
Queen Egg

Celebrations were getting underway as Egg returned to the atrium. Confetti rained down on hundreds of dancing and cheering people and trumpets crammed the air with triumphant blasts of abrasive sound as the storks led her past the dead dragon and, she was very relieved to see, the yellow soldier, who was alive and well and posing for photographs beside the stricken beast. She wanted to congratulate him too but so many people flocked around him it was impossible. Instead, she followed the storks through the crowd, down the gold and marble staircase where an assortment of mythical characters chanted noisily, warriors and monsters of all creeds, colour and cosmic persuasion, waving swords, spears and streamers. A few giants had been employed as climbing frames for the shorter spectators to scramble up and get a better view of events. People were already selling newspapers with the headline *DE ZOET DEFEATED BY LITTLE GIRL*! Baluster the Bravado was being carried around on the shoulders of a large, elephant-headed man, the Knight limply wafting a hand under his chin as though curdling the air, the joyful mob misdirecting their gratitude towards him for old Scorcher's downfall.

When a hand grabbed her arm and almost dislodged de Zoet's ornate blue box, she whisked around to come face to face with Davis, one of the men in ill-fitting tuxedos, complete with scary teeth and cannibalistic menace. He glared at her, terrified, but with the hint of a sneer as he licked his lips and began to grovel. 'Forgive me, Your Grace,' he said. 'I had no intention of nibbling on your dainty pink fingers and toes or gnawing your chewy cartilage or sucking the savoury marrow from your skeleton. I am rarely mistaken for a herbivore it is true, but had I known you were our impending Queen, I would never have proposed eating you. Not that I ever have tasted human flesh, you understand. I have no latent impression of the texture of an eyeball popping on the gums or the lingering sensation of blood spurting from an aorta. Be assured, these are alien paradigms to me.'

Another grasping hand turned her round. This time she came face to face with Red. 'My, what a lovely blouse you're wearing,' he said, smiling falsely, shivering and sweating profusely. 'I don't think we've been formerly introduced. I'm Red, multifaceted poet, author and champion of small fries and underdogs.'

'*Ooh, fried underdog*,' Davis slavered over her shoulder.

'I was wondering if, now you're leaving, you might require an assistant, a PA or subordinate of some kind. Somebody to…' he glanced at the object under her arm, 'carry your luggage? You *are* leaving, aren't you? We haven't known each other long I know, but in that short while I feel like a bond has grown between us, that we've been through a lot together and the experience has made us brilliant friends. Could you possibly find it in your heart to take me with you, Your Majesty? I'll be your personal slave forever and ever and…'

'I bet she doesn't even remember who you are,' groaned Grimes, just as Sweet appeared and asked, 'Do you want to see some magic?' and, before Egg could respond, produced a hammer and whacked himself on the head with it, collapsing and sliding down the steps.

'Out of the way, *peasants*!' announced one of the storks and people all around the lobby turned to look. They knew instinctively a bigwig was approaching when storks demanded breathing space so distastefully. And then the celebration quieted until the only sound in that great span of reflections, dripping jewels and glitz was the occasional sniff or mucus cough. And then suddenly, everyone inhabiting the atrium bent the knee to their new Queen.

'I'm not really a Queen,' Egg told the stork next to her.

Leaning in close and whispering out the side of its beak, the stork said, '*Just milk it, love!*'

A little boy emerged from the sea of bowed heads. He was covered in muck and bruises, was wearing rags and walked with a limp. 'Is it true,' he asked, 'is the Frenchman defeated?'

Egg smiled, glancing momentarily at the stork who decided to ignore her and then back at the boy, nodding her head. 'Yes,' she said, 'he was no match for the mighty Egg.'

'The mighty who?' asked the boy, curling a lip in confusion.

'Me,' she said. 'I'm Egg.'

'Oh,' he replied as somebody called out, *hooray for Queen Egg* and the cheer was taken up by all in the lobby except a few storks and, of course, Sweet lying comatose at the bottom of the stairway.

As the populace rose from its knees and began to flock round her, Egg asked one of the storks, 'Where's the way out?'

'The what?' the stork replied as she was hoisted onto euphoric shoulders.

'*The way out*,' she said again.

'I don't recall there ever being one,' the stork informed her, turning to confer with one of his colleagues. 'Vole, do you remember the Peculiar Palace ever having a way out?'

As she was swept away on a wave of excitement Egg heard the stork called Vole say, 'There isn't one. Never was. What would be the point of having a way out? A way out is a way in. And the last thing an impenetrable fortress needs…'

And that was the last of their conversation she was privy to as the crowd surged and she was carried away on the shoulders of the populace.

As she passed Baluster the Bravado astride the wide neck of the man with the elephant head the Knight tried to high-five her, calling out, 'I killed the dragon.'

'*I beg to differ*,' she said, under her breath.

Travelling by shoulder up and down the atrium, Egg began to consider the possibility of being trapped forever. It was one thing to steal the Peculiar Palace from under the Frenchman's nose but quite another to reign in his absence, and besides, there had been a dreamlike quality to battling de Zoet and all one had to do in a dream was summon rainfall and puppy dogs where the subconscious offered fire and werewolves, but what if she was expected to conjure up original magic the next time something dangerous happened? She was uncertain if she had the capacity to produce magic out of thin air and had, so far, relied upon pilfering her opponent's powers and turning them to her advantage. It was easy to plagiarise and expand upon de Zoet's monstrous metamorphosis and she found nothing difficult about turning his Gods Vein homunculus into a monkey. She had even exploited one of his mechanical dioramas to travel back into the palace, but could she craft her own, unique glum arts, bespoke enchantments and specific illusions in order to fight other foes? Could she, for instance, beget an exit out of this exotic prison?

If she couldn't then she had to admit that the Peculiar Palace wasn't the worst place in the Known Universe to live, not if she really was its Queen. It might actually prove an entertaining existence governing a population of strange and bizarre people and creatures.

She tried, by majestic decree, to mentally summon an exit into shape, casting her eyes about for a peculiar peculiarity, at the mirrored perimeter walls where a thousand reflections glimmered with shades of silver and gold and the gem-encrusted ceiling where looping vines of jewels sparkled high above the lobby, but nothing denoting a way out caught her eye. The only noteworthy occurrence was that the sum of people who had initially raised her up had diminished from a clumsy horde to a group of three and then, briefly distracted by the sound of trumpets, she looked back to find only one person beneath her: a man with long, brown curly hair giving her a donkey ride. They were moving swiftly towards one of the reflective walls and Egg saw their mirrored representations approaching fast and watched with wonder and excitement as the other little girl opened her mouth wide and screamed.

CHAPTER THIRTY-FOUR
Azzarello Risso

Leontine Pryderi dropped her cargo and watched it tumble over the damp grass, rolling and bouncing clumsily off imbedded stones and other earthly protuberances, chafing elbows and knees until it came to rest, face down, in a clutch of ferns, arms and legs comically spread-eagled while she settled effortlessly a few metres away.

It had finally stopped raining but the fields and farmland surrounding them, what was visible of it anyway, sparkled where the light of the moon shone on damp surfaces.

The witch cast her eyes down at the inert body on the ground. 'Do you know where you are?'

When Pierpot didn't respond she leapt across the saturated mire, landing beside him. She placed a hand on the back of his head and cruelly pressed his face deeper into the earth until he began to cough and splutter and struggled to upend himself, waving his arms about. Eventually she stopped and stepped away allowing him to drag himself free. A sturdy breeze combed the hill, whipping Pierpot's clothes about him as he sat up. Tendrils of hair danced over his pink dome of a head.

He removed his skewed spectacles and attempted to straighten and clean them.

'This is Edgeworth Moors,' Pryderi said, staring out over invisible meadows and fells towards blinking urban lights in the distance. 'I have reason to believe you know absolutely nothing about my sister, but we shall soon discover the truth. I have brought you here for the purpose of inquisition.'

Pierpot replaced his specs and located the witch's position through two smudged lenses. He shook his head to rid it of the whistling ache that accompanied being carried over a hundred kilometres at high altitude in the talons of a witch.

'Edgeworth Moors? Isn't that...?'

'Where the Harbinger, Azzarello Risso is entombed, yes.'

The wind howled as it passed through and over ancient stones that littered the site, the remains of primordial dwellings and ancient markers only glum magic knew how to translate. Of course some vestiges were not so arcane. After the Futilities, when the Harbingers were officially disbanded, Thicket, Nabokov and Boon continued to work for the Plan in one fashion or another while Azzarello Risso chose self-exile, entombing himself in the earth beneath a large natural monolith.

Pierpot scanned their location, rendered barely discernible since the sun went down, but eventually he spotted the rectangle of rock.

'Risso was a loyal soldier,' the ex-Planner stated. 'He was devoted to the survival of humanity and fought for the Contingency Plan. I have nothing to fear from him.'

Pryderi approached the hill beneath the headstone. She closed her eyes and began to mumble incantations under her breath. A moment later the mound of earth and grass began to tremble. By the time she opened her eyes stones were rumbling to the surface like self-excavating minerals, popping out the ground and tumbling down the hill, the entire mound turning itself over. A whole section of ground became inverted, dry soil and sand, worms and beetles spewing forth from the organic wound she had inflicted upon the knoll. Her glum magic continued to churn up the area until a filthy pink dome followed by two hefty shoulders swathed in grubby orange rags came into view. The creature born of the embankment plummeted head first, performing a full forward roll to the base of the hummock and Pryderi backed up a couple of steps as it came to rest where she had been standing, two solid legs sprawled out, upper torso hunkered over and, for a long moment, remaining inanimate, but then slowly, painfully, the pig lifted his head.

Pierpot had never met the man, but recognised Risso's famous ungulate features instantly.

The witch stepped into shadow, unnerved by the sacrilege of renting a creature from its tomb, and watched as he shook his big head and squinted through raw and weary eyes, blinded by moonlight, at the man directly in front of him. 'What's the meaning of this interruption?'

'Mr Risso,' Pierpot spoke out in panic, 'you have to help me. I've...'

Pryderi was suddenly behind him with a hand over his mouth.

The pig coughed up earth and worms. 'Who are you?'

'It is I who released you from your tomb, Azzarello Risso,' the witch said, knowing full well that the Harbinger would sense lies, no matter how long it had existed in the earth, and so was ready to communicate only truth, or at least a broad version of it. 'I bring this prisoner before you, a man who betrayed the Contingency Plan and collaborated in the conception of a demon child with an incarnate witch. I need you to open up his mind to me!'

'Do we have to do this now?'

'There is no time for questions,' the witch urged, frantically. 'The safety of the Known Universe is at stake. This prisoner is a fugitive of hell. Open his mind.'

There was a moment of silence as the pig sat quietly giving the impression of not having understood the task he had been set. Pierpot hoped beyond hope Risso did not believe a word of the witch's blether despite its construed validity.

And then the pig coughed up soil and spoke his truth hex. '*Kepolomitakinastic*!'

With an inadvertent gasp, Pierpot sat up straight and stared directly ahead. Inside he prepared for resistance.

'Tell me about my sister,' Pryderi demanded.

'*Your uncle had a man brought to the Black House and tortured*,' his mouth said, surprising him. Pierpot tried to recall all of the pointless facts he had forced himself to learn to usurp top secret disclosures. '*This was before the end of the Futilities*,' he continued unintentionally, '*a long time before I served the General, but the Black House staff told tales about the sisters who tread separate paths, the traitor and the champion. They said that by the time General Galbi finished with Karl Buhrmann all that was left was a mouth, but he still refused to betray his beloved.*'

'And you heard this *gossip* from your dungeon deep beneath the Black House?' the witch asked, sceptically.

'*The General employed me as his librarian,*' he said, pushing his spectacles up the bridge of his nose and, based on this physical gesture as well as the tweed he wore, Pryderi laughed as if to suggest this was obvious '*I earwigged many of his private conversations. Felix Buhrmann worked on a smallholding the General kept in Leipzig. That's where he and Biel met. They ran away to Olsztyn in Prussia, seventy-four kilometres north-west of the Wolf's Lair!*'

'And does my sister still reside there?'

Pierpot felt relieved as a sliver of resistance slithered up his spine, a sign that Risso's curse was starting to fade, but heard himself saying, '*She became a turn-harp during the war and was taken prisoner when the Futilities ended. All trace of her was subsequently... subsequently...*'

The witch realised Risso's spell was waning and so decided to take full advantage of what remained of it in the librarian's skull. 'Tell me what you know about Egg. Is she Chaos Likely?'

Morecambe Pierpot looked petrified now as his limbs stiffened and face turned purple under the pressure. The Harbinger's curse left him feeling violated having unlocked every cerebral door against his will. Telling Pryderi what he knew of her sister hardly seemed damning but divulging information about Egg?

'Egg is... is...'

'Yes?'

'Is… is… *the onion, the most broadly used vegetable in the Known Universe. Tomatoes and potatoes are grown in the largest measure, but it is the onion…*'

Pryderi slapped him hard across the face, staring at the ridiculous man with frustration. '*Is she Chaos Likely?*'

'She is… *apple pips contain cyanide.*'

'*IS SHE CHAOS LIKELY?*'

'Chaos… Chaos… *there are no black flower blossoms in nature, the ones that look black are actually dark shades of purple.*'

Light suddenly swept the hillside as if day had arrived sooner than expected. Risso fell to the ground, screaming in agony, covering his delicate eyes with an arm. On seeing a number of figures silhouetted on the crest of the hill the witch became airborne again, Pierpot's lapel firmly grasped in one fist. She ascended at breakneck speed to such a height the illuminations around the opened tomb soon became no more interesting than the streetlamps of distant towns.

The air grew colder the higher they went and Pierpot clenched his fingers into fists as he realised the digits were threatening to freeze solid. He watched the moon grow so big he wondered if she was taking him there, mentally noting that the witch might be able to survive on the lunar surface, but he certainly couldn't.

It occurred to him, in regions of his mind now unimpaired by the Harbinger's truth spell, that Pryderi would surely know a way around his Plan-induced defence mechanism and that, one way or another, she would discover the only detail he did know about Egg, that she was the daughter of Chaos Likely. The next bout of interrogation might, or might not, include torture, but would certainly result in his death. He had never been a brave man, but he liked to think not even he would put an eight-year-old's life in danger. Pierpot slipped both arms from his jacket sleeves and, to his horror, fell much faster than he had risen, much faster than he had plummeted towards that street back in Manchester when the King saved his life. But no selfless companion was about to save him this time. In a moment he would impact with the earth and that would be it. He fell like the Seraph fell in the old tales, only their descent had brought, albeit glum, mystery to the Known Universe, whereas his would bring only a large crater in the Lancashire countryside.

DESIRE SANCTUARY AND IT WILL BE PERMITTED, a jolly voice bellowed inside his head.

Two hundred feet below, John Fate and a team of Witch-Finding Planners gasped at a haunting sound they first mistook for the blustery wind blasting that high region, but there was no denying what they actually heard; it was a human voice screaming, '*DRAG ME TO HELL*!'

CHAPTER THIRTY-FIVE
The Rescuer

It felt nothing like she imagined crashing through glass would feel, they simply passed through the mirror as if it didn't exist and emerged into pitch black on the other side. To Egg's horror, the man continued to move at no less a pace, though there appeared to be no ground to run upon and no obvious point of direction. And when she looked over her shoulder at the illuminated rectangle of atrium behind, she witnessed the gap grow smaller and repair itself.

'Am I being kidnapped?' she enquired, receiving no response and contemplating digging her heels into the man's chest to register complaint, a thought which was quickly replaced by an overriding air of wellbeing. Despite her circumstances, or perhaps because of them, she sensed no danger.

The gloom continued to breeze by, the only sound the hectic slapping of the man's feet on a concealed floor and the frantic bellows of his lungs.

After a long time passed, the urgency to escape and strength of her bearer began to wane and he stumbled to a clumsy stop, almost dropping her. He lifted her down and stretched his spine and limbs and attempted to replenish his store of oxygen with deep breaths. Egg could only just make him out in the dim light but recognised her rescuer immediately. It was his long dark hair and rugged, bristly features that gave him away. She had seen him earlier, in the Unfastened Room. 'You're Ashok Kumar,' she observed.

He was studying the concealed path they had travelled, inspecting it for signs of pursuit. Then he turned and placed a kind hand on her head and asked, 'You okay?' The place where they were, behind the mirror, in some hinterland between the Peculiar Palace and reality, didn't seem quite so gloomy now, as though an invisible sunrise delineated the space, though the space appeared no less a void for all its brightening up. And then Ashok Kumar smiled, sadly and said, 'This must be very confusing for you.'

Egg giggled and replied, 'Not really, this whole day's been full of weird goings-on.'

He crouched in front of her, looking very serious. 'Aren't you wondering why people called you *Queen* Egg?'

She briefly glanced the way they had come and when she looked at him again, stared into his deep brown eyes and nodded her head. 'Yes,' she said, 'I suppose I am a bit.' She felt giddy about meeting her father while at the same time felt something squishy in her belly, a sense of foreboding. Why *had* they called her Queen Egg? She was no Queen. Her grandfather was sort of a King but that did not necessarily mean…

'Has something happened to my grandfather?'

Kumar nodded. 'He's dead,' he said.

She felt emptiness invade her entire soul, a thousand times worse than amnesia. All this time she had desired remembering and knowing stuff, when possessing certain knowledge was truly more painful than not possessing it. A tear trickled down her cheek. 'How did he die?'

'To be honest, I'm not sure,' Kumar told her. 'The truth of the matter, which will sound even more puzzling, is that I only know he's dead because *you* know he's dead.'

With a blank expression on her face, she said, 'I don't understand.'

The living legend sighed, looked briefly at the non-existent ground and then confessed, 'I'm not a real person, Egg. I don't exist any more than Old Scorcher or most of the people back there. I'm like a ghost, but I'm not even that. I'm just a memory. I contaminate the Peculiar Palace because I died here and you don't kill something adulterated with so much glum magic like I was without leaving a stain. When you defeated de Zoet, his kingdom and all of its inhabitants became yours and, essentially, that included my residual existence. I'm part of the bundle you might say. I exist only to the degree that your subconscious recognises me and, as part of your subconscious, I can only provide your questions with answers you already know but have forgotten. It sounds complicated doesn't it?' She nodded. 'Don't think about it too hard,' he smiled, settling on his knees in front of her, resting both hands on his thighs. He looked happy and sad simultaneously; the way adults typically modified their facial expressions to explain complicated stuff to children. 'The whimsy of the palace has turned me into some sort of filter,' he told her. 'I'm a receptacle for the secrets of your past, like where you come from and who your parents actually are. You know the answers to all these questions but they're presently lost inside your head. The palace's role, my role as a part of the palace, is to help you locate them.'

She ignored his comment about *who your parents actually are* and asked instead, 'So you're not the real Ashok Kumar?'

'This is like explaining right and left to an alien,' he laughed. 'Okay, here goes, I'm all that remains of Ashok Kumar.'

'Like a ghost?'

'Yes, like a ghost, but as I said, not even that.'

And then it suddenly struck Egg that they had met before. She remembered it with crystal clear clarity and the surprise almost toppled her over. Prior to seeing his recorded image in the Unfastened Room and long before she revelled in his cartoon representation in a pop-up book, Egg and Kumar had been friends, but he had another name then. 'Why do I want to call you Mike?'

'*Eureka!*' he exclaimed and waved his arms in the air. 'Mike Joyce is one of my many names. That's the name your mum gave me after she escaped from her facsimile, which hasn't happened yet but will.'

'So you're from the future then?'

He nodded. 'And so are you.'

And then other things came back to her that immediately expunged the delight out of remembering them. Her mum was a bad person. She had Egg and Mike held prisoner, locking them in a filthy dungeon. That's why, when she arrived in her grandfather's garden, she was dressed in rags and encrusted with dirt. And then she remembered that her subconscious

359

mind had delivered her into the King's hands because she had been told stories about how honourable and brave he was. Mike had told her, or at least the *entity* her mum called Mike, the entity Sally Cakes brought with her when she escaped from her facsimile. While incarcerated, Egg had listened to the legend of Reginald Fielding, activist and war hero; the famous defender of migrant mud men and champion of Roquefort Ridge. He was murdered by a witch with fiery hair on a day that would be consequently considered ground zero for the chaos that followed, the same day John Fate was relieved of his post, Azzarello Risso was awoken from sleep and the disgraced Harbinger, Wilhelmina Hippocampus tried to murder Egg's mum and the Harbinger, Rose Thicket. She knew these things because Mike told her about them. But what was the use of remembering it all now? Perhaps if she had remembered it days ago she might have been able to intervene, at least to prevent her grandfather's death. 'Time is back to front,' she said. 'I haven't even been born yet.'

He smiled and ruffled her hair.

There was more, much more, but that was the crux of it, that was the strangest truth to bear fruit. She wasn't supposed to exist yet, at least not for a few years. Everything came flooding back as she stood staring into her father's eyes, sniffing back tears of sadness for a dead man she was never meant to meet. 'My father's name was Albrecht Krause,' she said. 'He was a soldier my mum fell in love with. Her real name is Karen Fleischer but now she's the Sinister Vessel they call Sally Cakes. My real name's…'

'Belladonna!' he said, which made her laugh. It sounded silly. She much preferred Egg. But *egg* was never a name, it was just a word she said when she arrived in the King's garden, just as Kumar had said it thirty years earlier to the ARP wardens who dragged him from the ruins of a bombed-out church. Her real name was Belladonna Krause, nay Fleischer, nay Cakes. 'Sally named you after a *Siouxsie and the Banshees* song,' said Kumar. 'As for Albrecht Krause, he died at Seelow Heights when the Rapture Bombs fell. Bombs, ironically, made from my flesh when I travelled back to 1944. When the Plan captures someone, they put them in a facsimile implanted with familiar looking people. It's meant to make the prisoner feel more comfortable I suppose. That's where I come in. Mike was based on your dad and fabricated as a love interest for your mum. When she escaped... or should I say, when she *escapes* in the not so distant future, she'll use glum magic to reanimate me and in doing so infuse my synthetic chromosomes with her glum ones, so when I travelled back to 1944, my powers, which are really Sally's powers, were harvested by the Plan.'

When Egg visited her mum's facsimile earlier, Sally Cakes said she remembered a world populated by dog people. Egg remembered it too now, an entire universe where a species originated from a canine called *Buster* had existed in virtual harmony until the arrival of Chaos Likely. Her mum ruled over that world like a tyrant, coldly condemning hostiles to death and disregarding famine and poverty. From atop a towering citadel called *the Basilica*, she reigned like an impassive god and whenever Mike disagreed with how Sally treat the masses, which was frequently, or attempted to interfere with the wanton nurturing of her daughter, often protecting Egg from her mum's casual cruelty and neglect, she would throw him across the room with a simple hand gesture, bounce him painfully off a wall or through a high window. But Mike proved immune to her bouts of vicious anger, always returning unscathed, to continue his protests. Eventually, tired of his constant interfering, she locked him up with her wayward daughter and, night after night, he whispered the history of the Known Universe to her.

'Sally was afraid of you,' Krause/Joyce/Kumar announced, 'afraid that your powers would dwarf hers and as you grew older you would pose a threat to her authority. She loved us both, in her own way, but her fondness for glum magic surpassed that affection and she began to recognise sentiment as a failing. When she didn't know how to engage with a problem, she did what the Plan had inadvertently taught her to do; she built a prison for it. But no prison cell could hold you. One minute you were incarcerated and the next, as quick as a flash, you were on the other side of the bars.'

'*Arcadia*,' she said. 'The city was called Arcadia and the tower was called the Basilica.'

Kumar nodded again. 'That's the place. Our plan was to leave together. But you couldn't make it work. You grabbed my arm and teleported, but left me in the cell every time. You were too stubborn to leave without me though. When Sally found out I'd been telling you stories about the Futilities she put me in another part of the Basilica, but you came and found me. You always came and found me. You would just pop up out of thin air and keep me company.'

'And so she decided,' Egg gulped at the memory 'to find a way to kill us both.'

'But she couldn't do it,' said Kumar. 'She kept trying and failing; poisoned soups, demon hexes, readings from magical books, nothing seemed to work. Not until she found a tried and tested magic, a destructive power that had worked on other magical forms. But when she came to the cell with the intention of using it, your anger got the better of you and you finally managed to teleport us out together.'

'We left together,' Egg remembered and the excitement of owning these memories was far overshadowed by the sadness.

Kumar patted her on the shoulder. 'We left together but somehow got separated. I travelled back to the war.'

'And I arrived three weeks ago.'

'In the garden of the war hero I told you all those stories about,' Kumar reasoned.

'And we both said the word, *egg* because…'

'Because it was the last thing we heard *her* say.'

Sally Cakes glared at them through the rusted bars of the cell, a spiteful leer twisting her face before it erupted with hysterical laughter and she began to explain how she intended to destroy them. 'Who needs god-kissed swords and haunted books when there's something a thousand times more powerful right under my nose? You, my child, you from the past are the answer to my prayers.'

Bella clung to Mike. Under her breath she told him everything would be okay, that neither of them would die. His tears kissed her cheek.

Two of the dog-headed soldiers dragged the girl forwards. She was a few years older than Belladonna and they gasped at the sight of the poor wretch.

'A paradox,' Sally laughed, 'all that's required to destroy you is a humble, unremarkable, run-of-the-mill paradox.'

Bella shook her head. 'I won't let you hurt us,' she said.

'There's not a thing you can do to stop me.'

'I don't have to stop you, not today,' she replied and looked at the other Bella. 'That's me. One day I'm coming back.'

Her older version looked up and said, 'you can change this future.'

Sally laughed. 'And exactly how do you...?'

But her words petered out when the two prisoners vanished before her eyes. Sally stared at the spot on the ground where squashed straw gently stretched back into shape, uninhibited by a prior weight. She felt rage grow inside her. Absently, she realised why history had recorded the word egg *significant; it was because* egg *had been the last syllable her daughter and that zombie heard before they disappeared.*

'What's that you're hiding behind your back?' asked Kumar.

Egg produced the blue box to show him. 'I took it off Pierre de Zoet. It has something called *Gods Vein* inside it.'

'A terrible creature came out of that box,' he said. 'I was too powerful for de Zoet and that creature was the only thing he could control me with. I think it's what he used to kill me. You need to be very careful with it, Egg. The thing inside is extremely dangerous!'

'Not any more,' she replied. 'I turned it into a monkey.'

Kumar laughed with incredulity and asked, 'You turned the poisonous remains of Orgo the Posthumous into a monkey?'

'Yes,' she said, nodding. 'Did John Fate send *you* here too?'

He sniffed a gloomy laugh and said, 'John considered me a joyous gift from heaven, but after I helped to win the war and the incarnate retreated into shadow, he was at a loss what to do with me. So he had de Zoet bring me to the Peculiar Palace. I don't think John wanted me dead, but after what happened here, he should be ashamed of himself for delivering you to this madman. When you leave,' he said, 'you will forget most of this. But you must remember one thing. Remember that the other you that Sally intended to kill us with, she said to change the future.'

'That was me,' said Egg, puzzled slightly by the incongruity of it all. 'I'm going to say that when I'm her.'

And when Kumar considered the absurdity of her statement he laughed. 'What I'm trying to say is that Sally wasn't always a bad person. Perhaps there's a way to avoid Arcadia and the Basilica and all the suffering that occurred there?'

Egg sighed. 'She's Chaos Likely, isn't she?'

He shook his head. 'No,' he said. 'You are. She was one of five potentially Sinister Vessels. Sally was expecting a child when the Plan captured her. She was never a vessel for chaos; she was a vessel for you.'

Egg almost dropped the ornate blue box with surprise.

'But chaos doesn't have to be a bad thing,' Kumar advised. 'Look at what I achieved with your mum's glum powers.'

Egg heard the faint sound of cars and saw the vague outlines of buildings as the void between two very diverse worlds began to fade.

'Oh, and there's something else you need to remember,' Kumar said, '*a shoeless ghost.*'

Her forehead scrunched up with puzzlement. '*A what?*'

'A ghost with no shoes,' he reiterated and laughed. 'It's important somehow. You used to know why but must have forgotten. Try to remember. It has something to do with saving the life of a Sinister Vessel.'

Confused, Egg nodded her head and heaved another sigh. 'I'll do my best,' she said as the hinterland melted away. 'Wait, what happened to…?'

*** **

'Mr Pierpot?' she said, finding herself in the middle of a busy Manchester high street with traffic hurtling past, car horns belching at her, people on the pavement shouting, calling her a *crazy kid* and other, less polite names. It was like awakening from a dream only the dream was still there, an amorphous haze suspended in the air, like when she left the suite at the Elysium Hotel. The Peculiar Palace was now nothing more than an ethereal, disconnected universe. De Zoet had exploited her imagination to maintain the surreal environment. That power was hers now and the location might come in useful in the future. Currently however, she watched it disappear along with the man who was a replica of her father and a war hero until she was surrounded only by the grey city.

Egg looked at the ornate blue box in her hands and remembered something about a shoeless ghost.

CHAPTER THIRTY-SIX
A Necessary Evil

A strong gust of air came off the sea as the ever-tumbling, ever-merging, serpentine attempted to crawl ashore. Distant crashing whitecaps overcame the sound of the tide lapping the toes of his pumps. Lord Sacheverell shivered and cast his gaze over the watery expanse, watching the frothy, grey wash, where, here and there, bleached white waves pirouetted in the moonlight. He had no desire to return to the underworld, and even less to wade through a polluted liquid mass of brine and Om-knew what else, risking further adulteration by a diverse range of human diseases all the way from dysentery to *dreaded lurgy*.

A mortal could do one of two things confronted by this boundary. It could surrender to despair and walk forward until the water consumed and drowned it or go back to the pitiable hovel it called home where a pair of net curtains and a Chubb lock ill-protected it from his kind. The glum Lord could not drown which gave humans an advantage over him at that specific moment because his melancholy had mined such a level that he envied the ability to do so. Unfortunately, he could walk into the sea and, detached from the compulsion to breathe, simply remain there. He could just be with the fish, lord over whole societies of crustacean and sea rocket for millennia and crawl from its salty milieu thousands of years from now to find human civilisation inevitably wiped out by its own hand, but then he would be no better than the morbid pig who preferred being underground to killing. He could drain the entire, sandy basin where the Irish Sea had slapped and slurped for billions of years if he wanted and pour its contents over the Plan's HQ, snuffing out a thousand unsuspecting human souls while aiming solely for the destruction of just one: *John Fate*. He could freeze every sea and ocean, boil and burn them in fact, or turn them to stone and fossilise every marine inhabitant, defuse an entire requisite of human consumption and starve those who depended upon its scaly fruit. The gulls would take to scavenging inland, convert to carnivores and pick off sheep and cows, further reducing mortal food supplies and, eventually, develop an appetite for human flesh. He could sit down and turn to stone, a stubborn, guerrilla-monument; an exhibit to the frustrations felt by all true Seraphs or he could remain at the shoreline randomly killing passers-by. It would take twenty-four hours at least for local law enforcement to work out why the town's idle teenagers, dog-walking pensioners, kite-flying juveniles, insipid romantic couples and rambling losers were rapidly diminishing. But although it would gratify him on a personal level, even cheer him up a bit, it was definitely behaviour unbecoming of nobility. Besides, he calculated several million humans would be required to erect the monuments, temples, pyramids and villas he would require once earth was his.

He could blight the sea, contaminate every organism that lived off its bounty, curse all marine life so that when humans tucked into their seared corpses, his poison would infect bodies and minds, hearts and souls and drive them all mad (he was certain madmen were as good as sane ones when it came to slaving, they would just require more organisation). He could do all these things at the drop of a hat but it would be futile. Other parts of the world had Rapture Bombs now, not only Manchester. Whether they were French or Russian, Spanish or Iranian, a Rapture Bomb was a Rapture Bomb.

He sniffed the air, infused with saline and sewage, shivered with cold and indignity as the wind blew out his hood like an air sock and, sighing, Callous Sacheverel realised he was lost. It was not a topographical forfeit of direction, his misplacement consisted more *how's* and *why's* than *where's*. But standing there in the North of England, neutered by (human) law and the complicated parameters of armistice, he existed in absolute isolation.

And then something touched his leg. Callous Sacheverell looked down to see a stray dog standing at his heel, a scruffy mongrel with a shaggy grey coat and a stupid complexion. The hairy newcomer was staring out to sea too. And then the glum Lord laughed with frustrated recognition and, returning his attention back to the dark waters, enquired, 'How's your mother?'

The dog ignored the question, noting instead that, 'It's a long, cold swim back to the underworld, Father.'

'My, how you've changed,' Sacheverel remarked. 'I barely recognise you these days.'

The mongrel chuckled. 'It's imperative I remain incognito,' it said, glancing up at him and taking in his father's strange attire, 'which, I suspect, is the excuse for your disguise. We can't afford to be seen together, not if our glorious plan for the future domination of humankind is to reach fruition.'

The clear, irksome rattle of a discarded fizzy drinks container blowing along the promenade behind them shattered the calm for a moment.

'How did you know where to find me?' Sacheverell asked.

'They always know.'

'*They* being?'

The dog looked up and said, 'Nefarious Logistics.'

'*A necessary evil*,' Sacheverell evoked and laughed. The sound was eerily out of place in the stillness. 'So you still throw your hat in with those weirdoes, do you? Fate must have been out of his mind not to close that operation down decades ago.'

'You don't approve?'

'Approve of *organised* chaos, absolutely not!'

'They are great admirers of *yours*, Father,' the dog said and bent to sniff one of the glum Lord's pumps. 'Good and evil are two sides of the same...'

His words were interrupted by a distant screech, a gull or an owl, or perhaps even the last vocal expletive of some nocturnal creature seized in the spiteful talons of a gull or an owl. 'I am aware of the axiom,' was Lord Sacheverell's delayed response, 'but like all axioms, it does not leave room for practicalities. Such legislation advances only a malicious appetite.'

'That's only a bad thing if you're not on the side of the malicious,' the dog pointed out.

'Personally, I prefer the thrill of war. Fire-pious simpletons consigning sin to all asunder take all the excitement out of sentencing souls.'

'Try saying that when you've had one glass of merlot too many,' the dog remarked with a howling laugh. 'Nefarious Logistics are willing to broker a deal, Father.'

'Are they now?' the glum Lord grinned.

The estranged silence that followed was commented upon by the biased opinion of the tide as it swilled over the man's pumps and the dog's paws. 'Very recently, indeed about an hour ago,' the dog said, 'they came into possession of some rather interesting information.'

'Oh yes? Let me see now, would it have anything to do with an arcane text in the hands of a madcap clown?'

The dog laughed again. 'You seem well-informed, Pater, but this information is far more interesting than the hopeless literary endeavours of Lord Crowberry's offspring. I mean, really, Father, did you…?'

'What do you mean *Lord Crowberry's offspring*?'

'Oh, didn't you know?'

'That pencil-limbed freak was Roderick Crowberry?' the glum Lord enquired angrily. 'I ought to have took the traitor's head the moment I laid eyes on him.'

The mongrel drew a deep breath and puffed out its canine cheeks before saying, 'As I mentioned, Nefarious Logistics admire you, Father. They have plans that, given your cooperation, may result in glory. John Fate underestimates them, tolerates them out of an obligation towards moral equilibrium. They're monitored by the Plan but the Plan only sees what Nefarious Logistics allows them to see. They have their own ways of spreading disinformation.'

The glum Lord was growing impatient. 'So what *are* their plans?'

'World domination, obviously!' said the scruffy hound.

'Obviously,' Sacheverell sniggered.

'And since the recent acquisition of rather curious information, this objective appears more imminent.'

The glum Lord sighed, gasping on the salty air, allowing it to fill up his lungs and, with a clemency he generally reserved for less tranquil activity like murder, said, 'I am at a crossroads in my life.'

The pooch looked up at him with concern and said, 'I'm not a seeing eye dog, Father.'

'Convey this deal of theirs,' Sacheverell advised, 'while I am in an amenable mood.'

'I'll be frank,' said the mutt, 'which is a rubbish name for a dog.' It laughed but when its father refrained, said, 'All right, I'll come straight to the point. Waffling on like this is getting us nowhere fast and it's bloody freezing out here *and* I'm dying for a slash so, I'll get to the nub of the issue and discontinue with all this dilly dallying and beating about the bush which, let's be honest, is rather vexing. So, the fact of the matter is, in a word, well, in several words, my patrons, sponsors, employers, whatever you wish to call them...'

'I'm not averse to killing my own flesh and blood,' Sacheverell advised.

'They've discovered the whereabouts of all five Sinister Vessels and request your involvement in planning their next move,' the dog said in a single breath.

The glum Lord silently sucked in air to avoid displaying his astonishment. There was another high-pitched squeal from the near distance, some tiny rodent forced to meet its maker in the dark. A sturdy breeze threatened to unbalance them both as the tide continued to lick at their ankles. And then Lord Callous Sacheverell looked down at his son and said, 'Take me to your leader.'

CHAPTER THIRTY-SEVEN
Long Live the King

Many of his friends attended, though Egg was certain many more did not. For a man who played a major role in fighting glum Seraphs and their hellish minion all his life, Reginald Fielding's funeral deserved more of a turnout. But a part of her was also glad because she could no more tolerate Hill House being overrun by nosy parkers than she could Spare Clowns.

She could not decide who was the most irregular. By far the most striking of the bunch was a tall, stocky individual with an eye patch and one silver hand. Another, the largest of all the mourners, resembled a giant, anthropoid beetle with four hairy arms, antennae and a set of clicking insect mandibles extending from his cheeks. There was a woman who was half man or maybe a man who was half woman, his/her attire separated into either camp down the centre of her/his body. An alien Queen with blue skin wrapped from neck to toe in exotic silks and who communicated in a cadence resembling a swarm of bees was carried by a group of men in black cloaks and cowls. They had arrived by way of an Astral Causeway, a hundred-foot pyramid of wrought iron, intertwined with metallic conduits and knotted steel ducts that currently resided in a distant section of the estate in a deep, square crater. The recently exhumed Harbinger, Azzarello Risso was also in attendance and having a man with the head of a pig staring at her throughout the service was quite unnerving. In the pop-up book in the Hill House library there was a page dedicated to the Harbingers and if one rolled a cardboard wheel at the edge of the page, each of the war heroes slid past a window with a corresponding speech bubble. Risso's had said, *hell cannot hold me*! He was accompanied by another Harbinger, the elderly witch, Rose Thicket. Her speech bubble read *you and whose army, fish-face*?

Many humans came to pay their respects. At least most of them appeared human until one got up close and discovered a flesh of scales or skin-tight synthetic sacks protecting them from earth's atmosphere. Many spoke in accents Egg couldn't interpret and some simply fizzled out of reality entirely when she attempted to communicate with them. Several mourners hid bulging wings beneath their black jackets and overcoats and during the actual internment, three grey men in white suits had materialized on the other side of the grave from Egg, glanced about awkwardly, apologised and then disappeared, apparently having gate-crashed the wrong cosmic event. And then there was Gladstone, the King's cat, recently liberated from Grace Plateau's quarantine section, currently winding in and out of the ankles of the bereaved, in a constant search for his owner.

Although it was the only funeral Egg remembered attending she was certain it was not a standard state of affairs.

As many of the achievements of the man in the coffin were conveyed, his heroic adventures and long, loyal service with the Plan, Egg wondered why the eulogy circumvented other topics, the animated way he read a pirate story for example, or how he calmed a fretting soul when the weather turned stormy or how he made marshmallows melt in hot chocolate or how he melted cheese on toast in the most mouth-watering fashion or how he filled an eight-year-old girl with the confidence that he would always be around to protect her. There were a thousand and one other things Egg remembered about her grandfather that the various orators overlooked and by the time the funeral party began its long trek back up the hill, past the scorched section of lawn where Mr Pierpot's biplane had exploded, she started to wonder if any of the other attendees had ever truly known the King.

That was when Azzarello Risso chose to address her. 'I'd like to offer my condolences,' he said, trudging along at her side until she stopped and gazed at him coldly. 'I was wondering, might we have a chat?'

'About what?' she asked.

'Well, a number of things really,' the large man said, nervously playing with his own fingertips. 'I was thinking perhaps we might discuss what happened…'

'If you want me to put in a word for John Fate, then you have another thing coming!' Egg told him.

Following a series of unforeseeable blunders, the death of the King foremost in Egg's estimation, Fate had been dismissed from the Plan and consequently arrested on a charge of gross dereliction of duty. In a single day the Plan's HQ had been bombed by the Real Salvation Army, the Tetrad had been assassinated and a Sinister Vessel had almost been abducted. It was fair to say his role as Captain of the Home Guard was untenable. Coupled with the illicit appointment of Pierre de Zoet to detain an eight-year-old girl and a bungling attempt to have Fletcher Kerguelen brought in for questioning resulting in the demise of eleven highly decorated Planners, the former Captain was now an inmate of Seven Gates Penitentiary.

The pig looked embarrassed, two fat pink cheeks blushing bright red while behind him, the hag sniffed and rolled her eyes as if to say, *I told you so!*

'What John did…'

'If I hadn't been abducted I could have saved my grandfather's life,' Egg interjected, stepping up to the brawny war veteran.

Molly Salter, a woman who often cooked for the King when he hosted dinner parties at the house or when he required more sustenance than a pot-noodle and a packet of biscuits, and who had, along with her husband Ted, been caring for Egg, Gladstone and the King's estate since his demise, took the opportunity to intrude upon their conversation.

'If all you've come for is to sway this child towards mercy,' she said, striding over the grass and wagging a finger in the pig's face, 'then you can think again.'

'Molly, I'd appreciate…' Risso started to reply.

'And I'd appreciate it if you lot wouldn't keep poking your noses in our private affairs,' Molly told him. 'Who invited you anyway? We don't want no friends of John Fate up at the house, I don't care who they are. I wasn't up at six o'clock this morning buttering bread and piercing sausages and pineapples for folk like you what mingle with traitors.'

'It's okay, Molly,' said Egg, placing a placatory hand on the woman's arm, concerned about her blood-pressure as she witnessed the cook's features boil with rage. 'Actually, I would like to talk to Mr Risso.'

Molly glanced back and forth between them, before saying, 'All right love, but I'll just be over here if you need me.' She wandered away to stand beside her husband presently conversing with a chimpanzee in a spacesuit.

Egg looked at Risso. 'My grandfather had a book with you in it,' she told him. 'He told me you were a hero. But if that was true you would have saved poor Mr Pierpot's life instead of helping that witch interrogate him.'

Her words clearly hurt the Harbinger. He looked at the ground with evident shame while behind him Rose Thicket chewed on her gums, hands thrust in her cardigan pockets, demonstrating calm.

'You're right,' the pig said, looking up. 'I've spent thirty years feeling sorry for myself, buried in the ground and ignoring my duties. I'd like to put things right, starting with John. He's in a lot of trouble.'

'Good.'

'He's not a bad man.'

'*I* don't like him and neither did my granddad.'

'Even so, without him the Plan will fall into the hands of worthless and contemptible bureaucrats, people who will turn it into a pantomime. Do you really want the Known Universe protected by pen-pushers, desk-jockeys and third-rate typists? If you put in a good word...'

Egg laughed. 'He let a murderer take me prisoner. He stood by and let those monsters kill the King.'

379

'Egg, you need to understand, there's far more at stake than the King's life,' Risso explained, looking grave. 'Even Reginald would have agreed with that assessment. There's more at stake than one person's morals and principles.'

'Does the Plan know where Mr Pierpot is?'

Risso shook his head. 'They think he's back in hell, but it's only a rumour. Nobody knows what happened to him.'

'What about Leontine Pryderi?'

'I don't know.'

'Can I have five minutes alone with Rhodeburt Raven?'

Realising they were being watched by most of the attendees, Risso looked nervous as he said, 'Raven's crazy. He thinks his father is still alive.'

'You didn't answer my question,' said Egg.

'What would you do to him?'

'I'd drop *him* off a building.'

'Revenge is no basis for a judicial system.'

Egg laughed, bitterly. 'Then we have nothing left to talk about.'

The weather had been bright earlier, but seemed to imitate the temper of the funeral party now, growing grey and gloomy, showing signs of irascibility. The pig cast a look at the ground and saw the late King's cat eyeing him with equal suspicion. When Egg looked down the hill to the spot where her grandfather had just been buried, he said, 'There's another matter we need to discuss. You're going to require guardianship and there's the small problem of where you'll live.'

'I'll live here,' she said, looking at him sternly.

'I doubt that.'

'I'm going to live in my grandfather's house,' she reiterated, adamantly, 'and there's nothing you can do about it.'

The pig puffed out his cheeks and said, 'You can't live in this great big house all by yourself. You're only eight-years-old!'

'She was only eight-years-old when Fate entrusted her to that murderous megalomaniac, de Zoet,' a buzzing voice spoke from behind them and Egg turned to see the blue woman perched on her litter.

Risso smiled, awkwardly. 'With the greatest of respect, Your Majesty, this is no concern of...'

The tall man with the eye patch and silver hand stepped forward now, offering Egg the shiny limb to shake. 'Sir Charles Waterhouse,' he said and, touching the cold steel, Egg recalled the hairy limb displayed in John Fate's office. 'I fought alongside the King many times and in many, many worlds away from this one.'

She noticed others had forestalled their journey to the house and its humble promise of a banquet to come and introduce themselves.

'Jimmy Jenny,' said the half woman half man.

'Queen Eschew wishes to extend her deepest commiserations,' said one of the hooded litter bearers in a deep, humming voice, bowing without upending his cargo.

When Egg looked up at the Queen, the blue woman also bowed and said, 'I present my deepest compassion over the loss of your grandfather as well as my highest regards for your assistance in defeating *my* mortal enemy, Pierre de Zoet.'

'Bug,' said the man with six limbs, holding out four for Egg to shake in turn.

'If the child wishes to remain at the King's home,' Sir Charles said to Risso, that metal hand placed on her shoulder, 'I see no reason why it cannot be arranged. With our guidance and support, she will be more than sufficiently cared for. I, for one, will not see her given up for dissection by the Plan.'

Egg smiled warmly as Molly and Ted wandered over to join the group and by the time she turned that smile on Risso it was twisted into cold indifference again.

'It would be quite irregular,' Risso responded, 'but I suppose, under the circumstances...'

Sir Charles Waterhouse stepped around his new charge and came face to face with the Harbinger. 'I wasn't asking for your permission. The girl is our responsibility now. I think it's time any friends of John Fate...' he lent to one side to include the old woman in his proposal, 'left. Your continued presence is one of profound disrespect. *Goodbye!*'

Risso appeared sincere in his sadness and looked at Egg. 'I had hoped we might be friends,' he said. 'I apologise for everything you have been though in the last week.' And then he turned and walked away, with Thicket in his wake, neither one looking back as they strode over the grass. Oddly, Egg felt sad as she watched them cross the lawn, an assortment of strangers filing in around her as if they were posing for a photograph.

Gladstone sniffed at a daisy, stretched his hind-legs, shook out his ruffled and carroty fur and trotted over the sundried grass towards the house. He circumvented a gravel pathway that bordered cherry blossom saplings because the stones hurt his paws, preferring to pad over smooth sward, up the incline of lawn and across a patch of crazy paving where the dulled but colourful vestiges of vanquished clowns tarnished the stone.

He went up the single step and through the mansion's grand entrance where his cant hooks clicked on buffed hallway tiles, entering the first room he came to. Staying low he, ambled over a Kashmir rug, under a selection of recently repaired chairs, a buffet-laden table and a *Steinway* before mooching over to the wall and leaping effortlessly to the windowsill, where he deposited himself elegantly between a priceless cobalt vase inhabited by azaleas, the only urn to survive the army of toys, and a receptacle for monsters the little girl had brought back from her adventures.

Peering out the ground floor window, watching the strange ensemble of creatures approach the house in their small groups, Gladstone languidly unfurled his long, serpent-like tail and, in doing so, inadvertently toppled the ornate blue box from the sill. The cerulean ampule tumbled and smashed on the floor, startling the cat and causing him to leap from the ledge, landing fluently on the back of a leather chesterfield and then dropping back to the rug. If he had been at all interested in scrutinising the wreckage before leaving, he may have observed a lone speck of oozing black matter dribble from the broken receptacle and trickle between two polished floorboards. But Gladstone, as smart as a whip, was more concerned about placing distance between him and the scene of the crime, understanding that cats got the blame for everything.

Epilogue

A fly landed on the back of his hand and as he flapped the buzzing pest away he used his other hand to press the channel button on the TV remote.

Harry dragged his fingertips over a recently shaved skull and watched a bunch of puppets and adults interact in the name of children's entertainment. *What a load of bloody rubbish!* He repressed the little rubber key and the image on screen changed. The hum of the fly increased in volume as the barmy critter dive-bombed his right ear. He waved the remote hand in front of his face and caught the smell of fried food. Was it time to change his T-shirt? Was Beverley frying onions? On the TV a man with a nice haircut dished out herd ethics to two clueless teenage parents in front of a baying audience. He pressed the rubber key to skip channels. The fly came back and Harry tried to hit it with the remote but missed. Now he could smell damp and thought he should do something about the downstairs toilet before Beverley got a cob on.

His son, Michael came hurtling into the room chasing Spartacus, grappling with the scruffy mutt in front of the telly, obscuring Harry's view of the screen, their unruly noise drowning out the volume of the show.

'Will you take that mongrel outside?'

Harry pressed the button. The channel changed. It was the news. Harry pressed the button and got sport.

'It's raining,' Michael moaned and continued to torture the dog, tumbling noisily over the furniture with it. The wiry, white and brown Jack Russell looked like it couldn't make up its mind if it was having fun or not.

'Then just *play somewhere else*,' Harry snapped. He pressed the button and John Wayne was striding through a packed saloon. Harry hated John Wayne. There was something fundamentally and irredeemably sanctimonious about men like John Wayne.

'Harry, the washer's making that funny whistling noise,' Beverley called from the utility room.

What does she expect me *to do about it? What do* I *know about bloody washing machines? Anybody would think I'm some kind of bloody genius the way this lot expect me to solve all their problems.*

Harry worked in a car park toll booth in the town centre three days a week, dishing out ticket stubs to fat and useless plebs with more money than sense. He also worked two nights at a local warehouse as a security officer. He preferred the night job because he only had to converse with people while clocking in and out. The warehouse stored everything from toilet rolls to Austin Allegro wheel trims, pencil cases and plastic beakers, guinea pig cages and electrical extension cables. Sometimes he patrolled it with a toy gun he'd whipped from Michael's bedroom and pretended he was hunting zombies. He knew where all the cameras were pointed and avoided those sections of the premises. Neither job required much handyman skills and even less training, especially surplus to requirement instruction in how to fix a *whistling washing machine*.

The fact that Harry was a total plank when it came to DIY had been a charming trait when he and Beverley first met. She used to make endearing remarks about his inability to bang a nail in a wall or screw a bracket under a shelf or plumb a toilet in without involving a subsequent six hour wait in a casualty department. But after fifteen years of marriage, she viewed his failure to learn how to do any of these things a dereliction of duty, tantamount to infidelity. It was okay for *her* not to know the shortest route to the supermarket or the most efficient motorway junction to access on a journey out of town or the nearest car park to whatever amenities they were using; these were dubbed *moments of geographic dyspraxia*, a low spectrum disability, but if anything Beverley's low spectrum disability had gotten worse because they lived in the same town and she still went up Burnley Road, along Accrington Road and then Harwood Street to get to the local supermarket when it was much easier to go down Hereford Road and along Gorse Street. And every time he stated this obvious short cut Beverley's excuse was, *I'm used to going* this *way*! When the council briefly closed Accrington Road to replace water pipes, rather than finally utilise his suggested route, she went shopping at an entirely different supermarket altogether for the duration of the works.

'It could be the spin bearing,' Beverley called. 'It only whistles during the spin cycle.'

Thanks for sharing that with me, Bev. What do you expect me to do now, write a four-hundred-page thesis on the unreliability of spin bearings?

'I'll get Jim to come and have a look at it,' he said. Jim was a bloke Harry knew from the pub. Jim could build book cabinets, wire plugs, connect gas-pipes, insulate lofts, dig foundations, service car engines, bleed radiators and even set the timer on the oven. Jim was Beverley's ideal man.

'Don't get Jim,' said Beverley. 'He doesn't have a clue. The vacuum cleaner hasn't worked properly since...'

The fly had the cheek to land on his cheek and Harry brushed it away again just as Spartacus jumped into his lap swiftly pursued by Michael. Harry hated that bloody dog.

'*Take the dog outside!*'

'And the iron won't spray water any more,' Beverley added.

Michael was still strewn across his father's lap. 'Can I have money for football cards?'

'What do you want football cards for? Try reading a book once in a while. Sport's for unimaginative people,' Harry told him and pushed the child onto the floor. Michael jumped up and chased the dog from the room.

'And the outside tap hasn't stopped leaking since he last used the hose.'

'I'll get a plumber from the yellow pages.'

'Plumbers charge a fortune,' she said.

'Then we'll buy a new washing machine.'

'We can't afford a new washing machine.'

'Then I'll magic one up from a cardboard box and some toilet roll tubes like they do on *Blue Peter*,' said Harry, contemptuously. He pressed the button and the channel changed. He sighed regretfully when he recognised the closing credits of *The Sweeney*. 'It's called austerity measures, Bev. I've had to lose a quarter of my income because of austerity measures. If we can't afford to have it looked at by a professional or get it replaced, then we'll have to get Jim to have a look at it. It's called black magic economy.'

'I think you mean black *market* economy.'

'You know what I mean. Anyway, the thing still washes, doesn't it? So what if it plays a tune at the same time?'

Harry pressed the button.

Saturday afternoons were supposed to be about relaxation. They were about taking time out from the busy schedule of the working week. He didn't get every Saturday off and so the opportunity for respite was rare, especially since the council had cut back on staff and let three car park attendants retire early. He was lucky if he got one weekend off out of four these days so he wanted to make the most of it. He dragged a palm across his shorn scalp, smelt onions and spotted the fly bothering a geranium.

The doorbell rang. Harry sighed, switched channels, closed his eyes and tried to remain calm. He attempted to count backwards from ten to one but when he got to seven he heard the doorbell ring again and further scrunched up his eyelids in mental agony. He listened to the sounds in the house, Beverley and her squealing washing machine, Michael attacking the dog, Samantha upstairs listening to her *Thrash Metal*. From the multifarious noises he registered, Harry was certain none resembled a pair of feet heading towards the front door any time soon.

The doorbell went again.

'Can somebody please get that?' he asked nobody in particular and at such a low volume it served only as a herald for his own frustration; more an angry prayer than a stated request. He opened his eyes and saw a TV commercial for a travel agent. 'I should be so bloody lucky!' he announced aloud and pressed the button until he saw a fiery-haired woman on the moon. He pressed the button and saw a dog running over a hillside in slow motion. He pressed the button and saw two men in a boat.

The doorbell rang.

'*WILL SOMEBODY ANSWER THE BLOODY...?*'

'Can you get that, Harry, I'm a bit busy with the washing,' Beverley called from the utility room.

'*Right*,' Harry said, through gritted teeth, leaping to his feet. 'You carry on with whatever it is you're doing. I wouldn't want to interrupt you scrutinising your undies whirling round and round behind that little window. Om only knows what effects such a disturbance might have on the delicate fabric of your life. It's not like I have anything better to do on my first day off in ten.'

Harry stomped backwards across the living room, eyes never leaving the TV set as he continued to channel-surf. When he finally reached the hallway Samantha came bounding down the stairs past him. 'It's for *me*, Daddy, it's Bobby, we're going to the pictures.' She opened the door and the long-haired drip that was Bobby Duncan stood grinning at him from the doorstep. Behind him was a short, fat man Harry wasn't supposed to see.

Harry hated Bobby Duncan.

''Ello, Mr Robinson,' said the benignly happy hippy, waving a hand. ''Ello, Sam.'

'See you later, Daddy,' his daughter said, standing on tip-toes and kissing his cheek before slamming the door in her wake.

Back on the sofa, Harry continued to channel-surf, trying not to notice the visitor who was currently plonked in an adjacent armchair. When Harry was younger, Saturday TV was a treat for kids and adults alike; cartoons, pirate movies and action-packed serials with a pre-Bond Roger Moore. These days it was just endless spools of incoherent drivel. Even *Scooby Doo* was oddly unintelligible and Harry used to love Scooby Doo. He knew where he was with Scooby Doo.

'You're looking well, son,' said the visitor in that dry, sardonic tone Harry had somehow come to know despite having no recollection of ever meeting the man.

'Oh bloody hell,' Beverley called from the utility room. 'I think it's leaking now. There's a big puddle of... I don't... *Michael, get in here at once, Spartacus has wee'd all over the kitchen.*'

'It wasn't him, Mum,' Michael shouted from somewhere in the house.

'What do you mean it wasn't him? If it wasn't him, who was it, your bloody dad?'

'I don't know, maybe it was next door's dog, it's always in the back.'

'Don't be ridiculous. The back door's been shut all...'

Harry looked at their visitor and rolled his eyes, sighing apologetically and scratching the bristles on his head. He tried to blank everyone out and concentrate on the TV. He couldn't see the fly so it had either left the room or the geranium had some Venus Fly Trap in it and had eaten the pesky little beggar. If they let him alone, the TV could be his salvation. He could be immersed in two of the worst jobs this side of cleaning toilets in hell as long as he was left in peace to watch

TV on a Saturday afternoon. It was the only thing that kept him sane. Once upon a time he enjoyed the football, but when Milgram Orient started hovering around the relegation zone, sitting in the freezing cold for ninety minutes a week lost all its former fizz. When people stopped going to matches there wasn't the same atmosphere and he was expected to pay the same ridiculous ticket and shirt prices. It occurred to Harry, as recently as a week ago, that his entire world, his wife, kids, that bloody dog, neighbours, work colleagues, two bosses, life-long favourite football team and even Jim and the rest of the blokes who supped in the *Dead Rabbit* of a Friday and Saturday night, had all been put on earth just to cause him mental anguish. He pressed the button and an episode of *Star Trek* appeared onscreen. He pressed the button and saw a bunch of old men in soldiers' uniforms. He pressed the button and saw a man chop off another man's head with a sword. He pressed the button and saw two men in a prison cell and heard canned laughter.

'How apt,' the visitor said, 'the penitentiary I mean.'

Absently, Harry wondered what Samantha and Bobby were going to see. He had always liked the cinema when he was young. He remembered going to see *Jaws* with Beverley and she thought it was the best movie she'd ever seen and told everybody it was *their* movie. He should have realised things were amiss then. He always considered *The Godfather* to be *their* movie, even though they'd only watched it on TV while babysitting.

Harry pressed the button and saw a man stood before a weather map. He pressed the button and saw a crocodile leap out of a river to feed. He pressed the button and saw...

He saw a clown.

'It's time for you to come home,' the short, fat visitor said.

The fly bounced off his bristly scalp and Harry snapped out a hand and finally caught the annoying little bastard. He squeezed his fingers into a fist and felt the insect's juices pop inside. He pressed the button and saw another clown. Inner fury surpassed the emotions that had currently been inspiring his temper, a wanton rage that had been smothered recently by the trifling aggravation of washing machines, ungrateful kids, a wife that got lost between the house and the end of the road and the droning sound emitted by filthy flying insects and Harry glanced at the man in the armchair and visibly shivered when he recognised him. Then he scraped his hand across his mouth, depositing the tiny corpse on his tongue and pressed the button on the remote several more times.

'All is not lost,' the visitor said. 'We will face this obstacle together.'

Clown was replaced by clown and so on and so forth as Harry repeatedly jabbed the channel changer with his thumb.

His Thumb.

'You know it makes sense!' said his father, smiling.

Clown after clown after clown after clown after clown after...

Harry hated bloody clowns.